UNDER THE BONE

UNDER
THE BONE

Anne-christine d'Adesky

Farrar, Straus and Giroux

New York

Copyright © 1994 by Anne-christine d'Adesky
All rights reserved
First printing, 1994
Printed in the United States of America
Published simultaneously in Canada by HarperCollinsCanadaLtd

Library of Congress Cataloging-in-Publication Data
D'Adesky, Anne-christine.
Under the bone / Anne-christine d'Adesky.
p.   cm.
1. Haiti—Politics and government—Fiction.   2. Young women—
Haiti—Fiction.   I. Title.
PS3554.A243U53   1993   813'.54—dc20   93-11962   CIP

This book is dedicated to the victims of

Duvalierism: May they rest in peace.

And to

my mother, Vivian Marie Berthoin d'Adesky,

and my father, Raymond Georges d'Adesky

I wish especially to thank my siblings, Katherine Marie, Serge Patrick, and Philippe Yan; and my dear friends Megan and Mary McLemore, Jennifer Monson, Harriet Hirshorn, John Cook, Toni Fitzpatrick, Laura Flanders, Sarah Pettit, and Sarah Schulman —for their love and continued support.

Many people—loved ones, friends, and strangers —share the novel with me because they not only nurtured me but protected me in moments of physical danger and fear. I wish to salute and remember in particular three outstanding human rights activists: Michael Hooper, Jean Blaise, and Lafontant Joseph. I also extend my deep gratitude to (in alphabetical order): Jean-Bertrand Aristide, Alix Arty, Daniel Arty, Ronald Aubourg, Jean-Claude Bajeux, Bettina Berch, Greg Chamberlain, Marie-Marcel Deschamps, Bruce Dollar, Marino Etienne, Anne Fuller, Lionel Legros, Mike Levy, Jocelyn McCalla, Kelly McKaig, Stephen Machon, Brenda Miller, Jacquie Misho, Antoinette (Annette) Salomon, Hannah Taylor, Amy Wilentz, and the Writers Room, NYC.

Finally, special thanks to my editor, John Glusman, for his interest and insights, to my agent, Joy Harris, and to designer James Conrad and photographer Maggie Steber.

KENBE FEM!

UNDER THE BONE

Prologue

I remember the bells of the church. How they rang to wake me from sleep. In the dead of night I stumbled, groping for the light switch, worrying about the rats. Heard the gunshots already, pop-pop-pop-pop, then faster, thuk-a-thuk-thuk, the machine gun. And felt the fear knocking like a trapped bird inside my chest. I opened the door and ran out to the balcony.

There I saw something I had never seen. An orange glow in a corner of the city. A fire so big it set off huge sparks in the distance, like an explosion of lava consuming everything with its amazing heat. Giant orange sparks and the bells of the church and all around me a sense of urgency and sudden fear. Terror. Panic. Because a crime was taking place. A slaughter; some new loss of human life. And I was standing on the balcony trying to see it, to follow the headlights I could see making their way. Ambulances and trucks with the criminals. Who else would dare to go out in such a moonless black-as-pitch night?

The fire consumed the night. Burned into the day. Sirens ricocheted up to my ears. With the light, the sound of the guns slowed, then was gone. In a gray dawn I passed the site. A dark still-smoldering heap remained, the stone wall licked by black tongues at its base. People stood with buckets of water drawn from the sewer nearby. Passed them head to hand to cinder block. Like a silent movie. I never saw the bodies, traced the gunshots. No one has.

So it is that I witnessed a great crime. One that offered beauty as it destroyed and lit a city that is too dark at night. A fire I will never forget. A mystery, a hundred small mysteries that were created in my brain as I stared at the valley that night. Where is that car going? Who is driving it? Is anyone down there? What exactly is happening?

Now when I sleep I wake with the sound of those church bells. Frantic clanging church bells with an unknown hand pulling at the end of the rope, sounding the alarm. And sometimes I push myself *to go downstairs and out into the driveway when I hear the thuk-thuk-thuk. Out into the deadly stillness. The houses and the walls and the dogs going crazy being tormented by the sirens. And I imagine I can see men in the darkness doing the crime. Men whose faces I would recognize by day.*

1

Elyse woke when the sun was still an hour away. The night was huge, arching over the mountain like a deep blue bowl spiked with pinprick stars. The moon shone on her arms and illuminated the room, divided into two by a hanging piece of burlap.

On the other side of it, she could hear Grann snoring softly. She slipped on her dress and lifted the burlap. Her grandmother's cheeks were like folds of suede as she unconsciously worked her jaw. Grann's face was angelic; small and heart-shaped, with a fine white mustache edging thin plum lips. Part of a gold cap protruded as she wheezed, sucking in the room's damp air through her remaining front teeth.

Elyse kissed her lightly on the cheek, then carefully arranged the cotton shift over her skinny thighs. Grann always complained of a chill now, even during the day. She was past ninety, and dying. The light, she would tell Elyse, I feel it, behind the door. When I close my eyes, I see it. Death is white, Elyse. Death is lighter than this air we breathe. Death is a big white light behind the door. But I don't want to open it, I'm scared.

Elyse passed a hand over her mouth; Grann's breath was damp but steady. She felt the temperature of her callused feet, the mis-shapen bones of her toes big and shiny, like pig knuckles. They were warm enough. Elyse squeezed them a last time and left.

A dog barked in the far distance. She listened for other sounds. Satisfied, she rounded the house and picked up the big basket of wash and a bar of detergent soap. The straw ribs of the large basket were worn with age.

She made her way past the other darkened houses, balancing the wash on her head as she scanned the sky, already lighter with the passage of a few minutes. Through a thin canopy of trees, she emerged into a clearing that led directly to the ravine. From here, one could trace the slope of the mountain, the flamboyants with their brilliant red flowers and sinewy, muscular branches extending upward like supplicants.

Behind her, the small mud house where Grann had been born leaned unevenly to the left. It was perched close to the edge of the mountain, in the shade of two large trees. These days, the rain heightened the faint pink color of its walls, red earth undertones bleached by limewash. Elyse looked at the house critically. It resembled a starving animal to her, raw wooden ribs exposed and jutting at the corners, the frame sagging under the weight of heavy waterlogged thatch. After last week's storm, she had added stones onto the thatch to keep it from blowing it away, but the water kept leaking in. She had balled newspaper and rags into the cracks, but still the mice and insects found their way, burrowing inside the walls to nest. And little fruit bats, who sought refuge in the warm thatch. At dusk, they suddenly spiraled out in a thick cloud, then disappeared into the trees. Elyse never saw them return, but would hear them, mewling like kittens, their cries faint but sharp.

The village had no name and was not marked on any map. It was located above the Fontamara district on the eastern side of the capital. People referred to the houses by their owners' names: kay Grann, kay Ti Pierre, kay Hyppolite, and so forth. Soon, the little house would be kay Elyse. She shivered. In the unseen distance, the dogs were barking again. She listened to their cries echoing across the valley.

Another dog had been found last week, stiff and wild-eyed. It had swallowed its tongue in desperation. The men who burned it said sparks burst from the animal's head. The tongue had been black and polished hard as a stone. As a child, everyone teased her: The dogs are going to come and get you. They'll bite you and make you crazy. You see that crazy person with his tongue hanging out of his mouth? A dog bit him. That's what happened. You see a dog coming your way, spitting like that? He's got a devil inside him. If the devil bites you, you'll become crazy too.

The dogs stopped barking. Elyse shook her head to clear it, rubbed a fingernail over her front teeth, scratched away the film of sleep. She stepped into an opening in the canebrake. The village behind her dropped from view. Farther below was the dirt track that formed a T with the highway, Route National One. With the rains, not even the Macoutes with their Pajero jeeps could get up the mountain. That was the only advantage to living up here; you could usually see the criminals coming, their jeeps stuck along the track.

The ground was wet. Her feet slid on moss covering the rocks. Already, the light had changed; she could make out the shapes of things. By now, the trucks coming from the Cape would have arrived. They were two days late because of the collapse of the bridge at the Artibonite River. She imagined the scene: chaos, panic, everyone fighting for the rice. Now that the price of rice was going up, nobody was selling. Everybody was waiting, hoping the price would go up even more. Thieves, thought Elyse, replaying her conversation with Pierre yesterday. All of them thieves. Not one of them an honest man. And now they want to tax the meat. Who's going to pay for that? Not me. Not us. None of us can afford that.

She remembered her hunger at the thought of meat. Last night's headache was gone, but the nausea remained, and under it, the hollow gnaw, like a coal burning a hole in her stomach; it made her want to throw up, except there was nothing to vomit. She had left the little bit of creamed corn on the fire for Grann; with her sick gums, it was all she could eat. That, and the little bits of boiled meat in the soups. With a little luck, Pierre will find some meat, she told herself. We'll manage somehow.

She slowed down to look for snakes. They liked to sleep here, under the roots of the big trees. The big fallen log was next. She walked along it toward the little goat path, staying all the while as close to the side of the ravine as she could without slipping; it was so steep. Soon, the mouth of the stream appeared. She dipped her hand into it, rinsed her face, and quickly stepped onto the oval stones named Dlo Nan Je Moiz, Moses' Tears, that bridged the stream.

A short distance farther, she put down the baskets, lifted her dress up and off, and waded into the shallow current. She liked coming here early to bathe in private. She rubbed the soap on her body and into her hair, watching as the foamy bubbles dissolved. After a while, she got out, dressed, and removed the wash. Only a few articles were hers and Grann's, the rest belonged to Pierre and his children. They were alone now that Eugenia, his wife, was dead of the fever. The others had left with Ignatius' group to cut cane in the bateys. Pierre was Grann's cousin, the only man who had stayed behind.

His shirts were dark at the collar and stained with kenep juices. They reminded her of Ignatius's, the stains stiff like dried sugar crystals. Ignatius had explained to her how they would keep some of the cane for themselves, make a sirop, and let it ferment. He always had visions drinking the cane alcohol. Checking the sky, she thought about him now, already at work, his broad back sweating. He was smiling at her, winking. The water was cool this morning but the soap was not taking out the stains. She redoubled her efforts, scraping at the brown spots with her fingernail. It was no use.

She thought about the news she had heard on the radio, about how the Dominican soldiers were using the old Tontons Macoutes to control the men in the camps, and how those who had rebelled had been beaten but were not receiving medical attention. She wondered if Ignatius was all right with his bad leg. If he hurt it again, he would probably never walk. Maybe he would be sent back with the others who were sick.

Secretly, although she knew he needed the money—they needed the money—Elyse was hoping he would. Then she could tell him in person what remained her secret. I'm pregnant, Ignatius. I'm pregnant with your baby.

The image of his face, his surprise and joy at the news, made her smile again. She rubbed soap more vigorously into the stains, then pushed the material harder against a rock, repeating the process with each shirt, then setting them to soak. Grann's Sunday dress was next. Elyse looked at it carefully. Somehow, another button was missing. It's finished, she thought, holding the near-transparent cotton between her fingers. We'll bury you in it. She rubbed a bit of soap into the dress, watching as the water filled it up for an instant, then removed it and set it to dry along with the other clothes on the bank.

The air was warmer. She thought about the rice again. Too many people selling the same things, that's the problem. I agree with Pierre. We should make a group. Tout moun ansanm. That's the

best way. We can't give them any more tax money anyway, we
don't have any money to buy food. So what are we going to give
them? What have they given us? Nothing. Look at the water. We
paid for the pipe, three times we paid a tax, and we know that water
is carrying fever. That's what they give us, a pipe with fever in it.
I say we keep the money and make a group. That way at least some
of us can eat. This way we are killing ourselves. Gwo vole, big
thieves, that's all they are.

She remembered an incident Pierre had told her about just yesterday, about the little boy who had been shot in midday by the
police. A boy standing in front of a store, minding his own business.
The boy jumping up and down, his stomach shooting blood like a
fountain, a little human fountain, and the soldiers just walking
away, nobody arresting them, nobody saying anything. They're just
thieves, Ignatius—she had his face before her again—we can't continue this way. When you come back, we have to find another
solution. Look at me, I'm waiting for a baby and I can't afford to
buy meat. No, this can't continue. And you know even if we gave
them this tax, they'll come back next month asking for something
else. So I'm going to refuse. Let them shoot me. Gwo vole!

She unbraided her hair, knowing what Grann would say. Stay
out of it. Don't get involved. It's all politics. But that wouldn't be
Grann talking; that would be an old woman who was afraid of the
white light. I'm more afraid of not eating, Elyse argued back. If
Pierre doesn't find us some meat today, what are we going to do?
She massaged her scalp with her thumbs in little circles, the way
the Nivea woman had demonstrated on television, trying to get rid
of the headache that was lasting longer every day to the point where
it hurt her eyes. She wondered if it hurt to put your head in a big
drying machine as that Nivea woman did . . . why didn't her hair
burn if it was so hot?

She rebraided her tresses, pressing water from the damp strands.
She wanted to make a crown for the party this weekend, a crown
like the Nivea lady had, like a princess, she thought, laughing, I'll
put something shiny in my hair. She settled instead for a fat tress
in the center and six little ones, three on each side. Braiding quickly,
her fingers felt and pulled the hair into shape. She hummed, her

thoughts shifting from the image of the high crown of the white woman's hair to Ignatius's leg. Was he suffering now? Was he hurt? She thought of the crowd arguing with the tax man in the market, of the idea of the heart as a little pump, that's why the boy's blood had shot so high.

She was staring at her own arms, thinking about the little pump that would grow in her baby, whom she would name Paul if it was a boy, Marie if it was a girl. And worrying more now about Ignatius and whether she should try to send him a message. But who could she pay to go over there? Just then she saw something out of the corner of her eye. Something long and dark in the distance, just beyond the curve of the stream. For a second, she thought of the mad dog and drew back, grabbing the wash off the bank and throwing it into the basket. She dragged it with her behind the bush.

Peering out again, she stared at the spot. Whatever it was, it was not moving, maybe it was sleeping. She strained her eyes, trying to make out the shape. A fallen tree, that's what it might be. But it was too far away to make out. I have to get closer, she thought, her heart beginning to pound. She took a step, then another, noticing as she did that the crickets had become silent.

It took her a few minutes to go the long way around. She jumped over the stream at a narrow point, wetting the hem of her dress. The bushes were dense on this side; the roots hurt her feet. She grabbed a low branch and leaned over the water to see where she was. Just then the smell hit her, an odor of rotting eggs she recognized instantly.

Death.

"Tonne!" she swore, revolted, as her stomach rocked and bile threatened to rise up her throat. Damn! She held her dress to her nose and breathed through her teeth. Then she took another step, placing her foot in the soft mud of the stream, seeing at last the outline of a corpse, half submerged by the tall grasses, an enormous, bloated thing that smelled so bad she could not go farther. The corpse was face down, turned away from her toward the grasses. A length of rope was stretched tight around the swollen back; the skin on both sides of it appeared ready to explode. Elyse turned away, then back again, then away. Her mind had gone blank, her body stiff. "Tonne!" she swore again, but to herself this time, not out loud.

A mass of green-backed dragonflies beat the air above the corpse. She watched them land on the rubbery-looking back, then head over to the riverbank like royal messengers. She felt shocked, not by the sight of a corpse, which she had seen before, but by the sight of this one, decaying at the edge of the stream where she had been baptized. She picked up a pebble and threw it at the body, watching the circles of water that spread as it ricocheted into the water. She half crouched, noticing at last the ash-colored light between the trees. An outline of a gray cloud hovered above the mountain far in the distance.

Her entire being was shivering, she couldn't control it. She gripped a tree branch to balance herself, hearing an inner voice demand, not for the first time: Go! Get out of here! Now! She tried to move her left leg; it felt like wood.

Batting the air right and left, she tried to stop the smell of death from entering her nostrils, but in vain. It was settling on her skin like a film, disgusting. She could feel the blood pounding in her ears now. I should get out of here, she agreed with her inner voice, I should go. But again, she stood rooted to the spot, fascinated by the sight of the insects hovering and the quiet stillness surrounding the rotting corpse. Who was it? She couldn't make out anything from the clothes. Only that it was a large person, a man, she assumed. She was unable to see anything below the water.

I'm going to get sick, she thought suddenly, I'm going to faint if I stay here another second. She heard a noise, something cracking, then saw that her own hand had snapped a twig off the tree, she had clenched it so hard. She managed to step back out of the water, back to a spot where the sweet-sour smell of death was fainter. She listened to the crickets, which had resumed their chatter. It's just a body, she recited. It can't hurt you. But she crossed herself twice for protection and moved to a position at another angle from the corpse. The smell was less intense here. She could also see where the weeds were crushed and there were imprints in the mud. The end of the rope trailed in the weeds.

Whoever had dragged the body here had worn shoes, hard shoes.

These were heel marks. And the rope . . . was this a murder? But by whom, and why and when? Questions flooded her mind now. She thought about finding a long stick to push the corpse over. But she could not get closer, the smell was too much. I'm going to be sick, she thought, feeling a sudden swell of nausea.

Her leg muscles were cramping; she rubbed them, looking all the while at the corpse. From here, it looked less sinister, less menacing, hidden by the grasses from anyone who would be walking on the path toward the waterfall. Now she saw something else. She maneuvered around the low bushes by the stream's edge, pushed through another thicket of thorny bushes, and picked it up. "Sen Kristof," she whispered aloud, picking up the silver medallion, St. Christopher. She held it in her hands, debating whether to keep it. She kept her head away from the smell of death, felt around the base of a tree and hung the medallion over a branch. Sen pou moun pedi, saint of lost souls. If the dead man's spirit was lost or wandering, it might be looking for someone to help it. St. Christopher could do that. She gave a last look at the corpse and quickly hurried away.

Upstream, far away from the smell, she stopped to wash her arms in the little trickle of water. In her panic, she had nearly forgotten the wash. She took out the bar of soap, and rubbed it on her arms, rinsing quickly, not wanting to let death enter Grann's house. A few minutes later, she spotted the first house, then the others, then Grann's. She slowed down to even her breath, to press her palm under her ribs, to calm the feeling of sickness, to swallow down the bile. It wasn't a mad dog, she was telling the others already, it was a person. And somebody killed them, they were tied up with a rope. I saw footprints in the mud, somebody with shoes or boots. The army, that's who I think it was, the Tontons Macoutes.

Inside, the house had not changed. Grann was still snoring. A trio of roosters crowed in succession as she sat down on her sleeping mat, then got up again, remembering the wash. Then she was back inside again, pulling her mat closer to Grann's. The curtain hung just over her head. Grann's breath was as regular as a child's. Grann, Elyse wanted to wake her, to whisper, I saw a dead man. Somebody murdered him. Grann, I feel so sick.

The old woman did not stir. Elyse placed her hand close to her grandmother's elbow. Grann, she edged her face even closer, the man lost his protection. Sen Kristof. I found it and left it on a tree for his spirit to find. She breathed deeply, pressing on the knot of nausea that was so hard it was hurting her. She didn't bother to strip off her dress, still somewhat damp. Instead, she stuck her fingers in her ears, listening to the blood pounding. Grann, she wanted to tell her, the light you keep seeing in your dreams, I saw it. It's like the edge of the night, just before the next day, isn't it? Just the next day, except you don't get to see it when you die.

2

Along Route National One the traffic was dense and moving fast. Top-heavy trucks vibrated out of nowhere, passengers leaning dangerously over the sides. Emmanuel slid the car onto the dirt bank and slowed as the truck zoomed by. Exhaust swirled over the road with no wind to drive it away. He closed the car windows, then opened the vents. Ten minutes later, his childhood friend and lawyer Gerard Metellus reopened the window to smoke a cigarette. Hot damp air struck their faces.

It was an hour after the quick storm and already the sun was beating down. The gray strip of the highway had become two black lines in the center of the asphalt, the shoulder crumbling into muddy puddles. A car flashed its lights behind them. They heard honking; the Mercedes-Benz passed them at a speed Emmanuel estimated to be over 100 kilometers, the gleaming trademark fender of the import blinding him for an instant. A young mulatto couple waved.

The priest slowed down to avoid the cloud of dust already enveloping their car. "Did you see?" he asked Gerard. "That was General Lucerne's youngest daughter. She must be coming back from the beach. You heard they're going ahead with the marriage, didn't you?"

Gerard nodded. He found a piece of newspaper under the seat and wiped his arms, which were already covered with dirt.

"Fifty cases of Dom Pérignon," the priest continued. "Directly from Paris. And not Brut—Rosé." A small smile played on his lips as he shook his head in disapproval.

"I got my invitation this week," said Gerard, who searched his pockets for a handkerchief. He had forgotten one. "I'm surprised the Duvaliers weren't included," he added, pulling discreetly on his nose to clear it. "They've invited that French minister, you know, the one they say helped the Duvaliers to stay in France."

The wedding invitation had been printed in embossed gold leaf, and listed twenty-five "distinguished foreign guests" who would be attending. Gerard had noted the Panamanian military envoy's name, a man alleged to have laundered money for a close Duvalier associate. Gerard had read the dossier only last week. "It's so crass, I'm almost tempted to go," he added, turning back to the conversation. "It will be like Michèle and Jean-Claude's wedding."

Emmanuel accepted the sooty newspaper and wiped his pant legs. "The Lucerne girl wants to be a model too, just like Michèle," he said sarcastically.

Gerard noticed that when Emmanuel smiled the corners of his lips turned slightly down, as if he were embarrassed. "Is it true what I heard?" he asked the priest.

"About her being pregnant? I wouldn't doubt it. That girl has been having sex since she was sixteen, even if her family wants to pretend differently."

"Now how do you know that?" Gerard laughed. "Did one of her boyfriends confess that to you?"

"The benefits of my profession." Emmanuel smiled, pulling unconsciously on his wispy beard with one hand. "You hear everything but you say nothing, contrary to our Haitian tradition."

"No wonder they're so afraid of you," Gerard remarked. The smell of something burning had infiltrated the car. In the distance, he could see a column of smoke in the middle of the plain, but no signs of life.

"Not that a teenage pregnancy would stop our famous bishop from celebrating the wedding," Emmanuel continued, braking smoothly and removing his sunglasses as they approached a village. "You'll see, Bishop Privat will perform the baptism too."

Just off the edge of the road, a group of women squatted beside piles of charcoal. They stood up, anticipating a sale.

"Didn't you see the editorial about him in *Le Nouvelliste*?" he asked Gerard. The women held the baskets aloft. "They are calling Privat 'the new voice of morality in the Catholic Church of Haiti.' "

"I saw that headline. Do you think he wrote it himself?"

"Probably." The priest grinned.

The women waved for the car to stop.

"I'll say this for Privat," Emmanuel added. "He's clever. This way, he can show his support for military men like Lucerne, without having to do so openly. I read another article recently claiming that

General Lucerne shouldn't be considered a Duvalierist because he refused that post in Jean-Claude's cabinet. But you'll remember, he refused before he was even nominated. It was an offensive move. He already knew there was too much opposition to him. Anyway, everything they're doing now is for the Americans. Lucerne is the only one whose hands are clean enough for them."

The women continued to shout as he slowed the car even more. Their dresses were black from the charcoal. "Non mesi," Emmanuel said to them, extending his hand to touch theirs. "No, thank you. Not today, thank you."

"Pe!" they cried out. Father! "Gade sa!" Look at this!

Emmanuel trailed an arm out the window to signal his regret, then turned back to Gerard. "I'm not so sure that all those pseudo-democrats who want to be deputies won't end up backing Lucerne. Don't forget, the post of ambassador is still open. If I wasn't opposed to games of chance, I would place my bet that one of these gentlemen flies to Washington very soon." He added as an afterthought: "It's all a sign of how desperate the hierarchy of the Church has become. They're afraid of us . . . afraid of the real Catholic Church." He looked at Gerard with a grim expression. "That's the kind of alliance our bishop will be celebrating next Saturday—a renewal of vows between Rome and the Devil." His tone was bitter.

"Plus ça change . . . " Gerard said, seeking to lighten the mood a bit.

"Hélas," the priest agreed, pulling on what passed for his small beard, "hélas."

A group of children played in the street. They scattered, tapping on the car as it slowly circled the concrete pole marking the entrance to the town.

The market was crowded. People recognized Emmanuel and pointed. The smell of outdoor cooking filled the air. The priest refrained from honking, waiting patiently as a woman whipped a recalcitrant mule with a branch. The animal resisted, deaf to the woman's curses. She dismounted to whip it more fiercely, ignoring the children, who mocked her until she moved to whip them too. "Makak! Maledve!" she screamed at them. Monkeys! Brats!

"Since the day they announced the election, Privat has been going out of his way to praise the army—'the new army'—that's what he calls it," Emmanuel continued. He turned his windshield wipers to the wash position and sprayed the window, clearing the dust. "And be careful. Rome is becoming more sympathetic. Privat's opinion is gaining support. Up to now, they still haven't issued any response to the attack on the parish in Labadie. That's what I went to see about this morning. I stopped by to see Hubert Sansaricq— he's being cared for by the Sisters of Perpetual Mercy. He's in poor condition, I have to say, worse than I had been told. I think the shock is just too great. He barely talks. And the sisters told me he cries all the time. All he wanted to know was if another novena could be said for his wife and daughter, the poor man. I told him we were pressing the authorities for an investigation, but I don't even think he heard me. Really, he doesn't hear anything. He's having a total breakdown."

Gerard listened, hearing the little catch in Emmanuel's voice. He did not personally know Sansaricq, the lay minister from La- badie, but had listened to a news report detailing the burning of the parish, in which the minister's wife and eldest child had perished.

The mule was bucking but slowly giving in, the woman pulling hard on its rope harness. The car inched ahead. "I took the step of personally speaking out about all of this to the Papal Nuncio last week. I told him a number of parishioners had identified the at- tackers as the men of the section chief, a Macoute. I told him I would send him a copy of their testimony. I told him what they didn't mention in the newspapers, that both the wife and the girl were raped. That's something no one is talking about. I don't even think Hubert accepts it. But we have two witnesses who will testify. They were forced to stay in the room and saw it. Shall I tell you what his response was? You won't be surprised: 'The Church does not involve itself in politics, Père Emmanuel.' That's what he told me. 'Our mission must remain strictly spiritual.' Can you imagine? What a hypocrite!" The priest shrugged his shoulders, disgusted. He sighed, pulling harder on his beard. "I've decided to send copies of my reports to the Vatican as well. Might as well let them know we are perfectly aware of their complicity." He added, touching Gerard on the arm: "I trust you'll keep this to yourself? . . ."

"Evidemment," the lawyer replied. Of course.

"As for Bishop Privat"—Emmanuel's voice was unbridled reproach—"I think we know everything about him that matters by now. Do you know his family made a large contribution to Papa Doc's campaign? And there's the little question of his family's property in St.-Marc. I'm sure Rome is not entirely unaware of Privat's patrimony."

"Actually it's technically a matrimony, no? From his grandmother's side?" Gerard thought he had read that somewhere.

"The blood on both sides is dirty," Emmanuel replied dryly. "Did you know his great-grandmother was the daughter of a slave? She married for reasons of color—the grandfather was so light he denied he was mulâtre." He looked quickly at Gerard, who was light-skinned. "No offense."

"Not at all." The lawyer chuckled. "I don't know the family, but I've always known Privat had some color in his blood, even if he claims it's Italian."

They laughed.

"Yes, well, don't all roads lead to Rome?" Emmanuel said wryly, yawning. They were leaving the town behind. "To change the subject," he added, stretching his arms, "are you going to touch upon the question of color in your play? There are some who are resurrecting that now with these elections—the noiristes." He himself was very dark.

"Oh, I don't know," Gerard replied. Emmanuel was the first one he had talked to about the play. "I don't know where any of this will really go. Right now I'm happy if something interesting comes out."

"Always modest, Gerard." The priest patted his friend on the knee.

"Honest, not modest," Gerard corrected. "I find writing much more difficult than practicing law."

"Although both require an active imagination, and, I imagine, an ability to suspend reality, no?" Emmanuel teased him.

"Quite true." Gerard laughed. "In that sense, I suppose I'm well prepared."

The high noon sun produced odd images: an old woman wavering as she watched the car pass; a group of young boys playing soccer, the aluminum panel of a store reflecting their near-nakedness. They drove on, past fields of bright green, women bent down in the distance, planting. A sign indicated the beginning of a malarial zone. More villages, mud houses built too close to the road. Two cars were stopped by the side of the road, the drivers arguing. Emmanuel honked, giving them a wide berth.

There were so many accidents each week that many considered the coastal highway an occupational hazard. Passengers were literally ejected from rickety trucks onto the tarmac, itself an occasional display of squashed watermelons and bananas. Emmanuel drove deftly, weaving the car from right to left to avoid huge potholes, many filled in with garbage. Gerard shifted his weight, leaned his head against the window frame to enjoy the warm breeze. He looked out at the land again. There were low trees, fields of aloe and prickly weeds, the sea cropping up from time to time, bright turquoise in the distance, now the flat brown marshlands close to the road. He thought of sailing, felt the heat sinking into his shoulders, caught a flash of yellow as a little girl dashed across a dirt courtyard, then entered a house. Scenes like these reminded him that Haiti had not lost all of its charm, despite the assault of natural and human forces. My poor country, he thought, still so beautiful. His finger drew a line along the distant horizon, his thoughts turning to Hubert Sansaricq and Privat, to the wedding and Lucerne, to the Panamanian envoy, to the Duvalier accounts, which an American legal firm had contacted him about, requesting assistance. He felt hungry, but sleepy. The sun felt so good on his shoulders.

Emmanuel reached over to lock the passenger door. His old friend had fallen asleep. No use adding to the statistics, he thought, looking affectionately at Gerard, whose lean café-au-lait face needed a shave. He's depressed, thought the priest. He needs a vacation. But I hope he's not serious about quitting his practice. Even though I understand his frustration. We need good men like him, more now than ever. I wonder what his wife knows . . . she would hear if Lucerne's daughter had an abortion. Dom Pérignon Rosé . . . it's as if February 7 had never taken place . . . do you hear me, Lord? Fifty cases on ice from Paris . . . there's the problem right there. No refrigerator—no vote. Now there's a platform for the pseudo-democrats. Poor Hubert, he thought, grimacing as he drove, what a terrible thing to endure.

3

A flash of heat lightning broke out below the wing of the American Airlines plane as it advanced toward the island of Haiti, illuminating the dimmed cabin for an instant. Leslie stared at her profile in the window before it disappeared. From her place of relative safety, the storm outside looked bad. A rumble of thunder had followed the lightning by seconds; the plane shook and entered a dense cloud. The thunder continued. The plane bumped and dipped as it passed through a seemingly solid gray mass and continued its descent. She pulled her seat forward and gripped the handrail, heard the "ding" of the intercom system a moment later, and the expected announcement: "Mesdames et messieurs, s'il vous plaît, retournez à vos sièges et attachez vos ceintures de sécurité. Nous vous prions d'éteindre toutes cigarettes. . . . Merci."

She stared at the ceiling as the voice outlined oxygen mask instructions in Creole: "Si oksijen vin koupe, mask yo ap soti nan plafon otomatikman . . ." If the oxygen is cut, your mask will automatically drop from the ceiling. "Me mask la kouvri nen ou ak bouch ou epi respire nomalman . . ." Put the mask over your nose and mouth and breathe normally. "Le ou fini, w'ap ajiste pa ti moun yo byen delika . . ." When you've finished adjusting your mask, adjust it carefully for your child. She checked her translation against that of the announcer. Not bad.

A large Haitian woman with two young children lifted the armrests separating them and pulled her brood in close, ignoring the anonymous advice. She smiled briefly at Leslie, who sat across the aisle from the trio, and crushed the children's small heads even tighter against her bosom. Leslie handed the woman a blanket and she took it, covering the children's heads completely. The plane trembled.

Leslie's eyes felt bloodshot. Another clap of thunder, more lightning. Her knuckles were white. Rain spattered the windows. They were in the middle of the black cloud. Please, she addressed a higher power, feeling her stomach drop with the plane in a sudden free fall, please stop now. As she looked out, the dark edge of the storm was outlined in pink, heat lightning revealing a dark, gaping hole in the middle of the cloud, like a cotton ball dipped in ink. The plane stopped vibrating. She closed her eyes and swallowed to relieve the pressure building inside her ears. Thank you.

When she opened her eyes fifteen minutes later, the storm had passed. The last beads of rain crawled up the window. Soon they would be above the island of La Gonâve, with its famed profile of a giant sleeping lady. Leslie could not make out the underwater reefs she knew were there, visible like dark fans on bright days. Instead, the sea was the color of slate, its depths unfathomable.

She craned her neck to look down, spying a tanker, then, near the shore, a trio of fishing boats. As the plane crossed over land, the dark water changed to green, but only momentarily. The narrow, fertile coast was replaced by a dull brown color. Although she was prepared for it, the effects of the continuing erosion were still shocking. The island's stark mountains looked like prehistoric caymans pressing craggy snouts and mud-dried bodies together, trapped in what had once been a fertile valley of rivers. Primeval, but futuristic, life before and after man, surreal. Here and there a handful of trees stood out, singular and pathetic like the few remaining tufts on an old man's head. Jesus, she muttered, there's almost nothing left. She continued to stare at the balding mountains, stunned.

The landing announcement was made. She turned her attention back to the stewardess, whose Creole bore a Midwestern accent, the *r*'s flattening like *w*'s as if a rubber band was around her tongue. She was always impressed when she heard other Americans speak Creole, instantly comparing their fluency with hers. "Medamn . . . Mesye . . . nap swete yon bon voyaj pou tou moun e toujou kenbe fem ak American Airlines . . ." Kenbe fem? We wish you a pleasant voyage and always hang on to American Airlines? She chuckled at that one; a literal translation would not do. Kenbe fem: Hold tight. Keep the faith. Don't give up. Survive. It replaced "goodbye" among friends. "Kenbe fem!" Gerard would add as a postscript to his faxes. And now American Airlines was using it to sell tickets. She shook her head, both amused and annoyed. Those capitalists don't miss a trick, she thought. Gerard is going to love hearing about this one.

The plane flew in a wide circle as it approached the runway. They passed over checkerboard fields of green and yellow, brown, beige, here and there a grouping of thatched-roof houses with dirt roads that trailed into the hillside and disappeared. Closer to the airport, the corrugated roofs of factories reflected the plane's shadow. She felt a tightening, a feeling of excitement as the wheels of the plane were released. Moments later, the cabin broke out in spontaneous clapping as the plane smoothly touched the ground.

The airport was no longer called the François Duvalier Airport, but the International Airport of Port-au-Prince, a benign title. The renaming of streets and public buildings had begun immediately after the hasty departure of the notorious family. The process of redressing history was ongoing. Leslie had obtained a last-minute fax of the tourist map of the capital from Gerard. Scrawled next to the printed names were the new popular ones: Cité-Simone, named after Simone Duvalier, was now Cité Soleil; Duvalierville had reverted to an earlier designation, Cabaret. Next to the airport, he had scribbled: Maisgate, the name of the district. She made a note to ask him about more recent changes.

Six months had passed since the hot spring of the dechoukaj—the uprooting, as the popular purge of the Duvalierists had been termed—but the campaign to erase any vestige of the dictatorship continued. Leslie had followed the process on television and by shortwave radio, glued to the news, and surprised at how quickly the brutal regime had crumbled after such a long reign. Even now she could recall the feeling of exhilaration and power that had crackled through the static as the Haitian newscasters proclaimed Duvalier's fall to the world. Some of them had lost their voices, too overjoyed to keep reporting. She had so much wanted to be there.

She felt a shiver of anticipation, wondering what awaited her. A tall fence separated the landing strip from overgrown fields bordering the industrial zone around it. She stared at them as if she might see the former Tontons Macoutes militia that were rumored to be meeting by the airport at night, regrouping. Are you out there? she asked the invisible menace. Are you waiting for me? There were four Sea-Land shipping containers by a small cinder-block shed, unmarked. Two goats grazed freely in the field beside it.

Instinctively, she felt for the letter she was carrying in her jacket pocket. A kind of letter of credentials, explaining her mission. She had written it herself, upon Gerard's advice. "Make it look official," he had said, and she had, stamping it and including her boss's signature. The letter stated simply that she was in Haiti to visit several cooperative "self-help" projects that had applied for assistance from the Funding Coalition, the nonprofit organization she represented. It was true enough. They did need to know if the political climate was stable in order to reassure their donors. But her real motives were personal. She wanted to visit Haiti again, to research an oral history project about women who had been imprisoned under the Duvaliers. The idea had been brewing for years, ever since she had gotten to know women migrant workers employed on a Maryland farm who had discussed their plight back in Haiti.

Until now, everyone, including Gerard, had deemed the political situation too dangerous, especially for an outsider, even one like her, who knew the country. But with things in flux, there was a window of opportunity, and people might feel freer to talk. Gerard had written as much in his last letter, urging Leslie to take advantage of the chaos. And with Marisa more grown up, and her own finances in better shape, there was no reason not to. Of course, everything would depend on how things felt. For now, what mattered was to be open, to observe, to talk to people. Despite Gerard's letters, and the weekly Sunday news broadcasts she listened to, she felt out of touch with Haiti. Somewhere in the back of her mind, she was also toying with the idea of living there year-round, to experience the country without dictatorship. Before, she had never felt free to move around, to explore independently.

She looked at the area beyond the fence a last time. It was easy to imagine the Duvalierists' meeting, just beyond her line of vision, hidden behind the Sea-Land containers. You're taking a risk, but it's not crazy, she reassured herself. It's calculated. And if something doesn't feel right, you won't do it. You won't put yourself into dangerous situations. I won't do anything stupid, she repeated to herself. It sounded like a mantra. I'm just going to see what's there. Anyway, it's now or never. The goats ran so clumsily, they were adorable. Marisa would love one as a pet, she thought. The plane had stopped. The air in the cabin was heating up since the air conditioning had been turned off. "Stay in your seats," the stewardess was urging, gently pushing people back down. "Tanpri." Please. "We'll be moving in a moment. The captain has not turned off the 'no smoking' sign. Keep your seat belts fastened."

Leslie waited patiently, mentally reviewing her agenda. She had scheduled three weeks for this visit. The first would be spent in the capital, the second and third visiting areas of the countryside. With Gerard's help, she was planning to contact as many human rights and women's groups as possible, and maybe gain access to a prison. In preparation, she had reviewed a barrage of private notes, legal and hospital reports that Gerard had sent her, as well as interviews with reporters. The majority covered the Duvalier period; some were about the current situation. But almost all were inconsistent or incomplete.

She quickly filled out her landing form and checked her passport, tucked safely into an inner pocket of her jacket. It was there, of course. The jet began to move again, braking repeatedly. She could feel the sweat forming between her breasts. Let's get there already! she thought. We're late!

This time the passengers were up and in the aisle before the stewardesses could rush forward to protest. The protective mother and her children were among the first standing. People began pressing their faces in twos and threes against the thick windows, looking at the terminal. The big woman caught Leslie's eye. "This is going to be their first time in Haiti," she explained in English, caressing her children.

"Li pale Kreyol?" Leslie asked. Do they speak Creole? She had decided to wait and let everyone else get off. She hated rushing.

"No." The woman replied in English, smiling at the children, who eyed Leslie with shy curiosity. "This is John, this is Susan. They have Canadian passports," she said proudly.

Looking around, Leslie wondered how many other passengers were returning for the first time since exile. Over the past months, she had spoken with a number of Haitians, particularly taxicab drivers, about the changes taking place in their homeland. She was continually surprised at how initially detached and unfamiliar they appeared with events in Haiti, given how passionate they could become on the subject when she pressed them. Yes, they had viewed the dechoukaj on television, and wasn't it exciting? Unbelievable, that's right. Sensing her interest, they would describe elaborate plans for returning, the blueprints for the new home or factory of their dreams worked out down to the smallest details, every penny of the long years saved for just this opportunity. Of course, they would laugh in that way, I've had a lot of time to think about it, I've been driving this cab for fifteen years wondering if this day would ever come. Driving around a foreign capital speaking the foreign language to strangers who mistook Haiti for Tahiti—isn't that in the Pacific? Driving through winters. Raising children to speak English and forget Haiti and Duvalier and the Tontons Macoutes in their dark sunglasses and their easy habit of torture. Why? Because the past is the past and my children are the future. For months, she had been hearing the same responses over and over. How many like them were on this very flight, wads of bills bound in tired envelopes, stuffed deep into handbags, a gift for the relatives?

What do you expect to find? What do you think will be different? It was here that the pause often inserted itself, a blank in the image bank, an inability to know how it would feel to finally be back, even if only to look, to see what had changed. Could it really be different? The joyous crowds who danced on the television newscasts and waved quickly printed blue-and-red flags of liberation. Were they really free? Or just drunk with the notion of it? Did some nightmare await them like an inevitable hangover? I'll wait, many of them had said to her. I'll wait and see. Until I'm there, I won't know for sure.

The Duvalierists had been chased out of the palace, the Tontons Macoutes hacked down in the streets. In some cases nothing was left even to bury. Papa Doc's tomb had been destroyed; Leslie had seen the pictures in the newspaper, young children standing victoriously on top of the graffitied crypt. But until these taxi drivers could do it themselves, walk in the streets unafraid, dance after dark, until they had accumulated enough new experiences to replace the old, the change was something that had taken place on television. Inside their minds and hearts, the Haiti they knew remained, a Haiti they had physically escaped but mentally inhabited to this day. The devout subject and object of their most intense love and fear, their own personal Haiti. There are no guarantees, everyone had said the same thing, no one can promise us that.

At the airport in New York, Leslie had overheard a group of Haitian businessmen discussing "the big question": whether to return or stay. "The Plight of the Exiles," a Brooklyn-based weekly had headlined it. Those who had assumed foreign citizenship would be welcomed as native sons and daughters. Incentives were being promised. But among the group was an older man who had disagreed with his colleagues. He was returning to visit a dying relative. In response to Leslie's questions about the end of Duvalierism, he had replied, "Joumon pa janm bay kalbas." The pumpkin never bears the calabash. Loosely translated, it meant: Like father, like son. She wasn't sure what the old man was referring to, and when she asked, "Are you talking about the elections?" he had merely repeated, emphasizing each word: "Joumon—pa—janm—bay—kalbas!" as if she were unusually slow. He had left her like that too, still wondering. A dictatorship doesn't produce democracy? That seemed like a good guess.

Men in gray overalls rushed toward the plane. From where she watched, they looked like silent cheerleaders, their arm movements large and animated as they directed it to the terminal. A line of people stood on the second-floor balcony of the building. Leslie didn't recognize any of them. Maybe Bertrand didn't get my message, she thought. Maybe he sent someone to pick me up.

She saw the businessman getting out of his seat a few feet behind her and let others pass her, waiting for him to catch up. The man offered her a broad smile, revealing a triptych of gold-rimmed teeth. "At last," he said in his heavily accented English, "we are arrived. I see my brother there—look." He indicated the airport balcony. Leslie nodded politely. The man was older than she had first thought, the nostrils of his broad nose badly veined, his fingertips yellowed with tobacco stain.

"The players are different," he whispered, "but the game remains the same. I tried to tell them"—he indicated his colleagues—"but they don't want to know." He removed a handkerchief and sneezed into it. "Some people want to forget the past," he added. "I understand that. Since I have been living in Queens, I no longer think about the Tontons Macoutes. But I never forget them. That's what people don't understand. Duvalier was only the head of the animal—la bête. The real monster was all those people who did his dirty work, all of those who participated, who accepted, who kept their silence."

He gave her a long, defiant look, then shrugged his shoulders and smiled again. "My children tell me I've become too old, that I repeat myself. But I'm not too old to be wrong, am I? I'm like an elephant, my memory hasn't deserted me yet." He pointed up to the balcony once more and added, this time to himself: "You'll see, they're easy to spot. They're the ones who want to forget." And he smiled again, nodding to himself.

Reaching into his vest pocket, the man retrieved a small card and held it at a distance to read it before handing it to her. "When you are in New York"—he watched as she read it—"you can have dinner with us. I live with my son's family in Flushing. I always like talking to people who care about my country."

"Sodex Incorporated. Alexandre Desfils. Manager. Thank you," Leslie said, putting the card in with her passport.

"That's my son, Alex. He's in charge now. I'm Henri. I retired five years ago—on my seventieth birthday."

"And are you going to return to Haiti now?"

He gave her a strange look, then shook his head. "Return? But I never left. I told you, I'm an elephant. We can travel, but we know where the bones of our ancestors lie. If you stay in Haiti a while, you'll see, you won't be able to leave either."

She laughed, but inside, the thought made her uneasy. Following the older man out, she leaned down for an instant to get another look at the fields and the goats. The man behind her was impatiently pushing into her legs with his bag. "Okay," she said, adding: "Mwen ale." I'm going.

I remember: The cave was so black I could not see my feet. A man-made cave, just a hole in the earth as wide as my shoulders, my son, they dropped me into it like I was already dead. How can I describe its blackness to you? It was thicker, more sour, more suffocating, hotter even than you might imagine the hell they teach you in school. A solitary hell. Remember your papa's words. If the blackness comes upon me now it is because I am hiding once again and once again there has been no warning, no time, no preparation. Death is stalking me, son, and I am hiding like a rabbit in my hole. Again I am in a cave but this time of my choosing. This time I have plunged into the earth without worrying about the viper or the rat or the dirt that makes a second skin that might embalm me in a coat of dust, mummify me in my sticking clothes. I have found refuge in the place I so feared. I have made a friend of darkness, son, as you must do if you are to survive. Here I can stretch my hands out, I can breathe, I can sleep. I have enough space to move, to burrow myself deeper into this mountain hole if I hear their dogs. They will not find me tonight, even a dog would be afraid to come inside. But I have no fear. Because I already died a hundred times in their dark prison, and yet I survived. It does not matter if the dirt touches my face now, or I feel the insects crawling on my feet. I am safe. The darkness is my mother.

These are things I did not tell you. I withheld my knowledge from you, my fears, my suffering. Now I am beginning to regret my decision. I wanted to shield you from the stink of your own urine, instead of teaching you how to drink it a little at a time, as I did to survive. Even when the earth had me in its grip, when my legs were full of pain, I found a way to move, to relax. Even when I could not feel my bones, I moved them. In my head, I forced myself to take a step, to walk, to escape the devil who was crushing me. The last hole on earth, that is what we called it. I could not see my arms, I could not move my neck. They dropped us into earthen coffins and starved us. And every time they opened the wooden square above our heads to see if we had died, more earth would fall and that's how we knew we had survived.

I walked, son, I walked and talked to you, I imagined you a man already, as I did again tonight, wondering what I will face tomorrow. I wanted to spare you my terror. I wanted you to know only your papa's courage, his triumph. Will anyone ever tell you about the man who was dragged by his bare feet from the prison cell, unconscious? That was me. I could not drink or chew. I was the man whose teeth could not stop rattling. I was their drum. They put their knives in my mouth and listened to the rhythm of my fear. Make music for us, Cedric, that's what they would say, and laugh. There is no one to tell you this story, the others are all dead. And those who escaped are too far gone in their heads, they only recall the glory now.

By my fear you will know me, son, that is my lesson for you today. When they put a scorpion on your head and tell you to sit still, think of the ones you love or your mother or me with our hands on your face and you will cease to tremble. You will become a rock like I was, like I have become in this cave.

I left you with songs and little sculptures. Sing and play, that is how I wanted you to spend your young life. Not frightened, not buried in your mama's lap waiting for the knock on the door. Knowing you are safe, I am rocking you tonight, my sweet son. Did they tell you I cannot have more children? About the iron bar that squeezed my testicles? I taught you the alphabet, the words of my mother's songs. But I never wanted you to taste the metal of a gun in your mouth. Cold acid in the darkness, like the memories I have of that dark place. With their death in my mouth and my teeth chattering and my stomach vomiting. No, I did not make a pretty sight. I was not a strong man. But I held you in my head, whatever image of you I had created from those short months we had together. I held you and rocked you in my arms and the bullet was not greater than our life force joined with the life force of my own father and his father, your great-grandfather.

These are the lessons. I was taught them and I learned, but now I have made my father's mistake, wanting to shield you from the knowledge. I told your aunt, my sister, that I feel death riding my back again, not Baron Samedi, but my own shadow catching up with me, sleeping as it does, as I do, in this little cave I have found to rest in for a few hours. My dearest son, I would wrap you in my arms and teach you to draw a short breath, to move your muscles inside without moving the skin outside. The tricks of survival I was taught by others and have been too foolish, too selfish, to share with you. Not seeing it as something valuable. It is my debt, my father's debt, and perhaps his father's too, each of us wanting to pretend the next life will be easier.

That is another lesson, son. Because you must never walk on the land without thinking of who has walked here before you. Walked just as I have been walking, with a sore hip and a heavy bundle, without food in my belly, with another harvest to be gathered and stolen by a thief with a friend's face—I never suspected him of treachery. Hard lessons, son, made softer through tricks of a heart that prefers to love, not hate, that is why we choose to forget. I know so little of my father's life, or of your mother's in the short time we lived together. We were not thinking of a hard life, but of our future. And I did not set out to make her suffer the uncertainty, the constant terror. It was not my intention to heap the darkness upon her.

The history of the cave. The story my father refused to tell me about his foot, how he lost his toes. Was it in the cane? Or with the bottle? In a fight? Only once did he mention the boats to me, and then he was drunk. He took me to a beach to go fishing. It was one of our few times together when he was not working. There was a feast for a cousin of his and my own brothers were swimming in the water and he said, Watch the current. See how the tide is coming in over there but not over there? When the water is pulling back like that there are rocks, it is not a good place to launch your boat. If you need to launch your boat, make sure about the current. And choose the night after the full moon. When I was older I learned this was the place the Maroons used. It was a famous beach. It was there our ancestors planned their rebellion.

Another story: When I was in prison for the very first time another man became my best friend, Edouard, even though he was older than my father—your grandfather. His head was completely bald,

not even a single white hair. But he knew all about the Maroons.
He talked to us about the oar, La Vogue. How if we had been born
in an earlier generation or had been the bastard light-skinned sons
of Frenchmen we too might have become La Vogue, that's what
Edouard called it, a kernel of five men lashed together to an oar
for life. La Vogue, it was the word he used to describe everything
that happened to us in that place. They crammed us like animals
in their underground prison and we were six, sometimes seven, in
a cell no bigger than a large closet without windows, with only a
hole that pretended to let the light slip in, but only for a short time
in the morning, so that we slept in shifts. Domi kanpe. Only two
at a time could we fully stretch out on the concrete floor. It got so
cold at night we could not forget our misery and had to press our
backs against one another to share our warmth and energy. That's
what Edouard called La Vogue.

We were not permitted to speak and one who tried had his tongue
cut out with a knife. And the rest of us were not given any food
that week either. That was La Vogue. We spoke with our hands
and our eyes, and Luc, the one who lost his tongue, he could not
eat. But before he died, he went crazy. And even then they did not
take him away from us. He remained our brother.

Shall I describe Edouard to you? He was a big man, very strong,
even at his age. He had been whipped so often his back had scars
like the roots of a tree growing between his shoulders. And when
people talk now of taking the boat they forget the oar and the dark
galley, and the nerf de boeuf, a bullwhip with leather knots that
lifted the skin off our bones. When Edouard would talk about these
things I would tell him to stop. I wanted to forget my indignities.
But Edouard would say, Cedric, nothing dignifies a man like the
knowledge that he is part of La Vogue, that he is part of something
bigger than himself.

Now I am tiring, I need to sleep. But before I close my eyes I'll
say my prayer for you, son. That by some little miracle you will
think of me and when you do my thoughts will be blown into your
ears and your dreams by this current, the one that lets me breathe,
the greater current of freedom and hope that will always blow
stronger and higher than the little wind of death that has chased

me away from you and into hiding again. And if my prayer does not reach you tonight where you are sleeping in your mother's house, hopefully in peace, hopefully safe from harm, then may it reach you on some night when you need to feel your father's love and hope.

Embrace the darkness, son. And when you do, think of me. And if my fate is to die and you have trouble remembering my face, then close your eyes as I do now. That is one trick of darkness, that it can reveal more clearly than any flame what is hidden. That is how I am seeing your face, my child, as I always see it in my mind's eye. With you in my head I am never alone. With your small face and your voice and the daily recitation of your lessons. Even though my tongue is dry and my bones hurt because this rocky ground is so hard. With my eyes shut I will rise like Lazarus from this cave in an hour and find my shadow waiting for me, ready to blend in with the night. And you will be my guide, son, my heart and my breath. You are part of La Vogue, the short and long end of what keeps me moving, my little oar. Good night.

4

The warm bay air was sweet and damp and full of salt. Leslie took in deep breaths, relishing the smoky mix of outdoor cooking she associated with Haiti, the smell of corn blackening in the pit. The storm above was moving away; already, a pale sun was penetrating the low cloud cover. She stood inside the terminal, away from the crowd waiting at the arrivals gate. Bertrand was nowhere to be seen. Maybe he was trying to park.

The airport was modern and relatively clean. It didn't matter that she had seen it this way before; what still stuck in her mind was the old mustard-colored François Duvalier terminal, the one where she had waited as a teenager for her father to pick her up, a shy stranger afraid of the armed, unsmiling soldiers with their sunglasses. She half expected to see him now, arriving with his battered briefcase in hand, his glasses perched on his head. Pwofese Paul, that's what the Haitians had called him. And her, tifi Paul, the professor's daughter. He had been on another sabbatical then, tracing the route of the cocoa bean from east to west, fascinated by such phenomena as the pattern of the winds swirling around the tip of Hispaniola, as he preferred to call the island.

"What matters is your frame of reference," he liked to lecture strangers. "All the history you need to know about a place you can find through agriculture. In this little seed lies the route the traders took from India past the Horn of Africa to the port of St. Domingue. No need to look any further."

Thin, given to bouts of depression and excited insomnia, he had been a classic academic, absorbed in the letters of eighteenth-century scholars, his intellectual appetite voracious. It was only later that she had come to view his perspective as too narrow, more attuned to the precision of science than the unruly nature of humans. That, along with shyness, had kept him at a distance from the cultures he studied.

"What's the difference between destiny and choice?" Questions like that had been a game to him, a philosophical exercise. As a child, she had reveled in the challenge, wanting to prove her knowledge, to match him. Later, when she realized the game was a form of one-upmanship, information rather than true knowledge, she lost interest. It was his way of relating to the world, but not hers and not Mother's either. Leslie was like her, a social creature more inclined to spend time with people than in a library, Father's favorite pastime.

Now, in a few thick breaths of tropical air, she remembered that first summer, the humid sleepy afternoons and the mosquitoes and her growing sense of isolation, left alone with Father, who was always reading. Once she had fainted, poisoned from a day in the sun, and woken to find herself lying on a soiled mattress, a young black man wearing a pair of shorts sponging off her face with a rag and rinsing it in an enamel basin. She could recall the details perfectly. The boy had had ringworms on his face and on his neck and she had been terrified of catching them. He had brought her a warm Coca-Cola, she remembered that too. And she had lain there until after dark, when Father arrived, a book in hand, surprised but not upset at her disappearance. Pityriasis versicolor—he had looked it up for her in his big encyclopedia—ringworm. Also called tinea versicolor, a noncontagious fungus. The information hadn't helped; for months, every mark that appeared on her skin was a budding parasite she inspected with great fear.

Every individual is a product of a personal and social history. How many times had Father said that? He had been right about the need for a frame of reference, but had remained ignorant—willfully so, she had come to believe—of the bigger picture. Pityriasis versicolor, a condition caused by colonization of the dead outer layer of the skin by a fungus. That's as far as he had cared to look, no deeper. He had had no interest in the social roots of the condition; his curiosity had remained academic. She couldn't recall that he had ever discussed Duvalier with her. Nor had they seen the kind boy again. It had been an odd, intense summer, the last trip they had spent alone. Now he was dead and his friend Bertrand was coming to pick her up.

The cacophony in the terminal was getting louder, the throng outside pressing against the glass exit door, wanting to come inside.

She debated going outside, wondering if Bertrand might be waiting in the parking lot. But if she did, she wouldn't be able to come back in. He had said to wait in here.

In countries where travel by air is not a given in one's life, a person's departures and arrivals are important. She watched a family greet a young boy of grade school age with familiar kisses on both cheeks and maternal hugs. How was your flight? What did you eat? Doesn't he look good, so grown-up and handsome! The boy was blushing from all the attention, his younger brothers fighting to carry his bags. A porter picked up a large Sanyo carton. With more exclamations and back-patting, the family piled into a bus like a herd being corralled.

"Leslie?" She heard her name being shouted and lifted her hand in the air.

"Bertrand?" she yelled back.

"Is that you, Leslie?"

Bertrand was smiling, looking older and heavier but otherwise the same as she remembered. His tan face was sweating; there were huge wet rings under his armpits. He wore an embroidered light blue guayabera shirt, his belly testing the buttons. "Enfin!" He reached through the crowd to pull her into a hug. "We didn't see you at first."

"We? Did Marie come?" She looked around for Bertrand's wife.

They kissed each other on both cheeks. "The traffic was bad. We left late. Marie is home in bed." Bertrand spoke in a string of sentences, looking around as he did. He pointed to the garbage bag she was holding along with her suitcase and handbag. "What's in there? Did you bring us your laundry?" His grin was so wide it looked comical.

"No." She laughed. "Pampers. Gerard asked me to bring them. But I had to throw the boxes away at Kennedy. They thought I'd try to sell them on the black market."

"They really exaggerate." Bertrand clicked his tongue, vexed. "Not that any of this surprises me. Why do you think I am retiring from my business? Because they are impossible."

Leslie wasn't sure who "they" referred to. Bertrand was waving to someone approaching. "Now we have everything?" he asked.

"Everything's here," she replied.

He introduced a young black man with a quiet, but genial expression. "Clemard, this is Madame Leslie Doyle." They shook hands. "The daughter of my good friend the professor. I told him all about you, Leslie," he added.

She smiled. "Bonjour, Clemard . . ."

"Rameau," he softly interjected.

Bertrand ignored him. "Clemard is my new chauffeur. I'll put him at your disposal during your stay. It will be better than renting a car if you don't know the roads. He drives very well." The man had already picked up her bags and was walking away.

"I'll carry this," Leslie said, keeping hold of her handbag. She smiled broadly at Clemard, wanting immediately to disassociate herself from Bertrand's behavior. He probably didn't even know Clemard's last name, she thought, following the older man's large back as they pushed through the crowd. I'm glad I decided not to stay with him and Marie.

"This is my new car, Leslie," Bertrand said, opening the door for her. "It's the same model Diahatsu as the old gray one—remember? Except this one climbs better." She got into the back seat. "The Japanese are so skilled," he added. Bertrand joined Clemard in the front.

They ignored the vendors pressing wooden sculptures and bowls through the cracks in the car windows. Leslie smiled at a toothless old man whose pants had a broken zipper. "Non mesi," she said. No thanks. Despite Clemard's protests, the old man kept pressing the wooden forms against the window. The car accelerated away.

"The economy's gotten so bad, these poor devils are selling absolutely nothing," Bertrand remarked, seeing Leslie glance back at the vendors. "It's terrible. You can't believe it." He turned back to survey the oncoming traffic. "We'll take Delmas," he instructed Clemard, who merely nodded. Leslie rolled down her window, smiling at the sky, still dotted with threatening clouds. The smell of diesel and dust hung over the highway. The Diahatsu passed people walking, riding donkeys, pushing handcarts. A young woman kneeled by a bicycle with a flat tire. Small knots of people waited for tap-taps, the brightly painted red jitney buses adorned with slogans. *Adieu, Tristesse,* Leslie read on the front of an approaching tap-tap, and on the back, *Jesus No. 1.*

She looked out the window as Bertrand made small talk, discussing her lodging arrangements, the food at the guesthouse, his business difficulties, Marie's latest operation. She didn't interrupt him, but was distracted. The signs of change were everywhere: new technology, consumer products, videocassettes, advertisements for satellite dishes and computers. They passed the triangle of the industrial park, once touted by the younger Duvalier as Haiti's hope for the future. As far as she knew, it functioned as a tax exemption for the multinationals. In the paper, it was reported that two companies had threatened to pull out if the minimum wage was increased, a central demand of the new unions, along with collective bargaining.

"What about the strike, Bertrand? Is it going to happen?" There had been an analysis of the labor negotiations in the newspaper she had left on board the plane.

"Oh, they've been saying that for a month now." Bertrand turned around in the front seat to answer her. "Last week, this week, next week . . ." he added sarcastically. "Here they're always threatening to strike. That way the economy remains in chaos. If you ask me, it makes no sense at all. We need some stability right now, a climate to invest. This strike is just a political thing which is hurting us." He looked out the window, adding quickly: "If anything, they're making the situation worse. More people were laid off last week. And who's to blame? The owners are losing money."

Gerard hadn't mentioned this in his last fax. "How many people?" she asked.

Bertrand shrugged. "A few people, you know, to make an example." The older man suddenly pointed to a group of children walking in the middle of the highway. "Look at that!" he exclaimed. "Idiots! It's a miracle they haven't all been killed. Slow down, Clemard!" He leaned out the window and shouted to the children. "Faites attention!" They laughed, dancing out of the way of the oncoming traffic. Bertrand rolled up his window again. "You see," he complained. "Idiots."

Leslie squeezed the bottom of her handbag to make sure her

Newsweek was still inside. In it was also a petition signed by American labor groups that Gerard had requested. He would probably know if it was true that the American baseball manufacturers were pulling out. She had heard the rumor from Max, a reporter friend at the *Miami Herald*, who regularly came to Washington to attend State Department briefings on Haiti.

"They're using the maquila argument," Max had informed her. "Haiti won't be able to compete with Mexico. Nothing new, except State seems to be pushing it. It's all election crap." He had used the expression the unionists had coined: men-nan-poch, the hand-in-the-pocket policy.

Glancing into the rearview mirror, Leslie saw Clemard smile. Their eyes met. She smiled and looked down. I wonder if he's married. The thought came automatically. She glanced discreetly at his hand. He wore silver rings on the third finger of each hand. Now what did that mean? To her, he looked young to be married, but then, everyone married young here. What was he, thirty-one, thirty-two? Twenty-seven?

They passed a new building with shiny red Datsuns in the parking lot. Gerard was right. The Japanese really were sinking in their money. Next to the Datsuns were three lines of jeeps, one black, one tan, one white. The white ones were used by the foreign NGOs, the nongovernmental organizations. She wondered if any were automatic. She didn't like stick shift. But they couldn't be if they were jeeps, could they?

She was thinking about how much there was to do, whom she would have to contact, and whether she would be able to travel on the coastal road given the storms, when Clemard suddenly slammed on the brakes, screeching to a dead stop. A man pushing a wooden cart piled high with stacks of cut timber glared at them and pushed on across the highway. "Idiot!" Bertrand cried out again. He looked back at Leslie. "Nothing broken?"

"I'm fine." She smiled. To Clemard she quipped, "Good reflexes." He nodded, glancing apprehensively at Bertrand. I wonder what kind of relationship they have, Leslie thought, as she watched Bertrand urge the chauffeur to push ahead.

"Tell me more about Marie," she said a moment later. "How is she feeling?" As Bertrand described the chemotherapy and Marie's loss of hair, Clemard gunned the engine, passing a half dozen cars before slipping back into the right lane. Not bad, Leslie thought, impressed. The news about Marie saddened her. "Six months," Bertrand was saying, "that's what they are predicting." He added: "My wife is a strong woman. She'll go when she's ready. Or maybe she says that for my sake."

Leslie looked at Bertrand with empathy. "I'm so sorry, Bertrand," she said. "It must be terrible for you."

"It is. Worse than terrible—I would rather it be me. That's what I can't stand, you know, to see her in pain like this. Enfin"—he straightened up, pointing to a road on the right—"life is like that. You can't predict. Right?" He shrugged his shoulders.

Clemard was taking a back road that was unfamiliar to her, by-passing a congested area. Up a curving road, then quickly down the other side. Leslie recognized the intersection of Delmas ahead of them. As they pressed into the center of the capital, she looked down narrow alleys that branched out from the asphalt road into corridors of dirt that separated small concrete houses from one another. Despite gay pink and green exteriors, she knew their interiors were dark, without electricity except for a single lightbulb in most cases. People lived out of doors; houses were for sleeping, or taking refuge from the afternoon rains.

Still she smiled, amused by the comic painting of a chicken and a cow on the side of a grocery store. I love it here, she thought, feeling more relaxed now that she was on the ground. I can't believe I was nervous about coming back. It's great.

The intersection of Delmas and Martin Luther King Avenue was a gridlock. "Allez-y, messieurs!" Bertrand shouted as Clemard accelerated into a small void. "Rete!" he commanded in Creole. Stop! A tap-tap driver nosed his machine inches from Leslie's door. The driver grinned at them, his shirt open to the navel. In the rear, the passengers, all of them black, looked over at them. Leslie felt self-conscious in the air-conditioned car. She smiled at the passengers, but none smiled back.

The driver moved the tap-tap back a foot. Clemard inched forward, narrowly avoiding a concrete piling. He drove quickly after that, slowing only to edge the car around huge potholes that Leslie knew could snap a car axle in two. It had happened to Father's car that first summer and it had taken three weeks to repair.

Leslie saw newspaper vendors at the next intersection and asked Clemard to stop. Bertrand pressed a few gourdes into the hands of a young boy and his partner, handing Leslie the weeklies. The boys were already arguing over the money, one pulling on the other's arm. "Half for each—share," she urged them, but they ignored her, the one pushing the other.

They continued past the ocher wall bordering the military airstrip. Leslie saw two armed guards stationed at opposite ends of the wall, submachine guns in hand. Haitian journalists had attributed the sudden flood of Uzis into Haiti to a covert Israeli arms deal. But Max said they had been bought in the local gunshops near his office. She tended to believe him. His sources were always street.

The car turned into the wide, dusty intersection of Portail St.-Joseph, where Delmas met Route National One. Leslie's nostrils filled with the odor of the market: smoky piles of discarded orange peels and other garbage, frying foods, animal and human excrement. The rain had left an overpopulated stretch of black, ankle-deep mud. Wooden stalls teetered with boxes and baskets of goods piled on top of them. Quite a few were closed, covered with colored cloths.

La Saline market looked the same as she had remembered it, only more crowded. Imported mops next to straw brooms, tall columns of ceramic plates and Tupperware bowls, vegetables and fruits arranged in geometric patterns on the ground: circles, squares, small pyramids. Women squatted on small chairs or on blankets in the drier patches selling beans, maize, rice, sugarcane, tomatoes, limes, mangoes. She saw a group of pigs tied together by their tails, a donkey drinking, a youth without legs crab-crawling through the market, plastic flip-flops on his hands.

She wondered where the fire she had read about had broken out, the one in which a woman had been badly burned trying to recover her merchandise.

"I read about the fire." She leaned forward, aware that Bertrand had a hearing problem. She caught Clemard smiling at her and smiled back. "It sounded bad."

"Vandals," Bertrand replied matter-of-factly. "They arrested the man who set it." He tweaked his nostrils. "What did the newspapers say?"

"They said it was arson. That the army was behind it." She kept her tone deliberately neutral, wanting to see Bertrand's reaction. Clemard was watching her through the rearview mirror.

Bertrand nodded. "I see you are well informed."

What did that mean? She could feel Bertrand sizing her up.

"I don't think it was the army," he added. "They always say that. Now it's mostly thieves. Little acts of revenge that the people make into something else."

Aha, she thought, deciding to push the situation a little. Pep-la, the people.

"What about you, Clemard? Do you have any information?" she asked.

The younger man glanced quickly at Bertrand, who was amused.

"Just what you heard," Clemard said, adding: "That is to say, that the man received some money for doing that."

"A bribe—who told you that?" Bertrand pounced. "Someone in the market?" His tone was gruff.

Clemard shook his head. "Not the market—my wife."

So he was married! Leslie was surprised to feel a pique of disappointment. He still looked too boyish to her. I bet he isn't even twenty-seven, she thought, studying her own hands, which were ringless, pink, and swollen. Clemard drove slowly to let her look at the blackened scene of the fire.

The hawkers repeated their calls. The sound they made reminded Leslie of muezzins calling the faithful to prayer. She couldn't make out any of the words. People pounded on the car roof as it passed, their bodies pressed against the fender and the doors. A young boy held a shiny toaster aloft, his feet caked in dried mud. Hands and faces demanded money, watches, her sunglasses, anything. Smiling, Leslie rolled down the window halfway and placed a few coins into outstretched hands. She had long ago learned to come prepared.

Cigarettes?

No, sorry.

The old woman shook her head at Leslie. I'm sorry too, she was indicating. I want one.

A group of boys teased her as they departed: "American girl? Miami lady? Foxy New York City?" Peals of laughter. All but one child ran away from the car. He solemnly watched them pass and held up a hand to wave goodbye.

5

Emmanuel glanced at his watch. He was running late. He dropped down to the floor and began doing his daily push-ups. "One, two, three . . ." His stringy forearms flexed and relaxed, the veins popping as he counted. He could feel a ridge of tension developing on one side of his spine as he reached fifty, and kept his slim, taut frame level with the straw mat. By seventy-five, the sweat was dripping from his nose and mouth. His underarms stank. There was a soft knock at the door. He ignored it. "Eighty, eighty-one, eighty-two"—he grimaced—"eighty-three and eighty-four . . ."

"Pe Emmanuel?"

"Five minutes," he said loudly, his stomach muscles aching. A slight shadow fell away from the crack; Joseph the caretaker shuffled away. He kept going. "Ninety-eight, ninety-nine . . . and, oh, one hundred! Phew! Oh . . ." He blew away the dripping sweat from his nostrils and lay breathing heavily on the mat, his heart pounding wildly. On the wall Christ wore a benign but intense expression, his Ethiopian eyes liquid black points. The Saviour was sitting on a mountain, surrounded by doves. The birds perched on his knees and shoulders. The graceful branches of a royal palm spread out behind them. The scene was peaceful. Emmanuel stared into Christ's eyes, relaxing until his head was devoid of all thought.

With the arrival of the rains, the Confession hours had shifted; he didn't know how many parishioners would show up today. Normally, he celebrated Mass every morning at 7 a.m. with special Masses at 5 p.m. on Mondays and Wednesdays, and a full Sunday menu. During the rest of the week, he divided his time between his duties at the parish and visits to villages in outlying areas.

He was a man of simple tastes. Aside from enjoying an occasional iced beer, and his one hundred push-ups, he spent his free time reading and practicing the flute. His quarters in the parish were modest but comfortable: a sink, desk, chair, mat, and wardrobe closet. He had also added a small desk lamp, a portable radio, and his Bible in its painted wooden box. Joseph regularly rearranged the makeshift altar on the windowsill. Today a fresh vase of yellow jonquil flowers had replaced the limp rainbow of white, violet, and blue larkspurs. Above the altar hung his crucifix, a plain brown wooden cross. While he had received more ornate crucifixes over the years, this was his favorite. He had prayed before it as an altar boy, and then in his room at the seminary. It was at this intersection of wood that God had first spoken to him. Why look elsewhere for Him? he thought now, admiring the simple cross.

He opened the drawer to the desk and removed a towel and a deodorant spray. Drying himself, he sprayed each armpit twice for good measure, then his back and stomach. It was a mild scent he had borrowed from his mother during a weekend at home and never returned. Although it was marketed for French women, he liked its musky edge.

He began his meditation, breathing slowly in and out, feeling his chest expand and his heartbeat slow down. The thoughts of the day, the many errands, his mother's birthday, the need to pick up a delivery at the wharf . . . all fell away. He no longer detected his breath entering and exiting. His mind was a still lake, framed by pine trees, unmoving, and a clear blue sky.

He lifted himself from the mat, stretching his well-shaped calves as he touched his toes. As he leaned back, then to the side, then from his waist again, he wondered how the national team was doing. Too bad I'm missing the game, he thought. I'm surprised Gerard thinks they have a chance in the World Cup.

"Pe?" The knock was more insistent this time.

"I'm coming right now, Joseph," he replied.

"There is someone in the left booth, Pe," Joseph whispered into the crack of the door. "He has been waiting for a long time. I told him to go away and come back, but he didn't listen to me. I think he might be asleep."

Emmanuel smiled, not surprised. He often found people sleeping in the pews in the afternoon. "Thank you, Joseph. I will come now. Please tell anyone else to wait in the hall. It will be more comfortable there than outside."

He licked his fingers to pat down a few stray hairs, and wiped his glasses. Then he reached for the peg on the door and removed the white cassock and purple sash. The sash was still damp from where he had rinsed it after spilling some wine on it earlier. The stain was imperceptible. His thin feet slipped into a pair of well-worn sandals. He adjusted the sash to fall evenly on both sides. Then he surveyed his image a last time, checking his teeth for threads of corn. After inspecting his fingernails, he pulled open the door and walked across the corridor that separated his private quarters from the rest of the church.

At the end of the hall, he entered a small room, opened a door, and stepped directly into the center confessional booth. Sliding partitions divided it from the other two on either side. He kneeled and crossed himself, then sat on the small chair.

He could hear the person breathing. He could also smell musk. You sprayed it too close to your neck, he thought. He wiped a finger against his skin to dilute the scent. A fly crawled up the crack in the paneling of the booth; he reached up and held his hand motionless to capture it. But the fly got away. He pulled back the crosshatched partition, ready at last.

There were sounds of a throat being cleared. He recognized the familiar sound of a body adjusting itself to the cramped, uncomfortable booth, imagined a pair of knees sinking into the worn knee cushion. He sighed inwardly, feeling tired, but alert. It was cool here in the confessional.

"Pale?" came a child's voice, high, uncertain. Talk? Not a child's voice exactly, the priest thought, but fuller, an adolescent's perhaps, nasal, poised to crack.

"Pale," he answered in Creole.

A silence followed. After a few seconds, the priest asked, "Do you wish to make a Confession?" He could hear movements, sighs and exhalations. But the person on the other side remained silent. Emmanuel glanced at his Timex. He had started late; it was already one-thirty. Luckily there was no one else waiting. He felt the place on his forearm where a little knob of something hard rolled under his fingers. His mother was expecting him for dinner; he had forgotten to stop by the florist to buy her some flowers. Maybe he could take the ones in the office.

"I didn't come to confess . . . not exactly," the voice began. "I just came to talk. . . . Are you the parish priest?" The accent was southern, thick, with a roughness that suggested tobacco.

Am I the priest? Emmanuel was charmed by the question. Obviously not one of his regular parishioners. "Yes, I am the priest of this parish." He's from Jérémie, the priest guessed, revising his initial opinion. The voice sounded more mature now, though he still couldn't pinpoint the age. Usually he knew right away.

"But you're the one . . . you can be trusted, I was told. That's true, isn't it?"

The one who could be trusted. Which one was that? Emmanuel considered his answer. "Whatever you tell me you are telling God. I am only His messenger. Whatever you say to me now I will keep in confidence." It was a standard reply, but already he was paying closer attention. He heard a grunt that sounded like satisfaction.

"Is there a problem? Is something troubling you?" he asked, then added: "Which priest are you looking for exactly? Someone in particular?"

"I . . . well not the fat one . . . you're not him, are you?"

That was Père Antoine, his colleague. Emmanuel chuckled at the description, then grew serious. "Does it matter who I am, if God is the one to whom you are confessing? He is the only one who matters. Or did someone send you here to talk to me?"

A moment's silence followed. "Yes . . . and no. I mean, yes, someone told me about you, that you were honest. But nobody knows I've come here. Not even my wife. I—I just needed to talk to someone . . ."

Emmanuel shifted closer to the mesh, his hands folded in his lap. It was his position of greatest attention. He smelled a fart, and then alcohol. The person was drunk, he suddenly realized.

"I have a problem," the voice was saying. "I don't know if you can help me . . . but I need help."

Once again Emmanuel was struck by its odd quality, thick yet clear, like caramel heating under a flame, he could visualize it. It's rather extraordinary, he thought, definitely from the south, a broad peasant voice. He had detected fear now too, in the pauses where the high voice thinned and dropped, the words cut off. Comme un homme qui a soif, he thought, like a man who's thirsty.

"I'm listening," he said. "Please continue."

"It's . . . I . . . it started about a month ago, the problem, I mean."

Emmanuel heard a sniffle. The voice had a cold.

"I, uh . . . sometimes I say, No it is not a real problem because it goes away," the anonymous voice continued. "But then it comes back. And I can't sleep, even with a capsule. All this week I didn't sleep, and last week I only slept a few hours in the afternoon. I feel like I'm going to go crazy . . . like I'm going crazy . . . I'm so tired, you see . . . I've tried drinking, you know that can work, but it only made it worse . . ."

Emmanuel had no idea what the man was talking about. The basic facts had registered: a not so young married man, drinking to curb his anxiety. Unless his instincts were wrong, there was guilt operating here, although this type sounded different from the usual variety. Nine times out of ten the Confession began: "It's my wife . . . it's about a woman . . ." Although this man had also mentioned his wife, that she did not know anything about it, or might not approve of his seeing a priest. Emmanuel was intrigued.

"What exactly is the problem?" he asked. He was looking at the spot where the fly had disappeared. The wood on the walls needed to be sanded and finished, he noted, knowing as he did that he would probably forget to mention it to Joseph. The confessional was almost thirty years old: the wood warped at the corners. He looked down; the burgundy knee cushion was pink where it was worn out. He unconsciously flexed his calves and fingers, feeling stiff from his earlier exercise.

"The problem? Yes . . ." There was a long pause, then repetition. "The problem? . . . Well, it's not easy to say. I mean, I'm not sure what the problem is myself. I mean, I think I know, but I . . ."

"Why are you having trouble sleeping?" Emmanuel cut him off, sensing a rambling Confession. He spotted the fly again in the little crack, rubbing its forelegs together, attuned like himself to the slightest shift of atmosphere. Distracted, he closed his eyes.

"I don't sleep anymore," the voice continued, "because if I do, I'll sink—I'll sink into the ground from the weight of all their possessions."

"You'll sink?" the priest repeated, confused. "I don't understand."

"Wait," the man answered. "Wait a minute and I'll explain . . ."

Emmanuel heard a hiccup. He waited. This time the pause was even longer.

"Like . . . like"—the voice returned abruptly, more loudly now—"like the way you take a step and then you've taken it. You know you can go back, but somehow you can't."

Emmanuel looked at the mesh, wondering what the man looked like. He was settling on age forty at the very youngest. The priest was also familiar with such delays. He heard another hiccup. "Start at the beginning," he suggested softly. "You can take your time. I'm not going anywhere. Don't forget, God is listening. You mustn't be afraid." For an instant, he wondered if the man was one of the mentally ill patients from the nearby asylum. They sometimes wandered off the grounds and ended up inside the church courtyard. Of course, he might also be a real alcoholic: the only time they made sense was when they were drinking; sober, they were incoherent.

"From the beginning . . . no, that's too far away . . . We might be here all night." A giggle followed, revealing a childlike sense of humor. "You wouldn't sleep, and you'd become like me." This time the laughter was loud, richer. Fascinated, Emmanuel leaned further forward, placing his ear directly against the mesh. He had detected a note of confidence, of trust.

"Anywhere, then," he encouraged. "Begin at any point."

"My name is Jean-Marc," the voice said finally. "Jean-Marc . . . Benjamin. You don't know me; I'm not important. I don't have an important job, I mean. That's why I came. I told myself that someone in your position might be able to help me. You will help me, won't you?"

"Of course," Emmanuel replied. He felt a familiar tightening in his gut, a sense of danger. Something was keeping the middle-aged man with the narcotic voice from sleeping. Something was frightening him.

"I live here, in the city," the voice continued. "My wife and I have seven children, although two are dead. A boy and a girl. My wife still cries for them." A pause. "All the time. But then she and

I are not alike. She's a woman, you know, she feels every emotion . . . do you understand? Me, I consider myself stronger." Another pause. "No, no, that's not true. She's the stronger one. I'm the one who made the mistake."

Emmanuel's face was a study in concentration. The voice had suddenly softened. The priest felt the fly on his shoulder and shrugged it off, but did not open his eyes.

"I say that for a reason, Pe," the voice resumed. "The reason is this: We have known death, my wife and I. A lot of death. The first time my mother died, I cried. Then my father. It was hard, I was still young. Then, with my son, it was already easier. I cried inside, but no one saw it. Then my little girl, she was just a baby. Three weeks old, but she didn't survive. She couldn't take my wife's milk. Like a little angel that appeared and was gone, do you understand? So I've become a rock, because what good is crying? It wouldn't bring my children back. If I had had money, I could have saved them. The ones who survive are hard, harder than you or me, believe me. That's not true for my wife, she's different. She always believed. In God, I mean, and in voudon too. I'll admit that to you as a priest. Her faith is very strong; every day, she lights her candles for the two of them, you see what I am saying? She speaks to them every day, and she says they answer."

Emmanuel heard joints popping, the man moving around. "Do you think the dead can hear us, Pe? Because I don't think so. My wife is a smart woman, a good woman, but a simple person, like me. She believes. But I . . . well, why would God take away my two children? There's no mercy there. She says—my wife—that they are waiting for us, that they are safe. But she cries all the time. Ever since the baby girl died, she doesn't care about anything. Forgive me for saying it, but sometimes I think my wife, even though she is Christian, she wants to join them. She would prefer to be with them than with us here on earth."

Emmanuel was tempted to interrupt, to console, but the voice picked up again.

"She was praying but He wasn't helping us, was He? That's what made me do it. Seven of us, and I was the only one with a little job. All those mouths to feed, how could I do it? It was impossible.

Every time they promised me more money, a promotion, each year. But nothing. They never did. That's why . . ." The voice faltered, stopped.

Emmanuel waited. "That's why? . . ." he urged. "What?"

A deep breath, a loud sigh. Emmanuel smelled the alcohol again. "You won't understand, Pe. A poor man, that's what I am, from a poor family. From the countryside. Since you're a priest, I won't lie to you, I won't pretend. You want to know? I'll tell you the truth. My son died of hunger. He had worms, he couldn't eat. He looked like a skeleton at twenty-three. And my daughter, why did she die? Hunger, Pe, hunger. That's why I did it. That's the only reason. Like the poorest in the village, we weren't eating. I thought with all my children, it would help. Children are riches, you know what they say. Well, it's not true in my case. Every mouth eats like two."

Emmanuel had noted the change. Anger had transformed the mellifluous voice. "Pe"—the tone was almost conspiratorial—"do you recognize this? 'Je suis le drapeau, Uni et Indivisible.' " It came out lilting, the French eerily singsong. I am the flag, One and Indivisible. "You recognize it, don't you? He used to come and see us in the barracks, to hear us recite it, like . . . like children."

Emmanuel heard the bitterness in the laugh now, and more self-pity. "I remember it," he said evenly. "Why?"

"Notre Doc, qui règne dans le Palais National à vie," the voice was haughty, bitter. Our Doc, who dwells in the National Palace for life. "Yes, we had to pretend to worship him, but we didn't, we hated him. No one understands that. They judge us. But we were afraid. He treated us like animals too."

Emmanuel scratched his hand where the fly had set down and departed. The voice was sliding toward self-hate.

"Well, I for one was never a Duvalierist, Pe, even if some of the others supported him. I was Fignolé's man, I voted MOP, Mouvman Ouvriye Peyizan. My father was a peasant and I am the son of a peasant. I trusted Fignolé. But when he didn't win, I signed up to work for the government. I was in Les Cayes, then I came here."

Emmanuel felt a flush of satisfaction. A peasant from Les Cayes, just as he had guessed. He made a quick calculation: 1957, the year

Duvalier stole the election from Fignolé. That would put the man's age closer to fifty than forty. He had erred there.

"I worked in many services, Pe: the police, traffic, customs, but never important jobs. I was a driver; I never enjoyed fighting or hurting people. And I did my job well, not like most people who have no respect. I traveled all over the country, even to the Dominican Republic, and I never had an accident. Not once. You would think I deserved a medal just for that, no? You know how the roads are. But never one accident. I never lost any cargo. And I didn't get anything, not a medal, nothing, just their promises . . ."

Emmanuel thought about the highway he and Gerard had been on that morning. A truck had overturned, stuck in the mud near the flooded Artibonite River. He held Hubert Sansaricq in his mind's eye for an instant, before the voice brought him back to reality.

"Once I drove all the way from the farthest point south to the northern border with the Dominican Republic without resting, with just a little bread to eat, you can see how hard I worked. But you know what they did? They cut all of our salaries. Because the prices went up, and we never earned more money. Year after year it continued like that, but I never saw my reward."

There was a cough, then the rack of phlegm. Startled, Emmanuel leaned back, worried that the man might be tubercular. More and more of the poor were these days. He sat back to listen, his eyes still closed.

"I'm saying this to explain to you, Pe. Because I want you to believe me. I was never—not for a moment, the entire time I worked for the government—I was never a Duvalierist. But I needed the money, there is no argument about that. My wife earned a little money here and there. But it wasn't enough. My oldest children had to stop going to school. I thought about quitting, all the time I wanted to quit, to take all of us away, to go somewhere else, but how could I? I didn't even have money to buy gasoline for the truck. Believe me, I would have gone, I would be in another country if it was up to me. Not that I'm not a patriot, Pe, don't misunderstand me, because I am. But not with that devil in the Palace."

Emmanuel opened his eyes, looked at the wooden wall, imagined the sneer he could hear in the voice, the sarcasm.

"Moun sadik—moun kriyel," the voice said. A sadist, a cruel man. "I'm telling you this in secret, Pe, but I was the first one to applaud at Jean-Claude's departure. Because I knew about it, as you can imagine. I called my wife and told her. That day I drank a whole bottle of rum to celebrate. We danced in our house, all of us, everyone, all the children . . ."

Emmanuel cut in, but gently. "You said something about possessions earlier. What does that have to do with your story?"

"It was the money, Pe," the voice answered with resignation. "My wife warned me. At first, she didn't want me doing that job, transporting the dead at night. She said it would only cause problems, because the dead have their own power. I didn't think that at the time, but now I see she was right. I thought the dead were dead, right? Why be afraid of them? All of us are going to die, that's how I thought about it. But I was wrong, I can see, I can see that now."

Emmanuel felt the sash where it had been stained. It was dry. He held his Timex up to the crack to see what time it was. Quarter to two. "What exactly do you see?" he asked.

But the voice had ignored him, was saying, "No one completely accepts death, do they, Pe? Even you, you must be afraid, you must wonder. No? Well, maybe not. Sometimes, you know, I see my children's faces—the ones who died. My oldest boy was a good young man, braver than I am. And I miss him. My wife is wrong about that. She thinks I don't care because I don't talk about him all the time like she does, or about our little girl. But that's the part of me that got hard, Pe; the soft part died with them."

The word *aigre-doux* came into Emmanuel's head, bittersweet. He wanted to reach through the mesh, to touch the pain and soothe it. He considered his response. "But you carry them in your heart," he said at last, sensing the inadequacy of his words. "Don't you? And they're with God."

"God? Oh yes, yes. That's what my wife says too." The voice sounded unconvinced. "My wife—my wife was right about the dead. They won't leave me alone. And it's my fault. I was hoping to escape my suffering, to escape my lot, Pe—my poor man's lot. But who was I fooling, right? Nobody. Myself. They won't let me escape."

Emmanuel rubbed his kneecaps. He could feel the truth surfacing at last, like a hooked fish. "Who?" he asked quietly. "Who is persecuting you? The government?"

He heard a sniff. "Not the government. The poor—the mendicants."

The mendicants? Now where had the son of a peasant learned a word like that? Emmanuel shook his head, surprised. "I'm not sure I understand," he said truthfully.

"If it wasn't me, it would have been someone else, Pe. Not that it excuses me, but it's true." The voice paused. "And if the others hadn't done it, I wouldn't have had the idea. I followed their example. I acted like a child, right? Not like a man. Forgive me, Pe," the voice implored. "Please forgive me."

"Forgive you for what?" the priest asked. "What is it exactly you've done?"

"I *stole* from them, Pe," the voice said, hushed. "From the dead! Not every time; at first, only when there was something to take. I only took what I thought I could sell, you know, jewelry, rings and bracelets—things the dead have no use for, how could they—that's how I justified it to myself. Why does a dead man need a watch? Life is over for him. Like that. Nobody knew who these people were, that's what I wanted to believe."

The voice was full of grief. The priest heard an intake of breath, then the awful cough again. Was he crying? Emmanuel couldn't tell.

"I—I just received the orders, Pe. I would go to the morgue or to the prison to get the body. You didn't ask questions. And anyone could see these were poor people, just like me, they weren't rich. I know sometimes they were political prisoners, but often it was someone who had died in an accident. We didn't know if they had a family, but they were dead, right? And they didn't have money for a funeral. So we wouldn't even bother to call an ambulance or take them to the morgue. What for? We didn't know who they were. So we would take them straight to Titanyen."

Titanyen. Emmanuel saw the garbage-strewn marshland, the coils of discarded razor wire and leather cutouts from the shoe and belt factories. And the bones. He stopped rubbing his knee, began chewing his inner cheek instead. Forgiveness, he spoke to the One who listened, whose ears heard everything, the One for whom he now strived to empty his own head and allow the bittersweet voice to be heard. He asks Your forgiveness. Emmanuel put his hands together in prayer, waiting for the response.

But the man's voice interrupted him, broke through the calm Emmanuel was trying to achieve. It was full of need. "Let me tell you how it happened, Pe, all right? Because at first, like I've already explained, it was different—I was different. Maybe I even believed them, that these were just beggars, people without anything. I was doing my little job, following the orders. I worked during the day, went home to my family at night. The first time they sent someone to wake me at three in the morning, I was scared, I thought I was maybe under arrest, although I hadn't done anything wrong, hadn't distinguished myself, so to speak. Anything is possible, isn't that true?

"So that was the first time I did that job. I was paid extra, of course. It was simple. I went with two soldiers—we were all dressed in our own clothes—and we picked up a dead man. He was lying on the side of the dirt road near the airport. Several times after that, I was sent to that zone and it was always the same thing. A body, shot. Sometimes I found the shells, so I knew our soldiers were involved, but like I told you, we had to keep our mouths shut. Nobody talked to us about anything. When it was done, I gave my commander whatever I had found in the pockets. I saw that he trusted me and I became the one who kept the envelope."

"The envelope—with their personal effects?" Emmanuel was finally getting the picture.

The hacking cough followed. "That's right, Pe. And after a few months, he let me take the envelope home first and bring it to him in the afternoon. I did that for almost two years, regularly. I was one of three drivers. We picked up the dead at the hospital morgue on Wednesdays and Fridays, and on Sunday nights, I mean, very early in the morning, we would go to all the prisons."

Emmanuel listened to the voice with one ear. With the other, he was creating a clear channel, for Him. I am Yours, he said to God, I am Your vessel. I am Your servant.

"One day, it was a Thursday in the summer, I saw another soldier wearing a watch just like the watch I put into the envelope and gave to my commander. You see, I realized my commander had taken the watch and given it to this man, to reward him. I paid attention, and found that he had rewarded others like that, they were getting richer while I was still waiting for my promotion. I was burying the dead to feed my family and still we were going hungry. You understand that, don't you?"

Emmanuel didn't answer.

"Well," the voice said, "I couldn't accept this. I thought, these people, who are they? Nobodies; no one knows they have died, no one is going to come and claim this envelope. I had been fooled by my superiors. I was naive. And these dead people, well, I thought, their lives were over, their children would never know they had died, but I, I, well, I was still here, on this earth. And my children needed to eat, we were hungry. Better for us, who were poor like they were, to benefit than those other soldiers who are criminals. Better for us who will die hungry the way we were born, better for us to live. That's right, Pe, they are true criminals. I worked with them, I know what they did. I witnessed it. They had no respect for anyone else. My commander, he had two cars, but what did I have? Not even the money to put a ring on my wife's hand. Did I say that already? Are you still listening, Pe?"

"I'm listening." Emmanuel opened his eyes momentarily, then closed them again. He knew he ought to push the man along, to draw the Confession to a close, but he sat back instead. "Please continue," he added.

"Well, that's what she wanted—a real wedding in a church— like a rich woman. With a gold ring. Who put that idea in her head I'll never know. Because she's not like that about other things, I told you. But she started to talk about it after our son died. It became an obsession. So I started to think about it. And I'll tell you the truth, I thought it might help, to take her mind off the children. You're the only one I've ever told.

"I started to think of the envelope as a gift, Pe. A gift that was being given to me, a poor man who lost two children and knows no one will help him. I said to myself that this was the way my dead children were helping me, by bringing me these things to sell.

I didn't feel good about it exactly, but I didn't feel bad either. I accepted it. Once I decided, I didn't think about it. I felt it was my fate. Because I needed money and there was never going to be my promotion. That much I finally understood. And I was no longer young. They were going to get rid of me sooner or later. So it was almost my duty to take these things, my duty as a parent, to my wife and my family."

The voice no longer sounded drunk, Emmanuel noted. Nor was it completely truthful. It was only rationalizing.

"I only took what I could sell, Pe; I wasn't greedy. And I had to be very careful—if they caught me they would have shot me too. So it was a risk."

The voice was slightly gruff now, challenging. It wanted approval, understanding. Emmanuel tilted back his head, but no instruction came. He remained silent.

"I was a good criminal, Pe," the voice said matter-of-factly. "I sold every last object. I even enjoyed it, to tell you the truth. Everything"—it paused—"except the ring I gave to my wife. We were married in a big ceremony exactly two years ago. I gave her a gold ring with a red stone I took off a fat woman's finger."

A little high laugh followed this disclosure, an unhappy laugh, Emmanuel noted. "That's terrible, isn't it?" the voice added, honesty breaking through, "but I didn't think so at the time. After I stopped doing that job, I even thought about asking her to give it back to me, or to trade it for another one, but I never dared. You see how I lack courage. But I don't think she would understand it."

No, I can't imagine she would, Emmanuel thought to himself. He was losing his concentration now, tiring. "What does she say about it—your insomnia, I mean? Does she know about it?"

"She says I worry too much. She thinks I should see a doctor and take a cure. But I know no leaves can fix something like this. If the dead want to punish me, what can I do? I have no power to stop them. They want their possessions, that's what I see. But I can't give them back, can I?—it's too late."

The voice had an edge of hysteria in it.

A long silence followed. Emmanuel broke it. There was something the man was not talking about. "You talk about the dead. You feel haunted, don't you?"

"I see them." The voice had dropped to a whisper. "Their faces. Their hands with their rings. Not only when I am going to sleep but during the day, sometimes the first thing when I wake up. They are waiting for me, Pe. They want it all back. Even though it's been two years since I stopped doing that job and I don't go to Titanyen. Before, I never thought about them—those people—I never saw anyone's face. It just started one night, just like that. And now it's all the time, constantly. And I can't stop seeing them. The objects, I mean. It happens all the time. I'm talking to someone and I see the ring they are wearing or a bracelet, and I remember the bracelet I sold. Once I offered to buy a watch from a friend, I was convinced he had bought a watch I had sold someone else, that's how crazy I was becoming. And you know, I could see he was afraid of me. As if he knew that something was wrong. He refused too; he said it wasn't for sale. And he was a poor man like me, so why would he say that? That's how I know the dead have a hand in this. But like I told you, it's too late. Even if I got another ring for my wife, I couldn't put it back on that fat woman's finger."

The voice was leaden, exhausted. "I feel so heavy, Pe. I close my eyes and tell myself to sleep. If the Devil wants to take me, let him take me. Because it's no use. I can't fight them. All I do is I wonder. I want to know who were they, you know, who was that fat woman, was she someone's mother? And who is her family, her husband and children? It's the same with the others. In my mind, when I'm awake and I can't sleep, I'm walking along the street with them, or we're driving in my truck. Sometimes they're taking me to see their relatives, so I can return the envelope. Even in my dreams they're still dead and I'm alive. And each time, we're getting close, we're near the house or the village, and I'm holding the watch or the bracelet."

Smack! Emmanuel jumped as a fist hit the wall, startling him. The man was softly hitting it.

"Boom!—just like that, it starts," the voice was saying. "Each time, just as I take a step toward the house. That's when I start to sink. I start to *sink*, Pe. Because the bracelet is getting so heavy and I can't take it off. It won't come off although I'm trying to get it off. It's a nightmare, my dream; the dead want to drag me down with them. I feel my feet sinking into the ground and I can't resist them. And so I panic, and I'm shouting for my wife and my children, but nobody hears, nobody is there, I'm all alone, just like that, I'm sinking. Now I can't sleep at all, because I know what they want. And the last time, I almost failed to pull myself up. And if I close my eyes, it's like I'm under water or under the earth already, I have no strength to fight them. And I can't open my eyes, I can't get out, I'm sinking. So you see, Pe, I'm convinced, I'm certain; the next time is the last time—I won't wake up."

6

Elyse opened her eyes. How much time had passed? The room was dim; the sky outside an indiscriminate wedge of gray. She looked up at it from the bed, through a hole near the ceiling created from fallen bricks. Tears welled up, but she held them back. She could still feel the salt on her cheeks.

"Dios padre de Jesús infante de la Virgen María, ayúdame en mi hora de . . ." Elyse did not turn at the sound of the woman's voice. She did not want to know if the woman was staring at her. She did not understand the words, but knew it was a prayer. Li pale ak Jezi. She's talking to Jesus.

The other woman began to cough again, an ugly racking sound that would end in a dry, breathless gasp. Elyse balled up her fists and pressed them into her ears. She heard voices outside, heard the old woman who was cursed say something. It was starting to rain. She listened to the sounds of the other women taking cover, returning to the rooms. Hers was the last of the row of cubicles, narrow spaces without doors, the broken walls letting the rain blow in. Each space held two beds, broken wooden rectangles with slats missing, some without pallets. Elyse had been put in with the Dominican prostitute and been given a pallet. It stank of mildew and was stained brown where women before her had bled. It was chewed upon; she had found mouse droppings in between the straw weave.

On the second day, they had thrown her a thin dirty sheet. She doubled it under her hip bones, to fill in the holes where the slats were gone. The bed was hard and uncomfortable, always damp, sticking to her skin. She shifted her weight, pulled the sheet down with her toes to soften the wood under her ankles. Let me rest, she thought now.

It was raining in the courtyard; the wind blew harder. She heard loud drops falling into the outdoor well, full of fetid water and mosquito larvae. The rain rustled the leaves of the small tree by the locked entry gate. Water was leaking from a hole in the ceiling onto her left foot. She closed her eyes and imagined the sun, the heat baking a deep dry well, and took refuge there; Ignatius and Pierre had helped build it in the summer. The rain tickled her but she ignored it, concentrating on their hands, packing the earth, the sides of the well, smoothing the cement, attaching the pipe. The sun so hot over their heads. Hot and dry.

Thunder cracked. The naked lightbulb in the middle of the room swayed. It was broken. In the dimness it looked like a faint white pear, a pencil outline against the dark wall. Minutes passed, then hours. She was alert to the sounds of traffic, however distant, an engine turning over, the three-note horn of a tap-tap. Each time, she would lift her head from the bed, look at the wall as if she could stare through it to see the car arriving, know by the sound of the engine what kind of car or truck it might be, whether by some miracle Ignatius had come to save her. Ignatius with his friends, driving with the car lights out and the windows rolled down, quietly shouting her name: Elyse! Elyse! She pressed her ears against the wall and listened. Elyse, are you in there? Is that you? The honking became fainter, then was gone. The woman in the other bed was praying again and coughing.

She put her hands back up to her ears and imagined Ignatius, driving like the race-car driver she had seen on television, accelerating when he arrived at the corner, smashing through the wall of the prison, freeing her even as the guards ran to stop them, shot at them, let the dogs loose to try to catch them. How strong could the wall be? Not stronger than a car. It looked old to her, older than Grann. He would need a big truck, an army truck. He would have stolen an army truck. There would be no hesitation. He would crash through the wall, and before anyone could respond, she would be out of here, off the big road, gone, escaped. Make it happen, she said. Make it happen.

A match flared. She smelled smoke. The Dominican placed the candle on the floor. It made the room look smaller, the upper walls still dark. Elyse extended a finger to trace the names scratched into the wall: Tata Alphonse, Marie Carmel. Below the bed, in a brown finger paint that had to have been blood, someone had written in script: Philiberte. Who was Philiberte? Did she escape? The brown substance came off under her nail. The Dominican woman, Luz, muttered to herself.

The policeman had beaten her up before arresting her. Elyse had understood that much of the woman's story. He had refused to pay Luz for sex; she had protested and now she was in here and her children were out there. Out there! Out there! Luz, who was now staring at the candle, had pulled on Elyse's hair to emphasize her point. "Loca!" she kept whispering. "Loca! Loca! Loca!" Crazy! I'll go crazy! Elyse agreed. She could see it happening, just the way Grann had described it: it was making Luz crazy and it would make her crazy too.

There was shouting coming from the place beyond the wall where the men were held. She had listened to their yelling the night before. How many were in there no one knew. A lot, someone had told her. One woman had a husband and son in there too. Only the youngest child had been left untouched. There was another court-yard for the men, a concrete yard like this one, but bigger.

Elyse listened to the Dominican woman praying. Up to now, she had said little. She was keeping her mouth shut, as the guards had ordered them to do. If they talked they would be punished, that was the rule. But no one seemed to follow it at night. She could hear the other woman whispering if she got up and listened by the other doorway. She listened now. But the shouting on the other side of the wall had stopped. Just like it would start and stop when the tap-taps in the street hit each other and a policeman had to be called to stop the fighting. Elyse saw Luz cocking her head toward the sound of the whistle too, a policeman's whistle. Something was happening inside the prison, not outside, Luz indicated.

What time is it? I didn't hear the church bells. It's warm but I'm cold. I'm shivering. I hope I don't get sick like she is. Elyse studied Luz's face, as impenetrable as a mask. The Dominican had showed her the sores on the inside of her mouth, a large spot by her eye that looked painful. Luz was absorbed in her own thoughts, her hands stretched outright as she opened her eyes and stared back at Elyse, her eyes saying nothing. The candle sputtered and went out. The room fell back into blackness.

.

The wind rose quietly at first, then grew louder. She was standing in a big room. The room was full of paintings—big paintings, little paintings, paintings on the ceiling, the walls, the floor. Pictures of a man being taken to heaven, the sky gold and the land purple, tiny cows and goats wearing bells. Of another, the lwas—the saints—circling the bed of a girl who was sick. Elyse saw herself, wearing Grann's Sunday dress. She was sweating, soaking wet. Her mother, who had been there, was gone. She knocked on a door. Mami? Mami, se ou-menm? Is that you? Mami, pale ak mwen! Talk to me! Ou la? Are you there?

She woke. The shot was not that close, near the market maybe. She heard it again. It was still raining. Luz was snoring. Elyse closed her eyes and tried to recall her dream. The room was wide, and there was a blue vase and a mirror. In one painting, the mermaid had blue eyes and wings. La syren was carrying a man. That's the man I found, she said to herself, in the river. She carried the picture over to show Mami, who was sitting on a big pink couch. But Mami was gone, Mami had disappeared again. She looked down at her feet and saw a bottle of Prell on its side. She reached for it; a green lizard darted out its mouth. Mami! she screamed. Mami, kote ou te ale? Where did you go?

The wind rattled the shutters. She was in a tree, high up, across from the prison. There was a shadow, a red bird landing on a branch below her, beating its wings. She was afraid of it. She hid. A car was coming, moving slowly down the street, out of sight. The bird was looking for her, was flying alongside the car.

The jeep with the men stopped at the top of the street. They blew the whistle, a sharp sound that shook the closet where she was hiding and hurt her ears. She heard her name being called: Elyse! Elyse! Mami was calling her! Mami and Grann! Mwen la! she shouted. I'm here!

She was standing on a narrow balcony. The second-story terrace of a wooden house. The wind had pulled everything down, the street was flooding, water was coming in everywhere. Below, what was left over from the market was rushing past, stalls broken apart, baskets and bars of soap and mangoes floating in dark water. Elyse could smell the sea and something else, a burning smell.

Back inside, she found the door. Mami had gone through this door. She heard music, laughter. She opened it. A Ra-Ra band was approaching, walking toward her down a dirt road. There was a giant field behind them, and the mountain. The men and women wore green shirts, their hands painted like a rainbow. They held wooden sticks, banged them on tin cans and sang. They moved like spiders, lifting their arms and legs sharp and high. The water crept up behind them, swirled around their ankles. She saw that they did not notice, cried out to warn them. But they were wearing cowbells around their necks; they could not hear her. The current swept them into a side street toward the car.

The men pointed toward houses, questioning the crowd. They were looking for her, had a small picture of her in their hands. The wind blew the door to the terrace open. She saw a basket full of dice. Dice and silver pearls. She heard a whistle, then another, and saw the bird, the silver medallion around its neck. Sen Kristof. The bird circled the house. Thunder shook the terrace.

Wherever the bird flew, a curtain of fat red drops followed. Elyse watched the red rain hit the sides of the buildings; the water streaming down the gutter ran pink.

The first in a line of boats sailed into view with a family aboard. Mother, father, two boys, Elyse counted them. Strangers. Next was a raft of cardboard boxes roped loosely together. A dozen babies were sleeping, one in each box. A giant sail made of newspaper blew the vessel along. The wind caught the edge of the paper tarp; the babies sailed past her. One of them had Gran's, her grandfather's face.

Ignatius! Ignatius! she cried. He had lost his glasses and could not see her without them. She watched him paddling a crutch in a white boat full of flowers. His leg had been cut off; he was older and skinnier and had grown a beard. She picked up two of the dice and threw them to catch his attention. But the bird caught them in its beak and landed on the jeep. Ignatius! . . . The wind drowned out her voice . . . Ignatius! A shutter opened across the street from her; a dog barked. The shutter closed and opened again, and the animal was gone.

The jeep moved slowly up the street, parting the red current. The bird was circling again. Elyse jumped down and began to run.

Everyone had disappeared. She was alone on the beach. The

waves had died down, the water was silvery, the tide leaving rings of dirt-specked foam. She could see fish in the waves. She walked slowly, picking her way over the smooth black stones. The sound was behind her, the motor dying, then catching, then accelerating. The men were whistling. They were closing in. The red bird dropped the dice on the sand in front of her. Elyse screamed. The black stones had begun to vibrate, were cracking open like eggs, a hundred eyes staring at her. The water was turning red, the tide coming closer. She slipped trying to avoid the eyes, slipped again and kept running. On the horizon, the ships were little points growing smaller as the jeep bore down upon her, the men shouting.

·

Luz had gotten up in the darkness. Elyse stood up with her. The shots were coming from beyond the wall, outside the prison, close by in the street. She heard another whistle, and a siren beginning to wail. "Escucha esto. Matan a los pobres. Y mis muchachos están allá." Luz was talking softly, looking upward. Elyse couldn't understand what she was saying. "Tengo miedo por ellos." The older woman was trying to light the candle again but was failing. "Solo Dios puede ayudarme. Dios y la Virgen. Les pido ayuda para mis niños . . . que ella les ayude . . . Escucha . . . hay otros tiros . . . pero no son fuertes como antes . . . deben estar más lejos ahora . . ."

Elyse looked at her, a short, heavy woman with long black hair, pressing a cross against her forehead. Only part of her face was visible as she stood in the doorway. "Se termina," Luz said finally, and Elyse understood. It's over.

7

They met at the restaurant. Gerard's usually impassive face twisted into a crooked smile when he saw Leslie enter. "Chérie." Gerard kissed her on both cheeks. "Te voici enfin." He held her at a distance for inspection. "Tired, but pretty as always. Did you sleep well?" He had already signaled for the waiter to approach. "What would you like? An aperitif?"

Leslie smiled. She had forgotten Gerard could drink at any time of day or night. It was not a serious habit, but one he enjoyed. As he would say to his critics: Just a little finger of rum to calm the worms.

"I might go right back to sleep," she warned him. She had slept late but still felt sleepy. "I'll have a rum cocktail. We're in the tropics, right?" She laughed and sat down.

Gerard nodded his approval. "Two rum cocktails, please, monsieur." The waiter smiled.

It was a modest restaurant with two dozen tables, half of them inside, half out. Red curtains separated the dining area from the kitchen. "They came here last year from Beirut," Gerard informed her in a low voice. "The war chased them out. Compared to over there, they say, Port-au-Prince is calm." He said this with a smile.

Leslie looked discreetly at the proprietor, a mustachioed Arab of fifty with a portly, circumspect demeanor. His scalp showed through his dark, thinning hair. Their eyes met; the proprietor tweaked his nostrils, and gave her a short, polite bow.

"He probably thinks you're my mistress," Gerard whispered. "He takes a great interest in such matters. He has four children himself—all of them girls. Only the oldest is unmarried. Youssef, that's his name, says he's heartbroken, but I think he loves it. No competition from other men, you see." Gerard smiled affectionately at the proprietor. "Actually, he's had a difficult life; he lost his parents and brothers in the same week. A bomb, on the Christian side. He's a Maronite and tells me there is nothing left of the French in Lebanon. Of course, I think that part is good."

She nodded. Through a break in the curtain, she could see an elderly Haitian woman pounding something in a large wooden bowl. Leslie caught the woman's eye; she smiled but stayed focused on her task.

"Why did they come here?" Leslie asked, looking around to see if smoking was allowed. There were ashtrays on several tables.

"It's hot. We speak French. And we're used to sleeping through gunshots at night." Gerard chuckled, getting up quickly to get her an ashtray. "Why really? I don't know. I know it's almost impossible to get a visa now for France. Anyway, he seems to like it here. We're beginning to have a thriving Arab population, you know."

It was still early for lunch. There was only one other party seated, all men. Leslie scanned the paintings on the wall, then caught Gerard's eye. He was watching her. He cocked his head and took her hand, lifting her fingers and dropping them.

"You finally came . . . after all this time," he said. "I'm so glad. I was beginning to think it was never going to happen." His brown eyes took in her face, her angular jaw, her gray-blue eyes. A practical woman, that was the way he thought of her. He could see her face had aged; the divorce seemed to have taken its toll. But she was wearing the same color lipstick she had always worn, a mild pink.

"You look well," he said. "Maybe a little tired under the eyes?"

She laughed. "A lot tired under the eyes—too much under the eyes." She automatically touched them, self-conscious. "I'm getting old." She had taken out a cigarette but was not smoking it.

"Non, non," he said, "don't exaggerate. Besides, you're in Haiti now. Don't you know we prefer women with experience?"

Leslie rolled her eyes, amused. "Sexist," she threw out lightly. She smiled, feeling how good it was to see Gerard in person. "I've missed you." She looked around for matches. "Letters and phone calls aren't enough."

"No," he agreed. "Especially with our postal system. Now it takes a month instead of two." He added quietly: "I've missed you too. And your little girl. How is Marisa?"

"Your adopted niece?" Leslie joked. "Oh, she's fine. Except she was so angry with me when I was leaving, she wouldn't give me a kiss goodbye. She begged me to take her to see Tonton Gerard."

"It's a stage," Gerard reassured her. "They all go through it. You know she adores you."

"Right now she likes my ex-husband better," Leslie remarked. "Not that I really mind. I can understand she misses him."

He nodded, venturing, "How is Mark? Do you see him?"

"He comes to see Marisa," she said evenly. "But no, we don't have much to say to one another. I really think of Mark as a chapter I'd like to forget—at least for right now. Except for Marisa, of course. In that respect I'm grateful."

He had known she was unhappy then, but to hear the bitterness now still surprised him. Of course, the man had betrayed her, and with a close friend. That was unforgivable. He took a drink, not certain how to respond.

The waiter came by just then to light her cigarette. "Thank you," Leslie said, noticing his thick green, yellow, and red woven cotton bracelet. Marleyists, that was what the Haitian Rastafarian youths called themselves. The proprietor was watching them carefully, and seemed satisfied.

Mark. The pain that had surfaced was already passing, his image and voice fading away. Leslie blew out a long stream of smoke. "I have something Marisa made to give you," she told Gerard. "But I forgot it back at the hotel. Really, she gets mad at me if I don't give her the phone when you call."

He laughed. "Why didn't you bring her this time? Too complicated?"

"She's just started a new school," Leslie said. "And she's taking music lessons."

"The piano?"

"No." Leslie kept the smoke away from Gerard's face. "The drum. She wants to be in a marching band. She asked me to buy her a little uniform, with the white boots. You've seen them?"

"That's too adorable," he remarked. "I wish my children wanted to study music. The only thing they like is television. And our television isn't very good."

"Well, her little drum is very noisy," Leslie said. "I've had to buy earplugs. But I actually like the idea. I always wanted to drum."

"Well, you could start," he said. "Here everyone likes to drum."

"All the more humiliating." She laughed. Then, lowering her voice, she asked, "Gerard, is it safe to talk here?"

"I think so," he replied, looking around. Two men, both Arabs, had joined the other party. "I asked Monsieur Youssef to give us privacy. Now that you are smoking, he'll be convinced you're my mistress. We can count on his discretion."

She smiled again. "You're impossible." He was probably right, though.

There was a soft padding sound behind Leslie. The Marleyist was back. He wore sandals with his uniform black pants and short red jacket. Leslie noticed he had shapely, very hairy legs. The waiter handed each of them a menu on which several entrées were penciled out.

"Chicken?" Gerard asked him.

The waiter glanced back at the proprietor, who shook his head.

"Pardon," the waiter said. "C'est fini."

"No more chicken. How about lamb or couscous? What will you have, Leslie? The couscous comes with vegetables."

A second waiter arrived with their rum drinks. The glasses had been frozen; there were no ice cubes. Leslie took a sip of her cocktail and felt a liquid flame shoot down her throat.

"Couscous . . . that's fine," she managed. "This is delicious." She took another sip, fanning her mouth. "But it's too strong."

A third waiter arrived with a wine list. Gerard put on his black half-spectacles to read it. They gave him a faintly academic air. For a man who favored plain living, Leslie thought, Gerard retained a gourmet's palate. "Would you like wine, Leslie? Or maybe later?"

"I'm fine, thanks. I'll be drunk with this." The third waiter reluctantly withdrew.

After a few more comings and goings, they were left in peace. Gerard had ordered the lamb. The Marleyist leaned against the wall at a respectful distance. Gerard raised his cocktail glass and tapped it against Leslie's. "Soyez bienvenue," he said.

"I want to hear more about this project of yours," Gerard began a moment later. "I think it's a good one. It's only now that we are beginning to focus on women here. I told you Jeanne is part of a women's organization. She can put you in touch with some people. There will certainly be some who suffered in Duvalier's jails." He added, squeezing the lime in his cocktail: "Le moment est . . . propice. I've told several of my colleagues about your visit. We'll put together what we have. It's not well organized, unfortunately. Will you be able to use what I sent you?"

Nodding, she said, "I used it to write my proposal. I won't get a response for a few months. But it's helped me shape my ideas. I've decided to limit it to an oral history project for now. That's what I did with the migrant workers."

"Yes, I remember. But you want to include a lot of documents, don't you?"

"I'd like to. Especially the prison and medical records. But from what you've told me, there isn't very much that's written down."

"That's true. We don't know if the authorities kept a log at every prison. They're supposed to keep track of any transfers from one prison to another, too, but it's very haphazard. That way there's no trace of the prisoner. I know some of the officers kept personal diaries. That would be something to pursue, although I can't imagine how we would get our hands on them."

"I have almost four weeks to do this first part," she said. "It's more than I originally anticipated. And I've arranged it so I can stay longer if I have to. They're being quite flexible at the foundation. Anyway, I think that I should be able to accomplish a good deal, don't you? Depends on who I can find."

"A month should be sufficient," he reassured her. "There are plenty of people who can help. Don't worry about it."

The waiter brought a small salad. She paused to remove a tobacco strand from her tongue. He slapped a mosquito that had landed on the tablecloth, leaving a red streak.

"Did they give you mosquito netting?"

"For my room? Yes. It's very comfortable. And I prefer the big fans to air conditioning." She looked up at a large ceiling fan spinning overhead. "I have one like that one, but smaller."

Gerard nodded. "And there is a gardien?"

Leslie grinned. "I caught him drinking tafia on the terrace last night. We're already friends." She wanted another cigarette. I have to stop smoking so much, she thought, taking another sip of the sweet rum drink. It left her teeth feeling oily.

Gerard laughed aloud. "So—you're already drinking with the

servants, hein?" He waved a finger disapprovingly at her. "I'm sure Bertrand will be happy to hear that."

"Oh, he probably expects it of me," she countered. "I think I offend him with almost everything I say." She added: "Maybe that's good."

He laughed.

Leslie took a moment to look at Gerard. He was skinnier around the shoulders. His eyes looked slightly bloodshot; otherwise he seemed fit, his complexion darker than it had been in Washington. Despite a set of permanent worry lines furrowing his wide brow, he appeared to be in good health. "Finally, it was the parasite, right?"

"Schistosoma mansoni," he clarified. "Bilharzia. More than capitalism or Communism, the real common enemy of the Third World. My spleen was starting to swell."

"Ouch," she said, grimacing. "But now you're all right?"

"I think so. I'm still eating my daily bowl of rice, but my eyes aren't yellow anymore . . . I had a touch of jaundice for a few weeks there." He patted his stomach. "Jeanne thinks I'm getting fat."

"Fat?" Leslie leaned forward to inspect the dubious swell. "That doesn't even qualify as overweight by American standards," she teased. "To us, that looks like a few beers on the weekend and not enough exercise."

He poked his paunch. "Jeanne likes to say that because she knows I have a horror of looking too much like my brothers."

"Aah." Leslie smiled, looking around for the Marleyist waiter. "The big bourgeois brothers." Now that she wanted some water, he was suddenly nowhere to be found.

"Exactly," Gerard replied. "A family of overconsumers." He patted his nascent stomach, pleased. "In any case, if I continue like this, I figure I'll qualify as a candidate in the elections. You should see our candidates this year. Every last one of them is a big man or woman. They like to eat. They look like they eat so much you would never imagine we are a starving nation. It's an image problem, you see. The poorer we are, the fatter we want our leaders to be."

She smiled again, appreciating his dark sense of humor.

"In fact, I think when they print the ballots this time, they shouldn't even bother to put the initials of the party, just the name of the candidate and a profile of the stomach. Trust me, the people would have no trouble knowing who to vote for." He pushed out his stomach. "What do you say? Do I have a chance?"

"Maybe—in the local elections." She finally spotted the waiter. "But definitely not the national elections."

"No," Gerard agreed. "We'll leave that to Bertrand."

"Bertrand?" This was news.

"Didn't he tell you? He wants to be a senator."

"Really? He just told me this morning how he hates politics."

Gerard laughed. "Everybody hates politics. But everybody wants power. That's why we'll have five hundred candidates for the presidency this year. Monsieur Youssef says it's the same way in Lebanon. One big family quarrel . . . all those tribes. It's the same here. It's not a question of ideas or having a vision, it's more an emotional thing. Ego," he clarified. "A lot of stupid ego."

She nodded but her attention was distracted. It was just after lunchtime. Marisa would be eating her peanut butter and jelly sandwich, drinking from her Snoopy thermos. She suddenly missed her daughter and felt jealous that Mark would be spending more time with her. Gerard had stopped speaking, was waiting for her to respond.

"So you're not very hopeful?" she asked, refocusing.

"Hopeful? About what?" He fished an orange slice out of his drink and inspected it. "The elections? Or democracy?" He dropped the rind back in, minus the fruit part. "Of course I'm hopeful. How can anyone afford not to have hope? It's like I've told the people at the American embassy. We Haitians always have hope. Hope is what allows us to survive. But hope isn't food. Hope isn't money. Hope doesn't produce roads or jobs. I say there's hope and then there's all this stupidity."

The proprietor appeared. "A telephone call for Maître Gerard."

Gerard excused himself. "That must be Jeanne. I'll be right back."

She watched him walk away. His weekend outfit was a pair of cotton pants and a short-sleeved button-down shirt squared at the bottom and untucked, his sockless feet in dark blue rope-soled shoes. His limp, somewhat curly hair stuck to his forehead and neck. In

Washington, Gerard had often been mistaken for a European due to his accented English, something he resented. She wondered if he ever visited his half sister, who had taken up permanent residence in France. The other members of his clan, it seemed, had adopted a more seasonal attitude toward the political situation, jetting for nearby Miami or the Bahamas at each hint of a new palace coup.

A few minutes later, Gerard made his way back to the table. "For each step forward, we seem to take one back," he said, picking up the conversation again. "That was Jeanne. We've finally received the computer I told you about. But they forgot to send us an instruction manual." He shook his head. "She is going crazy trying to set up the program."

Leslie had only a mental image of Gerard's wife, supplemented by a picture Gerard had sent her and by Jeanne's voice on the telephone. They had spoken many times, but always briefly. Leslie wondered what Jeanne would think of her and felt a little nervous about it. She wondered what Gerard had told Jeanne about their time together in Washington. Did she know he and Leslie had been on the brink of having an affair? That it was Leslie who had reconsidered, and somewhat reluctantly. Nothing had passed between them except desire, acknowledged but left dormant. Would Jeanne sense it? The thought preoccupied her.

The waiter brought an appetizer composed of semolina, tomatoes, and lentils. They both watched him attentively as he spooned the food out with a large wooden ladle. "You've never eaten Lebanese food in Haiti, have you, Leslie?"

"My first time," she said, lowering her voice. "It seems to be a *slow* cuisine."

Gerard laughed, waiting for the waiter to leave. After he had, Gerard said, "I'm telling you, they've become very Haitian." A moment later, he reached over to get a manila envelope he had placed, with his newspapers, on the floor. "Take a look."

There were documents inside and two cassettes. She edged the clippings out. On top was a photograph of a group of men standing under a banner that read, *Konbit Papay*. Attached to it was a photocopy of the picture.

"This was before Duvalier fell. They were just beginning to organize in Papaye then." Gerard had lowered his voice. "See the man in the middle? His name is Cedric George—Ti Cedric, that's his nickname. He's an animateur, an activist, and president of the cooperative, Konbit Papay. Last night someone called to tell us he's missing. He disappeared the same day the army came to arrest members of his group.

"I saw him not so long ago," Gerard continued, glancing at the picture as she studied it further. "He was imprisoned and tortured under Duvalier. The second time was in December of 1985, at the beginning of the hot period. But he was one of the lucky ones; they released him as part of the big amnesty."

The man had a rather round face and a sloe-eyed, almost furtive expression. Wary, Leslie thought. His thick eyebrows met over a wide, slightly crooked nose and high cheekbones. He was carrying a machete in his left hand, as were the other men. They also looked slightly dazed, as if the flash of the camera had caught them unprepared. It was clear from the way the group was arranged that Ti Cedric was the leader, although he stood a half-head shorter than the others. He was the only one not smiling.

"His nose looks like it was broken," Leslie observed.

"More than once," Gerard confirmed.

She grimaced, shaking her head. "From the torture?"

"I never asked."

She nodded, keeping the envelope near her lap. The waiter was leaning against the wall, a little too close to them for Leslie's taste. She was still feeling a little paranoid, despite Gerard's assurances.

"I don't recall his name from the lists you sent me. Did they tell you anything else on the telephone?"

"No." Gerard ate as he spoke. "I got the call from a colleague who said a member of the group has taken refuge with a priest over there. But we don't have any more details. We haven't even been able to confirm the arrests yet."

"Was he helping to organize the national strike?" She was scanning another clipping, this one from *Haïti Progrès*, the more radical of the diaspora-based weeklies. The article detailed a labor dispute in the Papaye region. It was dated September 1985. The other newspaper clippings also referred to labor disputes that had taken place in the region.

"The konbit certainly supports the strike; they're part of a coalition of cooperatives. But we really don't have any accurate information because the people there have to be extra-discreet. And unfortunately the telephone lines are working poorly with these storms. We've had trouble getting through; it's easier to call overseas."

She went back to the photograph. "What are his political views? Radical, I presume?"

Gerard smiled tolerantly. "What's radical? That's what my brothers call me. I think in our Haitian context Ti Cedric would be considered a nationalist, above all, because he's a peasant activist. They have their own particular agenda. He's worked with a lot of groups, including the literacy campaign, and now to organize distribution of the local products. Because the problem in that region is not that they can't grow food, but, because of the bad roads, they have to pay too much to have it transported to the big markets. Ti Cedric has a good head for organization."

"What party is he affiliated with? Any?"

"Honestly, I don't know. You could tell me he supports the Communists and I wouldn't be surprised. Because of all the parties, they are the only one with a solid land reform program. Now that it's legal to be a Communist, a small minority of people have registered, and so far, they're the best-organized for an election. At the same time, it's still dangerous to say you're a Communist, especially in the countryside. Not that it's the Communism of Russia, not at all. Here they want more decentralization. They don't favor the big state bureaucracy. Actually, it resembles the Maoism that was popular when I was a student in Paris. The ideas are rooted in the land—that is the main platform. They want to recover the communal property that belonged to villages and was given away by the Duvalierists."

"What's their position on armed struggle?" she asked. "Like the Shining Path?"

"Pas du tout," Gerard replied. "I mean, their rhetoric is definitely anti-imperialist and aimed heavily at your country. But it's more the idea than the action. For now, I'm sure they've decided that it would be a political mistake to declare a violent revolution—they need to gain supporters first. But a lot of them must privately support the idea, at least in principle."

Leslie had read about the purge of Haitian Communists in the

1960s and 1970s. François Duvalier had used the Red threat to tar and eliminate his closest intimates. Thousands had been murdered; hundreds of others disappeared, many of them prominent middle-class citizens, including women. It was another hidden aspect of their history she hoped to document.

The waiter arrived with a plate of hummus and olives. She dropped the clippings back into the envelope, held it close to her shins until he left.

"What are these?" she asked, pulling out the cassettes.

"Those are the testimonies I mentioned to you in my letter." Gerard followed the waiter with his eyes. "They're among the prisoners who were released in the big amnesty. But they're not official transcripts. I don't think these cases were ever presented in the courts. Anyway, the Red Cross doctor who did the interviews has left; I think he might be in Canada, but I don't have his address."

"Are all of these women?" Leslie asked excitedly. She wanted to listen to them right away.

"Men and women. Somehow in all of the chaos of that period, right after Duvalier left, the prison authorities decided to let the Red Cross enter the prison, but it was a secret. The authorities were trying to deny the rumor that prisoners were being killed. So this doctor takes his machine in, and no one says anything about it. It was pure luck, because he could easily have been shot for trying that."

"Did he do anything with the interviews? Was the information publicly released?"

"Only their names, but no details. I had thought about giving the cassettes to a journalist I know, but frankly, I forgot about them until you reminded me."

"What about that rumor, Gerard? That the army killed a lot of people in revenge the day Duvalier was leaving? Does anyone have any proof of it? Because we keep hearing different stories."

"It's difficult to know, actually. It can't be a large number of people, but you've seen the lists—there are still many names that we can't account for."

"What about Fort Dimanche?" she asked, referring to the notorious military prison.

"Nothing new there. They refuse to allow anyone in. They say they've closed it. But we know there are still soldiers there guarding the munitions. We have no way of getting inside."

She put the tapes in her pocket. "I'll listen to these as soon as I can and give them back to you."

"You can take your time," he said. "I wouldn't be doing anything with them anyway. Legally, they're not worth very much—unfortunately."

"Thank you, Gerard." She reached forward to squeeze his hand. "This is a big help."

"Pa fe rien," he said, shrugging, mixing Creole and French. No problem. "This benefits us."

They remained silent for a few minutes, enjoying the tranquil atmosphere of the restaurant. The waiters appeared and disappeared, fussing around the table, working for a higher tip.

The olives were huge and brown, the pits stringy. Leslie watched as Gerard ate deftly, scooping hummus onto a fat lip of bread and placing an olive on top. She drained the rum drink and considered ordering another.

"You mentioned the strike earlier," Gerard continued, wiping his mouth with a finger. "So I'll tell you. What's happening now is that the government made several promises to the unions and they haven't fulfilled them. The deadline was eleven days ago. All the workers want right now—as a minimum demand—is for the labor code to be enforced. The law already exists. But even the reforms they have suggested are minor." He drained his glass of water and refilled it, eyeing the cloudy water with distrust. Leslie smiled.

"That's very threatening to the barons and the factory owners and people like my brothers," he continued, attacking the hummus again. "They've had a free hand up to now; there's never been any enforcement." He sniffed, clearing his nose. "The first demonstrations happened independently in the south, in Miragoâne and Petit Goâve, and in the interior. Then they started organizing in Papaye and Hinche and the Artibonite. So far, the protests have been relatively peaceful, but the army has shot up in the air the last two times. A man was hit in the arm when a bullet ricocheted off a wall. That was in Hinche. They've also arrested people—you have those names on that list—and in general they only keep them overnight, but first they beat them and warn them to stop their activities. Anyone who is perceived as organizing the strike is vulnerable."

"Would that be a pretext for arresting the people from Konbit Papay?"

"If they needed one. But they don't. They make up their reasons afterward." Gerard tore the bread into quarters with his fingers, offering a sample to Leslie. "Just the fact that your name becomes known to the authorities makes you a suspect. Or else they arrest people while conducting a raid."

"Searching for drugs or contraband?" Max the reporter had told her all about it.

"Exactly. And I'm afraid that the closer we come to actually holding an election, even if it's not a clean one, the worse it's going to get. Because I hear my brothers and their friends and they are really frightened. They have a mentality like . . . oh, let's see . . ." He tapped his pursed mouth, seeking the precise word.

"A bunker mentality?"

"That's right." He approved of her choice. "Because this is like a war for them—a class war—the rich against the poor. Definitely. Most people do see it that way. Even if an election would be good for the elite and they know it. In the long run, they do know that, but they can't think that way. It's too threatening to their way of life. They can only think about what's good for them today, not next week or next year. It's really a crisis mentality."

He took another long drink from the cloudy water. She watched his large Adam's apple move, almost disappear, then protrude again. A new plate of vegetables swimming in oil and topped with cooked lemon slices had been placed before them. "Delicious," Leslie declared. The Marleyist waiter smiled at her.

Gerard wiped his mouth. "I think the army will use the election as a pretext for violence," he declared, touching his stomach. "Call me a pessimist, but I feel it right here."

They paused when the lamb arrived, and then a dish they had not ordered. "Compliments of Monsieur Youssef," said Gerard, sniffing at what appeared to be a vegetable puree of some sort adorned with parsley sprigs. Leslie saw two Arab women talking in the kitchen. Monsieur Youssef's daughters, she bet.

"I'll check with a contact in the hospital," Gerard added, picking up the conversation again. The puree tasted like yams to Leslie. "I know a doctor who's been helpful in cases like this, Dr. Sylvie—Julie Sylvie. In fact, you should go to see her. She might be able to help you get into the penitentiary. She's been in there several times."

"That would be wonderful," said Leslie. "Would she know of cases of Communist women?"

"Oh, I'm sure she does. But I don't think she sees the political prisoners, just the common ones. Not that I care about such distinctions, since most of the arrests are illegal. But the politicals are held in another section. In any case, it will take her a few days to check on this. She has to be very discreet. The hospital is still full of Macoutes."

"Still?"

"That's why we lack information about these student arrests. The people who are wounded are too afraid to go to the hospitals. The soldiers will come in there and shoot them in their beds. It happened just a month ago."

She hadn't read about it, but made a mental note to follow it up.

"I'll give you Dr. Sylvie's office telephone," Gerard added. "You won't find her at home. She lives up in Kenscoff, not far from our little cabin. You've been there, haven't you?"

"Not since I was a teenager, with my father. I don't remember it very well. Only that it was cool. But I hope I can find the time. I love the mountains." She jotted this information down, along with the details about Ti Cedric, on a fresh paper napkin. "What's her specialty?"

"Gynecology. She's Jeanne's doctor. But she also advises me about my parasites. She has a second degree in internal medicine, from Philadelphia."

There was a long pause. Leslie saw that Gerard had grown pensive.

"What is it?" she asked.

"I'm wondering if they would have killed him," he said after a moment. "I'm trying to see what their motivation would be—beyond the usual, I mean. I mean at this particular moment. It seems to me they could have killed him a month ago, it would have made more sense. But now, it's a foolish move, considering that the army is trying to play its democracy card. On the other hand," he added, "not everybody in the army is in agreement. And it's always a mistake to apply logic to men like that." He passed his hand over his face, wiped away a brow of sweat. "We'll just have to hope," he said, leaving it at that.

A different waiter came to clear their dishes. Then the maître d' approached with coffee. It was spiced with cardamom seeds. Gerard sipped it and wrinkled his nose, drinking slowly. A moment later, they heard the sound of an engine. It was Clemard coming up the long driveway. He was early, Leslie noted, glancing at her watch. Before she could protest, Gerard had handed the waiter a large bill. "You can invite me to dinner in Washington," he said, refusing to discuss it. As they waited for the waiter to return, Gerard said, "Before I forget, my sister-in-law said to thank you."

"I take it the Pampers were the right size?" Leslie took out her lipstick and quickly applied it, glancing in her compact mirror.

"The child is huge. I don't know why."

"Maybe because he's your brother's child?" Leslie suggested slyly.

He laughed appreciatively. "Why don't you come and live in Haiti with us, Leslie? I'm telling you we need more people who know how to joke."

"I'm thinking about it," she said. "Of course, I'd become an alcoholic."

"You're just killing the worms," he said sagely, leaving a large tip for the waiter. They got up to leave, saying goodbye to Monsieur Youssef.

"Another thing." Gerard stopped her as they started down the entrance steps. "You asked me to contact Pierre Lescot? Well, I'm afraid he's not going to be available. He got beat up this summer for helping a Canadian mission. I meant to tell you earlier."

"What happened?" She had wanted to ask Pierre, an interpreter she had met in Washington, to assist her on the project.

"A group of Macoutes. Young guys. He spent a few days in the hospital and now he's recovered, but not psychologically. He's ready to go back to Washington." Gerard added: "What made us so angry was the response of the American embassy. They refused to condemn the incident. I think they characterized it as an accident. It's very disappointing. They love to lecture us about democracy, then they hear about an incident like this and suddenly they aren't willing to find fault with the army."

Clemard had turned the car around.

"Bonjour, Clemard," Gerard said, shaking hands with Bertrand's driver. "How is Blan Bertrand?"

Clemard grinned. It was clear the two men understood each other regarding the subject.

"He's preparing his campaign, isn't that so, Clemard?" Gerard added.

The chauffeur grinned even wider. He held the door open for Leslie and rolled down the window. She got in.

Gerard came around to her side. "Don't forget to give Bertrand my advice. If he wants to win, he should eat an extra meal a day. That's the strategy."

Leslie reached out to lightly punch Gerard's little gut and kissed him twice on one cheek, once on the other.

"Adieu, chérie." He tapped on the car as Clemard carefully backed it out. "It looks like a senator's car, doesn't it?" he shouted after them.

At the top of the hill, Clemard stopped, waiting for her instructions. "I'm sorry, Clemard," Leslie apologized, realizing it too late. "I'd like to go to the hotel, if that's not a problem."

"No problem, Madanm Leslie. I'll go up here and come down behind the hotel. We'll be there in a quarter of an hour."

The white woman looked ill. At an intersection, Clemard hopped out, rolled up the back windows he had opened earlier, then his own, and turned on the air conditioning. Leslie, who had closed her eyes, thanked him. "I drank too much," she said, smiling a little.

Exactly fifteen minutes later he eased the Diahatsu over the speed bump at the entrance to the Hôtel Royale. The custodian was there, sleeping in a chair by the gate, his jug of tafia nowhere in sight. Leslie eased herself out of the car. "Mesi, Clemard." She shook his hand. Thank you. "That was a smooth drive."

He watched her walk inside the hotel. She had an awkward grace, he thought, noticing that her slip showed. But he was impressed that she spoke Creole, if badly. He turned off the air conditioner; Met Bertrand didn't like him to use it. Then he executed a careful three-point turn under the baleful gaze of the custodian, who had woken. The car's first gear stuck, then fell into place with a scraping sound. "Diahatsu," he muttered, swearing, "Gran bagay kaka!" Big piece of shit!

8

It was a quiet afternoon when Leslie approached the first of the houses with Clemard. It was siesta time and no one was in the streets. Even the lime sellers were asleep, slumped against the whitewashed walls of houses. The rain was gone today; the sun shone, soft and hot, through a low cloud cover that wrapped the mountain peaks like loose gauze. Leslie and Clemard stepped through the gate, which could no longer be locked, and felt the ringing silence contained by the high walls. Leslie's feet absorbed the energy, an invisible vibration.

They approached like tourists, stopping to examine debris in the grass. To Leslie, it seemed like a moment of history frozen, the entire drama revealed in the layers of left-behind objects, now torn apart and gathering dust. Yellowed newspaper clippings, a deck of cards, ceramic shards, odd bits of wood from the garage. They climbed a spiral staircase leading up to the front door.

She could not shake the feeling of an electric current causing her feet to involuntarily flex and release, her hands doing the same. Clemard led the way, took the steps two by two. Leslie moved more slowly, trailing her palm over the wide concrete banister and its ornate encrusted edge. Fingertips plump with blood, sensitive to the sharp tips of shell and coral and rounded stones. Clemard traced for her the angle of the roof down the drainpipe to the back, where the lower rooms once blended with the rear wall, sloping to fit in with the natural surroundings. Where, before the attack, the owners had raised native black pigs in a small pen. The house was set apart now, isolated from the cluster of trees behind it; there was no trace of the pen, only discarded bits of wood and corn husks. Even months later, there was no question of letting the house resume its previous shape or function; it was defenseless and exposed.

Leslie felt anew the thrill of the radio broadcasts as they entered the hall, a visceral experience as her feet scattered marble and china fragments, business documents, torn pages of the Miami telephone book, used checks. She could sense the presence of human fury, of bodies that had attacked the thick walls heedless of barriers such as metal, marble, stone. Everything had fallen prey: pipes, wires, windows, furniture, fixtures. Plants were uprooted, giant ceramic flowerpots lay in long halves on the floor, the dirt strewn everywhere. The house was still reeling from it, the release of a collective twenty-nine-year rage.

Leslie became a camera, clicking away, trying to capture the whole frame by frame, the details shifting in relation to one another like a moving collage. But she was unable to grasp it in its entirety. The house was too full of information. Every detail of destruction was part of the story.

Clemard stopped to smell the piles of shit, trying to distinguish human from animal. The elemental desire to shit upon your enemy, like fucking them or killing them, Leslie thought, watching Clemard count the piles. Thirteen in this room.

He finally broke the silence. "This is what we think of the Du-valierists." He pointed out the shit-smeared graffiti on a wall she had mistaken for old blood. *Aba Makout. Viktwa Pep.* Down with the Macoutes. Victory to the People.

They kept walking. The shit filled the other rooms as well. Another message of triumph was scratched into the space where a bathroom mirror had hung: a smiling face and the initials TTM, for Tontons Macoutes, crossed out with a large fecal X. The shit had been dropped in neat, deliberate piles and, outside, into the half-drained pool. Leslie could see the pool from where she stood looking through a broken window, the droppings resembling murky little turtles under a stagnant green surface. Reclamation, she thought, remembering her conversation with Gerard. Cleansing with shit.

You'd have to see it to believe it, she said to the invisible audience in her head, a lecture hall filled with academics—and her father —nodding but privately disapproving of such crude political expressions. Is it primitive or ultrasophisticated, a visual haiku? she asked them. The audience took up the question, deliberating among themselves. Ahead of her, Clemard picked up and dropped empty cartons, splintered shelves, rusted batteries. Anyone who has been violated to the core of their being, day in and day out, as these people have, needs no interpreter. She said this to the theory-heads, the glass-housed beings, to her father.

Clemard gestured to a drawing on the wall. "It's a monkey . . . Baby Doc," he explained. "See? He's being lynched by his own tail." Duvalier, Firm as a Monkey's Tail. Leslie nodded, remembering the dictator's infamous quote, broadcast around the world on the eve of his forced exile. She leaned forward to determine the nature of the graffiti. The faint odor was unmistakable. In her head, the lecture audience agreed with her. Definitely an advance, roots in the Claes Oldenburg school, a semiotic coup, beyond the oral into the anal tradition, transcending European structuralism and First World boundaries. She listened to their comments, amused.

Out loud, unnaturally loud given the silence of the day and the isolation of the house, Clemard began recounting the value of the objects that had been trundled away by cheering crowds, but only what was intact. "The people destroyed everything at first; the impulse to steal came later," he said like the best postrevolutionary guide. "For weeks after Duvalier left, the people stayed camped in the yard." Indulging in her fantasy, Leslie requested a slide for the audience: a picture of the people gnawing like lions on the bones of the Duvalierist houses. The lecture hall was breaking into applause.

Downstairs, the room was bigger and wider, with high ceilings. And airy, because the windows had been wrested from their painted wrought-iron frames. A decorative grille of white leaves and roses was now a skeleton of twisted metal discarded on the tile floor, except the tiles had been dug up, almost all of them. Nothing had been left that could be put to use. Leslie opened and shut her eyes, matching raw holes in the concrete wall with the objects they might have held. Light fixture, door, shelf, candleholder, painting. Leslie marveled at the destruction. On the terrace, huge urn-shaped clay planters were grounded like missiles still waiting to explode, their metal stands almost unrecognizable. Clemard tried to bend one back into shape, then gave up.

They went back inside. There was a cracked mirror in the upper bedroom, more graffiti. Names, insults, slogans, vindication. Shit and paint mixed together. The stuffing of a ripped chair had blown into corners, its springs stretched into uselessness. A perfect cone of shit had been dropped onto the velvet fleur-de-lis-imprinted seat. "Joli bagay," Clemard said as he stepped over it. Nice thing. In her head, the audience was taking notes now, clapping as each image she composed with her eyes appeared as a slide.

In this room, as in the others they had toured, the wall sockets were gone, live wires exposed. Leslie imagined the force it took to pull wiring from concrete; the idea rushed through her like a drug. She gritted her teeth, imagining the resistance, the incredible satisfaction as part of the wall gave way.

Clemard shouted to her from the master bedroom. At arm's length he held a dirty wedding invitation featuring the smiling presidential couple, Jean-Claude and Michèle, printed in embossed gold-leaf script. Not a local job, she told the audience; they used a printer from Paris or Miami. You can't get this typeface in Port-au-Prince. She invited the audience to pass the invitation along, to judge for themselves.

There were Polaroids strewn across the bathroom floor. Unknown children were grouped together in happy poses by the clean pool. A light-skinned man raised his glass to the camera; he was afloat in the pool. Now his lower torso was a purply blur from the pressure of too many fingers on the chemically treated paper.

In another, a woman vamped like a coquette, one arm thrown back dramatically, hip jutting, a pink hibiscus in her hair. They rearranged the Polaroids with their feet. Leslie was lecturing again. What do these pictures say? As they now exist, framed by shit? New pictures in a new context. They are no longer pictures of a family joking around the pool. Their significance depends on where the viewer is standing, which picture he or she looks at first, whether the pictures of the children are viewed apart from those of the parents, or in conjunction with them. And of course, by whom. Shitting, she countered her father's cocoa-bean view of things, is reductive, simple, an equalizer of men. He was frowning.

Leslie squatted beside Clemard. She thought of women selling in the markets, of giving birth, of herself rocking on her heels in grief at the news of her father's death. Clemard recognized a hibachi by the pool, an Armani shirt. He did not know any of the people in the photographs. To Leslie, they looked like middle-income Americans relaxing in the suburbs. There is nothing intrinsically wrong with a swimming pool in the tropics, she was saying to her father as he led the others out of the lecture hall. It's all a matter of context, wouldn't you agree? She saw him standing in the middle of the fields that first summer, inspecting the crops, oblivious to the heat. *Wouldn't you agree?*

She followed Clemard back to the car. They drove for five minutes, then parked alongside a house that had belonged to a military officer. A purported torturer. A shiny gray Toyota was parked in the driveway. Clemard knocked on the door. No one answered. Behind the house, they found a man in his fifties, with broad peasant features, salt-and-pepper hair, and a wizened, suspicious face. "Everyone's left," he told them without prompting. "No one's here."

"She's visiting from America," Clemard said.

"Bonjour," Leslie said, offering her hand. The man ignored it and repeated, "There's no one here. I'm just the gardien."

"She's not a journalist," Clemard explained. It was obvious they all knew the purpose of the visit. "She just wants to see the house."

The custodian looked at her dubiously, then at the house, then back at Clemard again. He did not say anything. After a pause, Clemard insisted, "We just want to see. There's no problem."

The man's eyes were on her. Leslie pretended not to care about visiting the house and turned toward the street.

"There's nothing inside. Nothing to see." He took a step forward, leaned on the gray car. "This is his son's car. He'll be here later. You could come back." This was said without much conviction. Clemard nodded, then looked at Leslie.

She spoke in bad Creole. "Pa gen pwoblem. Mwen pa jounalis. Me mwen pa kapab vini pi ta . . . tanpri?" There's no problem. I'm not a journalist but I can't come back later . . . please?

The man would not budge. Clemard removed a cigarette from his pocket, lit it, and offered one to each of them. The man smoked, but still stayed silent. Then he said, "They've stolen everything. The car wasn't here then. But they came back. See? They broke the locks." His tone was dispassionate.

Clemard looked inside the car, at the damaged seats. Leslie

watched the custodian watching Clemard, the servant guarding the master's property, except now the master had fled. It was clear that he was uncertain about his responsibility to the house, and to his past. He has been freed, but into what? A new life? A clean slate? How can that be when memory exists to call up the past and the past marks the point from which the future springs? The servant remembers the master, and vice versa. At any moment, the present may assume the qualities of the past and this will be the future. Leslie thought this as she smiled at the man, trying to win him over. What exists today may not exist tomorrow. Today you are free, tomorrow is the future. He's gone. Let us in.

The custodian smoked considerately, then ground the ashes with his big toe, spreading them evenly. One day the owner may return and another generation of masters will occupy the house. Is that what he is thinking? Leslie kept her eyes on his foot. Or does he harbor a desire for vengeance? The desire even the most loyal of servants must feel? The master was gone, dead, Clemard had informed her on the way down, killed by a crowd while fleeing. The rest of the family was keeping a low profile. Who was going to pay this poor man now?

Finally the custodian confessed. "I don't stay here anymore. I only come here to collect the mail. I take it to the police. I don't know what they do with it." He shifted his feet. Clemard turned his back to Leslie, said to the man in a low tone, "Just the house, nothing else."

The man gave the house a final look and relented. "No pictures. If anyone asks, you were never here."

There was no longer the surprise of disaster, only the feeling of a vacuum, a great void. The house had been targeted in the second wave of the dechoukaj, the descent from the houses of the Duvaliers to those of friends and supporters. The short lapse in time had blunted some of the fury here; not everything had been destroyed. There were a few large canvases on the living-room walls, and a couch whose surface was intact, although covered with footprints. Almost like a museum.

There was a painting of a wedding couple being blessed by Christ and the Virgin Mary, all black faces. To Leslie, it offered yet another glimpse into the Duvalierist vision of unreality. She studied the painting, transposed the blessing of the long-haired Christ over the piles of shit from the other house, then over the Polaroid of the coquette's painted face instead of the Virgin smiling at the assembly. Then over herself, standing next to Clemard among the spectators. Who I am depends on who you are, she said to her imaginary audience. It's a basic fact. You can't escape it. None of us can.

An image stayed with Leslie long after they had left: the custodian, graying hair and weathered face, leaning against the frame of the bedroom window smoking another cigarette, waiting for the visitors to leave, a sheaf of blue gourde notes in his other hand, calm eyes that had witnessed three decades of crime moving from the white woman to the glass on the floor out to the bright green branches of the wild trees in the ravine that had overgrown the master's property.

Soti 15 Out
Dosye Vyolasyon Dwa Moun   Paj 1

VIKTIM: Pran bal, li blese. Fanm, 17 ane, machann
KILE: 17 Out, ve 4 ze di matin
KI KOTE: Devan mache Petyonvil
SIKONSTANS: Yon gwoup moun ap monte nan lari Delmas. Yo rive devan
mache Petyonvil ve 4 ze di matin. Gen yon machann ki domi ate nan
lari nan gwo mache. Konsa gen milite nan machin ki komanse tire.
Fi-a pran twa bal nan janm dwat li. Gen yon lot moun ki rele la Kwa
Wouj pou li.
KONSEKANS: Li fe operasyon nan Lopital Canape Vert, fi-a te lage paske
li pa ka peye pou remed.

Period 15 August
Dossier of Human Rights Violations   Page 1

VICTIM: Shot, wounded. Female, 17 years old, market vendor
TIME: 17 August, around 4 a.m.
WHERE: In front of Pétionville market
CIRCUMSTANCES: A group of people were walking up Delmas Road. They
arrived near the Pétionville market at about 4 a.m. A market vendor
was sleeping outdoors near the big market. The army arrived in a vehicle
and began shooting. The woman was struck with three bullets in her
right leg. Another individual called the Red Cross for her.
CONSEQUENCES: She had an operation at the Canapé Vert Hospital. The
woman was released because she could not pay for treatments.

VIKTIM: Pran bal, li blese. Fanm ansent, 22 lane, estetisyen
KILE: 16 Out, ve 5 e 30 diswa
KI KOTE: Ri 4
SIKONSTANS: 3 milite ame an sivil ki te nan tap-tap ak estetisyen. Yon

milite te di anpil bagay sou madanm. Milite te vin kraze madanm sou tet ak ko. Madanm te mande pou yo sispann paske li gen gwo vent epi li fin gen doule. Milite komanse frape lot moun nan tap-tap.

KONSEKANS: Fi-a gen 3 ti moun, li ansent 5 mwa. Li fe operasyon nan Lopital Jeneral, men li soufri gwo doule epi li vin pedi bebe.

VICTIM: Beaten. Pregnant woman, 22 years, beautician
WHEN: 16 August, about 5:30 p.m.
WHERE: Ri 4 (Fourth Street)
CIRCUMSTANCES: Three soldiers in civilian clothing were in a tap-tap bus with the beautician. One soldier began saying a lot of things to the woman. The soldier ended by striking the woman on the head and body. The woman asked him to stop because she had a large stomach and was having pains. The soldiers began hitting other passengers.
CONSEQUENCES: The woman has three children, and was five months pregnant. She was operated on in the General Hospital, but suffered too much injury and lost her baby.

VIKTIM: Pran bal, li blese e mouri. Gason, 36, ansyen pwofese
KILE: 18 Out, ve 10 e nan matin
KI KOTE: Site Soley, anndan lakay madanm li
SIKONSTANS: Tout moun te anndan kay madanm la. Gen yon bal ki travese kay la epi pran gason nan tet ak nan do. Yo mennen gason a Lopital Jeneral.
KONSEKANS: Gason te soufri plizye jou epi konsa li mouri.

VICTIM: Shot, wounded and died. Male, 36, former teacher
WHEN: 18 August, around 10 a.m.
WHERE: Cité Soleil shantytown, in wife's home
CIRCUMSTANCES: Everyone was inside the house of the wife. A bullet entered and crossed the room, striking the man in the head and back. They took him to the General Hospital.
CONSEQUENCES: The man suffered for several days and then died.

9

Gerard opened the door to his office. It was a small room, with water stains on the low ceiling and a riot of ferns threatening to take over one corner of it. A little balcony looked out on a residential side street; he could see the cigarette sellers sleeping on the sunlit sidewalk. Nearby a donkey was tied to a gate; a woman repacked her basket of plastic bowls. He pulled on the old overhead fan to air out the room, and slid open the glass doors of the balcony. Then he sat in a chair to finish his breakfast.

He had woken before the others, showered downstairs where Jeanne could not hear him, and let the car slip noiselessly out of their steep driveway before turning over the engine. Usually he slept late on Sundays, but today was different. It was his birthday. How could I be forty-nine? he asked himself, turning to look at his reflection in the glass door. A long-faced man with a high forehead and large ears peered thoughtfully back at him. He was turning gray at the temples and was unshaven. Forty-nine. I look more like Mother every day, he mused, running a hand along the deep angular wrinkles that gave his face an exaggerated air of gravity. He tried smoothing the lines to make himself look the way he wished to appear, which was younger and less serious. Then he let his hand go, and the pensive man made a face. Forty-nine. How awful!

Driving downtown, he had stopped by the bakery near the office and persuaded the owner to sell him a dozen little meat pies cooling on top of the old black oven. They were still warm, as was the thermos of coffee he had brought from home. I'm having a picnic, he thought, wondering at the origins of the word. Pique-nique. The purist French had adopted it, like other imports lumped under the category of Franglais. Pique-nique. Such a funny word. What a strange coincidence to have seen it scrawled on a piece of paper in the bakery. *Pain Pyk-Nyk. Style Miami.* He assumed Style Miami meant a hot sandwich.

Crumbs littered the red Université de Paris T-shirt that Beatrice, his niece, had sent him as a gift. "For old times' sake," she had written. He thought about her, studying on a bench by the Seine, as he had done so long ago, taking naps under the archways of the low bridges, walking around the Ile St.-Louis. It had been years since he had been to Paris. He wondered if they still sold doves and flowers at dawn in the market. Strolling the streets of Paris and perusing the kiosks of old books along the river had been his favorite pastimes. He sighed, nostalgic. Beatrice was probably doing well. At least she had the sense to study business, not law. He was betting she wouldn't come back; she was more independent than he had been at twenty. He could barely remember what had occupied him then, what delusions of fame or success had bolstered the long, cold winters of study in his little chambre de bonne, nine flights up a rickety wooden staircase in the Marais. He had been a serious student, rising at dawn, dancing only on the occasional weekend. Far too serious, in retrospect. And too rigid. Not enough fun. Gerard smiled. C'est bien vrai.

He yawned, felt the little cracking in his jaw, no doubt another sign of impending old age. He had to begin exercising; maybe he could play soccer with Emmanuel's group. The little clock on his desk read 7:30. Emmanuel would be saying Mass shortly. He had enjoyed their short visit. It was the first time in weeks that they had had a chance to catch up.

Gerard let the sun warm his face. Emmanuel never took things too personally, that's what made him different. Maybe he really wasn't human, as Jeanne said. He yawned again, stretching his mouth into a grin, then blew a kiss to the sun. How can you call yourself a Haitian and not take things personally? It's almost un-patriotic. The man in the glass door smiled at him benevolently.

He felt the deep lines along his jaw with his finger. Getting old. Maybe too old to start writing. Maybe just a fantasy. A last burst of youth. But if I wait any longer, an inner voice reasoned, then it really will be too late. Perhaps he'd waited too long as it was. And if you succeed, what then? another voice asked. Then he'd be happy. He would have done what he wanted to do. At least one thing he really wanted to do. And nobody could stop him. He could tell them just what he thought. Even if they killed him for saying it, he would have said it.

How many times had he daydreamed about writing a book, sitting somewhere by the ocean, or in the mountains, up at the little house in Kenscoff? He bit into another meat pie. You can still redeem yourself, he thought. But would he? That was the question and it had always been.

He took a long sip of coffee, gazing at the mountain. In a few hours the men from Papaye would be arriving at Victor's. Gerard closed his eyes for a moment, saw Ti Cedric's penetrating eyes, his slightly suspicious expression. He heard his quick, explosive laughter. A short, tough man, uncompromising with his opponents, but generous to his friends. Gerard didn't know him well, had only met the man twice, both times at large meetings. They had never spoken privately. But the idea of Ti Cedric missing, kidnapped, or possibly murdered continued to disturb him. He narrowed his eyes, trying to make out details of the distant trees. He assumed that Cedric was in the maquis, underground, but he felt uneasy. Where are you, man? he wondered. What's going on?

He glanced at his watch, then got up and went inside, leaving the sliding glass door open. Across the room, he noticed that a fax had arrived during the night. The paper curled down to the floor.

LAW OFFICE OF

MITCHELL, LAKE & STRICKLAND

35 WALL STREET

NEW YORK, NY 10004

MEMORANDUM

CONFIDENTIAL

By Telecopier

RE: Haiti/Duvalier   August 26, 1986

TO: Gerard Metellus

FROM: Stephen Lake

Following our conversation last week, we are still trying to confirm a number of checks and wire transfers out of BNC and BNP accounts into foreign banks. Given your source at BNP, we are hoping to determine what kinds of accounts were used by JCD and MBD as well as which accounts were used to make payoffs or gifts to Duvalier associates. We suspect a Duvalier associate who arranged the visa sales along with the Haitian consul in Switzerland. Any information you can provide in this regard would be helpful.

We have officially put Martin Fabricant under contract as of August 1. He will be contacting you when he arrives. As you know, the Ministry of Justice has been assisting our investigation. But our sources tell us that certain documents are still being withheld by BNP and BNC bank managers. Again, we do not have underlying documents to indicate where funds from BNC state accounts were deposited into foreign banks. We do have documents showing that a number of our friends used Citibank, Bank of Boston, and Bank of Nova Scotia in Port-au-Prince, as you suggested in our first conversation last month. We are now focusing on Curaçao, New York, Texas, and Miami. Coincidentally, we have some transfers into Panama banks, so we will pursue the Noriega connection (the same with Marcos connections).

We have also confirmed the information provided to us by Jean-Claude Sanon of Central Bank regarding the eight secret accounts marked National Defense used by JCD and transferred directly into personal accounts abroad. So far, our estimate remains that $1 million a month was transferred, most into original U.S. dollar deposit accounts. Other accounts appear to correspond to a number of front companies in Netherlands Antilles and Liechtenstein. We have identified an investment banking facility in Geneva regarding Sanon 1983 transfers. Given Sanon disclosures, many of his friends appear willing to talk to us in exchange for good press. Can you give us background on them?

We are still trying to make a paper trail of funds taken directly from government agencies. Please refer to our fax 8/12, which updates the May list that the CNG interim government issued of the 100 "Presumed Accessories to Corruption." Our sources show that Duvalier received: 50 cents a bag from the cement factory; one dollar per hundredweight from the Minoterie, the state flour mill (these are the "zombie" accounts); regular payments from domestic oil refinery and lottery (these amounts vary, according to our sources). Luckily, JCD and cronies felt so confident they did not bother to hide direct transfers, so this will be easy enough to track once we get all the records.

In lieu of underlying documents, the account numbers for cash transfers are as follows:

BENEFICIARY	TRANS. DATE	ACCOUNT	AMOUNT	SIG.
CASH	9/5/74	454G	$1,050	JCD
CASH	9/9/74	383G	$832	JCD
CASH	11/3/75	962G	$11,560	
CASH	4/21/76	EMERG FUNDS	$150,000	JCD/AD
CASH	6/15/78	DIV DEB	$744,382	
CASH	4/6/84	7498	$64,000	MBD

SL: rt

Enc.

CC: Bill Farrow, Esq. (w/o enc.)

Strom Mitchell, Esq. (w/o enc.)

Gerard perused the numbers a second time and took a seat at the ornate desk his father had given him as a gift for passing the bar. The desk was ostentatious, the legs carved to look like climbing vines. It had a broad expanse, and best of all, a trick drawer, where he kept his notes on the Duvalier files and any personal writings. He found the key he hid under the desk clock and unlocked the desk. A wooden panel inside shifted and the little spring moved. Gerard lifted the partition and removed several folders from the secret drawer. He glanced by habit at the balcony; nobody could see inside, but he always worried about it.

He closed the desk and picked up the old Smith Corona typewriter from the floor. It was a wonderful machine. He tested the keys lightly, tapping "Bon Anniversaire à moi." It needed to be cleaned; the M key stuck a little. He opened the desk drawer a second time and took out fresh paper, then inserted it. He picked up the telephone on the desk and dialed the international operator. The line rang without answering, which meant at least it was operating. He put it back in its cradle.

August 27, 1986

By Telecopier

Stephen Lake, Esq.

Mitchell, Lake & Strickland

35 Wall Street

New York, NY 10004

CABINET METELLUS

40, RUE DES MIRACLES

PORT-AU-PRINCE,

HAITI

TEL/FAX: 2-2891

RE: *Haiti v. Duvalier*

Dear Stephen:

  1. I received your fax of 8/26 at 0540 hrs. and will pursue as requested. I cannot guarantee any success with regard to my source at the BNP. Regarding the visa scandal, this was widely known here for many years. I have located a source who worked at the Haitian embassy in Miami who will discuss allegations against consular officials in Miami and Switzerland based on his direct involvement and possibly in exchange for immunity from future prosecution. I will introduce him to Martin to discuss terms. Also, you might check into the sale of Haitian visas to citizens of Arab origin (Lebanese, Iranian, Syrian in particular). I have certain names but no proof at this point. Perhaps U.S. Immigration Service could assist in this matter?

  2. The situation at Banque Nationale de Crédit remains in flux and the majority of employees are still in favor of joining a national strike. Their complaint is that Duvalierists remain in control of the bank (which is true). I can work with these employees to gain access to any hidden accounts. Your information regarding the state agency transfers made by Duvalier is correct. I would suggest pushing Sanon for more about this.

  3. Reconfirming the names of the accounts you are pursuing as mentioned in your last fax, here is your list with my commentary added in parentheses:

IDENTIFICATION/ALIAS

NAME

Simone Duvalier: Duvalier's mother (Maman Simone/Mama Doc)
Nicole Duvalier: Duvalier's sister
Michèle Bennett Duvalier (check Bon Repos Hospital account 6251)
Marie Denise Duvalier Théard
Ernest Bennett: JCD's father-in-law (check business accounts)
Ernest Bennett, Jr. (check business accounts/companies)
Joan Bennett
Joan Thiesfeld
Aurore Bennett
Auguste Douyon
Théo Achille
Jean-Claude Sanon: Central Bank governor

Frantz Merceron: former Minister of Finance

Jean-Claude Sambour: decorator for Michèle (we call him Johnny)

Luckner Cambronne: former Defense Minister (was implicated in 1972 scandal of plasma of poor Haitians exported to U.S. Also JCD's courier, according to my sources)

Claude Raymond: former ambassador to Spain

Roger Lafontant: former Defense Minister (I have sources willing to discuss his funneling money through government accounts)

Colonel Albert Pierre: head of Secret Police (we call him "Ti Boulé"— Burning Spear. He is still in Brazil, but my source in the army says he may have left Fernando de Noronha off the Brazilian coast. I have no information regarding payments or other monies/property for Pierre, who is considered one of the worst torturers. He is currently the subject of several other complaints pending before the Ministry of Justice)

Prosper Avril: former member of CNG interim government (Avril critical to pursue—he was closest to Papa Doc. Knows where money and property would be. We should discuss this before proceeding)

Samuel Jérémie: former presidential guard (now in jail for fifteen years after June conviction. Jérémie might be in a position to assist with names, etc.—perhaps in exchange for immunity against other charges being brought against him?)

Alexandre Paul: former consul in Miami (brother of Colonel Jean-Claude Paul—alleged to have trafficked in visas while at embassy in Miami. Also my sources suggest checking into allegations of drug trafficking by the Paul clan. You might check with Miami DEA officials—apparently DEA's "Group Six" unit is actively pursuing this information)

Rosalie Adolphe: female head of Tontons Macoutes under elder Duvalier (I don't have any information about current status of "Madame Max," but she is rumored to have escaped Haiti, possibly disguised as a nun. I would assume she might be in New Jersey or New York—she has friends in both places. No information regarding cash payments or property, though)

That's all for now. S.V.P. tell Martin to fax his arrival. —GM

Gerard scanned his reply. It was succinct. He removed the paper from the typewriter and slipped it into the fax machine, then dialed.

The line was busy. He tried again, then again, and finally gave up. Back at the desk, he skimmed the memorandum another time. Madame Max, he thought, spinning around to his big cabinet file. He should give her dossier to Leslie. She might want to include information about the Macoute women in her project. After searching, he found a bulging file and removed several news clippings as well as a picture of a middle-aged black woman in a broad, tricornered hat, her expression hard. Madame Max, a woman of modest means, was said to have personally overseen the torture sessions at Fort Dimanche. She was a fervent voudonist, like many of the Macoute chiefs. Gerard had once stood next to her at a party; Madame Max had worn a simple dress, a far cry from her sadistic image. He set the documents and picture aside.

He quickly compared the bank account numbers that Stephen had inquired about with the account numbers he had been sent over the past months by the New York firm. The numbers went on for pages, over forty of them in one file alone. They had already surpassed their original estimate of $120 million for Jean-Claude's stolen fortune; privately, Gerard had told Stephen the amount would be many times that figure, and even then they would only be scratching the surface, because so many individuals had benefited.

After twenty minutes, he found account 383G, a government account, and a record of four other deposits made to it. He also found a corresponding date for a cash transfer on April 21, 1976. He looked at the memorandum again. The initials were JCD/AD, which meant that Auguste Douyon, Duvalier's financial courier, had probably authorized the transaction. Satisfied, he removed the pages, and used the fax machine to make copies. These he circled and added the pages to the fax for Stephen. The telephone line was still busy.

It was already 8:15. With some difficulty Gerard slipped the news clippings and photo of Rosalie Adolphe through the fax machine to make a copy, then put the original documents back in the folder and returned the file to its place. As he was doing so, he noticed Madame Paule's file and, with a smile, removed it. Madame Paule, another woman named Rosalie, but an altogether different creature from Madame Max, as different as day from night. Gerard had never met a kinder woman.

He took out the photograph he had taken of Rosalie Paule with his little Minolta. The quality was poor. Rosalie stood leaning on a broom, her white dress and white head kerchief overexposed. She was squinting in the picture, her expression almost comic. Thin as a twig, she had barely reached his waist, yet borne ten children. A poor woman whose land had been usurped, she had plied him with cassava cakes for years as payment for his legal services, which he had freely offered. The case had lasted fifteen years and never come to trial. He had not recovered a cent for her. Of all his land cases—the majority of which remained unresolved—hers was the one he most regretted. She had placed unwavering faith in him. Blind faith. He judged himself harshly. He had failed her; he should have been able to find some compensation for her. Maybe if *you* had had more faith, you wouldn't have failed, he said to himself. Maybe that's what you're missing.

He sat down again, tracing the pretty leaf pattern of inlaid mahogany and pine that decorated the edges of the desk. Arching his back, he could feel in his lumbar region where a disk was out of place; it felt stiff there. He put the Duvalier files back inside the trick drawer but kept the one marked "personal." It was a thin folder and contained loose pages of journal writing and unfinished essays he had attempted over the years. It had been months since he had read its contents. He lifted up the first page.

. . . *Shakespeare was the one to say, "The law hath not been dead, though it hath slept." He might have been writing about the state of our country over these past 250 years, for after our brief awakening from the sleep of slavery, we have fallen into twilight. We have lived without living, died without ever having lived, our existence a purgatory. The Great Judge, God, has He fallen asleep or is it too much even for Him to bear our suffering? To witness how little separates life from death for us, both become meaningless, an incident too banal to notice. My neighbor drinks with me in the evening, then murders me with his indifference. When he invites me to his parties, he does not see the ghosts of my friends dancing between us. Our children have no future to grow into, and no past worth recovering . . .*

Gerard read the fragment again. It was flowery, melodramatic. I must have been really depressed that day, he thought, setting the page aside. Just then an image of Mr. Singh came to mind, Rajiv Vijay Singh from Trinidad, his old teacher at the Sorbonne. A man nearly as small as Rosalie Paule, with long graying hair tucked under a formidable white turban and a constant smell of spices. He had tutored Gerard in English literature, and had taught him to appreciate Shakespeare. Professor R.V.—"Hervé" to his students—a passionate man of letters whose long front teeth overlapped a little. His religious faith had been sorely tested by the bottles of Barbancourt rum Gerard shared with him after their Shakespeare tutorials. Gerard grinned at the memory of Singh, a rabbit-faced man impeccably dressed in starched white robes worn underneath a sharkskin suit jacket, a tin of snuff in his pocket. His recitations from *Hamlet* had been flawless and inspired, fanning Gerard's long-held desire to write plays.

He opened the bottom drawer of his desk and found the bottle of three-star rum he kept there for anxious clients; he unscrewed it and took a little sip. To your teeth, Monsieur Singh, and to mine, which are getting just as bad. He savored the rum, swilling it around his mouth, imagining the distinct smell of Singh's clove cigarettes and body odor as if the man himself was in the room. What a great teacher he had been!

"To Rajiv and Rosalie," he toasted aloud, turning away from the desk to contemplate the crowded shelf of law books by the far wall, stacks of yellowing copies of Haiti's amended Constitutions, oversized volumes of international jurisprudence and economics. A portrait of Toussaint L'Ouverture hung above the shelf, a rather slender Toussaint, drawn with fine, sensitive features. He glanced at the fax he had yet to send, then at the picture of Rosalie Paule, then up to the fading portrait of Toussaint. An idea began to take shape.

"But in these nice sharp quillets of the law, good faith, I am no wiser than a daw," he recited from memory, hearing Singh's clipped British accent in his head. He pressed his tongue against a loose front tooth. Yes, he liked this idea. Jackdaw, a foolish little bird, a common crow. *Graculus* in Latin. "As for me, I am no wiser than a daw," he repeated, "just a little bird . . ." He inserted a piece of paper into the typewriter, ". . . a little shrill bird still hoping for a few crumbs of justice." He adjusted the margins of the machine and began typing.

A half hour later, the telephone rang once, then stopped. Gerard waited. The telephone rang again. He waited before speaking.

"Gerard?"

It was Jeanne, his wife. "Bonjour, chéri," she said. "Happy birthday. I didn't want to interrupt you, but Victor called twice. He said it's important, that you'd know why." She paused. "Do you?" She spoke in her sleepy morning voice.

"Remember the broken nose I told you about?" he said. They were speaking in code, as always.

"Oh yes, I remember," she said. "That's what I thought it might be about. Have you had any news?"

"We're expecting some this morning. At Victor's. I forgot to tell you last night."

There was a short pause. "Gerard?"

"I'm here."

"Your mother called too. She woke me up. That's why I feel so lonely in this bed."

There was a suggestive lilt in her voice. She was teasing him.

He chuckled. "What bad news did she have for us today?"

"The Pope has a cold. Someone else will be saying Mass this afternoon. She's very disappointed."

It had been Gerard's idea to buy his mother a shortwave radio after her husband's death. Since then, she had become addicted to the Vatican broadcasts from Rome, calling daily to recount what the Holy See had preached. Gerard now knew more about the Polish priest than he had ever wanted to know.

"Gerard?"

"Tell me."

"I have a surprise for you. Actually, it was a surprise for your mother, but a little birthday gift for you."

He waited, amused.

"I've decided your mother is taking the children this afternoon. She tried to refuse, poor woman, but I reminded her that the Pope wasn't speaking today. And it is your birthday. Should I feel guilty?"

He was delighted. "You should feel brilliant, because that's what you are. Have you told the children?"

"I told them their papa wanted the day alone with his lonely wife. Isn't that the truth?"

He smiled again, scanning the first lines of what he had just typed. *Afternoons at the Palace*, a play by Hervé Paule. He took another swig of rum, listening as Jeanne detailed what the children would do.

"Isn't that something?" she asked again. "Are you there? Did you hear what I just said?"

"I'm right here." He yawned. In fact, he hadn't heard a word. He reminded himself to try the fax again. "Are you going back to sleep now?" he asked her.

"Of course," she said. "But I'll keep the bed warm for you. Will you be long?"

"Not too long."

"Gerard?"

"Chérie?"

"Don't let Victor get you drunk. I want you to be awake later."

"Don't worry," he reassured her. "I may be an old man but I'm not *that* old."

She giggled, then her tone turned serious. "Call me before you leave Victor's?"

"Promise," he said.

"One last thing, mon amour."

"Yes."

"Even though you abandoned your devoted wife this morning . . ."

"Chérie, I told you, I had to pick up something here. It's important."

". . . on your birthday . . . and you didn't find the card she left you by the bed . . ."

He hadn't seen it. Where had she put it?

". . . she forgives you . . ."

"Thank you, Jeanne."

"Say hello to Edith for me, will you?"

"I won't forget," he said, and hung up.

He took a final sip of the rum, and reread the opening scenes of the play. He had been tempted to tell Jeanne, to say, I've finally started something, something I like. But he wanted to wait, savoring this small beginning, this little birthday gift he had given to himself. He picked up where he left off, and a short while later realized with a start that he still hadn't gotten through to Stephen.

Before leaving the office, he put the first pages of his play under the Duvalier folder in the secret desk drawer. From the latter, he removed two documents, and added these to the fax Stephen had sent. There were twenty-five names on each document and next to each the five-digit number of a payroll check. These were the zombie accounts Stephen had referred to, monthly salary checks paid to government workers at the Minoterie, workers who didn't exist. But somebody had collected the money since 1984, and somebody had authorized the checks. Given the chaotic state of affairs at the Banque Nationale de Crédit, Gerard sensed that he might convince a disgruntled employee to help him search the government accounts, possibly in exchange for free legal services. The ploy had worked before. After faxing he put all the papers back and locked the trick desk, then put the key under the desk clock. It was 9:30; he was late.

Outside on the landing in front of his office door, he pulled a hair from his head and glued it with saliva to the crack of the door. A young boy with a rag in his hand was sitting on his car. Gerard gave him a coin. A few minutes later, he passed in front of the National Palace. For twenty-nine years, it had been illegal to walk on the palace sidewalk. Driving slowly could result in a sudden gunshot, a mere warning. Now the lawn in front of the palace was overgrown with weeds. Only two armed guards were stationed at the entrance, casually cradling their rifles. Gerard looked up at the second-story window where the dictator used to greet the masses, but it was dark.

He gunned the car forward, veered right, taking the broad avenue that led to the Bois-Verna neighborhood. To his left, red graffiti covered the base of a long, low wall. *Aba eleksyons!* Down with elections! Whoever had painted it had obviously been in a hurry; the giant letters dripped like blood.

10

Here is what my baby feels like. Can you hear me, Ignatius? Like a seed. You know, the kind that grows in the tree with the red flowers. You know, that tree near your house, the long thing with the seeds inside you shake to make the music. It feels long like that, like you probably were when you were a baby inside your mother's stomach. I know this baby is going to like music the way I do too. That's why I'm singing to it already, because you know how my blood is going to go to the baby. Well, if music is in my blood, then it will be in the baby's too.

Luz told me that, and a lot of other things about having a baby. She doesn't think I'm really going to have one because my stomach isn't growing enough, but I told her I know I have a baby, it doesn't matter what anyone says. And it's going to look like you too. My stomach isn't growing, though, because they don't give us enough food. And what they do give us is so bad I can't even swallow it. So I force myself. I have to stay strong for this baby.

Luz has been in here twice before, did I tell you that already? But only for a few days each time. Now she thinks they are going to keep her in here a long time. She says if the guards like me, maybe they'll take pity on me. But I know what that means. You can go with the guard and then he doesn't do anything for you. And I won't do that anyway, not even to get out, you understand that, don't you? I know you would understand. But I'm so worried about everyone. Grann. Without me there, what's going to happen to her? Who's taking care of her? The last time there was trouble Pierre left. Remember? And I know Grann won't leave, she'll refuse to leave our land. Grann; I cry inside and I know she's crying for me too. I'm sure she's wondering what happened to me.

I told the guard here I'm innocent, all I did was report a crime. I didn't do it. But I can see they don't care, they won't take pity on me. They only want money and I don't have any. And I'm not going to go with them. Because they're liars too.

They let women in here at night, nobody knows that. Nobody outside of here, I mean. Every night. We aren't allowed to talk to them, but I'm going to try anyway. Somehow I have to get a message to Pierre. Pierre will know what to do if he knows I'm here. I don't know how to do it but I have to try.

There's one who's always looking at me, Ignatius, he's crazy. Luz told me about him, he's bad. They say he kills with his bare hands. And I can see it, he's crazy. It's in his eyes, I don't even like to look at him. He's a bad man. If he tries to touch me, I won't let him. He must know I hate him. If I could kill him just with my thoughts he'd be dead already.

I told all of them I'm having a child, no Macoute with blood all over his hands is going to touch me. Maybe they think I'm stupid, but they're the ones fooling themselves if they think the guards will take pity on them. These men are the worst. I'd rather die than let one of them touch me.

I hope Pierre is taking care of Grann. He must be. They must be going crazy wondering what's happened to me. I hope they don't think I went away to see Ignatius. That was just a joke I was making. Pierre must know a bad thing happened to me, why would I just disappear? He always knows when something is bad. He always said, Now the soldiers are coming. I asked him once, How do you know? And he said, I can smell them. I thought he was teasing me because I was young, but now I know he wasn't teasing. He was telling the truth. I can smell them, Ignatius. There's something, I can't even say what it is, but it's a smell. Not the smell like that dead man I found in the water. But a bad smell anyway. Luz agrees with me. She always knows right before they come in here.

The guard I hate, he's a big, fat man. I hate the way he looks at me. I would bite off his tongue if he tried to kiss me. You probably don't think I could do it, but believe me I could. I've changed, Ignatius. You wouldn't like to see me this way. I feel wild; I'd kill them if they touched me, if I had the chance, that's how it feels. Because it's torture to wait like this, not knowing how long it's going to last. Over two weeks, Ignatius, and I'm dying already. How long am I going to be in here? I can't bear it another day. All I do is pray one day this will be over and I'll be with you and we'll have our child and my life will be the way it was before. Even if it wasn't good, even if I was suffering.

I'm innocent, but they don't care. The others, they're innocent too. None of us is a bad woman. We're all victims, Ignatius. But they don't even listen to us, they won't even let us speak, only answer their questions. And they never ask us anything. We don't have anything to do, just sit. Sit and wait. Like I'm doing now. Not even cards or a pencil, something I could do, draw you a picture of our baby if I had some chalk. Because I have an idea how the baby will look. You might not believe me, but I can sense that kind of thing. And I know he'll have your green eyes. They say people with green eyes are jealous, but you've never been jealous, you're the most generous man I've known. I wish I could talk to you in person, Ignatius, I miss you so much.

The guard says we'd use a pencil as a weapon. Maybe he's right. I'd use one to scratch out that big man's eyes, I hate the way he looks at me. I want to kill him. I want to make him stop.

I wonder if you know what's happened to me, Ignatius. Does anybody know? I want to believe somebody knows. How could I be arrested and no one say anything? But I thought someone would come for me by now, at least Pierre. It's making me crazy.

I wish you could see this place, Ignatius. Because it's worse than I ever imagined. Remember how we wanted to know what's on the other side of the wall? Who was in there? What kind of crimes did they commit? Well, now I know. It's just people like you and me, Ignatius, not criminals at all except for a few thieves. And they must have stood by the wall like I do, listening to what's on the other side, wishing they could scream, Get me out of here! But if I scream, they'll shoot me, they already told me that. So I can't say anything, I just sit here in silence. Like a zombi, that's how I feel. Like I'm alive but it's as if I was dead, nobody is thinking about me, that's all I can think. Even though I'm not allowed to talk, I know what the others are thinking too, because we're all thinking the same thing. All we do is listen, all day long. I listen every time the gate opens, hoping it's going to be you or someone from our village. But it's always just another guard. I can't stand looking anymore, because I can see it makes them happy to see me sad, to see me crying.

If they ever let me out of here and I meet the man who told the police I was a murderer, I'll kill him, Ignatius, it's a promise. How could somebody lie like that? But he did, right in front of my eyes, this little man standing next to the policeman, he pointed right at me and said, She did it. I told them I don't even know this man, I haven't done anything. Here I am being an honest citizen and reporting a crime and you accuse me? That man is a liar, someone paid him to say this thing. So now I think it would give me pleasure to kill him. Even if it takes me the rest of my life, I'll look for him until I find him and I'll make him suffer. Like I'm suffering. Because I am suffering, Ignatius, I wouldn't lie to you. I feel like I'm dying, every day it's getting worse and I'm going crazy, all I do is talk to myself like this all day in my head.

I told the police, That man probably did it. He's trying to save his own skin. So you should arrest him, not me. I'm innocent. But I didn't have any money and that's what they wanted. They knew I was innocent. But they didn't care.

It's the same thing with the old lady. They just brought her in here one day, just like that, four months ago. For no good reason. Because she saw a policeman stealing from somebody's car. So! He arrested her. You see what's happening here? Just to save their own skins, that's why they do it. And they're cowards. If they didn't have their guns, they wouldn't have a chance. We would attack them with our own hands. That's why they don't like us to talk to one another. They're afraid of us.

Four months, Ignatius! I can't let that happen to me. I have to get out of here before that. Because I won't have my baby in here. They had two women who had their babies in here and one of them lost hers. There's no food and no water, only sickness. That's what will happen to all of us if we don't get out. Luz is already sick. Her head and her arms hurt her all the time. And she has sores on her body which are all infected. You can't know how bad it is in here.

I keep thinking, How can they keep a pregnant woman in jail? Everybody knows the government isn't allowed to do that anymore. The two women who had the babies, that was before, when Jean-Claude was still President. But they're San Manman, they don't know what it means to carry a baby. They only know how to kill people, not what it means to give life. They know that old lady is innocent, one of them even said that to her in front of all of us.

How can anybody be that cruel? First they put her in a little cell in another prison all alone for a week. Just to shut her up, that's what they said. But she wasn't going to open her mouth. Just like me, I didn't say anyone killed that man. All I did was find him. There's no crime in that.

There's a woman who works here, Ignatius, her eyes are so sick she can't even see. I think the light hurts her; she only comes in the evening. No one knows how long she's been here, but they say they kept her father and mother in here too, and her brothers. The whole family. And all of them died in here, except her. And now she won't leave, she likes it here.

Did I tell you a man on the other side hung himself with a belt? The guards didn't stop him. And they pointed their guns at the ones who tried to stop him. So he didn't die right away. Luz heard a guard talking, on the other side of the wall. We can hear them like that when they think we're asleep. Even sometimes during the day. They let his body hang for an hour and he had blood coming out of his ears. As a warning, Luz says. What kind of warning? I asked her. You see what I mean? How crazy they are to let a man die slowly like that. It's a sickness, Ignatius, to laugh when they see a man hang himself. You can even see it in their eyes, when they look at us through the little hole in the gate; they're laughing like it's funny, like we're funny. What else could it be but some kind of poison to make them laugh when they should be crying?

You remember that massacre in Carrefour? Well, that was the San Manman too. The same ones who come in here at night when they're drunk to bother us. They've never touched me or talked to me, not to Luz either, but one day they'll probably try. So I'm sharpening a stone I found, and I keep it under my bed for the day one of them tries. Remember how we used to find those little brown bottles in the street? After the soldiers did their patrol? It was a maji they take—magic. Because it's the only way they can kill like that without feeling anything. It's the same way with the fat man. That's why his eyes look so wet and shiny. Like he's enraje—crazy.

Last night, we heard the shots again, Luz and I. The others were sleeping. But no screams like the other night. Luz says they must be torturing someone in the upstairs room. The guards say no one is up there, but we know they are lying. And that's where that woman goes, the one who won't leave this place; we hear her singing when she climbs up the stairs. That's where they take people when they want to interrogate them. That's where Luz told me they took that man before he hung himself.

Ignatius, what am I going to do? If I keep talking to you in my head, doesn't that mean I'm already a little crazy? Luz thinks they put their poison in our food so that we'll get sick and die. I look at everybody here, everybody's getting sick.

I had that dream again, did I tell you? The one where you looked so old. That scares me. Because maybe it means I'll be kept in here until I'm old, if I don't die first. But it could mean that you're talking to me the way you promised you would. So I listen, I stay awake. Every night, all night. I know you must be thinking about me; you're probably wondering why I didn't send a message by now. But I wouldn't forget about you, how could I? All I do is think about you, about you and Grann and getting out of here and having our baby.

Did I tell you I want to call the baby Paul? That was my father's middle name, even if he left us. And there's a picture of St. Paul in the little chapel here, so that's a good sign. It's not really a chapel, it has some desks and some sewing machines. The guards keep promising they'll bring some material and we're supposed to sew some uniforms and dresses and that way we can make some money, but we know that's just another of their lies. Those machines are so rusty you can't turn even the wheel with your hand. And who's going to buy us the material to sew? The army? The government? Another lie.

Luz says I should rub my stomach every morning and every night to keep the cord of life from making a knot. That's what's happening because I'm so worried. She says I need a tea to stay calm, but I said, Just let me out and this baby will come and be healthy. She says if the baby knows something is wrong, it won't come, sometimes it will wait. It's true, I'm not growing, and I feel a knot, a big knot. I asked Luz, How can a baby stay inside you and not come out? But she's seen it. She says there was a woman in Jérémie who kept her baby inside for three years and it was so big when it was born, it had teeth and long, long hair. I said, My baby's going to have green eyes and sing.

You know what I've been thinking? When I escape, I might take the boat. I think that's what the dream is telling me. I know I'm afraid, but why else would I have this dream? Always the same dream three times now, and each time I see the boats.

Ignatius, you wouldn't take the boat without me, would you? I was afraid that was what my dream meant. But I won't let myself think that way. Instead, I'm praying that your leg is better and that you're coming here, right now, this very minute, to get me out. So I'll wait. I'll wait and think about you. About getting out of here and being with you and having our baby. About Grann, that she's safe. That's my prayer, I say it night and day. Do you hear me, Ignatius? I'm waiting and listening for you. Night and day. Talk to me.

I'm waiting for a sign, Ignatius, any sign. Then I'll know you've heard my thoughts. Just something—anything—to give me hope. Because I don't feel hopeful today, I feel afraid. Afraid that you'll forget me—that's what scares me the most. Or that I'll go crazy waiting for you to come and the day you do I won't even remember you, I'll be like that woman who can't leave or maybe I'll have given up like the man who hung himself. Because it wasn't the torture; he couldn't wait anymore. And I know that I'm not really like that, I have you, and our baby inside of me, but something has to change, Ignatius, can you hear me? You have to come and rescue me—soon. Because there's a sickness in this place and it's making me crazy. I can't tell you how, but I can feel it. It's happening and I can't stop it. As much as I try, I can't stop it.

11

"Would you like me to drive now?" Leslie leaned out the window of the passenger door. Clemard was checking one of the tires. They had stopped on the side of the road after hitting a large rock. "You're not answering me," she said. "I drive quite well, for your information."

Clemard grinned up at her. "Blan Bertrand would not like that. I could lose my job."

"Blan Bertrand"—Leslie liked the sound of his name—"isn't here. No one is going to see us. We can switch again when we go back."

No, he shook his head, laughing a little. "I can't." He licked his fingers, then put them on the rim to make sure no air was escaping.

How people worked without equipment fascinated Leslie. "Can you hear anything?" she asked. He shook his head again.

Clemard got up, rubbed his dirty hands on his brown pants. Leslie had decided he owned two pairs of pants, these and a pair of gray pants he wore on the weekends when he doubled as a gardener for Bertrand. Yesterday, he had shown her his method of terracing to prevent the heavy rains from washing away the pebbly soil. He had used rope to build up the ridges of earth and bits of cutoff hose under the ground to allow the water to filter evenly through it. Leslie, who knew a bit about gardening herself, was impressed. She had shared with him her problems with a yellow rose bush that had finally died last month. Yellow roses were her favorite. Noting her interest, he had stopped on the way downtown to point out a pygmy palm she had never seen before. Clemard kicked the tire a final time. Then he put his sunglasses back on.

"You look very mod, Clemard," she told him, adding in English: "A hipster."

A hipster? What did it mean?

She searched for the Creole equivalent, then gave up. "Like cool. You know, cool?"

"Wi, Madanm."

She laughed. "Do you like Jimmy Cliff?"

"The musician who died?"

"There's a movie he made—he looked just like you with those glasses. But he drove a motorcycle." I've got a Jamaican thing going, she thought to herself, first the Marleyist and now Jimmy Cliff. She admired Clemard's muscled arms in the short-sleeved gray-and-red-striped shirt. His style was actually more like . . . What was the name of that Yves Montand movie, the one that took place in Brazil? Or was it another actor? She couldn't remember. She knew it was the actor who had made *The Man with the Red Shoe*. No, that wasn't right either. Maybe Mark was right about her lousy memory.

"I like his music." Clemard brought her back to reality. "I sing too," he added modestly.

"What kind of singing?"

"Everything. Compas . . . Merengue . . . Michael Jackson . . . Madonna." He grinned. She noticed again how much more relaxed he was when Bertrand was not around.

He got back in the car, then waited as a huge Texaco truck blocking the highway executed an awkward version of a three-point turn. "I sing in a little band, and I play drums," he added.

"So you're an all-around guy." She smiled.

That threw him. "Excuse me, could you repeat?"

"All-around guy. That means you can do a lot of things, that you have a lot of interests." In her mind, she added: It means that you're probably good in bed. The thought amused her. There was no longer any question that they were flirting, albeit mildly.

He smiled in agreement.

"I appreciate that you came with me today," she said, adopting a more serious tone. "I'm not sure exactly where it is. But you know how to get there, right?" She had asked him before, but wanted to be certain. Pierre Lescot had pretended to know where he was going, even when he didn't. It seemed to be a matter of politeness among Haitians. Something about not wanting to disappoint foreigners who were lost. As a result, she was more aggressive than usual about where she was going. "Are you really sure?" she persisted. "Because if you don't know, that's fine."

"Trust me. We just take this road, then after the bridge we go left and we're there, right before the beaches. You know the beaches, don't you?"

"Yes." She followed the progress of the Texaco truck, not completely convinced. But it was a nice enough day, and she was happy to be getting out of the city, even if the reason for doing so was hardly a vacation.

Avenue John Paul II was in terrible shape. Potholes were more like long ditches beside two tire tracks of concrete. Passing the American embassy, she wondered if Peter Samuels had gotten her message. She hoped for a meeting, and possibly his assistance in getting into the national penitentiary. He hadn't returned her call. Gerard had also asked her to probe Samuels about the embassy's position on the strike.

The park near the port was run-down. She remembered it as well tended, full of blossoming hibiscus and labapen trees. Perhaps the recent storm was responsible for the damage. They rolled up their windows as vendors approached with paintings; one young man carried three or four at once, trying to deposit them on the hood of passing cars as they neared the traffic circle. Clemard honked at the man but braked. Young children ran toward the car, arms extended. Blan! Blan! they shouted. Gen grangou! We're hungry!

As they approached La Saline market, Leslie asked Clemard to slow down; she was interested in the foldup wooden cots being sold next to sacks of charcoal. She thought about taking one back to use at the beach; she could get a child-sized one for Marisa too.

"How much are those, Clemard?" She pointed toward the cots.

He shook his head, unsure. "You have to bargain," he said. "Offer them something."

"Ten dollars?" she asked. "Is that too little? Twenty dollars?"

He made a dismissive face, and began pressing the car horn again, leaving his hand on it for long periods. Leslie wanted him to stop but didn't say anything.

"Fifteen dollars?" She didn't like betraying her ignorance.

He chewed his lip, a habit, she had noticed. "Start with fifty gourdes. They'll say one hundred. But I wouldn't pay more than fifteen dollars."

They watched a woman selling water throw her cup at a man

who was laughing. Clemard suggested stopping at a stand displaying gourds with corncob plugs; Leslie had mentioned wanting one earlier in the week. The food was tempting; more smoking meats and corn laced with shallots and hot peppers and parsley. Several women stood at the intersection beyond the market, their arms outstretched, holding bolts of calico cloth. Leslie thought of making a little dress for Marisa. "You know what? Let's not stop," she told Clemard impulsively. "I don't want to get there too late."

They opened the windows, preferring the odor of diesel and the warm breeze to the stale-smelling air conditioning. Leslie pushed in the lighter, took out two cigarettes, lit one for Clemard and one for herself. "Mesi." He accepted it. They were beginning to feel comfortable with each other, although Clemard continued to call her Madanm Leslie.

"Clemard, can I ask you a personal question?" she ventured a while later.

He nodded.

"How much money does Bertrand give you? Does he pay you by the week or the month?"

"Almost nothing," he said quickly, then looked over to gauge her reaction. He added: "He gives me twenty-five dollars—in gourdes —a month. He's supposed to give me lunch, but all of a sudden it's one o'clock and he's forgotten to buy it. So what am I supposed to do? He has a meeting. I wait for him; he's late. So I have to buy my food myself, out of my salary. But watch out if I'm not there when he comes back. I'd be out on the street. So I have to pay someone to go and get a sandwich for me because I can't leave the car. You know what I call what he gives me? A little charity. It's not a salary."

He lifted his hands off the steering wheel as if to say, But what can one do? "Don't you agree?" he asked, his tone somewhat challenging.

She appreciated his sudden frankness. "Definitely. I definitely agree."

He nodded, his smile grim. It was his turn now. "How much money do you make? A lot?"

"A lot?" She shrugged. "No. Well," she clarified, "by Haitian standards, of course, it's a fortune. But for that kind of job it's a normal salary. When my daughter gets older and I have to send her to college, then it will be tight." She realized she hadn't mentioned the amount, because it embarrassed her. So she forced herself, adding: "I earned about thirty-five thousand dollars last year. Before taxes."

Thirty-five thousand dollars! His expression said it all. He exhaled out the window, shook his head. "You see how unfair it is?" he said softly after a moment. "It's so unfair. I'm a Haitian, but as much as I love my country, I can't survive here. There are no jobs, even though Duvalier is gone, even though they told us there would be more jobs now." He pulled the car into the oncoming lane of traffic, squeezed between two tap-taps parked diagonally across from one another, leaving only a small space in the center lane. How can people park like that? Leslie wondered. It's so dangerous.

A truck in front of them weaved like a drunk, the passengers looked fearfully at Clemard as he honked repeatedly. The truck moved into the center of the highway to block the car's passage. Clemard suddenly downshifted into third, let the wheels slip off the tarmac onto the dirt shoulder, and passed the truck on the right. Leslie braced herself as the car slid back onto the road. Clemard looked at her, arched his brow, then took up where he had left off.

"Blan Bertrand, he promised me when I took the job that he would help me to get a visa, so after two or three years I could go to Canada, where my brother lives. But he hasn't kept his promise." His tone was matter-of-fact, but angry. "He acts like it's a favor I'm asking, but it's a promise. That was part of our agreement."

Leslie wondered if she should say something to Bertrand, then thought better of it. "Is it hard to get a job as a chauffeur?" she asked. She felt a gust of wind undo her hair, blowing it close to her cigarette. She bunched up her hair with one hand, smoking with the other.

"Madanm Leslie," he said, "I think you know the answer." He was not being patronizing, though it might sound that way. "I had to wait six months to get this job. I don't like doing it. You heard Blan Bertrand; he tries to say I'm a bad driver. That way he doesn't have to pay me what I deserve. But I've never had an accident. I fix the car when it breaks. Where else can I get a job? If I could take a course to become a mechanic, I would like to do that. I might get a job repairing the airplanes at the airport. But I don't have time to take the course. I've been working since I was a boy. So you could say I am lucky, I have a job. But I say again, it's nothing more than a little charity."

"What about your wife? Does she have a job?"

"My wife cooks for some blans in Pétionville."

"Blans blans or blans mulâtres?" she asked. Because blan, which meant white, could denote wealth or social status, usually both at once. It could also suggest authority, regardless of one's color.

"Like Met Gerard . . . Blans milats."

She smiled. Gerard would have hated to hear how and when Clemard used words like *blan* and *met*—master. In Gerard's case, it showed that Clemard respected him. Her Creole tutor had discussed these kinds of subtleties with her too, but she found that there were no real rules. It could also be a question of tone. The receptionist at the hotel who called her Madame did so in a cool, somewhat contemptuous voice. She could tell he associated her with all foreigners and whites, objects of derision, even hate. Perhaps because he had seen her arrive with Bertrand that first night, and Bertrand was apparently well known to the staff at the guesthouse. With Clemard, Madanm was a polite term; she had yet to detect any sarcasm when he used it.

"My wife has to work from six o'clock in the morning until ten o'clock at night, sometimes," Clemard was telling her. "So neither one of us is home for the children. They stay with a neighbor until we come back at night. I don't like that, but there is nothing we can do. We both have to work. And even with that, I don't know if I can keep paying their school fees."

"I thought school was free."

"Yes. But there are fees, for the uniforms, and they have to eat lunch. And each time there is something to do, or somewhere to go. Last July, I asked Blan Bertrand for money because it was my son's graduation; you know they have a little ceremony with the certificate for the children. He said he would give it to me. But it's like the visa, I'm still waiting for the money. And maybe he'll give it to me, and maybe he won't. If he is in the mood for charity, then my son is lucky. If he's forgotten, then I'm not lucky. Because I had to borrow the money for my son to get his certificate."

"Your son, he's six, right? And the other one is eight?"

"Six and eight. The one who is six received his certificate in July. He's a good boy. They are both good boys." Clemard flicked his cigarette out the window. They passed a stream of pedestrians waiting for a bus at an unmarked stop. A woman rode toward them, sidesaddle on a donkey, a pipe in her mouth. She looked like a classic vision of Haiti to Leslie, a madanmsara, bringing her wares to market. The woman waved to them.

"I told you my little girl, Marisa, is five." She turned back to Clemard.

He smiled. "Marisa. That's a pretty name. Does she look like you?"

"The truth? Not really. She looks more like her father. Brown hair. And his eyes too. They're kind of hazel—the color of nuts."

"Did you want the divorce?"

The question came out of nowhere. Leslie looked at him hard for a second, wondering if and how he had overheard her conversation with Bertrand. The thought irritated her.

They passed a little village to their left where chickens and small dogs walked in between wattle-and-daub houses. Laundry was draped over the branches of trees. Women sat on the ground, snapping peas into a basket. "We were living together," she answered finally.

"Plasaj," he said. Common-law marriage.

"And I got pregnant, even though we hadn't planned for it." Leslie lit another cigarette. "And at first I was happy, of course. Anyway, Mark, my partner, my menaj . . ."

Menaj, okay, he was chewing his lip again, listening.

". . . convinced me that it was a good idea to marry. For the child, and financially, it was better for us, for the taxes. We don't have the same salaries now that we did then. And he still had some big loans."

A skinny white dog began to chase their car, running along a ditch full of garbage. Leslie watched it stop, then sniff the garbage, distracted, and start barking again.

"You don't love him anymore?"

The bluntness of the question struck her again, though there was nothing malicious or calculated. "No?" he asked.

"I . . . I don't know." His directness was disconcerting. "Most of the time I only hate him, because he hurt me. We didn't have a bad marriage, but it ended badly." She swallowed, then chose her words carefully. "He wasn't . . . fidel." That was as nicely as she could put it. "He was . . ."

Just then his hand interrupted her. A group of soldiers stood by the side of the road, leaning against their truck. Leslie felt her stomach tighten. They continued on, looking straight ahead, not talking until the truck was completely out of sight. Leslie couldn't help looking back. "What do you think they were doing?"

"Looks like they had a flat tire."

She hadn't seen it. She glanced at the empty highway behind them, suddenly reminded of the purpose of the day. They had all been armed with submachine guns.

She glanced at her watch. They should be there in half an hour. "Do you think we could continue this conversation later?" she asked, rolling up the window, leaving only a crack open for the smoke. "There's some work I should get done before we arrive." She knew she was changing the subject.

His expression was inscrutable. "No problem." He rolled up his window. "Should we turn on the air?"

She shook her head. "I'm fine."

He gave her another instant's look, adjusted the rearview mirror, and focused on his driving.

Leslie had worked out a system of abbreviation to make sense of the various lists: PN for the National Penitentiary. FD for Fort Dimanche. RC for the Criminal Research Bureau. P for prisoner. A for arrested. T for torture. B for beaten. D for dead.

"What's E?" he asked, glancing at her notebook. "Exhumed?"

"Exile," she replied. She hadn't even thought of exhumed. "Here," she said, pointing to various names. "I'll explain it to you. These are people who are missing, and here, the ones who were released from the prisons but haven't gone back to their villages. And here, if they're supposed to be in hiding."

He read down the page as he drove, nodding. "But you have the same name there twice."

"I do? Where? You're right," she said. "I didn't notice. That's because I haven't gone through these lists carefully enough. Gerard just gave them to me last night. They're from Dwa Moun."

Dwa Moun was the local human rights group. "I know them," Clemard said. "I know the sister of one of their members."

"And that man?" he asked a moment later, after she had noted the error.

"What man?"

"The one Met Gerard told you about."

"How did you know about that?" she asked, somewhat sharply. "Did he mention him to you?" Gerard had asked her not to discuss the case with anyone for the time being. Why would he say anything to Clemard?

"He asked me if I had heard anything on the radio," Clemard replied calmly. "Isn't he on your list?"

"What exactly did Gerard tell you?"

"He asked me if I heard any news about the strike, if they said anything about a man from Papaye who had disappeared. I told him no."

"Did he ask you to keep this secret?"

"Madanm Leslie." He smiled tolerantly. "Met Gerard trusts me. You should trust me too."

She felt instantly ashamed. "It's not that," she said defensively. "I do trust you. It's something else. But it doesn't matter. Anyway, he's on my list, yes." Liar, she said to herself, there's nothing else.

"Well, we could go there, to Papaye," he offered. "If you want."

Gerard had obviously told him that too. "Maybe," she conceded. "But we're waiting for someone from there to contact us—to contact Gerard," she clarified, feeling slightly peeved.

Okay, he agreed. Whatever.

She turned back to the list. Exhumed. That would be an interesting category to monitor: political zombies. She glanced up to study Clemard's profile. He was gnawing the inside of his cheek. The man was sharp.

"We're almost there," he said twenty minutes later. Leslie quickly put away her notebook and got out a small, pocket-sized pad and two pens. She stuffed her handbag and large notebook under the seat as Gerard had suggested, playing it extra safe. Her passport was in her money belt, which pressed against her waist, reassuring her.

"Have you ever come here?" she asked as they stared out at the plains.

"No."

"Why not?"

He shrugged, then downshifted as the asphalt momentarily gave way to packed dirt. "Only foreigners like to come here," he said. It was the first time he had referred to her that way. "We try to stay away from places like this. Why look for trouble?"

The road was pocked with puddles. Clemard adjusted his weight, driving slowly. Leslie caught herself looking at his body, the mat of black hairs on his arms and even his palms.

"Because it scares you?" she asked, curious.

"No. But I have no desire. I know what it is. Even without coming here. We see this in the streets all the time."

His cheek moved in and out, like a faint pulse. She wondered what he would look like with a full beard. As a child, she had made a game of opening her mother's mouth, putting in a finger to feel the little scars on her inner cheek. Watching Clemard, she wanted to do the same. Clearly, she was attracted to him. The idea unsettled her. Not only was he married and fifteen years her junior, and a Haitian, he was Bertrand's chauffeur. Inappropriate, she told herself. Pas question.

Why did she always fixate on completely unavailable people? It was the question that had dominated her therapy. At least with Clemard she could curb the fantasy before it had had a chance to unfold. She shook her head. You really are too much.

She liked his hands, though. They were broad, the thumbs flat at the tips. Practical, she decided, trying to figure out what the shape of his fingers could tell her. Mechanically inclined, but she already knew that. The little fingers were spaced apart from the other fingers. That meant he was loose with money, just like her. She looked back at the plain, dotted with cactus.

The sea was separated from the highway by marshland and murky canals. Leslie studied the horizon. The water was so blue here, she renewed her vow to go to the beach one day soon, take a day off, maybe sail to La Gonâve. Or an overnight trip, that would be fun.

She flexed her calf muscles. "I don't see anything. Have we passed it?"

Clemard slowed down further. Low trees on either side of the road made it hard to see.

"I think we missed the turn," she said. "I think it was back there."

He hesitated, then stopped and made a U-turn. She noted, with a touch of triumph, that he hadn't really known exactly where the turnoff was either. Now they were both looking for it.

Several children played in a tree at the side of the road. There had to be a village nearby; maybe they had come to the wrong spot. Clemard parked the car, just out of sight of the cars approaching around the curve. A boy jumped down from the tree and waited for them to approach. "Gade," Clemard said, offering him a cigarette. Look here. He turned away from the road and said quietly, "We're looking for the entrance to Titanyen—is it over there?" The youth nodded.

"Nou ka rentre?" Leslie asked. "Can we go in?"

The boy nodded again, but seemed somewhat confused. He looked back toward the other children, who had stopped playing and were trying to listen.

"Jounalis?" the boy asked, holding the cigarette delicately, not asking for a light. Journalists?

"Non." Clemard turned to Leslie. "It's over there. Come on." He added for the boy's sake: "Touris." Tourists.

They walked back to the dirt tire tracks. Leslie followed Clemard. She tried to recall what she had read about the place, but it just looked like a field with a lot of garbage. "Do you see anything?" They kept walking, going farther inside. She pulled her hat down. The sun was hot, and she was sweating hard.

There was a length of razor wire, scraps of leather and metal, what looked like industrial waste. The place smelled of dankness and decay, but not too strongly. Clemard picked up a shoe, gesturing to Leslie. She searched the ground, which was slightly damp, and littered with broken glass and bottle caps, fragments of cartons. They kept going.

Leslie saw it first, part of a jaw, with only two teeth in it. She picked it up. It seemed too small to be human. Then she began to find more teeth, and what looked like slivers of shale, which she now recognized were fragments of bone. A few feet ahead, she found a femur. Then a tooth, and another. She left Clemard, who pulled on a piece of concertina wire stuck to the bushes, and wandered up a hillock where the bushes were still thick. Then she saw the farmer and stopped in her tracks.

He wore only a pair of purple gymnasium shorts and tennis shoes and stood holding the rope halter of his mule. The animal nuzzled a branch.

"Bonswa," she said. Hello. She wasn't sure what to say, nor was he, she noticed. Clemard was behind her, walking up the incline. She stepped closer to the man. "Nou vin gade," she informed him. We're just looking around.

The ground was covered with wild grasses in some places; then it leveled off into what could have been a crude baseball field, except it was too muddy. She saw mule tracks.

The man looked like an ordinary villager. Leslie decided to take a risk. "Gen mo la?" Are there any dead people here?

He nodded. Behind her Clemard stepped forward and offered a cigarette to the man, who took it, but put it behind his ear. He patted the mule, which was fitted with a wooden saddle on top of a burlap bag. The animal's coat was coarse and mangy. Leslie noticed that the mule's legs were wet; the man must have been riding along the edge of the inland canal.

"Kote?" she asked. Where are they? She had half expected to see bodies rotting in the daylight, but there was nothing, not even the big stones that normally marked paupers' graves in the countryside.

He gestured in a circle with his arm. "La." All around here.

"La—ou?" She followed his hand. There—where?

He pointed where there was another small incline.

Up there?

"La. Tou la." There. Everywhere. He stroked the donkey between its ears. The animal's teeth were almost black, a dark yellowish brown like molasses.

Clemard started to go. "Tann mwen," Leslie said. Wait for me.

She turned back to the man. "I was told they're still bringing bodies here, dumping them at night. Is that true?"

He was getting nervous, she could see that. He shaded his brow with his free hand and looked toward the sea. He squinted, and nodded slightly.

"Anpil fwa?" Often?

"Wi." Yes.

"Chak nwit?" Every night?

Non. He shook his head. His expression now looked more like a grimace; the sun seemed to shine directly into his eyes. His teeth were spaced widely apart, like those of the old man on the airplane. He shifted his weight back and forth; he was visibly uncomfortable.

"The trucks come twice a week usually. In the evening. With the soldiers." He spoke softly.

"But have there been other bodies too? Do you know if they've brought prisoners here?" Leslie felt like one of those journalists she hated, the ones who thrust their microphones in front of parents whose children have just fallen out of buildings.

He paused, and she decided she didn't care about making him uncomfortable. The information was too important.

"Did they bring any bodies this week?"

Again he gestured: La, la. Up there. Then he relented. "We don't know who they are, and we're not supposed to be here when the trucks come in. Sometimes the people are dead, sometimes they shoot them. But if they find you here, they'll shoot you too." He mounted his mule. He had said enough.

Leslie persisted. "The people living in those villages"—she pointed—"would they know?"

The man smiled bitterly. "Everyone knows what happens here." He stretched out his hand again, then added, as if it were a joke: "It's better not to disturb your neighbors, especially if they're dead. Because one day you'll be joining them."

Leslie looked up at the hillock, and the land around it.

"Madanm."

She turned.

He had reined the mule, was stripping a branch to make a whip. He motioned with it to an area behind her and to the right. "Where it is green, madanm," he said.

"I see. Thank you."

Clemard had already found the spot, in between a thicket of bushes and a cactus. There were two graves, side by side. One was a freshly dug hole, the other a recently covered mound. She could see fragments of bones mixed in with dirt at the bottom of the open grave. There were probably layers and layers of bones; all around her and under her, bodies were simply decomposing. She wondered about those spots where the vegetation was unusually dense. Leslie turned to Clemard. His expression was hard to read.

She couldn't tell anything from the filled-in grave. There was no question of digging it up. They had already pushed the limits. Leslie worried that the man might alert his neighbors to the presence of strangers. Or that the truck with the soldiers had been heading this way. She looked at the packed dirt, smooth, as if a hand had patted it down.

Behind another bush they found a tennis shoe, farther on a bag, then someone's photograph, torn. She picked it up. They walked on, Leslie with her mini-notepad in hand, sketching the perimeter of the area. In some ways it surprised her, for a killing field it looked so ordinary and banal: a dirt lot covered with garbage. Far out on the water, she saw a fishing boat. She imagined Miami, its glittering lights, beyond the horizon. Only five hundred miles, but a world away. She looked up at the mountains, the same mountains she had seen from the air just a few days before. From here they seemed more verdant, more lush. Clemard was heading back to the car.

"I'll join you in a minute," she told him.

She walked back across the muddy black-clay field, toward the inland stream. She wondered what it felt like for the villagers to fish in these waters, where death leaked in. Her head began to throb. The heat. This is how they must feel in Brazil, she thought. The mundaneness of it. That's what makes it so tragic. And that it will never be recorded. That's why they call it Titanyen, a diminutive, to diminish death, to make it smaller and less frightening. She wondered if the mule could feel anything walking over bones. Horses know, it must know, they all must feel it, even the lone fisherman out on the water who casts his net into the sea.

Titanyen. She looked directly into the sun and remembered the custodian at the second Duvalierist house they had visited, wondered what he was doing, and whether he had talked to anyone about their visit. She saw the Polaroid pictures and the piles of shit. She removed her hat and closed her eyes, felt the sun burning her face, exposing the bones under her flesh like an X ray, like a living skeleton's.

Walking back, she sketched, making a map for Gerard, noting where the bushes were thickest, as well as how many bones she found. She thought about taking one back, but didn't. It was like museum or cultural theft, and what would be the use? A symbol, nothing more. She was beginning to appreciate what Gerard meant when he talked about the legal difference between evidence and proof. All of this was evidence, some would argue it was final proof, but none of it could be applied to an individual case.

She came across the dome of a skull with a small hole in it. Neat, unmistakable, a bullet hole directly in the center at the top. He must have been kneeling, the gun directly above his head. Or was it a she? Who are you? she asked. She put the skull down gently, noticing footprints all around it from the track she was leaving.

Ti-tan-yen, she thought. Ti-temps-rien. Little—time—nothing. Life; a little bit of time, then the great nothing.

LUTHERAN OFFICE FOR WORLD COMMUNITY
Representing the Lutheran World Federation
and the Evangelical Lutheran Church in America
INTEROFFICE TELEFAX MEMORANDUM

DATE: August 28

TO: Member representatives: CCS; DGM; LIRS; LOGA; LWF/Caracas; LIRS/NY; National Council of Churches; Lutheran World Relief; Mike Hope, National Coalition for Haitian Refugees; Anne Benning, Church World Service; Tim Patton, United Nations Inter-Act; Georgina Wells, Pax Christi

FROM: Benjamin Vera/LWF

RE: Pastoral statement from Bishop Eagle concerning Haiti

Dear Friends,

I am pleased to share with you a copy of this pastoral statement issued today by Bishop Robert Eagle with respect to the recent developments in Haiti and the attacks on lay workers and clergy. For more information, you may contact my office or Father Emmanuel Gabriel, Eglise du Saint-Esprit, PO Box 82, Port-au-Prince, Haiti. Te. 35224. Fax after 5 p.m. EST.

With cordial greetings,

Ben

A PASTORAL STATEMENT ON THE SITUATION IN HAITI

I am deeply disturbed by recent events in Haiti that indicate a new level of violence being directed at Haitian clergy and religious workers, particularly in the countryside. Reports from Catholic priests in Haiti suggest that their members are subject to increased threats and harassment by local military commanders and unidentified armed individuals. I call your attention to the case of Pastor Hubert Sansaricq, whose wife and daughter were raped and murdered on July 13 prior to the burning of the parish church by individuals identified as being assistants to a former section chief under the previous regime of Jean-Claude Duvalier.

I have also received a report that two lay members of the Ti Legliz community-based clergy, Didier Romain and Pascal Moraboux, were attacked by a band of local thugs when they attempted to inquire about the murder. Didier Romain received several blows to the head and was briefly hospitalized.

In February 1986, the Haitian people overwhelmingly demonstrated their desire to overcome a legacy of military dictatorship and embark on the road to democracy. While the Haitian authorities and the interim government appear to support this popular mandate, it must take firm steps to curb the resurgence of arbitrary and paramilitary violence. Attention must be paid to the fact that the Haitian Ti Legliz is actively supporting rural communities who are busy organizing for future elections.

The renewed attacks on the Haitian clergy demand a prompt and firm response from all our congregations. I ask you and all people of good will to urge the United States government to maintain its position of support for Haitian democracy by pressuring the interim government of Haiti to swiftly investigate these reported attacks on religious leaders and arrest those culpable in the vicious murder of Pastor Sansaricq's family.

Finally, I am urging you to join me in adding our voices to those of our Catholic brothers and sisters who are calling on the Papal Nuncio in Haiti to act in this affair and to unite Haitian clergy and lay and civic leaders to safeguard the lives of those working to bring about this much-needed democratic reform in Haiti. On this issue we must not stay silent.

Robert W. Eagle
Bishop
Evangelical Lutheran Church in America
August 28

⋙ 12 ⋙

Victor lived in a modest whitewashed house above the eastern curve of the bay. The paved road gave way to a dirt strip that dipped in and out of sight. Skimpy mud houses clung to the sides of the hills high above, a vivid red-clay jumble.

Gerard felt a familar kick of adrenaline as he passed the corner and saw a military jeep parked by the store. Several young men stood next to it. The policemen sat on top of the small outdoor freezer customarily full of lukewarm Fanta soda. They watched him pass without displaying much interest except to signal: Your back tire is flat. He acknowledged it with a wave, not stopping. The less attention he attracted, the better.

The neighborhood was freshly washed with rain. A young woman squatted in a corner of the street, catching spillover water from the gutter into her bucket. Gerard smiled, recognizing her from the neighborhood. He stopped the car near a closed red metal gate. A red Land-Rover was parked in the driveway.

The house was not finished yet; the new front area that was to serve as the union's headquarters was only a square of dirt with piles of concrete bags in one corner. A young man poured red and blue paint into plastic cups, mixing with a stick. On the ground, the banner he had painted was drying, along with a half dozen strike posters. $3.00 *ak Benifis!* Three dollars with benefits! Gerard read. *Ayisyen Fe Travay Bourik!* Haitians do donkey's work! That, he knew, referred to the famous proverb *Bourik pa travay pou-l chwal galone.* The donkey doesn't work for the horse to gallop. The poor man doesn't work for the rich. He nodded to the young activist and, knocking, entered the house.

"Chéri, you're here! Victor, look who's here!" It was Edith, Victor's wife. The union's feisty treasurer pulled him inside. "Hello, big man," she said cheerfully, offering him the two sides of her face to kiss. "We didn't know if you were coming. Happy birthday," she added, returning his extra hug.

"Sak pase?" What's up? Gerard said to José, spotting the Do-

minican photographer in the kitchen. The smaller man had stripped
down to his undershirt in the heat. He turned to Gerard, his smile
wide, his thick mustache dripping from the coffee he was drinking.
He said hello, holding up his cup.

Edith called Victor's name. "My husband's in back—he can't
hear us," she explained, grabbing Gerard's chin. It was a childhood
game they played: Je te tiens, tu me tiens, par la barbuchette . . .
You hold me, I hold you, by the tip of your chinny chin chin . . .
Gerard laughed, grabbed her chin in turn. They stood there like
that for thirty seconds, until abruptly, Edith gave up. "You win,"
she said breezily. "It's your birthday. Anyway, I've never had any
patience for this game."

José joined them. "Buenas," he said to Gerard, adding: "Feliz
cumpleaños."

"Gracias, José." Gerard shook his hand. "How's the fashion
business?"

The slim photographer laughed. He had recently set up a studio
that was popular with the aspiring teenage daughters of the richer
set.

"They get younger every day," he answered. "But I can't complain. I'm eating. They're all such princesses, though," he added.
"It's exhausting me."

"Princesses with teeth," Edith cut in, amused. "One of them bit
him. Look, show him, José. Look—right there." She lifted his shirt.
"How old was she, José? Not even ten, right?" She laughed.

José gave them a helpless, somewhat doleful look that said: It's
not my fault. "She got mad at me," he confessed. "But no, she
wasn't ten. And I don't think she meant it." When he saw Gerard
and Edith didn't quite believe him, he added: "Please, trust me,
she attacked me. I'm a gentleman photographer."

Gerard hugged Edith. "Here I thought you were sacrificing your-
selves for the cause on a Sunday, doing serious work, but instead,
you're having fun, huh?"

Edith tapped him defensively. "Don't tease me, Gerard. You
know I'm sensitive."

Gerard chuckled. Edith was widely considered one of the most
outspoken women in the country, far more radical than most union-

ists. She had been arrested three times in the past six years, and beaten once, though not badly. But each incident, rather than silencing her, had sharpened her tongue. She was not afraid to denounce the regime, and had done so just this week, urging shopkeepers to honor the upcoming strike, to close their stores, not to cave in to the army's threats. The national press had nicknamed her Ti Malis, naughty one, after the comic-strip character Ti Malice, who with her pet goat Bouki—that was Victor—inevitably got into scraps. Given how Edith dominated their relationship—Victor being shy and cautious in comparison—Gerard thought their nicknames were rather apt. Edith, of course, loved hers. Why don't they call me Grann Malis? she would ask friends. I don't want to be a little thorn in their side. I want to be a big knife making them bleed.

"How's the family? How are the children? Why didn't you bring Jeanne?" Edith asked all at once. "What are you doing for your birthday?"

"The kids are going to their grandmother's today," he replied, accepting a sip of José's coffee. It was too sweet.

"Oh." Edith arched an eyebrow, impressed. "Now there's a nice gift for their papa."

Gerard laughed. Everyone knew his mother was, in a word, a bitch. He was the first to admit it.

"Ah, the family," Edith sighed dramatically. "We can never really escape them, can we?" She opened a door leading to the back of the house. "I thought your mother was staying in Miami these days."

"She complains that Miami is too big and that the Haitian taxi drivers don't respect her over there."

Edith guffawed. "I'm sure they don't. Really, your mother is precious. There are a lot of things one can say about her but never that she lacks personality. I'll see if Victor's ready," she added. "Wait just a moment."

"I just got back from the bateys," José told Gerard as they waited, referring to the sugarcane plantations on the Dominican border. "They're having a big problem over there, you probably heard?"

"I heard the news this morning, on the radio. A dozen hurt, right?"

"More. And they're bringing in the Dominican army. There's one man in critical condition. If he dies, it's going to get worse. I'm thinking of going there to cover what's happening."

Gerard nodded. "What is your President saying? Is he going to honor the contracts?"

"I doubt it," José answered. "He maintains that the Dominicans paid Duvalier the money, so the poor Haitians have to do the work. It's not his fault that Duvalier stole the money. That's what he said just yesterday."

"Nice guy," Gerard said.

Edith was back. "Come on. Victor is ready."

They followed her down the narrow hall into a back room, which looked out onto the backyard. Victor sat at a wrought-iron table covered with papers.

"Mon ami!" The union president stood up and embraced Gerard, patting him on the stomach at the same time. "How are the worms today? Hein? Huh? Ça va? You okay?" He was a medium-sized dark man with a close-trimmed Afro and wire-rim glasses. He slapped Gerard lightly on a cheek. "Good to see you, man, really good to see you. Here, sit right here. I'll move these things. By the way, our friends called to say they'll be by. But we'll drink to your health first, okay? We have a surprise for you. José—do me a favor, those glasses in the cabinet? Thank you . . . and bring the you-know-what." He smiled broadly at Gerard, a mischievous look in his eyes. He pushed the papers on the table into a pile and set half of them on the floor.

They sat down. "So what were you doing at your office so early?" Victor asked. "Working on a case?"

"Writing," Gerard replied.

"Writing on your birthday? What? A brief?" Before Gerard could answer, José returned with an iced bottle of rare rosé champagne and four short glasses in hand.

"Stolen from Lucerne's wedding!" Victor said triumphantly, handing Gerard his glass. "José did it for us."

"I have another bottle at home." The photographer grinned, taking his place beside Gerard. Edith winked at him.

"Four hundred and fifty francs a bottle," said Victor. "And they had over five hundred guests." He peeled the seal off and let the cork pop; the champagne overflowed onto the ground as they clapped. "Bravo!" José said, catching the overflow and handing it to Edith, who traded her glass for his.

"To Gerard," Victor said a moment later, when the other glasses were full. "Happy birthday," he toasted.

"Ti Malis?" Gerard held his glass up to hers.

Edith laughed and clinked her glass. "How old are you now, Gerard?" she asked. "Twenty-five?"

"Eighteen," he replied dryly. "I'm just maturing." He took a long sip, held up his glass, and added: "Victor, José, thank you. Thank you all. This is a very nice surprise."

"Thank our Defense Minister," Edith added. "The leader of our new democracy."

"Really." Victor laughed sarcastically, draining his glass. "Come on, drink up, Gerard. This is a big bottle."

Gerard did as requested. It was excellent champagne, cold and very dry.

"So why didn't you attend the Lucerne wedding? You, one of the rich and famous invited guests." Victor examined the small bubbles rising from the center of his glass in a short, straight line. "Did you boycott?"

Gerard shrugged. "I had a headache, but we did watch it on television. Jeanne wanted to see who was wearing the biggest diamonds."

Edith cut in, "That's easy: Francine—what's her name, José?— from Seychelles."

"No, you're wrong. It was Guillaume's wife. I saw them up close. I have the pictures." The photographer licked the champagne off his mustache. "You don't believe me? I'll show you later. As big as an egg. She bought it in Luxembourg."

"How many carats?" Edith asked.

"Too many," Victor answered, laughing, his attention still focused on Gerard. "I'm glad you boycotted," he told the lawyer. "Not that I would have expected anything less of you." He patted Gerard on the leg.

"It was like watching the animals at the zoo." Edith pursed her lips in distaste. "The reception. Don't you think?" she asked Gerard.

"You see, Gerard?" Victor grinned. "She hasn't lost her wicked tongue. You should have heard her on the radio last night. Even I was scared." He was teasing Edith. She stuck her tongue out at him, then took a long swallow.

"I understand she doesn't like our future ambassador," Gerard remarked. "What do you call him—a mama's boy?"

"I was nicer to him than I should have been. Wait till next time." She laughed.

Victor shook his head. "See?" He nudged Gerard. "Fearless."

"He's a gorilla." Edith shrugged. "Did you see him and the Papal Nuncio in their little tête-à-tête? Disgusting, wasn't it? It made me sick."

Gerard smiled. Being around Edith always cheered him up, she was so direct. "I was talking about him with Père Emmanuel," he told them. "He says the Americans favor Lucerne."

"They're going to announce the ambassador's post this week," José chimed in. He had refilled his glass. Gerard stuck his own under the bottle.

"By the way," he told the Dominican, "I thought your pictures of the wedding cake were fabulous. It was like slow motion." José's pictures of the Lucerne reception had appeared in the centerfold of this week's local newspaper, including several of the ten-tiered cake, carried in by four porters, collapsing as it was set on the floor.

"It was a beautiful thing to see," José agreed, pleased with himself. "What a mess."

"But that wasn't the real scandal, was it?" Edith said slyly. "José, can I tell Gerard?"

The photographer considered it. "¿Cómo no?" Why not?

"You have to keep this to yourself—except for Jeanne," Edith demanded.

"I promise." Gerard was curious, amused. Victor was looking at him in a way that suggested: this is going to be good.

"First of all, she's two months pregnant—the bride. José heard it from her cousin who's trying to be a model. Isn't that right, José?"

The photographer nodded. "Sí."

Gerard could see Edith was relishing this bit of gossip, whatever it was.

"Now, the beautiful little truth is not only that she's two months pregnant but that it's not even his baby—not her husband's, handsome young man that he is. No." Edith shook her head in mock disapproval. "Of course it's tragic for the girl, and I suppose for the boy. And for her father, well, what could this do for his reputation, right? Our ambassador?"

Her expression, Gerard thought, was almost malicious, her eyes twinkling.

"So, who *is* the father?" he asked.

"Who knows?" Edith spread her hands apart, looking innocent. "The mystery lover . . . an old boyfriend . . . all we know is it's not her husband's."

Gerard looked at Victor, who chuckled. "So why get married?" he asked Edith. "And why would he marry her?"

"Well, I'm sure he doesn't know her history. But for her the reason is clear. Money. The boy's father is a Swiss millionaire."

It was Victor's turn. "He may be a dumb kid, but she's not. She has ambitions. And whoever her other Romeo is, he's not a millionaire. I understand the husband is really in love, though, poor guy. And you never know. If she wants money and she's happy, maybe she'll be nice to him."

"And he'll be getting an ambassador for a father-in-law." Edith leaned back, satisfied. "How was that for some sweet birthday gossip?"

"Rich," Gerard agreed. "Delicious."

"You saw Père Emmanuel. How is he?" Victor was turning businesslike, as he riffled through his papers.

"He seems well," Gerard replied. "Although upset about Bishop Privat."

"Don't get me started." Victor put up his hand. "I don't want to hear another word about that bastard. That's more than a disaster, that's a catastrophe."

José pulled his chair back. "Before I forget," he told Gerard, "I brought those pictures for your friend."

"For Leslie?" Gerard said. "Oh, wonderful. She'll be very grateful."

"They're not that good, but I can try to print some better ones this week. I'll be right back." He got up and went out toward the car.

Gerard looked around the room. There were two posters side by side on the wall, one of Martin Luther King, the other of Mahatma Gandhi. There was also the oversized sofa the couple had bought in Pakistan, a strange, slightly garish couch with embroidered leather cushions in different colors and a high back. Once he had taken a nap on it and dreamed of being Gandhi's best friend. In the dream, he and Gandhi were riding a motorcycle. The memory made him smile.

They drank in silence for a moment. It was edging past noon. A rooster crowed somewhere beyond the back wall, which was spiked with bottle glass since Victor and Edith's house had been broken into last month. Gerard pulled the documents with the payroll accounts he had stuck into his pocket earlier and handed them to the couple. "I would ask you both not to discuss this with anyone right now, until I can verify the accounts."

Edith read over Victor's shoulder. "What are these?" Edith asked.

"Someone slipped them under my door about two weeks ago. They are Minoterie payroll accounts. I called there and pretended to be one of the employees. That one right there"—Gerard pointed to the fourth name, Louis Sebastien—"I told them I had lost my check and needed a new one. They didn't have any record of my employment."

Victor read the list of names. "I don't recognize any of these names, do you, darling?" he asked Edith.

"No." She took the document from her husband. "No," she repeated. "Never heard of them." She turned to Gerard. "Any idea who gave you these?"

"I assume it was someone who works there, maybe someone who wants his bosses fired. The papers were in an envelope with my name misspelled. They wrote 'Metelluss.' So I'm inclined to think it's not someone I know. Also, my name was mentioned in the article about the labor negotiations. They said I was a lawyer willing to help any worker who needed representation, remember?"

"I think I told them that," Victor joked, teasing him. He tapped his knee. "Speaking of the negotiations, something like this could be useful to us, couldn't it, Gerard? If the management knows we have something on them, they might change their position."

"You're jumping ahead," Gerard told him. "We don't know what these accounts consist of and who's involved. Even if they are zombie accounts, we'd have to find some way to prove the crime. That may take a long time. I'm hoping that someone at the Banque Nationale de Crédit will help us out. But we'll have to be very discreet. And we won't have any answers by Wednesday." He paused. "I don't mean to discourage you, but this was given to me for a reason. I want to proceed quickly, but cautiously. We don't want anyone getting fired without good reason. Who knows? Maybe they're trying to throw us off, to distract us from something else."

"Such as?" Edith reread the names.

Such as the fact that I'm now helping the Americans track Duvalier's money, Gerard thought. Maybe someone found out I'm helping them. I can't see how they would, but it's possible. To Edith he replied, "I don't know. Such as helping you two. It could be any number of things."

"Gerard's right." Victor nodded. "He needs to investigate this first. It's too bad, though. I would have loved to dump this in their laps on Wednesday morning."

"I know what these numbers mean." Edith waved the documents, her tone bitter. "It means they're pigs, which we already knew." She handed the papers to Gerard, adding, "So—what do you want us to do? Anything?"

"I'll pursue my contacts in the bank. There's got to be someone there who's willing to do me a favor. If you wanted, you could check with your people to find out if any of these people exist." He pointed anew to the names of the Minoterie employees. "That would save me a lot of effort."

"We have people in there," Edith said. "We can find out very quickly." She turned to the window, distracted; there was something happening outside.

"I'll go look," Victor suggested.

"We'll need to get the current and back lists of employees." Gerard followed Victor with his eyes. "But it really has to be kept confidential for now. The last thing we want is to tip someone off. Remember, somebody is watching me—whoever gave me this. I'm hoping they'll contact me personally. So we must keep all of this quiet. Victor," he called over to the unionist, "did you hear that? I don't want you to say anything to anyone. Just find out for me who might want to cover his own back over at the Minoterie. Okay?"

"Bien." Victor was waving his hand to someone outside the window. Come in, he gestured, saying to Gerard and Edith, "They're here."

"We'll talk Tuesday night," Gerard told Edith. "No—even better—why don't the two of you come to my office? I have some other documents you might want to look at too. And I want you to sign those other papers."

There was a commotion. José walked in with two men behind him. Both wore T-shirts and carried straw hats.

"Victor, these are the young men from Papaye," José said. He handed a package to Gerard, saying quietly, "My telephone number is on the back. You can tell your friend to call me at the agency in the late afternoon. I'm usually there after four."

"Gentlemen, sit down," Victor said, as José pulled more chairs in from the other room. The union leader introduced himself and the others.

"Serge César," the older of the two men said, offering his hand.

"David Dezirab," said the other.

There was a moment of silence as they settled in. "We were drinking champagne," Victor explained. "This is Gerard Metellus, a lawyer. It's his birthday."

The men nodded in unison. They were shy. Edith pointed to the glasses and the bottle. "Would you like some?" she offered.

They hesitated. Okay. José disappeared to get more glasses.

"You must be tired," Victor said, adding for the benefit of the others: "These men are from Konbit Papay—Ti Cedric's group. Isn't that right?"

They nodded, holding their hats in their laps. David's left hand was missing three fingers above the knuckle. Gerard smiled at the men, as José returned, whistling. Gerard could see they were nervous; their eyes took in everything.

"They told us we could come and see you," Serge said, as Victor poured. "We arrived the night before last. The army arrested a whole bunch of us. My two sisters, his brother." He indicated David, who nodded. "We don't know what's happened to Ti Cedric. He's disappeared. The Macoutes came to our office and burned it. We lost everything. Nobody has seen or heard from Ti Cedric. One of our people was in the prison, he didn't see him. But anyway, we had to leave, it wasn't safe for us."

"When did you leave—in relation to Ti Cedric's disappearance?" Victor asked. He took out a pad of paper, began writing down information, then tore off a sheet for Gerard, who started to take notes too.

"The next day," Serge said. "In the morning, very early. Right after we put out the fire. We don't know if Ti Cedric is hiding," he added. "We thought he would have contacted someone by now if he was, but nobody's heard anything." He took a sip of the champagne, grimaced a little, set it down.

"What do the authorities say?" Edith asked.

"We don't know." Serge turned to his partner. "Nothing, right?"

"No."

Gerard thought they were about twenty, maybe a bit older. David, he noticed, had a wide scar on his wrist above his maimed hand.

"Was your group working on the strike campaign?" Victor asked. "Is that why they came to arrest you?"

"Well, we weren't doing much of that, mostly organizing our group," Serge said. "But my sisters—they're both at the college—they had gone to one meeting. Everybody supported it. We had already had one demonstration. We were waiting until after the results of the negotiations here."

"We should call that reporter in Papaye—the one from the radio," Edith interrupted. "She should know something."

"How did you get here?" José spoke now. "Did you come by car?"

"Bus," Serge replied. "But we had to get out twice. The army is stopping to check every one."

"Intimidation," Victor said. "So you haven't had any contact with your members since that day?" He was asking Serge.

"There are no phones. There was only the phone in the office. And that's been destroyed."

"I'll call Soeur Madeleine right after this," Edith chimed in. "Maybe we can put something on the radio tonight."

"Where are you staying?" Victor asked.

There was a momentary silence.

"Do you have anyone to stay with?" Victor persisted.

David looked at Serge, who replied, "He has a cousin," indicating David. "But we went to his house and he's not there. We'll go back after this to find him. He lives in Cité Soley."

"We'll find somewhere for you to stay," Victor assured them, "if you don't find him. Don't worry."

"Mesi," Serge said, looking at the floor. Thank you.

David appeared visibly relieved. He drank the champagne with his good hand.

Serge continued: "We were receiving threats. For about three months now."

"We read about that," said Victor. "Everyone heard about that, right?"

They all nodded. A dozen activists in Papaye had been detained last month, then released.

"That's when things s-s-started to get hot for Ti Cedric," the smaller man, David, cut in, stuttering. "They came to find our group one day and p-pointed a gun and t-told him we have to stop doing that."

"Who told him? The police?" asked Victor. "The army? Or a section chief?"

Gerard searched his pockets for another pen; the one he had was dried up. He found another one and tested it on his skin.

"Th-they weren't in uniform."

"Armed civilians?"

David looked uncertainly at Serge, who replied, "That's what we think. But we weren't there. Ti Cedric was the one they talked to."

"Gerard, you have a source in the police," said Victor. "Could you talk to him?"

"I can try," Gerard said. "But I doubt we'll find out anything. I would think some acquaintance of these gentlemen, who are living in Papaye, would be better placed to find out something like that." He turned to the tall one. "Does your group work with any attorney there?"

"No," Serge answered regretfully. "I don't know anyone, do you?" he asked David.

"No," David said. "I only know our group." He added: "W-we thought Ti Cedric might come h-here."

"If he was here, I'm sure we would know it by now." Victor shook his head in disagreement. "I can't see why he wouldn't contact one of us. I mean, he could have his reasons, but—" A look of doubt came over his face. "Chérie, what do you think?" he asked Edith.

"We would know," Edith agreed. "But we'll call around anyway. You never know, especially if he's worried about putting others at risk. But how would he have gotten here? I can't imagine he'd take public transportation. Not if they're patrolling, as you say."

David rubbed his hand against his knee, nervous. The sight of the rounded, digitless joints made something inside Gerard twinge.

"They had spies at our reunions," Serge continued. "After every meeting, we would get a telephone call and the person would hang up. That's how we knew they were watching us and knew what we were up to. But all we were doing was talking to people in our group."

There was a knock at the door. They all looked up. It was the sign painter, holding up his cup of paint.

"Come in," Victor said. "What is it?"

The man came no farther, but gestured behind him.

Victor looked annoyed. He got up quickly and went to the door. Edith followed him. "What's going on? Who is it?"

The two men from Papaye and José exchanged glances. "Don't worry," José said to David. "It's nothing."

"It seems our friends the police are in the street," Victor answered her. "Did you see them on your way in?" he asked Gerard.

"By the store? Yes. What are they doing now?"

"Sitting in their jeep. But they've moved across the street, just down there. I think it might be wise for us to end our conversation for now and escort our friends to their cousin's house. What do you think? It might be safer."

The two men from Papaye looked alarmed. Edith calmed them down. "Finish your champagne," she said. "We know those policemen. They do this all the time." But she shot a warning look at Gerard.

"José, you can go out the front and go around and come back here to pick them up, can't you?" Victor asked.

"I'm going," the photographer said, gathering up the equipment he had brought inside with him. "I was going to leave anyway." He went, closing the door quietly.

Victor pointed toward the door. The sign painter stood guard on the other side of it. "Our friend is keeping an eye on them for us."

They continued their discussion for another five minutes. The Papaye activists filled them in on other details of the attack, and together they made a short list of people to contact.

"I'm speaking at the rally this week," Edith told them. "Unless you don't want me to, I plan to mention Ti Cedric's disappearance. I'm of the opinion that it's better to let the army know we are aware of what they're doing. What do you think, Gerard?"

"I agree," he said. "What about you, Victor?"

"Me too. And we should get this to the press as soon as possible. But I don't think you two"—he indicated the Papaye activists—"should speak to anyone. Let us do it."

The two men whispered to each other. "We'll do what you say," Serge said. "But we don't want to cause more problems for our colleagues."

"They'll be more protected if the authorities know we're watching them," Victor assured them. "Trust me, I was in prison. If there hadn't been people outside putting pressure on them, I wouldn't be here today." He added: "They never like getting publicity. That's to our advantage."

José's Land-Rover arrived behind the backyard wall. The meeting was over. Gerard gave the two men his and Victor's telephone numbers. "Dial once, let it ring twice, then hang up and dial again," he instructed. They all shook hands; the men left. They heard José's vehicle leave.

Victor sighed. He looked at Edith, then at Gerard, and shook his head. He unrolled the flyer one of the men had given them. *Vote pep! Mande edykasyon nasyonal!* Vote for the people! Ask for national education!

Victor riffled through the other papers on the table. "Here is the latest management offer." He handed a thick legal document to Gerard.

"I'll read it today and tell you what I think," Gerard said. "Okay?"

"Fine." Victor nodded.

A little silence followed. "Are you coming to the rally, Gerard?" Edith asked, breaking it.

"I'll try to swing by, but I may be late. I have to be in court that morning." He added: "You be careful."

The couple walked him out. The sign painter pointed to where the police had stationed themselves. Gerard opened the front gate and walked in the other direction toward his car. José's envelope was tucked under the front of his shirt. His arms were crossed over it.

In the car, he slipped the envelope under his seat, then released the hand brake and put the car in neutral before starting the engine. He waved casually to the policemen, who watched him pass. Four streets and two intersections later, he stopped the car and pulled out the envelope.

The pictures showed a shallow grave with the remains of several bodies in a state of severe decomposition. They had been buried fully dressed. There were also close-ups of the women's clothing. On the back, José had written: *Artibonite: Mai 1981.* There were other photographs as well: of different prisoners; individual shots of several older women and young girls; and one picture of a group of women, hands behind their backs, a soldier aiming his gun at them. *Duvalierville: Juillet 1983.* The last set of pictures were small photographs, all of women's bodies, lying where they had fallen: in a gutter, in a courtyard, shot in a bedroom. Gerard turned them over. *Port-au-Prince: 3 Novembre 1985, Victimes Inconnues.*

Leslie closed her eyes. The buzz of words continued near her ears, faint static in little bursts like a radio never turned off, but never listened to either. Information that slipped into the brain unnoticed, shelved somewhere for future use. She only had to move her thumb, inch the tiny foam disk of the earphone over a bit, to better understand the words. But she didn't. She had heard enough.

She dozed. The ceiling fan spun slowly overhead; the wooden floor creaked as someone walked past in the hallway. The bed she slept in seemed age-old; she traced the carved floral pattern in the wooden bedpost absently.

The voices on the tape rose and fell. The lower tone was a man's voice, even and practical. She could hardly make out his questions. The woman's reply came a second later, a flurry of high-pitched sounds like machine-gun fire, followed by silence, then another rapid eruption. Bursts like flames, Leslie thought, smoke following each reply.

Leslie had an image of herself, face pressed against the window of the infirmary, looking in. The woman was dressed in a green hospital gown and sat on a steel cot in the corner. She saw her own tape recorder on the desk by the bed. Then she was standing at the entrance to the infirmary. The priest and the lawyer were there, waiting for her. Something had happened. She had forgotten the ampoules. She opened her bag and found the thin glass vials filled with the precious liquid. They contained the aqueous humor to cure the woman's eyes. The priest smiled at Leslie and blessed her. The lawyer stroked her cheek. Together, they stepped through the infirmary door.

The woman watched them through clouded eyes. Her cheeks were streaked with red. Here it is, here it is, see? Leslie held up the ampoules. The lawyer and the priest smiled too. See? We came after all. She stepped forward to give the woman a better view, but as she did, the ampoules fell from the tray and shattered on the floor. She heard a cry and saw that the woman was laughing, her thin frame bent over nearly double, her mucoid eyes dripping. Help me! the woman implored. Help me!

Leslie heard steps; the lawyer and the priest were fleeing. She heard her own voice asking questions on the tape: "What did the room look like? Did they give you a bed?" The woman had taken the bandages off her eyes. She played with the machine, turning the pitch button from right to left. The answers were grotesquely distorted: "Theeeerrrre . . . weeerrre . . . wiiinnndoows . . . buuuutt . . . there were rats and mice and snails and cockroaches."

She heard the tape screech, watched the infirm woman wrap the long plastic-coated wire attached to the earphones around her torso, around each breast, all the way up her neck. The woman placed the earphones upside down, like a stethoscope, a foam disk over each temple, listened intently. Leslie tried to step forward, but her shoes were nailed to the ground. They were covered with mustard-colored slugs. Her own voice from the machine was loud, amplified beyond recognition. The woman's head began to vibrate; the volume button was broken, she could not turn down the sound.

The words rattled the walls of the infirmary, threatened its foundation. "Enough!" the amplified voice shouted. "It's enough! We have enough!" Smoke began pouring from the infirm woman's ears, from her nostrils and mouth, spiraling up into thin columns of dark smoke and wrapping around her head like a loose bonnet. The pillars of smoke began to disperse as the woman mouthed, " 'No! No!' I said. 'I can't wait! I can't see! My eyes are hurting, my eyes burn!' I said, 'My eyes are sick! I need medication!' They struck me, to shut me up, to stop my complaining, but they couldn't shut my mouth. I said, 'Why? Why am I here? Why? I have my rights!' "

The tape clicked to a stop. Leslie opened her eyes, stared at the shadow the fan cast on the narrow, shuttered doors. The daydream was still with her. She could see the clinic door, the loose bonnet of smoke around the sick woman's head, Gerard and Père Emmanuel getting into their cars and leaving. She took a deep breath, then another. She was covered with sweat and her mouth was dry. She noted the position of the tape counter, marking it on her transcript. Then she removed the headset.

Yawning, she stretched and pushed the mosquito netting off her legs, then slid off the bed to get a glass of warm water. It was mildly sweet, and cloudy. She broke open a package of aspirin and downed two tablets quickly, then shook her head at the harsh aftertaste. It was four o'clock, still early. Bertrand would not arrive till seven.

She slipped on her sandals and dress and went out into the hall, locking the bedroom door behind her. It was quiet, everyone still resting. She walked silently along the corridor on the second floor, and admired a large sculpture of two intertwined bodies: long and sleek, they flowed into each other. Large floral paintings adorned the walls, the flower petals cadmium yellow. In a smaller canvas, dark abstract figures danced like shadows in a fire. Staring at the figures, she momentarily saw the woman again, her panicked face, her hands clutching the earphones, smoke pouring from her mouth.

She went downstairs. There was no one around. It was too late for lunch and too early for dinner. Maybe someone would be in back. She pushed open the door to the kitchen, but it was deserted. She shooed away a handful of flies that had settled on a covered basket, and took out a piece of stale bread to nibble on. Where was the coffee? There it was. She smiled at the sound of liquid swishing around the speckled enameled pot, then looked for the evaporated milk. She couldn't find it, but spied a tube advertising itself as a sweetened dairy product. It dissolved poorly in the tepid coffee. She pressed down on the mixture with a finger, trying to blend it in, then gave up. The pale dropping floated on the surface, barely lightening the coffee. To hell with it, she thought, sipping the espresso. It was so strong. She drank half of it and filled the cup to the top again, avoiding the sweetener. On the way out, she shook the bread basket, not content to let the flies rest.

She went back upstairs to bed and crawled under the netting. She loved its luxurious, self-contained feeling. She was one of Gabriel García Márquez's doomed South American women, living a life of unrequited love in some forgotten corner of the jungle.

She lit a Salem, alternately smoking and drinking, enjoying the acrid mix of caffeine and nicotine. Mark had hated the fact that she could smoke and drink and still want to kiss. One of his failings, she thought—to embrace life's sourness. She smiled, wishing she could transform the pleasant edge of rancor she felt into something creative.

Her mind wandered again. Images of what she had seen earlier in the day while walking along the edge of the bay, near the docks, passed before her mind's eye. The families that slept there cooking over the piles of refuse left by the tankers. The beggars, each younger than the next, crooked-limbed polio victims, sitting on the broken pier, fishing with lines tied to their ankles. The high wall that surrounded the city cemetery, the new graffiti on Duvalier's van- dalized grave. Smelling the horrible smell Clemard had warned her about, the smell she had expected but had not found at Titanyen. The tall, broken crypt, and inside it, what appeared at first glance to be a giant pile of thrift-shop clothing, until one noticed the charred bones jutting out. And stuck into the cracks of the two- storied crypt, dozens of soft, thin white votive candles, like those on a birthday cake, like waxen incense sticks that had left wisps of black smoke on the concrete. She shuddered, the coffee bitter. The pastel tombstones had been so beautiful, some decorated with bright tiles in Art Deco style. Horror and beauty, side by side. What to do with such contradictions?

The thought hung in the air with her cigarette smoke; she blew on it, blew the images of the smoked corpses away, moved the cigarette around, watched the smoke sift through the netting up to the fan and be dispersed. It was four forty-five. Back to work, she sighed, glancing at her notepad. The details of this woman's story already confirmed her suspicion that no one had paid attention to the experience of women in Duvalier's prisons, and to what might still be happening to them. She reread the last lines she had written down: "Inside the cell there were three other women, one 62 years of age at the time, the others 21 and 16. I think all of them were killed, because I never saw them again."

She took a long drag on her cigarette, let the smoke fill her mouth, swallowed it, imagined it coming out her ears, the way it had in her daydream. *Inside there were three other women.* Inside, versus outside. *And me*—she rose up on an elbow to study her reflection in the mirror—*where do I fit into all of this?* Through a hole in the netting she saw the infirm woman standing behind her own reflection in the mirror, and behind the woman, the broken crypt with its ragged skirt of thin candles. They were called baleine candles, because once they had been made of whale oil. They burned quickly.

She lifted up the netting, tied it above her head in a knot. In the mirror she was thinner, her bony, freckled shoulders bore deep pink moons, the peeling skin painful to touch. She struck a pose with her cigarette, crossed her thin legs at the ankles, admired her black silk slip with its lace border. She was a 1950s television housewife waiting to greet the police detective after killing her husband, no remorse. Lana Turner—Leslie cocked her head to one side—or Marlene Dietrich in that Western, what was its title? Maybe one day she would remember the names of movies or songs. Maybe it was a disgusting habit to smoke and drink and roll your tongue in another person's mouth. Maybe Mark had been right, and she had never really wanted him. Maybe she was deceiving herself about everything. Her fingers left pale marks on her shoulders when she pressed them down. I have the glow of a tourist, she thought, how unattractive. She looked over at her green dress, hanging in the closet without a door. Should she wear it tonight? Or her black dress—which was more formal? Such decisions. She pulled a gray strand out of her hair, smiling at the incongruity of it all. Here she was documenting torture, and she was preoccupied with what to wear. She leaned back down to the bed and read the woman's testimony a third time. Nobody cares what happened to you, she thought, but I do.

She finished the cigarette, then pressed the tape to rewind and dated the testimony: Period 1979–82. Subject: Marie-Thérèse Dubossy, prisoner at the National Penitentiary, La Salette, Port-au-Prince, Haiti. Interviewed by the Red Cross on April 2, 1986. Unedited transcript.

There were places where the woman's words were garbled. The official who had questioned her had been careless; there were several questions left unanswered. She doubled-checked the position of the counter, making sure it matched the testimony. It was obvious listening to the tape that the woman had not understood all of the official's questions, his Creole had been too limited. And, it seemed, he had asked leading questions, had been more interested in the details of her medical treatment than in her emotional state. The dates were off too. Leslie wound the tape back again and concentrated.

(0:00)

RC: You were released March 10. Do you feel free?

MTD: Free? Is it freedom if each time I walk in the street the Tontons Macoutes can stop me for no reason? Yes, then I suppose I am free.

RC: Let's discuss your case. When were you first arrested?

MTD: The first time was in the summer of 1979. For eight hours that time. The second time was also the summer of 1979 and this was for two days, and again for two days on the third and fourth times. It was the same thing. They arrested me and asked me questions, a lot of questions. Then they let me go. Each time I said, "I'm innocent," and there were protests by my friends. But the last time—

RC: The fifth time?

MTD: Yes, the fifth time. It was more serious. The fifth time I spent six months. I still remember the day. July 7, 1981. You know why I remember it especially? It was my aunt's birthday. When she found out I was arrested again she got in her bed and never got up again. She was dead before I was released. So you can see that they didn't succeed in killing me but they killed her.

RC: Did they arrest you because of your uncle's activities?

MTD: My uncle had been a candidate in the municipal elections of 1979. Even though we all knew they were not real elections, my uncle posted his candidacy. He ran against a Macoute. Just before the election, when it looked like my uncle had the support of many people, he was arrested. They beat and tortured him in jail. He died after six months. And after that, they came to get the rest of us.

RC: The other members of the family?

MTD: My two brothers and me. My parents had stayed in the Plateau Central, where I was born. Luckily, my brothers had left to find work in the north. I was the only one they caught.

RC: Tell me about that day—the day they arrested you.

MTD: On that day I was at a friend's house ironing some clothes. There was someone who said, "Marie-Thérèse, Marie-Thérèse, they've gone to your house—you have to hide!" So I stayed with my friend. But eventually I had to go back and so it was on that morning, the morning of the seventh of July, that they finally found me.

RC: What happened then?

MTD: They took me to the Casernes Dessalines. There was General Henri Lucerne. When I was taken to see him he forced me to strip in order to humiliate me. Next he told me to walk back and forth fifty times and he invited all the Tontons Macoutes to watch and they cursed and spit on me. But no one touched me; not on that day. They sent me to La Salette.

RC: The women's section of the National Penitentiary?

MTD: Yes. Inside the cell there were three other women, one sixty-two years of age at the time, the others twenty-one and sixteen. I think all of them were killed, because I never saw them again. They were taken away two months after I arrived, so I was alone for four months in the clinic.

RC: Why did they put you in the clinic? Were you sick?

MTD: They were telling the world Duvalier had no political prisoners, so they put me in the clinic. The common prisoners were in the cells. They called it a medical clinic—an infirmary—but it didn't really have any medicine or anything, just a bed. It was a place to keep me, that's all. I was there alone—they never brought anyone else in, except sometimes a doctor would come there to do an examination and they would bring a prisoner from the cell. But the doctor did not come often—only twice during the whole time I was there. Even when women were dying, they didn't call a doctor.

RC: What did the infirmary look like?

MTD: It was a room, big and long, with separate compartments, a toilet like . . .

"Words garbled here," Leslie wrote, marking 1:21, "bad tape quality."

MTD: There were windows but there were rats and mice and snails and cockroaches.

RC: Did you have a bed?

MTD: They gave me a steel bed, a mattress, and a pillow but no sheets. They said I could hang myself with a sheet.

RC: Was there a shower?

MTD: Yes. If you can call that a shower. It was a pipe, that's all. But there wasn't any soap, nothing like that.

RC: Did you receive visitors?

MTD: At first they denied I was there. But later they let me receive food because I was losing weight. I couldn't eat the food in the prison—it gave me diarrhea. All I had to eat at first was a little creamed corn that was never cooked well. The food they give you causes diarrhea. So I was lucky because my family brought me some rice and paid a guard and so they cooked it for me. Otherwise I would be dead.

RC: Tell me about a typical day in La Salette.

MTD: Well, I'll tell you about one day. On this particular day I felt very angry, very vengeful, very bad. I was crying and saying, "Why am I here? I haven't done anything. I'm innocent." They had killed my uncle and I thought they were going to let me die too. After that, the entire staff came to the infirmary except the one who was nice to me and they beat me and told me to stop causing problems. They tied my hands to the bed and beat me all around my head. But they couldn't shut my mouth. I said, "You killed my uncle! You're going to kill me! I haven't done anything!" It was my worst day . . .

RC: Was that when you lost your vision?

MTD: When they beat me I started to bleed in one eye and I couldn't see well. There was a sickness in my eyes after that called conjunctivitis. They brought the doctor to see me and he said I needed some ampoules of medicine. So I asked them to let my friends send the ampoules of medicine for my eyes. They agreed, and I waited, but the ampoules never arrived. I protested: "No! No!" I said. "I can't wait! I can't see! My eyes are hurting, my eyes burn!" I said, "My eyes are sick! I need medication." They struck me, to shut me up, to stop my complaining, but they couldn't shut my mouth. I said, "Why? Why am I here? Why? I have my rights!" The morning before they released me, the same doctor came to see me again but by then it was too late. I couldn't even open my eyes to recognize my family when they came to get me . . .

RC: In all your time in La Salette, did you ever appear before a judge?

MTD: I never saw a judge. I never saw a lawyer. I never saw anybody. All

I had was the rice that came from my family from time to time, and even that I had to save to eat all during the week. There was not even a letter or a word from my mother and my father. When they sent someone to tell them in the Plateau Central to come and get me, my family didn't believe it at first. Just the week before, someone told them I had died.

(2:02)

Leslie shut the machine off. She placed the notepad on her chest. Above her the knot of mosquito netting resembled a large gauze snail. She stared at the wall, hearing Marie-Thérèse Dubossy's soft, stilted voice, her desperation. Much later the church bells sounded, indicating it was time to dress.

Port-au-Prince
20 August
Dr. Gesner Frances FADH
Military Hospital
Port-au-Prince, Haiti

Dear Dr. Frances:

We bring to your urgent attention the case of the six cadavers recently discovered in a shallow grave outside Petit Goâve. (See attached copies of pages 14–15, Aug. 15 report by Dwa Moun and the Amnesty International Urgent Action bulletin sent to the Ministry of Justice.)

We urge you in your capacity as Chief Coroner for the Haitian Military to publicly release the findings of the exhumation you carried out as reported on the national radio last week. Any failure to do so will be viewed by the public as a breach of law and your professional duties as the chief medical officer of the Haitian army.

We remind you that the eyes of the world are on Haiti now. Given recent reports suggesting a rise in paramilitary and extrajudicial actions on the part of individual soldiers, it is important that the Haitian army disassociate itself from those forces opposed to democracy and constitutional respect for human rights. A full public disclosure of the Petit Goâve exhumation would be viewed as an important step in that direction.

While we in the international community are aware that the political climate in Haiti remains difficult, we urge you to take this action swiftly.
Signed,
Dr. Robert Morse
President,
International Commission on Human Rights
Geneva

🐊 14 🐊

Wristwatches gleamed in a pile atop an overturned carton; the young man hawking them picked one up and shouted at the well-dressed woman who had paused to pick mud off her white high-heeled shoes. "Madanm! You can go swimming with it. Madanm! You can go underwater! Look how beautiful! See? The numbers shine in the night. How about this one, madanm? One hundred percent sterling! Madanm! Why do you walk away like that? Madanm! I have many others! Madanm, I will sell it to you cheaper than any of those other persons. Madanm, you're not even looking!"

The other hawkers next to him under the archway of the Rue des Miracles laughed. The woman crossed the street to avoid them. She passed ten feet from where Jean-Marc was sitting alone in a truck. He turned to see her being accosted by the young man. "For your husband, madanm? Oh, you are not married? For your fiancé, then? Here, look at this fine man's watch. Yes, try it on. It's all right, you can try it on. No, it's not too heavy. Get away, all you swine! Leave this woman alone! She's my customer!"

Jean-Marc saw the watch again. The young man held it up in his hand, draping it over the woman's wrist. He felt his hands grip the wheel slightly. He forced himself to look at another corner of the market, to see if anyone had gone the wrong way on the one-way road where the traffic jam was most backed up. The tap-taps were five vehicles across, the noise they made so loud and prolonged that Jean-Marc wanted to scream, Shut up! I'll arrest you all! "Silence!" he said aloud, but only one woman sitting on the pavement heard him. She looked fearfully his way, then turned away. He felt ill-tempered again today, exhausted. It was too much to endure with the heat and the crazy traffic. Right next to him, a jitney bus let off a blast of three notes. Ta-ti-tah! . . . Ta-ti-tah! . . . Ta-ti-tah! Jean-Marc glared at the driver of the vehicle, who looked straight ahead, not moving, avoiding Jean-Marc in his blue traffic uniform, inside the small Honda truck.

Across the way, the young woman was laughing; her sunglasses were up on her head now. The young man was laughing too. He had removed another tray of watches and selected a thin silver one that caught the sun's glare and twinkled. Jean-Marc felt the dampness of his palms, and reached down under the front seat. He opened the bottle of alcohol and drank three quick shots, holding the last one in his mouth as long as possible, swishing it around, then finally swallowing it. It gave a pleasant shock to his insides. You're having visions again, he told himself sternly, staring at his reflection in the chrome of the armrest.

He sat up again. The young woman was gone, the young man stood talking to his friends, laughing. Had he made a sale? Had she bought the silver watch or the gold one Jean-Marc had once sold to another man at this very same stand? He stepped out of the truck, held the door for support, pretended to survey the traffic. He made impatient signs for the tap-taps to move aside and let a car that was being forced into the vendors' stalls back into the stream of traffic. He took out his whistle and blew on it twice, pointing sternly to the car. The tap-taps offered the car an inch of space; it slowly edged back in. His eyes traveled up and down the street again. Then he spotted the woman, the silver watch gleaming from far away on her wrist. Satisfied, Jean-Marc stood there a while longer, watching as she rounded a corner and was gone. It was eight o'clock. The rally would be starting any minute now.

He heard faint static and turned the radio dial back and forth until the dispatcher's voice could be heard clearly. Headquarters was demanding additional reinforcements along the airport road and Delmas and on the downtown avenues closest to the palace. There had been two arrests this morning unrelated to the rally. Jean-Marc listened to messages going back and forth a while longer. His partner was not returning for another twenty minutes. Despite the heat, he closed the windows, half closed his eyes, stared at the man selling the watches through the dusty window. He replayed the conversation he had had with the priest.

Think about it, the priest had advised. *I'm sure you'll find your answer. And don't forget, He is listening. Talk to Him. He's the only one who can help you with your problem.*

Jean-Marc sipped the clairin. He says I should know. But I don't know. I wish I knew. A smart priest, talking to me that way. Saying I'm the judge. Saying if I sold those things to feed my family, it might be a crime, but it isn't a sin. I was right to keep my mouth shut. They would have put me in prison.

He heard a barking of the radio transmitter. The dispatcher at headquarters was putting out a general call to all free units. Jean-Marc looked at the cars around him, which had begun to move. His partner was snaking his way back between them, wielding his baton. "Back to headquarters," Jean-Marc told the younger man, who jumped in, whistle in mouth.

They made their way slowly toward police headquarters, passing near the government offices where the rally was taking place. Jean-Marc glanced down a side street and saw that many vehicles had been abandoned around the Labor Ministry. People sat or stood on the hoods and trunks of others. He heard the sound of a broadcast speech, but the words were distorted. His partner pounded on the roof of the truck, urging them away from the snarl of traffic.

An ambulance honked behind them, and Jean-Marc recognized the driver in his rearview mirror—Frantz, one of his former colleagues. Further along, he slowed the truck and parked near the police station. "I want to talk to someone a minute," he told his young partner. "Come and get me if there's anything important." Behind him, the ambulance had pulled up. He walked over to it.

"Allo, Jean-Marc!" Frantz gave him a warm handshake.

The policeman glanced in back. "Nobody in there, eh?" he joked. The other man laughed. They looked at the uniformed men coming and going through the entrance of the mustard-colored police headquarters.

"So you're in traffic now," Frantz said, offering Jean-Marc a cigarette. "Do you earn more money?"

Jean-Marc waved him away, laughing. "No."

"So why the change? I thought you liked it with us."

Jean-Marc smiled, shaking his head. But he remained silent.

The other man looked at him appraisingly. "Got tired of all those dead people, huh?" he said slyly. "Couldn't take the smell anymore?"

Jean-Marc grinned.

"I'll tell you what." Frantz leaned close to him. "You should have been here last week. A body"—he whispered—"smelling like a dead cow and just as big, even bigger. If it had been me I wouldn't have let them come inside. You couldn't get near that body. They wanted to bring it into the morgue, but the attendant refused. Can you imagine?" He let out a rich laugh. "It reminds me what we went through. Those were the days, weren't they?" He chuckled, then nudged Jean-Marc. "I can see why you don't miss it."

"Who was it?" Jean-Marc asked, curious.

"The stiff? Nobody special."

Jean-Marc nodded.

"They brought a bunch of people in there today," Frantz said, shaking his head disapprovingly. "A bunch of kids."

"To the morgue?" Jean-Marc was surprised.

"No, man, the prison." Frantz smiled collegially at Jean-Marc. "You ever go in there anymore?"

"I used to—to say hello."

"Yeah, I don't go in as often myself. They've got these new guys—they're suspicious of everybody. Even though they know me, they give me a hard time. So I don't bother."

They finished smoking. The ambulance driver looked at Jean-Marc with amusement. "So you got yourself a better job. That's good for you. I should think about that kind of job. At least you get to be outside."

"It's a headache," Jean-Marc complained, "especially on a day like this." He looked in the direction of the prison. A thought had come to mind. "There's a big traffic mess near the cathedral because of the rally." He turned to the other man. "Didn't you run into that?"

"Oh, that. No, I just got here. I'm on my way to pick up some supplies." He surveyed Jean-Marc for an instant, then leaned forward again. "Between you and me"—Frantz pulled on Jean-Marc's sleeve to make sure he was listening—"I'm for it."

When Jean-Marc didn't respond, he added: "They fired a good friend of mine. He's not a troublemaker. He's a quiet man. With six kids too. You know how that is. So I agree with them, even if I'm in this uniform. You know what I mean?"

"Sure I know," Jean-Marc said gruffly, "but you better be careful saying that."

They both looked around.

Frantz suddenly smiled broadly. "You're a friend, I can trust you." He laughed. "You always were a careful one. Always keep your cards close to your chest. I remember . . ." He gave Jean-Marc a friendly smile. "Say, why don't you come around and play some dominoes with us one night? We play every Friday after work. It's a good group. Nobody loses too much. We have fun. Now that you're a rich man," he added, teasing him again.

"Right," said Jean-Marc sourly. "A millionaire."

They heard a shout. His partner was signaling. "I have to go," Jean-Marc said. He shook the other man's hand. "Hey, Frantz, I'm glad I ran into you. It's been too long. Funny thing is, I was just thinking about the old days this morning. Coincidence, no?"

"Fate," the other man said. "Don't forget—Friday nights."

"I'll try to make it," Jean-Marc said. His partner ran up.

"What's happening?" Jean-Marc asked him. "Trouble?"

"Special duty," his partner said, making a face. "And they didn't say anything about extra pay." He handed Jean-Marc a sheet. "We have to fill this out and go get gas. Come on, we're late."

They passed the hospital on the way back out. Frantz's ambulance was parked in the courtyard. Jean-Marc half listened to his partner describing what was going on at headquarters, the arrests that had been made, the prostitutes who had been inside, and other gossip. His mind was on what Frantz had told him. Later, he thought, I'll stop by the prison. Just to say hello. They won't be suspicious of me. Why should they be?

I hear a great wind, sister, blowing from someplace far away, and it lifts the smoke rising from the charcoal pits along this mountainside. I trust that by now you have gotten my message, that I am safe and in hiding. I think about you and our mother and the mother of my child hoping nothing has befallen you and that you are all safe. I received the news today that they had not only burned our house but the konbit office. All of our tools burned, and nothing to salvage! The friend who brings me the news says the army knocks on all the doors of those who agree with the strike. He is not well either; he was caught on the road and beaten. But he is recovering.

He says all of our group is hiding, everyone in the bush. But not even the mountain is safe. They are patrolling all the small villages and paying fifty gourdes to anyone who sees people from Konbit Papay. I told him that it is too dangerous even for him to stay with me. I will keep moving to a new place every night. So far, I have gotten lucky, finding people who do not ask questions. But I can see my presence will bring trouble. It is better for me to sleep in the caves than in a bed. I told him that Pe Smit has taken my request for some protection to my colleagues in the capital. But I heard on the radio that they are arresting the students and the organizers there too and many have gone underground into the marron.

I don't know if it is safe to take any of the big roads. If I can find someone who has a truck I might risk it. I have no news from the friends who were heading for St.-Marc.

I have trouble writing this letter. My hand still aches from jumping off the balcony of the office. It was already weak from the torture in the prison. But I am blessed again, sister, my bonanj was watching out for me. I felt nervous about our meeting, like I had told you that afternoon. So I asked Daniel to stay downstairs by the door, just in case. And he was the one who saw them coming in the truck. I suppose he's in prison if he's not dead. But my friend has no news. He tells me the word is that no one should try to return home now. It's not that they will arrest us; they have promised to cut us into little pieces. But if you have news about Daniel, please give it to my friend when he brings you this letter and he will find a way to pass it to me. Do not write, though, just tell him you are well and that is all I need to know. When it is safe to come and see you I will do it.

I'm sure you have all the details of what happened to us, but I will tell you what I know. They shot at Mickey and me in the ravine but we were able to run away. And they had the truck and could not follow us. I left Mickey at the river. He did not want to go up to the mountain. He has a friend in Hinche and has decided to try his luck there. I have no news from him but I think it will be safer because he is not so well known to the authorities. But as I said to my friend, the life of a bird is worth more than mine right now. It will not be safe for me anywhere in this region. I have to try to find sanctuary somewhere else. Of course, the army is denying everything. They are accusing us of storing materials to make bombs when everyone knows there was nothing in our office except for the tools. There is a rumor they forced those in Thomonde who put up the strike posters to eat the paper and one boy choked to death. The news is terrible. I am surprised there is nothing on the radio. That is the kind of news that makes me want to cry and you know I don't believe in crying, in giving them any more of my tears. But the boy was only twelve—only twelve! Not even a man.

The only news the radio is carrying is to warn the drivers that they will lose their jobs if they participate in the strike. But I heard that the chauffeurs in Port-au-Prince have voted definitely to strike. So that is another small victory. And the students and teachers, even though they are being persecuted, they are going to close the schools. Because of my situation it is impossible to know how successful our own campaign has been, but already I can see that the people are beginning to say if there is an election it must be clean and there must be a promise of jobs and some security.

I have been hiding in the woods these last two nights. The farmers are being forced to pay the grandons twice the tax they used to receive. They said at first, right after Jean-Claude left, the grandons promised to return part of the land that had been stolen. But now *that they have made their claims and the Macoutes who went underground are back, the grandons are hiring them to enforce the tax. So nothing is really different. And it seems the Macoutes are promising to exact their vengeance on the ones who called for their heads. There is a lot of violence. The attitude of the grandons is the same as with our konbit. They say it is a Communist plot.*

There is a great wind, sister, and it reminds me of the last hurricane we lived through, you and I. Sometimes I think about the big eye of the storm, how terrible and yellow it was, and how we took our walk in the middle of it and you told me about what it was like for you when I was in prison. I feel that same stillness now, like I am standing in the middle of a giant hurricane but everything around me can be destroyed at any moment. In the middle I am calm but the danger is everywhere.

I have not told you enough how you remain my sister whom I love so close to my heart. And do you know what makes me happiest? Knowing that you will be able to read this letter, that you have taught yourself to read. So we are two in our family who have triumphed, but for you the road was that much harder than for me.

When I was sent away to live with that family, I remember being afraid that you would hate me because I was getting to go to school and your future was not as certain. I knew it was unfair. And I was jealous at the same time that I had been sent away and not you. Even though they were not bad people, I felt like a little slave to that family, having to clean their yard and feed the sick grandfather. A restavek, their little servant. I was ashamed. And I felt guilty too, because it should be you who was going to the better school. You were the one who was smarter, who was better with the math. I've never said any of this to you because it was so long ago, but I feel so proud of you. How many women from our village could teach themselves to read? How many women with four children and no husband to help her? Sister, my heart smiles when I think about you reading this letter and now teaching your own children to read. You are an inspiration to all of us. You are a rock I carry in my hand to hold on to when I am troubled.

My friend has just told me we must go now. There is a car that will be coming to the village, which is a half hour from where we are resting. With luck, it will take me on a safe road.

Sister, my sister Violette. When I survived that prison, I thought it was a miracle to see you again. Now I think it will be another miracle the day I can return, the day I feel safe enough to sleep in a bed at night. But the day will come. I am keeping my faith. Even though the big wind of death is all around me, I am comforted knowing you are with my son and his mother, that you are all taking care of each other. If for any reason God should drop me from His sight, do not cry for me either. I will be waiting for you on the other side. Be well, sister, and embrace all those I love. Take courage from what I say to you: God is on our side.
Your loving brother,
Sedryk

15

"I haven't been to the club in a long time," Bertrand remarked to Leslie as he turned around in the front seat. "Since the curfew, we don't go out as much." Blackie, a poodle suffering from a broken foot, was curled up soulfully next to her in the back seat. Clemard was driving. He was to drop the animal off at the veterinarian's this evening. Leslie hoped he would join them later. Clemard wore a white shirt with large orange flowers and his brown pants. She noticed his nails were freshly cleaned and trimmed after working on the engine earlier that evening.

"How is everything, Clemard?" she asked, gripping him lightly on the shoulder. Leslie caught Bertrand's look of annoyance. He did not approve of her friendship with his chauffeur. Leslie had decided to ignore this.

"I'm fine, thank you, Madanm Leslie," he said.

"Is Gerard coming?" Bertrand inquired, interrupting.

"Yes, with Jeanne," Leslie answered.

"Jeanne is coming to the American Club? I'm surprised. I had always heard she detested Americans."

"Oh?" Leslie asked, interested. "Why is that?"

"Her father suffered under the Marine occupation."

"Suffered how?"

"I don't remember the story exactly. Ask Gerard. I'm surprised he hasn't recounted it to you." Bertrand's voice bore a familiar sarcasm. She wondered why it was the two men disliked each other so much, beyond their political differences. It seemed more personal somehow, a mutual distaste. But Bertrand's remark had piqued her interest in Jeanne. She knew about Jeanne's teaching degree from the University of the West Indies in Barbados and her work with mentally impaired children. Gerard had also discussed her liberal views, similar to his, and Jeanne's good humor. Leslie had a picture of a lively, highly intelligent woman with an easygoing nature, one Gerard called complex.

Leslie looked up to catch Clemard trying to communicate something with his eyes in the mirror. What? she tried to ask. What? She saw him shake his head slightly, indicating he couldn't say. It was probably just a response to Bertrand, who was fiddling with the radio, leaving it on a Haitian ballad Leslie recognized. It was being played night and day. Staring at the older man's pate, she noticed Bertrand had liver spots on his neck, something she had never seen before. They were just like those her mother had on her stomach.

She felt a sudden pang of sympathy for the older man, whom she had been feeling at odds with since her arrival. She knew the reason had less to do with Bertrand than herself; having learned more about him from Gerard, she realized she seriously disagreed with Bertrand. But she had not been able to discuss any of this with him; nor did she want to, really. There was something so set about Bertrand that she felt it would be of little use, and could only add to the strain between them. Not that he was being anything but typically polite, going out of his way to make suggestions to Leslie about people she ought to meet and offering to make introductions.

She could also see how worried he continued to be about his wife's condition. Leslie had spoken to Marie on the telephone that morning, hearing a fatigue and weakness in her voice that had not been there before.

"Is Marie feeling any better today, Bertrand? I'm sorry she's not coming with us." Leslie tried to make her voice sound warmer, more affectionate.

"Oh, she doesn't like to go to parties anymore anyway," Bertrand said, turning around in his seat. "It makes her too self-conscious . . . with the wig, you know . . . she can't enjoy herself. We had a friend over for lunch yesterday . . . I think she enjoyed that. But she gets tired very easily."

Marie had described it herself: All my hair fell out. I was totally bald. Now I look like a young chick, my hair is as soft as a baby's. It's awful, though; I can't stand it. I feel like a Martian. And I know people are looking at me when I go out, that's the worst of it. Because they pretend nothing's happened. I'd rather you came here to see me.

"She was hoping you would come for lunch yesterday," Bertrand added. "Her friend is a painter. You would have liked him. And she made a rice djon-djon." Bertrand turned around. "You remember her djon-djon, don't you?"

"How could I forget?" Leslie smiled. "She's a superb cook. I'm sorry I missed it, but I didn't get back in time. We've made a lunch date for Tuesday, though." In her mind, she added, irritated: Marie did not make the rice, Bertrand. One of the two cooks made it. It's those little details you ignore. She hadn't lied about Marie, though. She was an excellent cook.

She looked at the back of Bertrand's head again, noticing how age puffed up certain people's faces, blurred the profile, while with her the opposite was likely to happen. Bertrand, who had a somewhat Greek cast to his face, looked like a lifelong alcoholic who had given up the bottle too late, his skin lacking a certain dynamism. She had caught him looking at her a few times this week too, sizing her up, as it were, thinking the assessment was probably not positive. He doesn't really like me and I don't really like him, she thought now. It's like a family thing; we're bound by some past but we have nothing to say to one another.

She noticed Clemard looking at her again and smiled quickly, feeling guilty that he might have been reading her mind. He smiled back.

"How is the work going, Bertrand?" She made an effort to communicate with the older man.

"I'm fine, Leslie, just overworked. We had a long day at the store today and two of my employees are sick. It's the third time this month. I'm going to have to let them go if it continues. It's not their fault, of course, but in the meantime I'm losing money . . ." He looked at Blackie as he said this, wagging his finger at the dog, who licked it.

She nodded, instantly angry again at his casual tone. How can you fire someone for being sick? she thought. What a cad you are.

"What's wrong with them?" she asked, knowing the question was slightly provocative. She couldn't help it, though.

He shrugged his shoulders. "Who knows? These people are sick all the time. They don't take care of themselves. If you see how they live, it's unsanitary. That's a big problem in the factories, you know, tuberculosis. We end up losing too many of them."

Well, she thought, if you gave them some health care and more money to buy food, they might not get so sick. But the comment stayed in her mind. At least for tonight, she was not prepared to confront him further.

"That's hard," she managed.

"It's hard for a man my age. I work eight hours a day. And there's Marie to take care of. I'm the one who ought to be taking time off."

There it was again. She merely nodded, looked out at the evening sky. She listened for a second to the radio, which was announcing the upcoming news. They were going to give an update on the demonstration. Earlier, she had heard a government official denouncing the planned action, and had called Gerard, letting the phone ring a half dozen times. It was too late by the time she remembered she should have let it ring twice, then hung up. By the time she called back to do that, she knew that if Gerard and Jeanne were home, they would not pick up. It was frustrating, but it had happened to her before. She was hoping he and Jeanne were still coming tonight; they hadn't been certain earlier. The announcer was repeating the government's statement now. "Any incitement to violence will be met by appropriate action"—a woman was reading the decree. What was appropriate action? Leslie wondered cynically. She had not made up her mind about attending the demonstration, which had been rescheduled after yesterday's report about a shooting at the Cape. There, police had used tear gas at a spontaneous protest, and a bullet had struck a child in the leg, though the police claimed that only blanks had been used.

"I wonder what the menu is tonight," Bertrand said, switching the dial without asking them. He found another music station and kept it there. "Not that anything can be as good as the food at the Lucerne wedding reception. I told you about the food, didn't I?"

She nodded, saying nothing.

"Grilled lobster and coquilles St. Jacques. It was quite a feast. I wish you had been here. You would see that our parties are as good as those in Washington."

She attempted another smile, but kept looking away, out at the sky. He's going to drive me crazy, she was thinking, he's doing it on purpose now.

"The bride's dress cost two thousand dollars. There were four of them carrying the train. Quite beautiful," he added. He was saying this for Clemard's benefit now, as well as Leslie's. She wondered if Clemard had heard it all already. Probably.

"The father-in-law's company is Swiss. Do you know of it? They make beautiful ceramics, plates, cups, very similar to Villeroy and Boch."

"I know of Villeroy and Boch. They're based in Geneva, aren't they?" Leslie had to say something; she felt like a model, being forced to smile too long while the photographer adjusted his lens.

"Geneva, maybe Lausanne. I'm not sure, to tell you the truth." Bertrand was whistling to the music, tapping his fingers in front of Blackie's nose. The dog kept licking them. "He's going to open a factory here—put the son in charge. I'm even thinking of investing." He sang a little part of the song, scratched Blackie on the head. Clemard was mouthing the music. Leslie felt the migraine she had taken three aspirin to get rid of returning over her eyes. She noticed that Bertrand had said nothing about the demonstration since his initial warning to her that she ought to stay away. It's more like a parent-child thing, our relationship, she thought. Like an undeclared war.

"Where there's money, there's money, that's what I told him. And that's all anyone needs to do business here." Bertrand added: "The son is a likable boy. Not as bright as his father, though."

God help this country if he becomes a senator, Leslie thought, shaking her head at Blackie, who had edged over to put his head in her lap.

The drive up to Pétionville and the American Club was pleasant. The lights of the houses on the hills sparkled; yellow spirals twirled from far away as cars moved down the opposite mountain. On the side of the road, geometric black-and-white rugs lay in piles beside straw mats and baskets. The ever-present smell of charcoal permeated the car. "I love that smell," Leslie said. "Even though I know it's bad for the country." In the rearview mirror Clemard smiled again. Bertrand pointed to pedestrians who were straying too close to the center of the road.

The night air was warm; people walked up the snaking road

carrying tins of oil and baskets of figs on their heads. A trio of boys rolled a car tire along the left side of the road, passing the tire from hand to hand. Children dragged hexagonal kites in their wake as they ran to catch the wind. They reached the entrance to the American Club, turning left sharply and accelerating to climb the steep drive. Lights shone on the empty tennis court. The ball boys had already left; a group of men stood by one of the cars smoking cigarettes. Clemard waved to them: most were fellow chauffeurs. Bertrand got out, holding the door for Leslie. "Don't forget to tell the veterinarian that it's for Blackie," he instructed Clemard for the third time. "He'll give us the special price." The chauffeur nodded, his eyes meeting Leslie's. See? he was saying. See how he treats me?

Leslie paused to talk to Clemard for a second. Bertrand did not wait. "I'll save you a rum punch," she told Clemard, maintaining a friendly tone in her voice, but trying to avoid any hint of flirtation. "Are you going to come in?" No, he shook his head, smiling. "Blan Bertrand would not like that. I'll stay out here with my friends." He pointed to the other men, one of whom waved.

"Bien," she said, locking the door on his side. "See you later, then."

She had ironed the black frock with its mildly scooping back, and worn a single strand of pearls. Her hair was tied in a pink velvet ribbon, rather stylishly, she thought. The moment she stepped into the airy room of the American Club, however, she felt underdressed and conspicuous. Most of the women wore calf-length dresses, bright, flowery, opulent, and revealing, and flashed expensive jewelry. Nails and hair revealed hours of attention. Leslie slipped quickly into the bathroom by the entrance. She was tempted to remove her ribbon, which looked schoolgirlish to her now. Two young mulatto women, dressed to the nines, left the stalls, glancing at her, their smiles professional. Relax, she told herself, inspecting her image in a long mirror in the hall. You look fine. No one is going to notice you're not wearing panty hose. Of course, she knew they would, but she had caught her only dark pair on the bedpost, causing a run. Come on, she said, stop avoiding this.

A waiter escorted her to the long table where Bertrand was seated.

Thank God, Gerard and Jeanne were already there. The couple embraced her. "It's so nice," Jeanne said to the company at hand, "to finally meet Leslie in person. How are you, Leslie?"

Gerard's petite wife was attractive and elegant in a coral-colored dress and a simple gold necklace; Leslie felt instantly envious. Bertrand stood to introduce her to the others sitting at the table, all couples she had never met. The room was almost completely mulatto and white, aside from Jeanne and two other couples nearby, and the waiters and musicians. She had been given the empty seat next to Bertrand, regretfully too far from Jeanne and Gerard to talk to them.

She accepted a rum cocktail from the waiter. Clemard had been right about not being welcome in such a gathering. She glanced at her watch; eight-fifteen. Blackie's appointment had been set for eight o'clock.

They had placed half the tables inside the large glassed room and the other half around the pool. Overhead fans spun slowly. Leslie listened to the music of the orchestra, a quintet of five young men dressed in gold lamé jumpsuits. Les Troubadours. The lead singer was short, and had a soft, melancholic voice. He kept nodding in her direction, winking at her. Oh great, she thought.

In all these years, the American Club had not changed. Leslie remembered the first time she had come, with Father, to play tennis. She had been uncomfortable, knowing none of the other American teenagers. The young ball boys made her embarrassed to be playing so badly, to be hitting the balls over the fence, so that in their bare feet they had had to wade through a thicket of bushes with thorns to retrieve the balls. She had not been able to stop them. Father had liked the place for the view and the foreign beer they kept on ice. The ladies' club, that's what she had called it then, and that's what it looked like to her now, a haven for the embassy wives and the upper-class Haitians with nothing to do but talk about who was sleeping with whom. For the most part, they were the same as country-club wives back home, a conservative, class-conscious group preoccupied with domestic dramas. Big fish in a little pond, Father had often said about the American Club. How strange it was to be back here now! She looked around the room again, trying to remember the expression Father had used. *Mulâtre pauvre c'est nègre riche; mulâtre riche c'est blanc.* A poor mulatto is a rich black man; a rich mulatto is a white. Something like that.

Leslie excused herself to sample the hors d'oeuvres laid out in gleaming silver trays on a long table. "Makes you miss Washington, doesn't it?" Bertrand quipped, coming up behind her. "Not at all," she said. "Anyway, everyone in Washington is on a diet. They only serve health food. Just a little roll of sushi, that's all."

He laughed. "You do miss our Haitian cooking, don't you?" They filled their plates. "Give me more of that conch." Bertrand poked her lightly with a toothpick. "Don't take it all for yourself." She was somewhat shocked at his doing that, but she relented. Was he drunk already? She wondered if he had been drinking before picking her up.

Back at the table, she listened in on a conversation between Bertrand and a businessman.

"But aren't you yourself planning to campaign for the Senate, Bertrand?" She heard someone ask the question. The patrician-looking Bertrand leaned back and took a sip of his cocktail before answering. Leslie could see he was planning a short speech.

"As a matter of fact," he turned away to answer, "I am considering my candidacy. But only if this election is properly planned. Only if it is a serious election. Because even though I consider myself as well qualified as any of these 'supposed' presidential candidates, I would not agree to campaign for President. I think it's absurd that we already have fifty candidates for President and only three for senator. But the job of a senator—if the Congress is well organized—is a very important one. That is where I think—in all modesty—I could make a contribution."

Gerard said nothing, but he caught Leslie's eye for a second. How are you doing? he asked with his eyes. Save me! she replied.

Bertrand wiped the sweat from his upper lip. "They're all dogs, really," he said. Leslie had lost track of his speech. Was he saying that about the Congress or the candidates?

Bertrand suddenly patted her arm, surprising her. "Not, my dear, that I am suggesting we have any more than our fair share of corrupt leaders. We just seem to have received a particularly vile dose of them. And it doesn't help that the particular gentlemen in question want to rule the country, now, does it?" He made a small grimace that soon turned into a smile. "Talk about politics." He smiled at the group at large. "Look who's just arriving."

They watched as the American ambassador and his entourage entered, along with several men in business suits whom Leslie immediately identified as embassy security officers. She recognized Peter Samuels in black tie, standing a few feet behind the ambassador; they shook hands with a table of people Leslie didn't know. A line began to form; people stood up at their tables to greet the ambassador. Leslie heard a scraping of the chair next to her; Bertrand had gotten up to join the queue.

She must have seemed bemused, because Jeanne slipped in beside her and asked, "You don't like your ambassador? Neither do we. Do you see whom he's talking to? Our Interior Minister."

Up close, Jeanne was even prettier; she had striking eyes and a flawless complexion, and wore a pale pink lipstick that matched her nails. Her long hair was pulled up into a tight chignon; a tiny gold mermaid sitting on a pearl dangled from her gold necklace. Leslie felt like an ugly duckling, big and plain, next to her. She smiled, feeling slightly shy now that she and Jeanne were finally able to talk. The couple seated nearest them had gotten up to dance.

"The minister has two mistresses," Jeanne added, accepting a fresh drink from the waiter. "Together their ages don't total thirty-five. He divorced his first wife when she turned twenty-five. Charming, no?" She toasted Leslie. "A ta santé. Gerard talks about nothing but you since you've arrived."

"Thank you," Leslie replied, blushing.

They watched the scene at the entrance, where the ambassador was having his picture taken by a news photographer. Leslie hadn't noticed the photographers before, but there was another one, near the orchestra. She wondered if either was José, who had taken the photographs Gerard brought her. He had stopped off earlier at the hotel to tell her about his meeting with several unionists. None had any news about Cedric George.

"Is that José?" she asked Jeanne. "Do you know the photographer?"

"No," Jeanne answered. "José is a Dominican. He's small and has a mustache. I don't see him." She added, "I don't know if he'll be here. The photographers are from the government paper."

"Oh, I see." Leslie accepted a light from the waiter. "Do you mind my smoking?"

"Oh, not at all. Unless it's a pipe. I abhor pipe smoke. Do you smoke one?"

Leslie looked at her strangely. Was she joking? No, she appeared to be serious.

"I read in a magazine the other day that young American women liked pipes. I thought maybe you had adopted the habit. Here, only poor women smoke pipes." She laughed.

What an odd sense of humor Jeanne had. Leslie found it refreshing.

"Gerard has told me all about your project," Jeanne said. "It sounds very interesting. In a way, it's sad to think that we don't even know this about our history. We have a number of women who have written about the situation. But these are mostly sociological analyses. I don't think anyone has focused on the experience of average women in the prisons of the Duvaliers. It's only now that we can even approach the subject, you know." She added, somewhat hesitantly: "I don't want to offend you, but I said to Gerard, 'It's a shame we don't initiate projects like this one ourselves. It always seems to be outsiders who see the value.' If I proposed such a project, people would probably be suspicious of my intentions. Do you understand?"

"I think so," Leslie replied, trying not to take what Jeanne said personally. "I've had to struggle with that question, coming from the outside. I'd prefer to work with women here. That's how I'm thinking about the project, as a kind of collaboration." She hoped she didn't sound defensive.

"That's good," said Jeanne, fingering her necklace absently. "Because, to be frank, you'll meet a lot of people who will ask you why you came here to do this."

"I understand that," Leslie interjected. "There's a history of exploitation."

Jeanne smiled. "Those are the same people that like to hide

behind their beautiful statistics, but"—she held up a warning finger—"you also won't find them in the street. Look at our Haitian intellectuals. They like to talk about the people—'le Peuple'—you know, but ask them to do some real work with 'le Pep'—the poor people—and suddenly they disappear. They have a meeting, or an appointment. That's always the excuse. They don't like to take a position. Well, I can't say that for all of them, because look what Duvalier did, he wiped out a whole class of intellectuals. But the ones who survived, a lot of them have lost their courage. They write books and poetry, but when you ask them to do something more difficult, to help your project with some money, or to sign a petition, they can't be found."

She shrugged her shoulders. "Gerard thinks I'm too hard on everyone, but I get tired of people who are so quick to criticize and don't act themselves. In any case," she added, waving to a tall woman who greeted her across the dance floor, "don't be surprised when you start getting attacked. That will probably mean you're doing something valuable."

"I appreciate your support." Leslie looked in the same direction as Jeanne; the tall woman tilted her head, as if to say, Come over here. Jeanne shook her head no. Then she turned back to Leslie. "Sorry, what were you saying?"

"Just that I appreciate your comments. Because I've had to think about that, you know, being an American, being white. These are important issues. That's not to say one shouldn't do projects, but I was hoping I would find women here to collaborate with me. They would give the project its direction. And eventually, it would become just a Haitian project, with outside funding. That's how we work at the foundation."

"Well, I'm sure you'll find a lot of women who are interested. And I hope I haven't discouraged you," Jeanne reassured her. "But it's like that here. You can't wait for people to like what you do. Ask Gerard. He can tell you all about that." She paused, then added: "I told him I would be happy to help you. I'm not a writer, and I haven't been imprisoned—not yet, at least—but if I can do something . . ."

"That's wonderful," said Leslie appreciatively. "I'm very grateful.

But do you have the time? Because I'm serious about looking for collaborators. This project is in a very initial stage. It could go in a lot of directions."

"Good." Jeanne smiled, adding: "But don't forget—I'm considered bourgeois too. I married up." She looked over at Gerard, still engaged in discussion. "Gerard must have told you about his family's reaction, no?"

"He did, actually."

"They're not bad people," Jeanne said, making a face, "just snobs. There's only one subject: the family. And if you don't show enough interest in the family, watch out!"

They ate more hors d'oeuvres and drank. Leslie described to Jeanne the daydream she had had while listening to the taped testimonies.

"I dream like that too," Jeanne confided. "In the early afternoon, before the children come home, very strange dreams, sometimes very bad and violent. But I never tell anyone about them. One day, I would like to do an analysis of my dreams. Have you ever done that?"

"No," Leslie admitted. "I've done therapy, but never that kind."

"Those poor women," Jeanne said, grimacing as she drank. "When I think about it, I don't know how I would have reacted to an experience like that. But I think I would crack. I really do. I don't think I could survive. Even the threat of being tortured, just the idea of it: I'd crack. I tell Gerard that all the time. If they ever arrest me, that's it. I'm finished." Jeanne smiled quickly. "You don't believe me, do you? Well, I know myself. I'm not that strong. I'd ask them to shoot me."

She was being serious. The waiter came around with a tray of fried something. Jeanne grabbed a few small plates and served them both. "Eat, Leslie," she said, "the embassy is paying for it."

They laughed.

"Gerard mentioned your new job to me." Leslie changed the subject. "How is it?" She bit into something unfamiliar. It was odd-tasting, somewhat crunchy. Seafood, maybe. She dipped it into a piquant sauce the waiter now offered them. "He told me a little about the school. I can't wait to come and visit."

"Well, I'm afraid you'll be disappointed," Jeanne said. "It's nothing to look at anyway. We have two classrooms. But it's a start."

"And the parents built it all themselves? That's incredible."

"We teach the children in the morning and the parents at night. So far, we have thirty adults."

"Men and women?"

"More women, actually. That's what a lot of people don't know. These are women who work in the markets, but they are eager to learn. And they bring their babies with them, and do the lessons. It doesn't matter."

"And you have some kind of peer counseling, some component like that?"

"That's right. Each student has a partner. That way they can work with each other when we don't have enough teachers. The minute they've learned something, they can teach someone else; we don't even have to ask them to do it. They do it of their own accord."

"Do the children ever teach the parents?" Leslie asked.

"The older ones sometimes. But rarely," Jeanne added, tasting the fried snack herself.

"Is the program being duplicated anywhere else?"

"One place." Jeanne coughed, blowing on her hand to indicate the sauce was hot. "In the south. But it's even newer than our program. So we'll have to wait to gauge its success."

"It must be rewarding," Leslie said. She admired Jeanne even more. "Have there been any problems?"

"Oh, yes." Jeanne lowered her voice, but kept her expression cheerful. Gerard was dancing with a couple on the dance floor as a trio. They watched, amused. "We've gotten our little warnings, like everybody else. It's very simple. They don't want people to be educated. Even though we're not doing any political education. But just the fact that one thinks the peasant deserves to be educated is considered subversive." She shook her head, her tone darkening. "That man over there—the Interior Minister—he's the one they say is responsible for the campaign against the literacy monitors. His father was a Macoute too."

Leslie looked over at the table where the minister was seated.

Bertrand hovered beside it. At the far end sat Peter Samuels. Leslie had been tacitly keeping an eye on him. I should go over, she thought, to make sure he got my message. She wondered if he knew about the events in Papaye.

"Did Gerard tell you about Cedric George?" she asked Jeanne a moment later.

"I'm the one who took the call," said Jeanne. "I don't know more than Gerard. He's the one who's following this thing. We're expecting the worst, I suppose."

"Really?" Leslie said quickly. "So you think they would kill him, even with the elections and everything?"

Jeanne gave Leslie a strange look. "Of course they would kill him. But first they would probably torture him. These are sadists, remember?" She looked over at the Interior Minister. "Too bad nobody's poisoned that man," she remarked.

For a second, the other Jeanne emerged, the one who would prefer to go mad, the one who had violent dreams, an ugly expression on her face. Leslie studied her, wondering what she was fantasizing.

Jeanne straightened up in her chair. "We're getting too melancholic," she said, rising. "Come on. Let's go dance."

Leslie held back. "I think I'll go and see how Clemard is doing. I'll be there in a little while. By the way," she asked, chewing, "what is this?"

"That? Brain. It's good, non?"

Leslie felt her stomach go queasy. "Cow brain?"

"That's right." Jeanne patted her on the arm, laughing. "Don't worry."

The orchestra slowed to a merengue. The lead singer gave Leslie a huge smile as she crossed the big room and walked out to the parking lot. It was nine-thirty. She found Clemard leaning against a car with his friends. He was eating a plate of the hors d'oeuvres.

"Mesye." She smiled at him, offering a cocktail.

Clemard accepted it, grinning broadly. She could see he felt shy about her presence around the other men. "Bonswa," she said to them, shaking hands all around.

"Bonswa, madanm," each one replied.

"How was the food, Madanm Leslie?" Clemard asked, placing the drink, untouched, on the car roof.

"It tastes . . . expensive," she said, looking away from him to the tennis courts. It was dark; there were no signs of the ball boys. "The music is nice, but I imagine your orchestra is better. Non?" The other men laughed.

Clemard took a sip of his drink. He was grateful Leslie had brought it. Earlier he had wanted to compliment her on her dress, because he saw how nervous she was. He wondered if it was he who made her nervous, or if it was Met Bertrand.

"They're an official orchestra," he explained. "They played for the Duvaliers at the palace." He reached into his shirt pocket and removed a pack of cigarettes.

"Non mesi," she said, adding: "Pa janm fimen Lucky Strikes." I don't ever smoke Lucky Strikes.

Hearing her Creole, the other men laughed approvingly. Clemard could see them wondering about her. He lit his cigarette, exhaling a long stream of smoke.

"You aren't dancing?" he asked her.

"No," she replied, embarrassed somehow by the question. "There's no one in there I want to dance with." Out loud, the remark sounded suggestive. "I don't really like to dance," she added quickly. Liar, she said to herself, why are you lying?

The group laughed. For a second, a look passed between them and Clemard, but Leslie missed it. Clemard smoked with his head down, shook his head slightly. He knew what the others were thinking but ignored them.

"We should invite Madanm Leslie to one of our parties," he said. "Shouldn't we? She would dance there." He smiled, trying to put her at ease.

"Wi," the other men agreed. Yes.

"Because they don't know how to dance in there," another of the drivers, a younger man, said slyly. At this, their laughter grew louder. "They dance like this," the youth said, holding his body rigid as he stepped forward and back.

The men laughed even louder at this. Leslie knew something

was going on, some private joke. She looked at Clemard, who was grinning too. Maybe he was drunk.

The others were still laughing as Clemard walked her a bit of the way back toward the entrance. "They're crazy," he said to her, still smiling. Was she offended? He could not tell. No, he decided, as she smiled, she was not offended. He stopped at the bottom of the steps.

"A plus tard," Leslie said to him. See you later.

She was going through the door when she heard "Leslie?" She spun around. It was the first time he had dropped the Madanm. "Mesi." He held the cocktail up. "Mesi anpil." Thanks a lot.

She blushed for the second time that evening. "No problem," she said, using his favorite Americanism. She added in bad Creole: "Pa fe rien." It's nothing.

The singer had finished his song and was on break when Leslie returned. Peter Samuels was still at the far table. She reconsidered introducing herself. She had done enough work for today.

"Here she comes." Gerard pulled Leslie into the center of the dance floor, where Jeanne, to her surprise, was dancing with Bertrand. To her further surprise, Bertrand was a smooth, fluid dancer. Jeanne winked at them as they passed close by.

"Look at her! She's even enjoying herself," Gerard exclaimed.

Leslie was glad to see he was having a good time, too. After a while, she relaxed as well, letting the music carry her along. During a break between songs, she thought she noticed Clemard watching her from the entrance. But when she looked back, he was gone.

They spilled out of the club well after midnight. Clemard did not speak in the car; Bertrand dominated the conversation, recounting all the gossip he had heard. Leslie watched the back of Clemard's head. "Bonswa," she said quietly to him, getting out. She waved to the custodian, Vincent, who was waiting with his customary flashlight. She kissed Bertrand good night. "A demain," she said to Clemard.

"Bonswa, Madanm Leslie," he replied.

Leslie followed the custodian up the stairs. By the time she had entered her bedroom and opened the doors to go out to the terrace,

Bertrand's car was already in the street. She saw the glow of its headlights, reflecting against the high walls of the hotel. Then it turned and vanished from sight. Clemard had wanted to say something to her, she felt. But what? She went to bed, the question still on her mind.

⇒⇐ 16 ⇒⇐

Gerard eased the Corvair over a particularly treacherous hole in the road, which quickly disintegrated into a red dirt track two feet in width. It was a feast day and he was free; Jeanne had taken the children to a party. Rather than working at home, he had decided on impulse to go up to Kenscoff.

The afternoon rain had arrived earlier than usual. It took him over an hour to make the trip. He drove without thinking about anything in particular, simply enjoying the scenery. At one point, he stopped the car on a wide curve to look at the metropolis below, flattened out and fraying at the edges like a tattered hat where thatch rooftops replaced concrete buildings. Another curve and an expanse of inland plains and low-lying hills came into sight.

He loved the cool piney smell of the air up here. It filled him with a feeling of purity and simplicity. He gazed at small plots of tended land and wildflowers lining the road. He wanted to remember to pick some for Jeanne on the way back down. Already he regretted not having come up sooner; it had been months since the two of them had spent a weekend in the cabin. Already the morning's pressures were falling away; even the judge who had angered him had receded from his thoughts.

He had made this trip so often as a boy that he felt he could drive it blind. The best trips had been with his uncle Louis on his big motorcycle—long, crazy journeys marked by continual dismountings. They had only had one bad spill in all those years, but Gerard could still feel the shock of it in his body. He had pissed helplessly all over himself, mortified. But Oncle Louis had not teased him, only examined his body for bruises. Memorable, exhausting trips. Gerard smiled. Before him was the face of the mountain where he had spent whole weekends walking in silence with the other boys, tracking small animals with homemade slingshots.

From this vantage point, pastoral life appeared unchanged, free from the suffocating mask of urban growth, closer to the picture of Haiti he had formed as a child. The mountains stood tall and majestic as they always had, the verdant slopes peppered not only with pine but with coffee, palm, coconut, and pygmy banana trees, flowering bougainvillea, berry bushes, and trees whose leaves had medicinal properties that Jeanne would cultivate and then be afraid to use. There were nervous, rough-maned horses with skinny legs and protruding spines, horses he had learned to grip as a boy with his own skinny legs, keeping his knees high up on the wooden saddle to race the village children. They ran barefoot behind, seemingly oblivious to the sharp stones and nettles, chasing the horses with stripped pine branches in their hands. The older peasant boys rode like daredevils, backwards, double and triple, balanced only on rough jute bags with rope harnesses, galloping down steep inclines. They were amazing to watch. He remembered Oncle Louis's voice crying after him: "You have to be one with the horse, one with the horse!" His words echoed silently across the valley below, across a gulf of time.

Long red patches of dirt streaked down the mountainside, great forked tongues of crumbling clay. For years, he had slid down them on his stomach, hands outstretched, eyes closed. There was nothing to match that out-of-control feeling, the speed and exhilaration, better than a modern roller coaster. Afterward, his stained clothes had been shredded into rags from the free fall. He could hardly resist the impulse now. Jeanne would kill me, he thought, laughing. With my bad back? But it would be fun to try again.

A final series of hairpin turns and he crossed a little gully in the road. He got out and locked the doors, placing rocks under the tires; the emergency brake worked poorly. He pounded once on the trunk, then stepped back to let it open itself. Inside was his sweater and the portable typewriter Victor had lent him. It would be cold inside the house.

Walking up the familiar road, he suddenly had an image of Jeanne's naked body, when they had come up here for a honeymoonlike week, although that first time they had been married for a year. Jeanne had wrapped herself with only a blanket; she never got dressed, not even to go behind the house to urinate. An ideal week in which they had made love morning and night, ignored everyone and everything. Gerard had brought her coffee and whiskey in bed, played songs on his guitar; sometimes they read together in bed. The memory made him smile. A sentimental creature, wasn't he? He wondered what had happened to the guitar. A perfect week, he thought, we should do it again. He imagined Jeanne's response to the idea. I'll stay in bed with you, old man, she would say, but I'm wearing my socks. He laughed.

A cluster of mud houses stood at the base of the upcoming slope. He hoped the caretaker had left the keys in the hiding place inside the pail. Near one of the houses, a woman stepped out, a child in her arms. Another child tugged on her skirt, and they watched Gerard approach. He nodded to them. The woman and children were barefoot, the infants clad in homemade shorts. The children were malnourished; their stomachs protruded like tight balloons. Gerard felt conscious of his sweater and shoes.

"You related to that man?" The woman pointed to a cabin in the distance, above the tree line.

"My uncle Louis's house," he said. "But now it's mine."

"Met Metelis." She nodded. "Li mouri." He died. The children were shy. Gerard smiled at them. There was an awkward silence. The older child broke into a fit of giggles, prompting a look from his mother. "Ret trankil!" she told him. Stay still! She pointed to the fire pit by the dirt houses. "Mais ou vle?" It's corn you like?

Her Creole was strange, the words inverted. He glanced sideways at the pit, where several ears of baby corn were smoking. He could see the woman's large, slack breasts through an opening in her flour-sack dress. The printing on it read: "Produit Haïti," the script running upside down in the back. The children's shorts were sewn from the same material. Gerard could imagine their little penises freezing at night.

"Manje pa vle?" She asked. Eat you don't want? He saw she had three teeth on top, four on the bottom. Her hair was braided in cornrows and ended in fuzzy points. Gerard put down the typewriter case. "Bon," he said. The smaller child took his hand to lead him to the pit. "Dife," the child warned. Fire.

He rarely had corn like this anymore, picked off the stalk, the cob thrown directly onto the coals. He sat down on a log; the woman and children squatted. She looked at Gerard with polite curiosity as he ate. "M'renmen sa," he said. I like this. The corn cracked under his teeth. "Sikre," he added. Sweet.

She pulled her smaller son away from the stranger and held on to him. "Dlo?" She pointed to a white enamel pitcher. Water? He considered it, then declined. Dr. Sylvie had told him about a cholera outbreak in this region.

I wonder how she eats this, Gerard thought. What kind of pattern do those teeth produce? It was a cruel but funny image. He ran his tongue over his own teeth, dislodging stubborn threads of corn. Then he felt around in his pocket and handed her a five-gourde note.

"Mesi." Thanks. The children stared at the money. She reached into the bosom of her sack dress and removed a safety pin; Gerard watched her pin the money there. She smiled at him, unembarrassed. The children circled around her legs, still eyeing him shyly. The older, bolder one held out a hand for money; his mother slapped it down and pulled the child roughly behind her. "Pa fe sa." Don't do that.

"No, no, it doesn't matter," Gerard said. "Tiens." He pulled a half-finished pack of mints from his pocket. He gave two to each of the children. The woman accepted one too.

"My name is Gerard," he said as he sucked bits of corn from his fingers. He looked for a place to discard the husk.

"Geneviève," she said, taking the husk from him and throwing it aside. "Geneviève Clovis." She looked young when she smiled, about twenty years old.

"Geneviève. That's a pretty name. And the children?"

"Ernest. And that one, Roosevelt." She gave the children an affectionate glance. They ran away at the mention of their names. Playfully, they grabbed the discarded cob and tossed it back. It landed near Gerard's knee. Geneviève Clovis grinned, shaking her head as she warned them: "Vakabons! Map kale ou! Atensyon!" Vagabonds! I'll hit you! Be careful! But she was joking. The children laughed and ran around in a circle.

"They like to play." Gerard caught sight of the time while brushing a fly off his wrist. "You'll have to excuse me," he said. "I have to go up to the cabin. But I thank you for the corn. Thank you again, Madanm Clovis." He waved goodbye to the children.

The older one followed him to the edge of the property, then heeded his mother's yell and went back. Gerard turned the large key in its ancient lock and pushed open the door. He set the typewriter down on the floor. The cabin felt like a time capsule to him, the air inside stale and heavy. It was also colder than he had anticipated.

He walked around, inspecting the house for signs of change. A screen door was broken. He opened the windows to air out the room, and got a foldout chair from the back room. A large bottle of Schweppes was left behind from a previous visit, and he pried off the cap.

He went out to the terrace with a blanket from the bedroom. With his hand, he brushed what appeared to be mice droppings from it, then smelled it for traces of Jeanne's perfume. It was musty. Although he could not see them, he imagined what the people in the village below were doing: cooking, drinking, gossiping.

A bluebird flew close by, settling on a branch. It seemed to look right at him. He placed the typewriter on the table and got settled. The machine he had borrowed was cheap, but it would do. The keys stuck a little. Tucked inside the cover was the play he had started. He had not looked at it since his birthday. He tested the machine, enjoying the smacking sound of the keys on the paper without the paper guard set in place. Loud and crisp. He thought about his meeting with Judge Daniel that morning. A coward who was afraid to exert his legal authority over the warden at the prison. He could have insisted that Gerard be allowed to see his client, Elyse Voltaire. Gerard concentrated, focused on the judge sitting in his dim chambers, as he read the beginning of his play.

AFTERNOONS AT THE PALACE
by Hervé Paule

CAST
(In Order of Appearance)
LAWYER
JUDGE ARSENIC
JUDGE BARBANCOURT
JUDGE CACAOUETTE

UNDER THE BONE

THE PROSECUTOR	THE JUDGE
THE JURY	THE CLERK
THE ACCUSED	THE WITNESS
RELATIVES OF THE ACCUSED	THE PUBLIC

Note to the actors: The characters of judge and jury are crows. Therefore, as author, I have disposed of the traditional concept of "character" as such. I offer you these guidelines: (1) Your characters are limited to these actions: speaking shrilly, preening, shitting, hopping, pecking, and flying short distances; and (2) you are vain, easily distracted, and unclean; (3) the role of Judge Cacaouette is designed with a female actor in mind, but an actor en travesti might be appropriate. The other judges are conventional male roles.

Note to the audience: As a modern and modestly civilized man, I offer my apologies in advance to crows in general, as they are certain to be metaphorically maligned in this play, as well as to members of the International Society for the Prevention of Cruelty to Animals, for yet another negative literary image.

Note to the lighting designer: There are no lights because the courtroom is open to natural light. Because of the rain, however, candles might be used and there are candleholders on the columns for that very purpose.

Note to the director: Let's keep the tone light, shall we? Remember, no one wants to feel any worse than they already do these days.

ACT ONE

The setting is the large hall of the Haitian Supreme Court, Port-au-Prince. The year is 2026. It is 10 a.m. The city looks much as it does today, except that it has been allowed to decline without any new construction or maintenance of buildings. Because the Haitian legal system is based on the Napoleonic Code, a portrait of Napoleon hangs above the justices' bench, located upstage. The bench has been carved by a famous Haitian artist with pastoral images decorating the surface.

Next to Napoleon are the portraits of Haitian national heroes Jean-Jacques Dessalines and Toussaint L'Ouverture. While the portrait of Napoleon rests in a gilded gold-leaf frame, the other portraits are unframed. If one were to turn them over, one would see a stretched flour sack tacked to a cheap wooden frame. A heavy coat of varnish has been used to try to preserve the portraits, but by now the varnish is yellowed and flaking, giving Dessalines in particular an unhealthy, sallow tone. The banner "Vive la Révolution" hangs above the portraits.

The courtroom is the coolest room in the city at the moment, due to a heat wave. Daily rainfall adds to the oppressive humidity. The courtroom is modeled on a Roman domus, circa A.D. 79, with a large open atrium allowing natural light to enter. At each corner of the rectangular courtroom rises a massive fluted Corinthian column with an Ionic capital.

Private chambers for the justices and jurors are off to one side of the atrium (left, midstage). There is a shallow trough to catch the rain; the jurors and members of the gallery flock there during recess to drink. Often, the justices will go to the trough to gaze at their own reflections as they determine the fate of the accused.

The justices' chairs are located behind the bench, with only their backs visible to the audience in the gallery. The chairs are Louis XIV style, with plush, but faded, burgundy velvet cushions. The straight-backed chairs of the jurors are less regal, though still fairly ornate, with turquoise velvet cushions and backs and arms and feet carved into lion's paws, painted black.

Several mango and lime trees have grown up in odd corners of the room where the original marble floor is falling apart; they are small but mature, with fat, ripe fruit bending their branches. They stand upstage left, by the jurors' box, center stage right, next to the door leading to the clerk's urinal, and front stage right and left, with branches arching over the edge of the stage. When the actors enter, they are framed by these branches; those in the audience sitting far to the left or right may be forced to strain their necks to see what is happening in the courtroom.

A hired orchestra should be warming up in a room offstage. The musicians are doubtless tired of working for the Supreme Court, but they are paid in cash (U.S. dollars, not gourdes) and receive bonuses of fruit. There is also the promise of an authorized (though unpaid) trip to Miami during the court's many recesses. Although tedious, theirs is a plush job.

The gallery is nearly empty this morning; two market vendors looking for shade wander into the courtroom to nap. The musicians check their watches. It is time to begin. The first chords of an electric guitar fill the air as the orchestra launches into the famous "Ballade Antillaise." The night rain has ended; the last raindrops slip off a rusting drainpipe into the trough.

Note to the audience: The public is forbidden to touch anything in the courtroom, since all objects are state property. This includes the fruit. Should a mango or lime fall to the floor, a clerk will retrieve it and take it to the kitchen (offstage) to be tasted by a kitchen staff member to make sure it is not poisonous. The best fruit is typically served to the justices as a late-morning repast.

This precaution has been Justice Arsenic's idea, given his particular interest in poison and, naturally, his family heritage. The judge is a connoisseur of poisons, but he is also a diagnosed paranoiac. He is convinced someone wants to poison him. So, please, do not eat the fruit.

SCENE I

Justice Arsenic enters from his quarters, stage left. He is a scraggly, ragged-looking crow who walks stiffly, his graying wings partially extended under his red legal cape. Despite the cloudy day, he wears a pair of imported Ray-Ban sunglasses, resting on his balding head. Behind him stands the prosecutor. A blind clerk enters, slowly pushing an ice vendor's cart painted in stripes of green and blue. The cart is stacked with different volumes of the Haitian Constitution with related appendices, and several Chinese pornographic magazines.

The judge takes his place on the back of his chair, fanning his wings several times to shake off the raindrops on his tail feathers. The clerk leaves the cart by the judge's bench. A moment later, the jurors enter, a noisy pack of crows; several clutch fresh five-gourde notes in their beaks. Each juror has a scarlet claw, having dipped it in dye in exchange for the gourdes.

The defense lawyer enters from the right. He is an old man, very black, with a thin crown of hair. He suffers from arthritis as well as eczema; his suit is covered with dandruff. He is carrying a bulging briefcase full of dusty newspapers.

JUDGE (snapping)

Hurry up, Counselor. We've been waiting for you for thirty-one, thirty-two, ah—finally—thirty-three seconds. Did you forget I have a regular luncheon date at the palace?

LAWYER

Pardon me, your honor. (*He opens the briefcase and pulls a brown bag with oranges out of it.*)

JUDGE

What's that you have there?

LAWYER

Oranges, your honor. I bought them from those young women over there. (*He points to the vendors, who are napping.*)

JUDGE

No oranges in my courtroom. No, sir. Every market is a den of thieves; the juice of that fruit may carry the poison that killed the son of Joseph Jolibois. That is why the sons of Trujillo continue to make war on us. Clerk, take those oranges to the kitchen!

(*The blind clerk feels his way along the banister to where the lawyer sits, and accepts the bag of oranges. He stumbles to the kitchen, stepping into an occasional puddle and clutching a giant column for support.*)

JUDGE

You have your first warning, Counselor. We'll have no disruption of our proceedings this morning.

(*The jurors titter. Many are well-dressed female crows with light brown and mahogany feathers. They crane their necks to examine the attorney. All of the jurors are new; the original jurors have long retired; most live in Florida. At least one of the female jurors is hoping to curry favor with the judge and become his mistress and eventually have her own house in Miami.*)

JURORS (*gossiping and looking at the lawyer*)

Doesn't he look terrible? He looks like his own great-grandfather.

I read somewhere that his great-grandfather wet his bed. Runs in the family, they say.

(*Several jurors fly to the ceiling to discreetly glance at the lawyer's crotch.*)

I can't see anything. But look how he's gone to seed. His pants are stained with berry juice. You can see he must have been handsome. But he's the opposite of his great-grandfather; that man had presence. This one looks more like a scarecrow abandoned in the field . . .

OTHER JURORS (*crying out in panic*)
Scarecrow! What? Where?

JUDGE (*pounding his gavel*)
Order! Order! Mesdames et messieurs, please! I understand your impatience. We're all very excited about this afternoon's game of canasta. Don't forget (*he flutters his wings*), I'm the defending champion.

JURORS (*clapping their wings*)
Bravo! Bravo!
(*The jurors like a judge with a firm hand. As they applaud, the blind clerk returns to stand by the judge's chair. The lawyer remains attentive. This is the third time in these last forty years he has appeared before the court; he wants it to be his last. He straightens the creased collar of his white shirt with a thumb he's just licked, and removes the remaining contents of his briefcase.*)

JUDGE
Clerk? What are we doing today?

CLERK
The court is now in session. Today's case is that of L'Espérance Fini versus the Government of Haiti.

JUDGE (*interrupting*)
Fini? I thought that poor unfortunate woman died. Poisoned, if my memory is right, which it always is even when it isn't. I remember the poor unfortunate—a thief, wasn't she?

LAWYER (*rising to protest*)
Not a thief, your honor. Please permit me to state the facts of the case. It is true the accused passed away, but her family has hired me as counsel in absentia on the grounds that the spirit of my client has informed them she will not rest in peace until her name has been cleared.

JUDGE

Highly unusual, highly unusual, but go on, Counselor.

LAWYER

Your honor, the family of L'Espérance Fini seeks compensation for damages. Since the honor of the accused, my client, has been ruined, no one will hire the other members of the family. I will remind you, my client was imprisoned on the basis of false accusations made by her employer, the Government of Haiti.

JUDGE

Come, come, Counselor. The Government of Haiti never falsely accuses anyone of a crime. If a theft is committed, there is a culprit. The accused was a thief, was she not?

LAWYER

No, your honor. That is precisely the accusation leveled against her.

JUDGE

Don't lecture me, Counselor. If there are any relevant facts, I know them. If I don't know them, they are not relevant.

LAWYER

Your honor, my client—the deceased L'Espérance Fini—died in prison due to malnourishment. She was confined for thirty-eight years awaiting trial.

JUDGE

Clerk! Note that the counselor for the accused has indirectly charged the Government of Haiti with the illegal detainment of his client. Counselor, I don't have to remind a lawyer of your experience not to identify too closely with a client's interests. Besides, I remember speaking to that poor unfortunate thief myself. Are you doubting my memory?

LAWYER

Excuse me, your honor, but the incident you are referring to was a chance meeting you had with my client in the market before she was hired to work for the Minister of Recreation. The record will show you asked her if she knew how to prepare a spicy cucumber salad.

JUDGE

That's right! And I could tell from her knowledge about cucumbers that she was capable of making a konkonm zombi, a zombie cucumber, a deadly meal. Why did the Minister of Recreation—who happens to be my second cousin—accuse your client of suspicious acts? Because she was a superb cook. And every Haitian knows that a good cook is dangerous. A good cook seeking revenge can mask evil ingredients inside a sweet cake. Prosecutor, the defense has spoken. Have you anything to say that might contradict what the counselor has presented? You do? Come forward, then, we don't have all day. Clerk, have you tested those oranges yet? Hurry up, everybody. They are serving salmon at the palace today and it's my favorite fish.

BLACKOUT

Gerard grinned, slipped out the page, and quickly reread it. He felt sublime. Across the mountain, the sun was dropping; it bathed the trees with a warm glow. His legs were chilled. Noting the lateness of the hour, he arranged the pages in a neat pile, closed the type-writer in its case, and carried them inside, shuffling like an inva-lid with the blanket still wrapped around his waist. He left several five-gourde notes on the bed for the caretaker, using the empty Schweppes bottle as a paperweight.

Geneviève Clovis was crouching outside the entrance of her house, washing small, dark green watercress leaves. Gerard re-minded her about the need to vaccinate the children and boil the water from the stream. She in turn offered him fresh, uncooked corn to take home. The children asked him what was in the box. A radio? A television?

He described a special machine with keys that jumped up and down and had letters that could spell their names. In the face of their skepticism, he put the typewriter down, put a piece of paper in, typed "Roosevelt and Ernest Clovis," and gave it to them to keep. "Bonswa, Madanm Clovis." He shook her hand. "Kenbe fem." Hang in there.

It was too late to stop and talk to Dr. Sylvie; the light was falling quickly. He drove carefully, smiling with contentment all the while. Near Pétionville, a car flashed its lights, the driver signaling Gerard to stop.

"An inspection," the young man warned. "About a kilometer down the road."

"Thanks." Gerard waved. He removed his driver's license and attorney's card from his wallet and put them in his pocket, then slipped the wallet and the play, along with the corn, under the passenger seat. At the roadblock, he handed a policeman his license and the other card. They were passed around and closely scrutinized, then handed back. A lanky youth with long sideburns and a whisper of a beard leaned past Gerard into the car. He ordered him to turn off the engine and open the glove compartment. Gerard complied; there was only a lighter and several pens.

Gerard smiled. "It's cool tonight, isn't it?" he said, making small talk. The men ignored him.

"We're looking for some thieves," the first policeman informed him at last. "You wouldn't know anything about that, would you?"

He was short, with a gun tucked into his belt instead of a holster, and he wore a yellow undershirt instead of the regulation white under his uniform.

They were stalling, hoping for a bribe.

"I'm sorry," Gerard said, more casually than he felt, "I've been in my house all day. Today is a feast day, you know. I'm religious. I didn't go out."

The short man looked at his partners, unsure of what to do next.

Gerard started up the car while they quietly debated. "Well, if that's all," he said, "I'll go now. Good luck," he added a moment later, pressing gently on the accelerator. They let him proceed.

He never looked back, avoided even the chance of catching their eyes in the rearview mirror. But he could feel them staring after him. At the bottom of the next curve, he relaxed, exhaling a long-held breath. The bullets that had been directed at him, that had pierced the back window and lodged between his shoulder blades, were already disappearing, slipping into that region of his brain where his subterranean fears lay. It had been a routine inspection, nothing more.

FROM: Leslie Doyle
TO: Rich, Pamela, Toni
DATE: Sept. 6   NO. OF PAGES: 1

PARTIAL LIST OF REPORTED ARRESTED STUDENTS
(Source, G. Metellus; Assoc. Dwa Moun Ayisyen)
(* for all names not on Aug. 15 list)
(** for incomplete/partial names)
Ronald Bien-Aimé
Fleur Jean-Baptiste
Serge Louis
Daniel Desrosiers*
Marie-France Desrosiers* (rumored dead/possible suicide)
Isidore Scot
Beatrice Songe (Songer)**
Ignace Fritz (possibly released)
Jean Ulrick*
Yviese César*
Marie César*
Chavanne Grapman
Thérèse Margaret Wilson (or Margaret Wilson and Thérèse)*
Rudolph* (no surname given)
Ti Momo* (no surname—probably nickname)
   GM also said that three women were raped during/prior/after arrest by
arresting soldiers and paramilitary militia: Yviese César, 17, and her sister,
Marie César, 16, and Marie-France Desrosiers, 20. No medical exami-
nation for confirmation, but eyewitnesses Jean Ulrick and Daniel Des-
rosiers (brother of M.F.D.) were forced to watch rape of Marie-France at
gunpoint. They say Marie-France was severely beaten with a whip ("ri-
gousasse") and with a metal bar ("crosse au fer"). Please pass this info. to
AI immediately and suggest urgent action. Cables to 28379 Ministry of

Justice (attn: Minister William Beaufort) and 22006 National Penitentiary (attn: Warden Vilvert Lamartin).

Also: GM's names come from several students who are now in the provinces. We are sending someone to try to get testimonies on tape, but this will be difficult. According to testimonies, any student who openly supports national strike is under threat, although authorities deny this. In several cities in the north (Port Margot, Limbé, Fort Liberté) students were beaten by individuals on order of the police and given death threats if they backed labor organization or called for a boycott of school classes next week. Students say there were spies at student meetings who attempted to disrupt. Also at August 6 demonstration in Les Cayes, police had paid individuals to disrupt and throw stones. One police vehicle was seen leaving the scene of a demonstration with a burlap bag of stones. GM not yet able to determine status of anyone inside National Penitentiary. I am hoping to gain entrance. Making a request via several channels: human rights groups (Assoc. Dwa Moun Ayisyen), Ministry of Justice, and American embassy. No response from anyone so far. Will keep you updated.

PS: Pierre Lescot unable to serve as guide. He was beaten after assisting Canadian Mission earlier this year. I am hiring Clemard Rameau as interim interpreter/driver at suggestion of GM.

PPS: Any mention of above in U.S. newspapers? Nothing here that I can find. Please clip and fax back if possible. Will expect your call at 24133. —Leslie

17

The first girl was pushed inside by a fat guard, who yelled at her. Elyse hung back; she noticed the girl's puffy face, the dark bloodstain on her light blue uniform. Against the wall to her left, Luz held her crucifix to her throat, muttering something.

The students were young, some thirteen or fourteen years old, and they were terrified. The guards forced them to the ground, holding rifles against their backs, mocking and cursing them. "Ti moun Kominis!" Communist kids! "Nou pa janm lage yo!" We'll never let you out!

Two of the girls sobbed. Another gathered her dress, which was ripped in half in the back, vainly trying to cover herself. Elyse moved toward the wall, away from the guards, trying to make herself invisible. She watched as the guards pulled the girl's hair, pushed her breasts, prodded her with the rifles.

"Pas un mot!" the big guard warned them in French. Not a word! "Sinon!" Or else! He held a whip in his hands, seven short lengths of rope fixed to a wooden handle. Elyse caught Luz's eye; they both looked down. The fat guard added, leaning his bulk close to the girl with the bloodstained dress: "I said stop it." But she could not stop crying. She kept her arms crossed over her head, her fingers laced together. All of the students had been shaved; they looked like ducks to Elyse. She involuntarily pulled on her hair, and kept her eyes to the concrete.

A tall, thin guard with long sideburns looked at the girl on the ground as if she were an insect. His boot almost touched her nose.

The girl looked up. Elyse saw the boot move, heard a cry, and saw the body bend in two as the guard kicked her again. All the while his eyes were on Elyse and Luz, daring them to move. Elyse wanted to close her eyes, to cover her ears. Rete! She silently begged the man. Stop! You'll kill her!

She felt the rush of a breeze. It was Luz, hurling herself on top of the girl, swearing in Spanish as the guard tried to pull her off. He struck Luz with the butt of his gun. The other guard came by, holding his whip, waiting. Then it came down with a crack on Luz's leg. She screamed. But he had not struck her, he had hit only the ground. Luz and the girl clutched each other, Luz trying to protect her face from the whip. Get her out of here! the man ordered his subordinate. Go on! Luz got up, the tall guard behind her. The fracas had drawn the attention of the other guards, who gathered at the cellblock entrance. They parted to let Luz through, but not before laughing, pinching, fondling her. Elyse wanted to cry out.

The stones around the edges of the room are crumbling. Elyse licks her fingers, touching the wall. She tastes the salt that hangs heavily in the air. She continues her sea voyage, the one she plays over and over in her mind, analyzing the dream for clues. She is certain there is something important in the dream. Why else would she hear it, the sound of lapping water, the tide of the bay, at some point in the night?

There are signs and meanings in everything, Grann has told her, in every action, in every object. She hears an old woman inside the wall, a baka, a dream image, a spirit that speaks to her, revealing messages. The wife of Agwe T'Royo, Met Dlo, the Master of Waters. A spirit she has not encountered before, the divine Metres, Mistress of Waters, who speaks to her in a familiar tongue, in Grann's voice.

The wife of Agwe T'Royo, the Queen of the kingdom of Agwe T'Royo, speaks from inside the wall; Elyse closes her ears to all other sounds. The spirit travels like a night creature, silent and furtive, borne by the wind and the rain.

She is not surprised to discover she is Metres Agwe T'Royo. The Mistress of Waters knows something important about what will occur. Is this a vision of her own future or the future of the world without Elyse? Look, Metres Agwe commands, listen. The river is here. Elyse feels the wall, feels the dampness, tastes lime and mineral and dirt and fish, the smell of the mud lining the banks of the river.

Every dream is a message, every object has a spirit. Every action has meaning and is preceded and followed by action. She listens to Grann, watches her tie sticks and herbs together, slide them into a bottle, then melt a seal of wax, create an altar. Grann explains to her the families and the saints: petwo, rada, ogun, ezili, sen jak maje. Metres Agwe speaks to her in Grann's voice because Grann understands the prophecies. Grann saw Mami's hair on fire a week before the fever came to kill her. Grann saw water pouring from Mami's legs, knew that Elyse would survive the birth. Grann knows

*the lwas, their natures, what pleases and angers them. Grann speaks
to her from a warm place in the wall, in the voice of the Princess
of Rivers, Metres Agwe.*

*Grann's face appears before her, a soft smile, somber eyes, hands
gently braiding Elyse's hair. Grann making a joke. Grann as a little
girl, laughing. Grann behind the wall, comforting her. Metres
Agwe, Grann's emissary, offering protection, to help Elyse make
the journey. Elyse shuts her eyes hard, concentrating on the sound
of wind, rain, night, dampness, stillness. The bay, the silent tide.
Grann's voice like light flowing through the bones of her fingers
into her blood; making her muscles tingle, the heat spreading
through her body. Grann inside her.*

*Elyse hears something. Birds. Music. A sound like insects in the
grass. Far away. Her fingers pulsate, thickening with blood, sen-
sation. The sound of tin horns and drums and bells like the sound
of glass against glass in the wind, the breeze an undertone encom-
passing all sounds within it. There is a clear place in a valley. A
band approaches along a stream. Elyse understands. The stream
will lead to the city of the dead, will flow into the street and blend
with the red rain, the flood that will carry her family away. But
why? And when?*

*She hears the high, thin notes of the tin horns above the sound
of drums. The parade laughs, jokes, as it moves. Pairs of feet glide
along the wet grass, like a slow-moving train, stopping often. Men
and women clap, slap their hands against their legs, snap their
fingers. A wet sound, the slap of flesh, sharp snapping like a pea
pod broken, the sound of legs stomping the ground, marking the
place, sliding forward again.*

*They advance slowly. Elyse feels her heart reverberating, two
heartbeats instead of one—hers and Grann's—in sync with the
rhythm of the drums. The heat in her hands burns, a wet heat
between the cracks of her fingers. Here they come. Metres Agwe's
voice is a dense whisper riding in on the edge of the wind, cutting
through all sound.*

*"Met, Lafrik Ginen se pwoteksyon . . . nou ap maide, se dlo ki
pote la vi, pwoteksyon . . . Met, dlo pou tout pitit li . . ." Master,
Africa Guinée is our protection . . . you can help us . . . water*

brings us life, protection . . . Master, water for all your children . . .

The dancers are youths dressed in school uniforms—sharply creased pants and skirts, white shirts with religious insignia on the pockets. The girls have neckerchiefs, the boys long ties. They wear black penny loafers with silver coins slipped into the flaps. Look, whispers the Queen, laughing. Grann laughs, escorting little Elyse to school.

The students sing: "Se gran Met ki pase avan nou, tou le sen, le mo, Marassas, Lafrik Ginen. Se yo ki fe, li defe . . ." The great Master comes before us, all the saints, the dead, Marassas, Africa Guinée. It is he who creates, he who destroys. Elyse sings along, "Se gran Met ki pase avan nou."

Push, stop, push, jump. The students break into two groups, boys and girls apart. They mime the sex act, arch their long backs, thrust their pelvises, move ecstatically. Grinding, arching, sliding, stomping, paying respect to the Creator. The girls grab their breasts, grab the sky, grab each other, grab hair, face, leg, stomach. The men penetrate the ground, the trees, one another. It is Carnival. A voice laughs. Grann is laughing.

The youths sing a new song. She hears Grann's voice singing along, high and thin, off-key. "Goldanbe . . . le fanm masay . . . le fanm tombe sou mwen . . . oh ho ho ou wo! Oh ho ho ou wo . . . ! Goldanbe . . . le fanm masay . . ." Goldanbe . . . the women are relaxed . . . the women fall on top of me . . . oh ho ho oh wo! Elyse holds herself, one hand between her legs, the other against the wall, waiting for the parade to pass close to this spot. Don't wait, Grann's voice tells her.

The heat leaves her wet with sweat. Her heels strike the soft ground. She thrusts her pelvis against Ignatius, his hips and stomach, grabs his wide, strong back. She is making his baby. The clouds in the sky spin. The dancers spin, then hop, kick, charge. Animals, frogs, asses, bulls.

Elyse is a chicken, pecking at corn, running on short legs across a field of dirt. She rejoices at the music, at the movement, at the feeling of sweat and spent passion. "Goldanbe . . . le fanm masay . . . le fanm tombe sou mwen!" Her fingernails are dirty from scratching at the ground, caked in mud.

Women come to join the parade, market women, carrying baskets with things to sell. A large, mustachioed woman smiles, picks a shiny pot, shakes it. She leads the band. Elyse listens to the giant, percussive sound of pots, metal cups, wooden spoons, plastic tubs. The women drum furiously, stopping to thank the sky, bowing to the spirits. Elyse drums against the wall, keeping time with the maman drums, three steel drums painted yellow, blue, and green: sun, sea, and earth. "Goldanbe . . . le fanm masay . . . le fanm tombe sou mwen . . . Oh ho ho ou wo! Oh ho ho ou wo!"

Grann's thin, strong arms inside her hold a basket aloft. Elyse dances with the market women, the base of her basket is the center of the universe. She spins like a planet.

The dusty path curves. There is a town ahead, a small city. The buildings are decorated with tin stars and plastic flags of all colors: Pepsi, Schweppes, Maggi . . . All of the products sold in the market are celebrated. More people rush to join the procession. Old men hang on to the waists of children; pregnant women rub their stomachs one against the other. The students have become long caterpillars, snakes, and they slide through the crowd.

The beat changes. Silence. The crowd becomes melancholy, sober, reflective, respectful. Heads and eyes are bowed. Elyse bows too. The first notes of the national anthem are trumpeted, a lingering, plaintive, cutting sound. A thousand arms are raised. Elyse raises her arms to the skies. The gods are revered, their power is supreme. The crowd roars its approval. The dancing begins again.

"Ayiti . . . pov ti cheri . . ." Haiti . . . poor little dear . . . The steel drums drive the rhythm. Elyse is carried along by the crowd, pulled by its centrifugal force toward the center of the town. Another cry erupts above the crowd; she cries too. Five giant papier-mâché pigs are dancing her way, drinking rum, carrying black parasols.

Is this a funeral procession? Elyse asks the queen, Metres Agwe. My funeral?

Dancing figures perch everywhere along the low wall of this wide street. Their costumes are colored dots, running together. Elyse feels a raindrop, then another. A shadow rushes toward her, a mud creature, a zombie covered head to foot in grayish mud, eyelids upturned. Then another, a procession of zombies tapping spoons against glass bottles, shaking handbells. *Death dances,* Elyse whispers to *Metres Agwe, death sings.*

"*Jodi danse . . . demen mouri . . . se pou sa nou bezwen kouri!*" *Today we dance . . . tomorrow we die . . . that's the reason why we run!* Zombies dancing with pigs, pregnant women suckling old men. The market women salute the spirits, blessing those nearby with fistfuls of rum. It is dusk. A great sun bathes the street. The rain is merely a pink mist, warm on Elyse's back.

A small girl with Grann's voice takes her by the hand. It is *Metres Agwe. Lift me up,* she commands. The child has no weight. She is air itself, her hair as light as straw. *Metres Agwe,* an angel. *Over there,* she tells Elyse.

A crooked ladder made of odd lengths of wood leans against a building. The procession moves past her, shakes the ladder. *Climb up,* the Queen insists. *Metres Agwe's* arms are like a monkey's, long and fluid, pulling them both up. *In here.*

The windows of the factory are broken. Rows of identical tables are stacked with spools of thread and leather strips. Elyse hears a siren. The workers file in, teenage girls, some carrying infants on their backs in slings. The child pulls her into another room. A mountain rises from the floor, a giant pile of leather tongues, heels, soles, all the parts of the black penny loafers of the students. The procession moves past them outside the factory. Drums boom, pots and bottles clang; the workers move their foot pedals, keeping time to the rhythm. "*Jodi travay, demen danse, jodi mouri . . .*" *Today we work, tomorrow we dance, today we die.*

The angel-child, *Metres Agwe,* leads her through a maze of corridors. The walls are filthy, the floor caked with garbage. Elyse smells sulfur on her fingertips. Children stack baseballs into a pyramid. The baseballs are shiny, and the pyramid, a temple. *Enter,* the Queen of the Waters commands. Elyse steps into a dark chamber. The smell in her nostrils is thick and sacred, myrrh and incense.

The walls of the temple are studded with fragments of mirrors and colored glass, beads and multihued feathers. On one wall is a painting of a waterfall baptizing the Apostles, a rose in each of their cleaved hearts. Christ hovers above them, his body spiraling down the cross. Above him, a giant, divine eye, the hazel color of the child's eye, Metres Agwe, the same color as Grann's.

A cold current blows into the factory, extinguishing the candles inside the temple. The factory is dark. The siren sounds again. The workers are leaving. Elyse enters another corridor, climbs a staircase. She stands on the balcony, the balcony where she will watch the rain come, then the flood.

"Mwen te ale nan simitye Sen Jak pou-l cheche ma tifi . . . mwen te soti nan simitye Sen Jak pou-l cheche ma tifi . . . Sen Jak pa la . . . Sen Jak pa la . . . se mwen ki la. . . ." I went to the cemetery, St. Jacques, to find my little girl. I went to the cemetery, St. Jacques, to find my little girl. St. Jacques was not there. St. Jacques was not there . . . It's just me. . . .

Elyse is singing. She holds her head between her legs, rocking. She shivers, feverish. The rain falls through cracks, onto her head. Luz has not come back, Luz may never come back. But Grann is with her. Grann holds her, rocks her. Grann and the spirits will guide her.

18

"Oh! Père Emmanuel? C'est toi?"

"Jeanne. Bonjour."

Emmanuel warmly embraced Gerard's wife in the aisle of the supermarket. He looked down at her shopping cart. It was filled with cans of evaporated milk and instant coffee. "Are you making a flan?" he asked.

"No, I'm bringing these to the school. The students have decided to keep a vigil there. To protest the arrests."

He nodded. "I went by there this morning. There were about a dozen of them. And several soldiers across the street. So far the police haven't said anything. But they're making threats. Ça chauffe," he added. It's heating up.

"They're more courageous than I was at that age," said Jeanne. "At the Lycée Ste. Anne we once talked about protesting like that. But it was right before the final exams. We would have had to repeat a whole year and we couldn't risk it. That was our logic. But it was really fear." She noticed that one can of evaporated milk was dented and put it back in the wrong place.

He smiled. "They aren't afraid, that's true. Even though I tell them fear can be useful at times. I think they've simply seen too much. They won't accept it anymore." He inspected the items closely, looking for their expiration dates.

"I won't take anything over six months on the shelf," she informed him. "Because it means it's been in the warehouse even longer than that." They moved farther into the store. "Will you be attending the vigil?" Jeanne asked. "I'm heading there after this."

"I'll go later, to pray with them. And I want to ask some women in my parish to prepare an evening meal to take over." He lowered his voice. "By the way, what's the Minister of Education saying about this now? I heard he's changed his mind again and plans to punish those who boycott classes the day of the strike."

She shrugged her shoulders. "The man is a worm. He has no spine. He'll never confront the army. He won't even meet with the parents of the students. A group of them went to the prison to try to speak with the warden. The guards refused to let them in. We still don't know how they've been treated."

The supermarket was packed. It was small, and stocked with mostly imported goods. Emmanuel only shopped here for items unavailable in the local markets. He held up a box marked Pop-Tarts. "Have you ever had these?" he asked Jeanne. "Would I like them?"

"They're like a dessert, but they eat them for breakfast in America. It's pure glucose," she added.

The priest set the box down. "Gerard passed by yesterday morning. Thank you for giving him my message."

"He told me," she said. "He also said you were planning to protest Bishop Privat's nomination." She grinned. "I'd sign that petition."

"We're not at that stage yet," he said. "But I'm glad to hear it. We'll need signatures from a lot of groups to make it less dangerous for anyone who signs. Fortunately, Privat has a lot of enemies."

"They're planning a whole day of television coverage of the nomination," she informed him. "People are upset, though, because they won't be able to watch *Dallas*."

"*Dallas*? What's that? American football?"

"The television series." She laughed. "Soap opera."

"Ah, yes." He smiled. "An oil story."

They passed a couple standing near the entrance: "Bonjour, Père. Bonswa, Pe Emmanuel. Sak pase, Pe?" Good day, Father. What's happening, Father?

"You're so popular, you should be the archbishop," Jeanne mused. "I can see why you never shop here. It must take you hours."

In the next aisle, an elderly mulatto man was pricing jars of manba, the local spicy peanut butter. "I'm looking for saccharin—for my mother," Emmanuel told Jeanne. "Do you know where they put it?"

"Over here," she indicated. "There are these little yellow packets. Or else right here, the bottle. You put in three or four drops. I prefer the bottle. It's easier to measure. The packets are too sweet."

Emmanuel unscrewed the little plastic top and turned it over, dropping the liquid onto his finger to taste it. "Awful," he agreed with her. "Too sweet."

"And cancerous," she added. "Which reminds me, I was talking to Bertrand the other night at the American Club cocktail party. He said Marie's condition has deteriorated, even though she's supposed to be in remission. She doesn't eat, so naturally he's very worried."

"I spoke with him last week," Emmanuel replied. "He said he was thinking of hiring a nurse to stay with her during the day. I think it's a good idea."

"Why doesn't he take her to Miami?" Jeanne shook her head, frustrated. "She'd find a better doctor there. I told him so."

"I don't think Bertrand is really opposed, although he mentioned his concern about their business. He's convinced his stores will be targeted if the strike becomes violent. The last time, they broke the windows of two stores on the Rue des Miracles. Marie is the one who insists on staying here. She doesn't think it's necessary to go elsewhere. If you want my opinion, I think she senses it's terminal at this point and wants to be home with her family. My uncle went through the same thing."

"It's so awful . . . the worst part is not being able to do anything." Jeanne grimaced. "Even though I have my difficulties with Bertrand, I don't like to see him like this. He feels absolutely helpless. It's hard to imagine how he'll go on without her—they've been married for over thirty years. She's his emotional anchor."

"Marie's an admirable woman," Emmanuel agreed. "They both need to be given a lot of support. That's all we can do. She's very religious and I think that reassures her."

The store was crowded. Emmanuel edged Jeanne over to one side to let the elderly mulatto man pass, clutching three jars of manba. "I have something private to ask you," the priest murmured, "after we go outside."

It took five minutes to pay for the goods. The cashier at the register punched a pocket-size calculator, converting dollars into gourdes, accepting both currencies. She held up the clear, tear-shaped bottle of substitute sugar. "Is it for you?" she asked Emmanuel, her expression doubtful.

"Yes. Well, no." He laughed. "For my mother."

The other customers smiled. Jeanne, who had paid and was waiting by the exit, observed the exchange. Emmanuel was the only priest she had ever known who wore tennis shoes. Today he looked like an overgrown child, his black pants and short-sleeved white shirt hanging loosely over his bony frame. As they departed, the cashier said aloud to the others in line, "He takes that artificial sugar for his mother, but you can see he doesn't like to eat. He's too skinny."

Jeanne poked him in the ribs. He grinned. "My mother would agree. She always says I'm not her child, because I won't eat her cakes. But I don't have an appetite for sweets."

"I wish I could say the same. I love everything that's sweet, especially chocolate. When I was little, my favorite lunch was a chocolate sandwich."

She rummaged through her handbag for her lipstick as they stood near her car. "So—you have something to ask me?"

He considered his words. "Gerard said you might know . . . It's not an important matter, but something I've been curious about. Although I generally try to refrain from this kind of gossip."

"I'm intrigued," she said. "But what makes Gerard think I would know? He's the real gossip. He's the one who ordered cable so we could watch *Dallas*."

She carefully applied the lipstick, then leaned to inspect her mouth in the side mirror of a car. If I had a wife, she would do that, Emmanuel thought absently. A truck went by, loudly honking its horn. "It's related to something someone told me," he added, holding her bag of groceries. "I thought you might have heard it too."

Jeanne waited.

"It's about an operation that a doctor—Dr. Frances—is alleged to have performed. Would you know anything about it?"

She kissed the back of her hand, then inspected the imprint of her lips. "How is it?" she asked him, smiling. "Okay?"

"Perfect."

"I know what you're talking about." She put the lipstick away. "General Lucerne's daughter. I heard about it the other day. But it was over a year ago, wasn't it? I heard she took a pill or something to lose the baby, but there was an accident. The mother wanted to take the girl to the hospital but Lucerne refused. So Dr. Frances did the operation in their home. I also heard the general ordered the doctor to sew his daughter up, so that, you know, she would appear to be a virgin." Jeanne shook her head, incredulous. "Unbelievable, no? To treat your own daughter that way! Why do you ask? Does it shock you?"

"The abortion? No, not at all. No, it's something else."

"They say Dr. Frances has been doing operations like that for years," Jeanne said. "He charges five thousand dollars. But I don't know anyone who's had one, aside from Lucerne's child."

"I also heard something to that effect," Emmanuel offered. He didn't tell her what Dr. Sylvie had told him, which was that Dr. Frances had recently operated on a young woman without anesthesia. Her screams had woken the neighbors.

"It's better than what they sell." Jeanne pointed to the vendors. "You swallow their tea and it kills everything inside, not only the embryo."

He put the groceries in the back of her car. "How is Gerard?" he asked. "He seems a little depressed to me. Is he all right?"

"Did he say something to you?" Jeanne rolled down the window, turned on the engine, let it idle. Emmanuel leaned on the door.

"Not really. It's just my observation."

Jeanne sighed, put her hand on his. He could see the issue had been bothering her.

"My husband works too hard. He doesn't know how to relax. Of course, Haiti is not relaxing. But he takes everything very personally. That's the problem. The news about Ti Cedric has affected him, I can tell. He doesn't like to talk about it, though. What did you discuss?"

He shrugged. "The situation in general." He added, smiling: "That's all we ever talk about. Did he tell you I saw Père Sansaricq?"

"He did. What horrible news."

Emmanuel drummed his fingers on the roof of the car. "The situation is deteriorating. It's obvious. We have to stop it. If we don't get rid of the remaining Duvalierists in the cabinet, we're doomed. There will be more attacks like the one against Père Sansaricq before they'll allow any election. Mark my words."

"I don't disagree with you," she said. "I can see it in the rising level of crime and anarchy; they're letting everything fall apart. But I find it hard to judge who's really behind it. Is it the army or are the criminals taking advantage of the situation? It's hard to say."

"The army is in disarray." Emmanuel stepped away from the car. "But ultimately, they're still in charge. What you have is a lot of cliques fighting for power, and they're all abusing the situation. They knock on someone's door and demand their television set. It's incredible. A total absence of government. Or else they see someone committing a crime and they do nothing. That way they can claim it's not political violence."

They were silent; Jeanne adjusted her rearview mirror. "Speaking of gossip," she said a moment later, "I heard a little rumor yesterday. They say Duvalier still calls all over town. Do you think he'll try to come back?"

"They'd lynch him," Emmanuel said. "He wouldn't get past the airport. But I don't doubt he calls. The thing about Jean-Claude is that his power was the palace, and his fortune. Now that he's gone and they're freezing his money, he's lost his power. There's nothing stopping the generals from making their fortunes—they don't need him."

Jeanne put the car in reverse. "I should be going. But I'd appreciate it if you talked to Gerard. He listens to you. I really want him to take a vacation. He says he can't leave right now, but I tell him there will never be a good time to leave. It's always going to be a risk. Would you talk to him?"

"Only if I can take a vacation too," he joked. "We should all take one together. Or better, the rest of the country should take a vacation and leave us here to run things. I like that idea."

Emmanuel always amused her. "Where would you go if you could take a vacation?"

He had to think about it. "Oh, maybe, let's see, Texas. I'd like a pair of cowboy boots. And you said Gerard likes *Dallas*."

"Perfect." She laughed. "I'm ready anytime."

They both knew it was a fantasy. The last time Emmanuel had left Haiti, he had been detained an hour at the airport before being allowed back in. To a lesser extent, Gerard shared the same risk.

"Speaking of America," Emmanuel added, "I spoke with Gerard's friend Leslie Doyle. She's going to come by the parish this week."

"We were with her at the cocktail party," Jeanne said.

"How is she?"

"Very nice." Jeanne smiled. "Different from what I expected."

He arched an eyebrow. "How so?"

She deliberated, screwing up her face. "Less . . . less . . . I don't know . . . less American. You know what I mean? She's not at all arrogant. And she was very kind to Gerard when he visited Washington. What do you think?"

"I don't really have an opinion," he replied honestly. "She seems informed. That's in itself something."

Jeanne laughed. "You don't love Americans either, do you? Oh, I forgot—you only adore God. Right?" He chuckled.

"Will you thank Gerard for the fax he brought me? I wasn't at the parish when he stopped by."

"I'll tell him," she promised.

The orange vendor hovered nearby. She rushed quickly forward with her basket.

"I'll take ten," Jeanne said, dropping the greenish oranges into the back seat. "For the students." She asked Emmanuel, "What time is the service?"

"Around six."

"Your mother's right, you know," she said, handing the woman a worn bill. "You don't eat enough. Look at Gerard. He's put on three kilos this month; he looks much better." She reached into the back seat, tossed him an orange. "Have a little natural sugar."

He caught it awkwardly with his left hand. The other held the saccharin. He put them together in a position of prayer. "Be careful, Jeanne," he said seriously. "If anything happens, call me. I'll be near the phone all afternoon."

19

Leslie felt apprehensive as Clemard passed a convoy of three military trucks heading for the central prison. The hospital was located just beyond on the Rue Monseigneur Guilloux, as if the original city planners had known that the distance between these two buildings would somehow be slight to many citizens in the years to come.

At the intersection, they avoided the stares of the guards holding submachine guns. The prison's small, barred windows were too high to peer into, but also impossible to ignore. Leslie wondered if any of them housed Cedric George or Elyse Voltaire. She had spoken to Père Emmanuel about the woman's case the previous evening. A source he would not divulge had confirmed her arrest. There were no other details. The priest had sent a contact to find the woman's family. She was being held without charges; so far, Gerard had been unsuccessful in his attempts to see her.

She had reviewed all the names on her list, narrowing it down to fifteen. There were thirteen men and two women who had recently disappeared in the zones nearest to the capital. She hoped Dr. Sylvie would be able to tell her more.

Clemard parked the car across from the hospital. A young man in khakis at the entrance gate directed them toward the reception area, but did not ask for any identity papers. They walked toward the end of a dimly lit hallway; several older women surveyed them as they entered the reception area. Leslie spoke quietly, "We have an appointment with Dr. Sylvie."

"You can wait in the courtyard," the receptionist said, after finding her name in the appointment book. "Is he with you?" She pointed to Clemard, who had taken off his sunglasses. "He'll have to sign in too."

She looked at Clemard suspiciously, then gave him a pen. Clemard's signature was regal, and he included his middle name: Simeon. Clemard Simeon Rameau, with a flourish to his capital letters. He caught Leslie looking over his shoulder.

The other women moved their legs to let them pass. They had

to wait outside; Leslie took a seat on a small wooden bench. Clemard remained standing. He lit a cigarette and offered her one, which she declined. She was trying to limit her smoking. Clemard smoked impatiently; he seemed more nervous than on the day of their visit to Titanyen.

They heard voices in the hallway behind them, someone asking who the strangers outside were. The receptionist's voice answered: An American. Leslie smiled at Clemard. "Don't worry," she reassured him.

"I've never seen the inside of the hospital, only the outside," Clemard said a few minutes later, finally deciding to sit beside her. Dr. Sylvie was late. "Are we going to be able to see the SIDA patients?" he asked.

Leslie nodded. She had mentioned the possibility earlier in the week. Someone had left a pamphlet on breast feeding on the bench; she scanned it.

"The 'piquers' caused the SIDA," Clemard remarked, reading over her shoulder. Leslie looked up; he was so talkative this morning. "They're parasites," he added. "They give you five gourdes for one like this." Clemard put his thumb and finger together. "One tube."

"I thought they closed the blood banks," Leslie replied, putting aside the pamphlet. "It was a big scandal, wasn't it?"

"A big scandal." He agreed. "But they still do it, except not openly. People sell their blood two, three times a week—as much as they can tolerate."

"Have you ever donated blood?" She immediately regretted asking the question. He might think she was inquiring about his risk for AIDS. She quickly added, "I've given blood a few times."

"Only when I was a boy. They would come to the schools. But they didn't pay us. And we didn't really have a choice. It was the patriotic thing to do."

She was about to ask him more about the practice when a mulatto woman appeared across the courtyard, waving. It was Dr. Sylvie. She was an attractive woman in her mid-thirties. Leslie was surprised to see she wore rather high-heeled black pumps and a bright flowered dress under the white lab coat. The only other concession to her trade was a stethoscope hanging around her neck. Her lipstick was mauve, a shade Leslie could never wear, it would make her mortuary.

"Hello." Dr. Sylvie greeted them warmly in English. "I'm sorry to keep you waiting." Her handshake was firm. "Bonjour, Clemard," she added, shaking his hand too.

Clemard smiled broadly. "Bonswa."

They followed her across the courtyard in the direction she had come from. "My office is over there." She pointed to a wing of the hospital to their left. "It will be easier to talk in private. But I'll take you through the hospital first, so you can see what it looks like." She had a brisk, efficient manner and walked with rapid steps. Leslie hurried to keep up with her.

Once inside, Leslie was again surprised by the dimness of the rooms. Dr. Sylvie read her thoughts. "These yellow bulbs are better for the mosquitoes; they're less attracted to them." They opened a door. Three dozen beds were pushed against three walls. Patients rested almost naked, with only a thin sheet to cover them. There were no individual night tables with flowers or radios. The bases of several freestanding IV units were rusted, the tubing yellowed from use. Tattered clothes and underwear were draped over the ends of the narrow cots. Beside each on the floor was an enamel basin; several were filled with urine. There was no question of privacy in the room. The communal stare of thirty-six adults seemed to follow them around. A silence had greeted their arrival; now it was broken.

"Doctor," called a woman whose elbows were bulbous. "Doctor, come here, please." Dr. Sylvie walked over to her bedside. The two spoke in low tones. The patient clutched the doctor's sleeve, held it for support.

"She wants to go home," Dr. Sylvie told Leslie and Clemard as they stood a polite distance from the bed. "She wants to be with her children in the village." She took the woman's pulse, felt her brow, then her glands. The woman's eyes were pools of supplication.

"We'll talk to your family, dear. Now try to sleep," she told her, making a note in the woman's chart attached to the end of her bed.

"These are the healthier ones, with only the usual share of maladies—parasites, stomach ulcers, fevers," the doctor informed them, whispering. "They stay a week or two, then we have them come to clinics for follow-up visits. Of course," she added, "not many of the clinics in the provinces have any medicine. But we try to return them to their villages as soon as they can walk, because we have so few beds." She glanced at the list of patients that had been posted on the wall of the second room, adding: "Medicine is a problem for us too. We give our patients, including the AIDS patients, aspirin. A half tablet for the babies, two for the adults. That's the most common remedy. And rest. Because, as you know, hunger is exhausting. By the time most of these patients are admitted, they're too weak to eat. We have to feed them intravenously."

A large man in a corner bed watched them from under lidded eyes. A bandage covered his waist on the left side. "How are you doing, Monsieur Nelson?" Dr. Sylvie asked, uncovering a long wound that had been stitched up but oozed an ugly purple and yellow. She introduced the man to Leslie and Clemard. "This is Figaro Nelson, who works at the docks. Monsieur Nelson was unfortunate enough to inquire why bags of rice were being unloaded off a ship at night into someone's truck, isn't that right?"

He nodded disconsolately.

"He got a knife as his answer." Dr. Sylvie shook her head. "Nice, no?" She felt around the wound, smiled, then patted Figaro Nelson on the shoulder. "Another three days, my friend, and you'll be on your way home. But try to be more prudent. You were lucky this time. And don't play with your bandage. The nurse told me you won't leave it alone."

"It scratches, Doctor," he said defensively. "It bothers me."

"You'll infect it," she told him firmly. "Leave yourself alone. All right?"

"Thank you, Doctor." Figaro Nelson tried to sit up. Dr. Sylvie gently pushed him back down. "Get some rest, Monsieur Figaro, please."

The next room looked identical to the one they had just visited, except that the beds were even closer together, the head of one meeting the foot of another, the space between patients less than a foot. There were also younger patients mixed in with the adults. A teenage girl with open sores on her face looked at Leslie; her thin arms batted away a fly. Her dress was open to reveal a framework of bone and shadow under flat, sagging breasts. An overhead fan listlessly pushed the warm air around the room. An elderly nurse dispensed glasses of water to the patients. Despite the relative cleanliness of the room, it was depressingly bleak. No one had expressed much interest in their arrival; everyone appeared to be suffering from the humidity. The room smelled of sickness and containment.

They passed through, smiling at the patients but not stopping. Down another corridor, then a right turn. Dr. Sylvie stopped them outside a door with a sign reading: *Salle d'Isolation*. It was the AIDS ward. Leslie looked at Clemard. His expression was somber, his earlier gaiety gone.

"You can wear these if you want." Dr. Sylvie pulled paper surgical masks out of a carton on a tray outside the door, and latex gloves for herself. "A lot of the AIDS patients have tuberculosis," she warned them. "We don't like to take chances. It's also for their protection." She opened the door. "We don't want to introduce any microbes to them; they're very vulnerable to catching things."

At first glance, there was little to distinguish these patients from the others they had seen. Most were skeletal, lying semi-naked on the mattresses.

"We have visitors," Dr. Sylvie announced to the room at large. The patients watched them wordlessly. "They aren't journalists," she added, walking over to the nearest of the beds. "They aren't going to take any pictures."

Leslie felt conspicuous and uncomfortable. "We don't have to stay," she said to the doctor, who dismissed her concern.

"Don't worry," she told Leslie. "It's only the journalists. We had some who came and took their pictures without asking anyone's permission. Now the hospital makes them sign a paper first."

Leslie followed Clemard, then said hello to the patients. Several smiled weakly at her; others closed their eyes as they approached. They looked more than exhausted. Leslie found it difficult to see how their bodies stayed alive. A bag of skin, like victims of famine, that's how they appeared to her. Her stomach twinged, it was so upsetting to see. Up close, the veins in their heads were visible, worms under the surface of dark but translucent cheeks, the cartilage of one boy's nose sharp enough to cut paper.

Dr. Sylvie was solicitous, massaging limbs, discreetly pulling back sheets, probing here and there, taking a pulse, checking eyes and tongue and throat, holding her own mask close to her mouth but lowering it to smile, offer comfort. She had a warm bedside manner; Leslie could see the patients liked her. Next to them, a man lay sideways on his cot, his legs bent like long matchsticks. Only his eyes and head, enlarged like a fetus's compared with his febrile body, betrayed the spark of human life. A nurse entered. Dr. Sylvie went over to a corner to confer with her. Leslie and Clemard stood back. The nurse pointed to the corridor; the doctor nodded.

"Nicole Deroncourt," she said, introducing them. "This is Gerard's friend Leslie Doyle—and Clemard . . . Rameau, isn't it?"

"That's right," Clemard said, extending his hand to the nurse. She held up a latex glove. "I can't shake," she apologized.

She was a lively woman, with a halo of black curls. She had pushed a rolling tray with test tubes into a corner, and gestured to them now. "I have to take these into the lab," she excused herself. "I'll be right back, Doctor."

"What they need are stronger painkillers, like morphine." Dr. Sylvie resumed their conversation, indicating the AIDS patients. "If they have a little money, we give them antibiotics, and try to make them as comfortable as possible. But at this point, they're really in God's hands." Her expression said it all. "It's an enormous tragedy," she added. "And it's not about to stop."

They stepped out into the corridor. A teenage girl lay on a gurney, an IV tube connected to her arm. Her eyes flickered like minnows, watching Dr. Sylvie's movements. The physician lowered her mask from her mouth and expertly examined the girl's eyes and mouth using two gloved fingers. A faint voice slipped out. "I hurt, Doctor. I'm dying."

The girl's tongue was nearly white. Her lips were cracked, and a pimply rash ran up her neck. Dr. Sylvie picked up a towel that had been placed on a chair by the bed and wiped off the girl's brow. "You have a fever." She felt her neck and glands, her armpit. "Have you had it for many days?"

Yes, the girl nodded.

Nicole had returned. She handed the doctor a thermometer, who placed it in the girl's mouth. Leslie and Clemard watched from several feet away. The girl closed her eyes. "A hundred and four," Dr. Sylvie said aloud a few minutes later. She moved her stethoscope over the girl's chest. "Breathe for me now. Good. Again. Good."

The girl whispered something. "You don't think your family will visit you? Hush, now don't worry about that. They'll come." Another whisper. "Your children are being cared for, don't worry. You'll see them later today." The nurse helped the girl sit up. Dr. Sylvie placed the metal disk on her back. "Once more. The last time." Leslie heard faint rasping. The girl coughed miserably. Dr. Sylvie tapped a finger to the girl's upper back, then nodded to the nurse. "Give her another injection in a half hour."

They walked farther down the hall. "Someone found her in the street, coughing blood. Her family's abandoned her with her two children. They're all infected." Dr. Sylvie discarded her mask and gloves and washed her hands in a large metal sink. "I'm afraid God has not heard our prayers this time. At this rate, she won't survive the week."

They heard a little cough behind them. It was Clemard. "Dr. Sylvie," he asked quietly, "what about the babies?"

"You mean her children? They're quite sick too. They're in the pediatric ward."

The tour was almost over. Entering the last of the rooms, Leslie was reminded of an army hospital, patients with bandaged limbs strung up like puppets. But the atmosphere here was more animated. She could see tins of food and homemade items placed next to the beds on the floor. "What I would give for even a dozen reclining beds," said Dr. Sylvie wistfully.

The doctor's office was cramped, with a desk, two chairs, and a small refrigerator in the corner. She offered them beverages, which they declined. Leslie sat; Clemard remained standing. Dr. Sylvie shuffled several papers into a semblance of a neat pile on her desk, then opened a drawer and took out a set of keys. "If you'll excuse me a minute," she told Leslie, "I'll go and see if I can find what you were looking for. I'm afraid I haven't had the time to check in the morgue yet." She added: "I can only go when the guard is away at lunch. If he's there, I might not be able to check it. But I'll be back in a few moments."

While she was away, Leslie scanned her lists. She and Clemard took turns looking at a vivid painting above the desk. It was a picture of a lougarou, Haiti's folkloric werewolf, half man, half beast, one leg ending with a cloven hoof, the other with a lion's paw. The werewolf's tail spiraled. Attached to it was a hexagonal kite.

Leslie noted the symbolism. The number six was the pagan symbol of the witch. The details of the painting were fantastic: the lougarou had a gray hide with bluish undertones, ears pointed and goatlike, and realistic horns. Most remarkable was its sweet, dreamy, androgynous face, Pan-like, but innocent. Leslie remembered the remark Henri Desfil, the elephant man on the airplane, had made to her. Blue devils, he had called the Tontons Macoutes.

■

Inside the morgue, Dr. Sylvie looked around for the attendant, but he wasn't there, as she had hoped. She would have to act quickly, before anyone asked questions. She shut the morgue door and proceeded directly to the first room. Three bodies were laid out on metal shelves, each naked and tagged. One of them was Madame Creuteil, a former patient. Dr. Sylvie examined the autopsy; it was a sloppy job—yellow fat oozed through the big black stitches.

In the second room, glass jars filled with formaldehyde contained vital organs: kidney, liver, and part of the large intestine. The liver, at a quick glance, looked diseased to her. She read the labels on each jar, and the chart tacked to the wall above them. A drunk, she guessed.

She looked around a little longer, and finally found the notebook she had been searching for. It was the monthly record of all the postmortems that had been completed. She riffled through it, noting with professional satisfaction that her diagnosis of stomach cancer in Madame Creuteil's case had been correct. The entire organ had been affected.

The postmortems were numbered in sequence and initialed by the pathologist or medical student who had performed the autopsy. She turned the book to its last pages, which dealt with cases in which a police or criminal investigation was involved. She removed one page, then closed the book and left the room, locking the morgue behind her. No one had seen her go in.

.

"Here." The doctor handed the log to Leslie. "This is the only case from the time period you mentioned to me. I'll translate for you if you want."

The report, written in French, was abbreviated in a technical shorthand. "Male. Twenty-seven to thirty-five years old," Dr. Sylvie read. "Negro. Probable cause of death: brain hemorrhage due to blow to cranium with multiple fractures. Estimated time of death: August 26 or 27. Perforation of left eardrum," she continued, "emission of blood and clear liquid from both ears. Bilateral conjunctiva ecchymosis—that means bruises which line the membrane of the eye—this was in both eyes. It's very common to find it in people who have been beaten in the face." She skipped to the end of the report. "Secondary blows to lower jaw, sacroiliac, both legs. Trauma of both ankles consistent with fracture of tibiae. Generalized hematoma suggestive of multiple blows to lower jaw, neck, chest, buttocks, lower legs, and feet." She looked up. "That's all."

"What about fingerprints?" Leslie asked.

"They're right here." Dr. Sylvie turned to the other side of the page. "But these aren't very good. They need to replace the ink stamp. I keep telling them that."

The prints were light, but legible.

"These aren't usually that helpful," the doctor was saying, handing the report to Clemard, who nodded, then passed it to Leslie. "It's not like where you come from," said the doctor. "Here, we don't have many fingerprints on file. Most people haven't been fingerprinted."

Of course, Leslie thought, I should have known that.

She read the report for herself. The information in it could potentially apply to three of the names on her list. She would have to see if anyone had fingerprints for them. There weren't any for Cedric George; Gerard had told her so. But the estimated date of death matched his disappearance.

"I checked all the reports for the last three weeks," Dr. Sylvie

added. "There aren't any unclassified ones—they've all been identified. But we only receive a small number of the dead. Most of
the time, especially if they are poor, they don't bother bringing them
to the morgue."

Titanyen. Leslie and Clemard exchanged glances.

"Do you know a man named Cedric George?" Leslie asked her.
"He's an activist from Papaye. He disappeared around the twenty-
sixth, according to his colleagues. The army attacked the office
where he worked. Konbit Papay."

"I'm afraid I don't. The name's familiar, though. Then again,
one hears so many names. Is he well known in the region?"

"Gerard and Victor know him. You know Victor, right?"

"I know his wife better—Edith. We went to the same school."

"They call him Ti Cedric. Gerard got a call about him last week,
and this weekend some members of Konbit Papay came to talk with
him."

Dr. Sylvie shook her head. "The name says something to me,
but I can't place him. Anyway, you see the scope of the problem."
She took back the autopsy report. "It's terrible, isn't it? Pauvre diable,
whoever he was." She scanned it a last time. "And you know, we
see dozens like this all the time."

"Could I get a copy?" Leslie asked. "I'm hoping to get some
documents that might have fingerprints so I could compare them."

"Certainly." The doctor smiled. "I'll do it for you later. Right
now I should put it back. We're not authorized to take anything
out of the morgue. In fact, there are a lot of things they don't
permit, but we do them anyway. If we waited for their permission,
all our patients would be dead. I'll be right back."

When the doctor returned, Leslie asked if she could accompany
her to the penitentiary on her next visit. "Gerard mentioned you
go there occasionally. I'd love to go in with you because I've been
trying to get permission through a contact in the American embassy,
but they haven't responded. Gerard said you were the one to talk
to."

"I do know the warden. His wife was once a patient. But he only
takes orders. I can make a request, but I can't promise anything."

"Wonderful," said Leslie. "Any possibility of doing that soon?"

"Why not?" Dr. Sylvie laughed. "I see you Americans don't like to waste time. Call me tomorrow. I'll have the copy of the report for you. We can talk then."

"Thank you very much." Leslie handed her a business card with the hotel's number on the back. "That's where I'm staying."

"The Royale. Very good," the doctor said. There was a low rumble in the sky. It was about to rain. "Every time there's a storm we lose our electricity," she complained. "We try not to schedule any surgeries for the afternoon." She blew a stray hair out of her face, sighing. "Ours is not an easy job."

They offered each other a cheek to peck. "We'll see each other soon?" Dr. Sylvie asked. "Maybe you can come up to my house for a visit. I live just a little way from Gerard's house, up in Kenscoff. You could come up on a Sunday. I always have guests for lunch."

"I'd love to," said Leslie, meaning it. "I'm here for a few more weeks. I really want to go up into the mountains."

"Maybe next weekend, then?" Dr. Sylvie shook Clemard's hand. "Monsieur Rameau, it was a pleasure to see you too. But, you know, you should stop that bad habit." She pointed to his cigarette. "You're a young man."

"Wi, madanm," he agreed. Yes, ma'am. Leslie got in the car. A military truck bearing a group of armed soldiers drove by.

The first raindrops began to fall, and in a matter of moments, their windshield was slick with water. They rolled up the windows, leaving only a crack. Clemard ignored Dr. Sylvie's advice and finished his cigarette.

As they made their way uptown, Clemard suddenly turned to her. "I didn't like the hospital. The next time, I won't go in with you. I'll wait in the car. I don't like to see all those people."

Leslie was taken aback. "The AIDS patients, you mean?"

"All those people." He gestured. "Too much sickness."

She didn't know what to say. He didn't want to see the dead at Titanyen or the sick here. Maybe he wasn't the best candidate to help her after all. She studied his profile; his expression was enigmatic. She wondered if Clemard, like Jeanne, would choose death or madness over torture.

Despite the rain, several children ran to the car, at the stoplight, their fingers prying at the crack in the window. "Grangou! Grangou!" they cried. We're hungry! Leslie rolled hers down further, dropped the few coins she had into their wet fingers. They were drenched. "Soti la pli!" she urged them. Get out of the rain! "Gen tonne!" It's thundering! They clung to the car, refused to let go. Clemard honked. "It's all right." Leslie touched his arm. "Just drive slowly." She looked back, imagining Marisa standing there among them.

FACSIMILE TRANSMISSION

TO: Leslie Doyle
FROM: Max Lieberman

STATE DEPARTMENT CHAIN OF COMMAND
FOR HAITI EMERGENCIES
RELATING TO ORGANIZATION OF ELECTIONS
AND NATIONAL STRIKE

I. Task Force
   (In descending authority)
   1. Bill Fielding
      Deputy legal adviser
   2. Peter Martin
         Phone: 202-647-5243
         Fax: 202-647-5994
   3. Arthur Sacks
         Haiti Desk officer
         Phone: 202-647-0893
II. Office of the Under Secretary for Political Affairs
   1. Under Secretary for Political Affairs
      Michael Brill
      Phone: 202-647-8330
   2. Special Assistant to the Under Secretary
      Peter Samuels
         Phone: (home) 301-663-7290
                (State) 202-647-0884
         Fax: 202-647-5533
   3. Special Assistant to the Under Secretary
      Tom Drake (former El Salvador Desk officer)
         Phone: 202-647-2295
         Fax: 202-647-7329

!!! Leslie: dommage qu'on n'avait pas reçu ça la nuit du cocktail . . .
j'ai fait une copie. —GM.

20

The water covers the body like plastic melting in the sun. The body glistens, black, shiny, hard, like a tree trunk underwater. The crowd shrinks back. Faces pull this way and that, stare at each other. This one opens her mouth; that one is silent. The body is pulled onto land. The priest kneels down. He embraces the dead one, speaking softly. The crowd leans forward to listen.

The priest looks up. Almighty God, have mercy on his soul. All of their eyes turn to Him as well. Eyes trace the pattern of the trees and hills, mountains and clouds, the sun shining over the wooden houses. The faces are hard, closed to one another; each bears a private thought.

It is time for prayer. The priest stands up, his slight frame bends with the weight of this new sorrow. His face is illuminated by the sunlight filtering into this narrow alley. The crowd bathes in the collective memory of others who have died, in the long history of their own struggle. The priest lifts his hands to heaven. The crowd echoes his prayer, each adding his own to his plea for forgiveness and redemption. Crying out to saints of earth and sky, saints of field and mountain and tree and river. God! God! Life is too hard! My life is too much suffering! My child has died! Embrace me! Help me! Bless us! Bless us! Banish the evil! Wipe away our tears! Give us your touch! God of Love! God of Peace! God of Justice! God of Sky! Rock! Tree! All that Lives! Met! Master! Mystère! Mystery! Suprême Majesté! See how I beat my breast, King? My legs move for You! My soul is Yours, take it! I surrender, take me! Deliver me! Have pity on me! Genius! Plenipotency! Salt of my tears! Milk of my breast! Blood of my veins! I surrender! My body belongs to You! Take it! Take it! Lift me up! Let me rise with You! Drink my blood! Make me one with You! Hear my cry. I am shouting for You! My Master! My Life! My Soul! My Heart! Divine Universe!

The priest lifts his hands to pray. Mesi Bondye mesi Papa mwen. Mesi pou tou sa-ou fe pou mwen. Thank you, Lord my Father. Thank you for all You have done for Me. Protect us, Lord, from all evil. *The priest hears an echo: Amen. Then another. Amen, Amen, Amen. He hears whispering, a gasp.* The moment comes. He watches it. A seizure, a fainting, a wail. The eyes are upturned, the gaze transcendent. The young woman is ecstatic.

The priest watches with the crowd, waits for the spirit to identify itself, its intentions. The crowd is frightened, draws back when the taken one moves toward them. The woman strokes a child's face, then a man's. Slowly, slyly, boldly, she circles the priest. He does not shrink back. He is praying. The woman takes the priest's hand, passes it over her own face. The priest feels the force of the blows that have struck the dead man lying before them, the sharpness of the knife that has cut his flesh in so many places, the pain of this woman, his widow, abandoned with eight children. She puts the priest's hand between her legs, a place of sorrow now. *Chante pou Bondye Granmet nou. Sing for the goodness of God Almighty.* The crowd sings with the priest. *Li-menm ki rwa sou tout te. He who rules over all the earth.*

The woman holds the sad place between her legs. Her body twists and jumps; her arms and legs and hands show how her husband, the innocent one, fought and fell and was slain. She falls upon him now, gently rides her husband a final time. *Take me! Deliver me! Free me!* The crowd encircles her, helps her, holds her, spins in a circle with her, cries with her. The priest stands back, respectful. He continues to pray. *God have mercy on this man's soul and the souls of all who loved him and suffer his death.*

The crowd embraces the woman. Hands comfort her, fingers cradle her head, pry her gently away from her dead husband. The priest moves forward to give blessing. He carries water in a small wooden bowl, water the woman has collected in a dirty bottle held under the tap of a nearby building. *In the name of the Father, the Son, and the Holy Spirit. There is no conflict between man and God, brother and sister, earth and sky and sea. We must live in love and peace. Let this man live forever in our hearts.* The woman nods her head. *Let there be justice,* the priest adds, *love, peace, and justice.* The crowd murmurs their approval. *This is the water of Life.*

The priest dips his thumb into water made sacred, then makes a sign of the cross. *Blessed be.* He lifts the bowl to his own lips, then *offers it to the widow, then to his neighbors, friends, relatives. Blessed be. Blessed be. Blessed be. Blessed be. The strongest in the crowd lift the dead man and place him in a wooden coffin. The dead man's children carry over the tall, narrow door to their father's house, a passageway during life now a gateway into death, and lower it on top of the coffin. A brilliant turquoise door through which his spirit passed a thousand times, now freshly painted white. Oh, blessed be.*

.

Emmanuel heard noises, startling him from his reverie. The memory of the funeral he had performed two nights before, changed and exaggerated in his mind, was replaced by moving figures in the doorway. The children giggled, watching him. He had fallen asleep leaning against the inner wall of the mud house. He smiled and pulled on the younger child's arm. "Vin la." Come here. She came shyly forward, her big eyes wide. "Ki laj ou genyen? Katran?" How old are you? Four?

He settled the little girl on his lap. She looked back at her brother, who was slightly older. The two were covered with dust; the girl's underwear was torn, her Mickey Mouse T-shirt filthy. Both had large heads and hungry bodies.

The little girl fingered the pen in Emmanuel's blue shirt pocket; he gave it to her to play with. The little boy came forward, took it from her. She gave the priest an uncertain look; he patted the girl on the head, lifted her hands and dropped them onto his own face. She laughed. So did the little boy. The room was dim, containing a hoe and some tools. A burlap bag was rolled up next to the tools. A large key hung on a nail in the room's center pole. Emmanuel had no idea what it fit, there was no door to this hut.

He leaned to one side, tilting the child with him. The man had not yet returned. An unpainted wooden chair, its thatch seat falling out, rested against a tree outside. The little girl suddenly jumped off. The children ran out, yelling.

A middle-aged man with a broad peasant's face was smiling, walking down the mountain path, holding his straw hat in one hand. His shirt was missing all but one button. He held a machete in the other hand, and waved to the priest with it. The children now clutched his legs, making it hard for him to advance. The man hit the children with his hat to make them let go, but they refused. They looked at Emmanuel, a potential ally, then back at their father, fearfully. Was he joking? Was he angry? He pushed them away.

Emmanuel had had no difficulty finding the place, although the soldier, Jean-Marc, had given him only vague directions. The villagers below had sent him up to see this man, Pierre, who had identified himself as Elyse Voltaire's cousin. He had immediately offered to take the priest to see an old woman, Grann, her grandmother.

Pierre's pants were held up with a length of rope. He was sweating; the front of his shirt was soaked. "She's up there." He pointed. "Less than a kilometer. She's waiting for us."

They didn't speak. Emmanuel was glad he had decided to wear hard shoes instead of sandals. The ground was slippery. The children trailed behind them. He listened carefully as Pierre recounted what he knew about the arrest. It was only after Elyse had not returned that they realized something bad had happened to her. He, Pierre, her second cousin, had personally gone to the police station at Fontamara to inquire about it. That's when a friend had informed him that Elyse had been taken away in a truck. The next morning he had taken a bus into the city to look for her at the police station there, but no one had known anything. And now the policeman at Fontamara had warned him that if he refused to pay the water tax, he would come and arrest Pierre personally. The government was tired of trouble and troublemakers.

Grann was too old, Pierre added. She didn't understand everything and couldn't really take care of herself. He was staying with her now, but he could not work in the field. And all the others had left to cut cane in Sabana Cruz, across the border. He wanted to take Grann and the children to his cousins in another village, because the situation was dangerous. He was afraid.

Ever since his wife had died, Pierre said as they climbed, things had gotten worse. The storms had destroyed the field for planting. He was lonely too; he missed his wife. And the children missed her. But he didn't want to leave the village, because where could he go? He was unhappy and nothing was getting better, as they had all hoped.

Pierre began peppering Emmanuel with questions. How did he know about Elyse? Had someone sent him here to talk to them? Was she in prison? Could he go see her?

Emmanuel answered his questions to the best of his ability. He was here to find out what he could. He had been told about Elyse's arrest—she was being held in the penitentiary. He had stopped at the police station at Fontamara to find out what they might know, but the police chief had been out. He planned to go back there after talking with Pierre, Grann, and anyone else who might have information. A lawyer, Gerard Metellus, who was his friend, was looking into her case.

"Does she have any other family?" he asked Pierre, looking behind him at the little girl, who refused to take his hand. He smiled at her. Whenever he slowed down, she slowed down. They were playing another secret game.

"No," Pierre said. "The mother died giving birth to Elyse. There was another child. But it was adopted. The father abandoned them when Elyse was small."

"What about aunts? Uncles? Other cousins?"

"They moved to another part of the country. Where the father is living. The land belongs to Grann, and Elyse decided to stay with her."

"What about the grandfather? The husband of her grandmother?"

"Mouri." Pierre shook his head. Dead.

"I see," Emmanuel said, panting a little. The climb was steep. He felt a little tug on his pants. The girl laughed and wanted to play some more.

"What's her name?" he shouted up to Pierre, who hoisted his son on his shoulders.

"Victoria, like her mother."

The little girl smiled. She had an enormous smile.

Emmanuel let her catch up. "Victoria-like-your-mother." He touched his shoulders. "Ou vle monte?" Would you ride up here?

She shook her head no.

"How old is she?" he asked Pierre, hurrying to narrow the distance between them. Pierre casually flicked his machete at branches that had overgrown the path. The boy tightly clutched his father's head.

"Seven."

Seven? Emmanuel took another look at the little girl. She was so small.

"She doesn't eat," Pierre said matter-of-factly.

The little girl looked down at the ground, avoiding Emmanuel's eyes. He caught her gaze. "Ou pa renmen manje?" You don't like to eat?

She shook her head at that too. Isn't she adorable? he thought, smiling. They reached a new path.

"There's the house." The man pointed. Emmanuel could barely make it out, a flash of white through the branches ahead of them. They stepped out of the dense underbrush, into a clearing. There were several houses farther away, separated from one another by surrounding trees. A pile of branches had been dropped into the center of the clearing, near a cold fire pit. He saw a pile of charcoal in a basket by the nearest house.

"I'll go get Grann," Pierre said.

Emmanuel watched as Pierre brought a tall chair from inside the house and out to the pit. He went back inside and emerged with a frail creature in a blue dress, sheltering her eyes from the afternoon sun. Her thin legs moved forward with help from Pierre and a walking stick. The little boy, William, positioned himself on her other side.

"Grann," Pierre explained in a loud voice, "this is the priest I told you about. Pe Emmanuel."

"Bonjour, Grann." Emmanuel came close to her. Without Pierre's help, her body would sink forward; the man held her shoulder firmly to keep her upright. Emmanuel took her hand, shook a palm that was soft and passive. It was obvious she was nearly deaf. She had very few teeth left. She looked up at him and nodded, still moving her lips, wetting them with her tongue. Beside her, William pushed Victoria, who was trying to get next to her father.

Emmanuel squatted before her. "Grann, ou konnen tet mwen?" Do you recognize me? "I'm the priest who comes to the parish in Carrefour to say Mass. No?" He looked at Pierre and smiled. "Well, that's all right."

"I think she understands," the farmer said. "Grann, do you understand what the father is saying?"

The old woman's eyes shifted from Pierre back to Emmanuel.

"That's all right," Emmanuel repeated. He took her hand again. "Grann, I have some news about Elyse, about your granddaughter. Elyse," he repeated loudly. "We think she's been arrested. Can you hear me? We think she's been arrested."

They watched as the purplish lips moved, and the old woman said, faintly, " 'Lyse."

"She understood," Pierre said. "Elyse!" he cupped his hand to her ear. "This father knows where they took Elyse. Do you hear that, Grann? We found Elyse!"

Tears had formed in the old woman's eyes, hung on her lower lashes.

"What are you crying for, Grann? She's all right. We found Elyse . . . Grann, stop that crying! . . . He's going to help her get out of there. Aren't you?" Pierre looked at Emmanuel, exasperated. "She's always crying," he added, imploring the old woman, "Grann, pa fe sa!" Don't do that! "There's no reason to cry, Grann. Here the good father has come to tell us Elyse is all right."

Emmanuel took his handkerchief from his back pocket, dabbed at the old woman's eyes. She looked directly at him, her expression miserable.

" 'Lyse," she repeated. It was almost a question.

"I came here to find out what you could tell me," Emmanuel continued, sensing the futility of his mission. "I have a lawyer—a friend of mine—he's going to try to see her. He's going to help your granddaughter." He turned to Pierre. "Do you think she understands me? I don't think so." He added: "Do you think there might be any papers, something with her name or identity on it, or a picture? That might help us get in to see her at the prison. Anything, any kind of paper."

"I'll go and look in the house," Pierre said. "She's not understanding."

Emmanuel put his hand where Pierre's had been, and held Grann upright. She was all bone. He looked down at her scalp, shining through thin, fine hair. The folds of her chin and neck were creased into a hundred tiny diamonds, like wrinkled carbon paper, flattened to be used again. Her hazel eyes were bloodshot. She looked over at the children. They had moved closer to the doorway of the house. Emmanuel saw Grann's lips disappear into the space between her nose and chin, then reappear as a dark line. She seemed to be smiling at him. " 'Lyse," she implored again.

"Don't worry," Emmanuel reassured her. "We're going to help your granddaughter."

Pierre came back with a picture and a yellow softbound exercise book, the kind schoolchildren used, with the name Elyse Voltaire written in large, childish script on the cover. The picture showed a tall young woman with a high forehead and a broad nose, with deep-set eyes and well-formed thin eyebrows. The overall shape of her face was long, her lips on the small side, her chin rounded. She was grinning, a gap between her two front teeth. It was a black-and-white picture. He turned it over. *E.V. 15 ans.*

He opened the exercise book. Each page contained three columns. In the first was a list of names, followed by items of clothing in the second column and varying amounts of money in the third. It was an accounts ledger.

"Laundry?" he asked Pierre. "Does she do that for a living?"

"Wi," Pierre confirmed. Yes.

"This will be fine," the priest answered. "I'll keep this in order to make a copy of her signature, then return it to you. I think that's all I need for now," he added. "Thank you."

Together, they helped Grann back into the house and lowered her carefully onto a straw mat. Emmanuel looked around for a minute. From outside, the house looked smaller than it was inside. A curtain divided the room in two. On the other side of it, he saw a large wooden dresser with a wooden bowl, a tin cup and plate, and toys: a straw horse and a wooden top. Pierre put the tall chair back in its place next to the dresser. A large empty basket and a smaller one with several tubes of Prell were stacked in a corner. An outdated Texaco calendar with pictures of horses was nailed to the wall; below it was a picture of the Virgin of Guadalupe. Several dresses hung from a peg in the wall. Emmanuel took the room in quickly, didn't want to stay too long. It seemed prudent, given what Pierre had told him about the police.

They left Grann resting in the house. Emmanuel asked Pierre to tell him all he knew about the days just before and after Elyse's disappearance. The farmer filled him in about the visit from the tax collector the week before Elyse's arrest, demanding that they pay more taxes on the water they were drawing from the well. They had refused. Pierre was certain the tax collector had sent the police to arrest Elyse.

The children accompanied the two men back to the storage shack where Emmanuel had fallen asleep earlier. He gave Pierre his telephone number and his address at the parish, as well as Gerard's name and office number.

"Let me know where I can contact you if you leave," he told Pierre. He handed him several ten-gourde notes. "That is all I have. I'll come back soon and see if we can do something to help you."

"Ah, Pe . . ." Pierre murmured gratefully, "Mesi, mesi." Thank you, thank you. He smiled, and shook the priest's hand. "Mesi anpil." Thanks a lot.

ANPIL ARESTASYON PAPAY

Makout ak milite ap fe e defe nan Papaye kont pep ayisyen ak drapo demokrasi a nan men li ki travay pou fasilite bon jan eleksyon. Se vye makout divalyeris ki arete sitwayen le yo vle, jan yo vle. Yo taye nenpot bonet mete nan nempot tet moun, sitout moun kap danse kole ak Konbit Papay. Se konsa fos divalyeris te arete tout moun ki te oganize pou reyalize bon jan chanjman ki nesese. Yo piye kay, yo volo lajan, you kraze pot, yo arete ti peyizan. Malgre tou peyizan yo pa fe bek ate. Yo kenbe rezistans.

Se konsa nan lannwit 26 Out yo mete dife nan biro Konbit Papay ki chita nan gran ri. Nandemen, komandan soudistri Enid Fleuris a voye arete: Mickey Ami (Konbit Papay); Daniel Dezirab (Konbit Papay); Violette Milfort George (peyizan, se Cedric Milfort George, prezidan Konbit Papay ki disparet lanwit 31 Out) ak anpil elev ki te sipote grev nasyonal: Ronald Bien-Aimé (etidyan); Fleur St. Baptiste (etidyan); Yviese César (elev); Marie César (elev).

Konbit Papay voye monte yon not pou lapres paske li setoblije leve lavwa pou denonse zak briganday gwo ponyet sa yo milite makout ap komet nan zon nan. Li vle denonse represyon komandan soudistri Enid Fleuris ki te gwo zanmi ak grandon makout Joseph Carena sou diktate Divalye.

Konbit Papay mande tout oganizasyon popile nan 4 kwen payi a pou sipote grev nasyonal. Antretan li mande tout moun ki sipote eleksyon ak demokrasi pou Ayiti vin rete mobilize. Plis nou plis, plis nou fo.

English version, translated by Leslie Doyle/Funding Coalition.
(Attn.: Check translation before distributing bulletin.)

NEWS BRIEF:

NUMEROUS ARRESTS IN PAPAYE

Former Macoutes and army soldiers have acted in Papaye against the Haitian people and the flag of democracy being held by those who are working to bring about a good election. It's the ex-Duvalierist Macoutes who are arresting people when they will, as they will. They trim any hat on anybody's head, especially people who are actively demonstrating with Konbit Papay. That is how the Duvalierist forces have arrested all the people who are organizing to bring about real change that is necessary. They have looted houses, stolen money, destroyed houses, arrested the ordinary peasants. Despite this the peasants refuse to bow their heads. They have maintained their resistance.

That is how on the night of August 26 they burned the offices of Konbit Papay collective that is located on the Grande Rue. The following day, army subdistrict commander Enid Fleuris arrested: Mickey Ami (Konbit Papay); Daniel Dezirab (Konbit Papay); Violette Milfort George (peasant woman, sister of Cedric Milfort George, president of Konbit Papay, who disappeared the night of August 31); and many students who supported the national strike: Ronald Bien-Aimé (university student); Fleur St. Baptiste (university student); Yviese César (high school student); Marie César (high school student).

Konbit Papay issues this press release because it finds it necessary to speak out and denounce the brutal acts of looting committed by the military Macoutes in this zone. It wishes to denounce the repression carried out by army subdistrict commander Enid Fleuris, who was a good friend of the landowner Joseph Carena during the Duvalier dictatorship.

Konbit Papay urges all popular organizations in the four corners of the country to support the national strike. In the meantime, it urges all people who support elections and democracy for Haiti to remain mobilized. The more we are, the stronger we are.

21

It was seven o'clock in the evening. Leslie lay in a reclining chair on the balcony, drowsy. But the day was still alive, the sky a Rousseau blue like the sky that towered over the man in the multicolored robe and the watchful lion in *The Sleeping Gypsy*, one of her favorite pictures. The rain clouds had gone away, hidden somewhere behind the mountains, gathering strength for tomorrow. Leslie had worked for four hours on the tapes. Her eyes twitched from fatigue.

She had woken from her nap feeling stifled. Her body was covered with a light sweat; the heat prickled her feet and hands. In the moment of waking, her eyes had been sealed shut and she felt they could remain so forever. Sealed in heat, like an Egyptian mummy's, her dreams ossified. There was a trace of something disturbing, something important, if only she could recall it.

She passed her hands over her body, felt the bubbles of sweat in the creases of arm and leg, along the bony ridge of her shin, where too many childhood accidents had left a series of hard bumps. Her hand trailed casually, sought only to confirm her being, to make certain that whatever had occurred without her knowledge during her long nap had left the world unaltered. She felt the pain of tired muscles in her neck, tasted the sour remains of a late-afternoon coffee on her tongue.

Small creatures had visited her, that was evident. She looked over at the crumbs of sweet bread on the nearby table where the custodian regularly played solitaire. There was a breadfruit on the table too. She wondered if he ever peered into her room, saw her lying naked under the mosquito netting. The setting sun slipped through the wooden rails of the terrace banister, creating diagonal bars of light on the floor. Near her hand, a line of tiny ants moved in an unbroken line up and down the ancient wall.

The Royale was a converted colonial house. It reminded her of her grandfather's house in Virginia, its sagging floor creaking so loudly no one could come upstairs unnoticed. There could be no simple spying in a house like this; one would have to move very slowly, stop the heavy doors from swinging on their iron hinges. But it was still ideal for an affair, she thought, reveling in the Indian summer heat, the barest breeze lifting the hairs on her arms. She listened to human voices, talking somewhere below and out of sight.

She sat up and her robe fell open. Below the terrace, hummingbirds flittered from blossom to blossom on the climbing vine. Beautiful flowers bordered the driveway, star-shaped orange and pink ones, gardenias, the ever-present bougainvillea, tall birds of paradise. The sky paled in the distance; a remnant of the sun illuminated the far side of the bay like the aura in a religious painting. That was toward Fontamara, where Père Emmanuel had gone to speak with the relatives of the imprisoned woman, Elyse Voltaire.

Directly below her to the left were the small tin-roofed houses of the kitchen staff, the domestics, as everyone referred to them. She thought the word was apt, in a cutting, cruel kind of way. Domestic as in homegrown, as in to domesticate, to tame the wild thing, to break it down. For a second, she saw Elyse Voltaire, whose Xeroxed picture Gerard had tacked to the wall in his office, being beaten with a baton, just as the guards had beaten Marie-Thérèse Dubossy. The image vanished. The sky was so lovely she wanted to paint the landscape; the deep blue soothed her somehow.

She missed Marisa, although they had spoken just this afternoon. She wanted to hold her, play cards with her at the little table with Vincent, the custodian. Marisa would love Haiti, Leslie thought, all the dogs and roosters and tap-taps. She reminded herself to buy the calico material she had seen in the market for Marisa's dress. There were such pretty colors.

The roosters were crowing again, making her smile. It would be nice to have a rooster in Washington, she thought, so much more natural than her tinny alarm. She was seeing roosters everywhere. On the road back from Fontamara, Clemard had stopped the car by a small gas station. In the lot next to it, behind a concrete wall, he had led her to a cockfight, invisible from the road. The people had looked at her with curiosity but no one had said anything. No one had broken off from their gambling to pay her any attention. Old women had clutched their finger purses to their bosoms and sworn liberally. The man in the ring taking money had shaken his hand like a rattle and spit on each bill placed there. It seemed to her that everyone had spit, young and old alike, even the birds. The owners had spit on their fingers, then massaged the spittle onto the heads of the cocks for good luck. They held the birds carefully under their wings, steel-tipped talons outstretched, out of harm's way, until a proper amount of money had been collected. Then it was: "Kraze li!" Crush him! And everyone had spit and cursed and laughed and elbowed each other as the birds circled, attacked, and retreated, only to be thrown back into the center of the ring. The inevitable dark red dot had appeared on the chest, followed by a final flurry of rage, and then it was over, faster than Leslie had anticipated.

She had enjoyed it, though, less the fight than the faces of the old women holding their mouths and blinking at each sudden rush, and the children, crouching by the side of the ring, at eye level with the fighting cocks. Crowds fascinated her, especially small crowds focused on a single intense event. Whenever she had accompanied Mark to amateur boxing matches, the emotions of the spectators, not the fights, captivated her. She had not bet on the cockfight; Clemard had lost two gourdes.

A long rain pipe ran along the outside of the terrace ledge. She leaned forward to shake it. The rusty pipe left an orange mark on her fingers; she rubbed the rust on the ledge, marking her initials. LMD. She shook the pipe, which was loose, listening for the drops of water she imagined were left inside.

Marisa would be in her pajamas already; Mark would be reading her a story. She felt tempted to call home again, but it took too long to reach the international operator. Everything at home had been fine. Marisa had drawn her a train and some flowers. Mark had been cordial, asking about Gerard. The babysitter was working out well.

She could smell dinner being prepared, but she was not very hungry. She felt a little nauseated from her period, and gaseous. Her menstrual cramps were getting worse; the aspirin was not taking effect. She farted again; the smell was awful. Maybe she ought to ask for her meal to be brought up. It would be embarrassing to sit next to anyone.

The tiny ants were devouring a lime-green caterpillar. The dead insect looked pretty against the white-and-black terrazzo floor. It almost looked alive, with the ants trying to move it along. She got down on her knees to look at the carnage. So systematic, so silent. Nature was merciless. She got back up, grimacing. My back, she thought. I'm completely out of shape. I can't kneel like that anymore. I've gotten too old.

She heard a noise and got up to walk around the terrace to the side of the hotel. Below, in the space between two of the shacks, a woman bathed. Crouching, she poured a yellow basin of water over her head. It was the woman she had seen talking to the custodian, an albino woman. Leslie hoped she would not look up and catch her spying. She was heavyset, with orangish hair.

Leslie lowered herself below the level of the banister, still looking. What would it be like to be an albino? In a black-majority country? Had anyone ever written about that experience? How did this woman relate to her blackness, her non-Caucasian features? That was the part Leslie found so fascinating, the idea of discordance between pigment and bone. What identity did it produce? She felt there was something so vulnerable about albinos, their skin too sensitive for a tropical sun, their light eyes unable to bear bright daylight. There were other frailties, genetic susceptibilities—hadn't she read that? Or had Father told her that? She wondered if this woman only washed in the evening, when her skin could bear exposure. Probably.

The woman turned away, offering a dorsal view. She had a broad, strong back. She had seated herself on a small three-legged stool; her arm moved back and forth, just out of Leslie's line of vision. Leslie stepped a few paces to her left, still hiding. Aha, the woman was washing someone. A child. Her child? It had to be. She held the dark infant in the crook of her arm, cupped water in her hand and washed the baby's tiny limbs.

Leslie felt a pang in her heart, remembering how it felt to bathe Marisa, her delicate hands and feet. The child was so tiny, how old could it be? Under six months, Leslie guessed. She wanted to hold it.

The albino woman reached for a blue cloth draped over a wash line nearby, dried and wrapped the baby. She was stark naked, except for a pair of pink flip-flops. Leslie drew farther back into the shadows. The woman disappeared, her infant in one arm, the yellow basin in another. Was she Vincent's companion? The custodian had mentioned having a menaj—a household.

She stood against the wall another few minutes, unconsciously cradling her breasts, imagined Marisa suckling. She had been a dream baby, sweet, rarely crying, not much colic. Now she was in her "No" stage, establishing her independence from Mommy. She had said "No" a dozen times on the phone today. Do you miss me? No. Are you having fun with Daddy? No. Tomorrow, she promised herself again, she would buy material for a dress and try to find a brimless straw hat for Marisa, like the Mardi Gras hat she had seen on the floor beside a patient's bed in the AIDS ward of the hospital. She pressed on her breasts again, soothing the physical ache centered there. Marisa, my little sweetie.

She went back to her chair. This side had a better view of the city. At night, it was unevenly lit; the poor neighborhoods were dark patches. Not far down the road was a house that had not been destroyed by vandals; a powerful Duvalierist still lived there. Clemard had driven her by it, a two-story gingerbread-style house surrounded by barbed wire.

Her days with him had taken on a routine. In the morning Leslie had appointments. If they were downtown, she would use Gerard's office to make calls or meet people. If the weather was good, they would venture out of the city for afternoon visits to projects in the suburbs. If there was any time to kill, Clemard would drive her around the city, introducing her to neighborhoods and the stories that accompanied them. Every day, she was learning new details about events she had read about in the human rights reports, attaching streets to names and cases. By now, a second city had formed in her mind, one where people had organized a protest in this square, pulled down the trees above Pétionville to stop the Macoutes living in Boutillier from fleeing after Duvalier's fall, set up barricades of burning tires at this corner, fallen prey to police bullets at another. She thought about the idea American feminists had initiated, marking every spot where a rape had been committed. What would Port-

au-Prince look like if that was done here? She marked the places
Clemard pointed out with a red X; by now the Xeroxed map Gerard
had first sent her was impossible to read.

Clemard had taken to recounting the history of the dechoukaj to
her, the incidents he had experienced and those he had merely
heard about, embellishing, repeating, adding more information
each time. His storytelling was a mosaic and passionate. After the
cockfight, passing the National Palace, he had slowed down the
car. There, see that cachot over there. Cachot? That hiding place,
that hole. Where? Over there, by the side of the fence, past the
guard. I don't see it. If we got closer, you could see it. That's where
Duvalier imprisoned his enemies. They had cells down there, underground. They have a tunnel and it connects the palace with the
police headquarters. That's how some of the Macoutes escaped, the
day Duvalier left. They hid in that cachot.

Really? Had anyone been down there? Had anyone actually seen
it? Oh, Madanm Leslie, believe me. Believe me! There are cells
down there, everybody knows it. Ask anybody, they would tell you.
But you can't ask just anybody, they might be a Macoute. Everybody
knows, though.

Everybody knows. Collective truth. Better than proof in Clemard's eyes. His was the teledjol—street gossip—mentality. She
was a nonbeliever, she wanted hard evidence. He understood it was
part of her job, the only truth accepted by outsiders. But the truth
is, he would argue to Leslie, everybody knows.

The best-lit section of the city was downtown, where the palace
was as bright as a stadium all night. From here she could see its
faint glow. Next to it was the prison, which remained in shadow,
though she could mentally place it. She was anxious to go inside,
to see the dimensions of the cells, the exact color of the walls. It
would be strange to actually go inside with Dr. Sylvie, as if her
daydream had foreshadowed it. If Titanyen was any example, it
would probably be a banal place: there would be no signs of torture,
no starving prisoners chained to steel posts on the floor. She felt
slightly nervous about going inside. What if they got mad, decided
to detain her? A foreigner trapped in a Haitian prison. She could
see the headlines, the interviews when she was released. Another

hero fantasy. No, it was just the unpredictable that was unsettling, knowing that something was going to happen and that it was likely to affect her deeply. That she could definitely sense, that was something she knew. Like everybody knows, she thought wryly, hearing Clemard's voice arguing with her.

She scanned the horizon. The city was shamelessly exposed, unable to protect itself, susceptible to the vicissitudes of weather and natural decline, from the noxious smell of smoldering garbage and the human waste that hardened like tar in the open sewers. Packs of rats ran along the port and in the big markets, dodging mangy cats, hiding under the stalls of the outdoor slaughterhouses where the flies drowned in jars of blood collected from the fresh entrails of animals. She had cut short her visit to the slaughterhouse in Carrefour; the smell and sight of pigs' heads black with dried blood had overwhelmed her.

The city was littered with fallen fruit that burst upon contact with the ground, then drew children to suck the overripe, wormy flesh. The city had tiny hexagonal kites that hung from telephone lines like bows in its hair and tall akee trees that bore deadly fruit if the pistil was not removed before cooking. The city, Leslie thought as she massaged her womb, was like the body of its citizens, with parts of itself that were cancerous, silently killing. The alarm clock went off in her room. Time to get dressed.

She shuffled inside, startling a lizard. It slipped into her room and she found it on the wall beside the mirror. It was a baby chameleon, striped with beautiful half-blue, half-green colors. It moved away from her hand, up toward the ceiling.

Leslie had read *The Whales in Lake Tanganyika*, a novel by Lennart Hagerfors, in which a character had observed that chameleons were the happiest of all creatures, though they had trouble abandoning their green color, a change which often preceded death. So far she had seen two burnt-orange-colored lizards and several dark gray ones. But none the midmorning color of gold or flashing silver, like slivers of glass at noon. And how had Hagerfors decided they were happy? Because of their soft smile, like a dolphin's? She moved up closer to the creature. Is it true you are afraid of death? That you hold on to your pretty green color too long? What if she got a tattoo of a chameleon on her shoulder that could change colors depending on her mood? Then the happiest of all creatures and one in tune with nature would remain a steadfast green and a comfort as her end approached.

The chameleons turned blue at night from melancholy, from remaining shadows frozen on the walls of the city: silent witnesses. Leslie had an image of the chameleons at Titanyen, their throats engorged with fear, pulsating with the final rapid heartbeats of the lives extinguished below them in the ground. Little blue angels to keep an eye on the lougarous, the blue devil, the Macoute. The chameleon's body was changing to match the color of the sky outside, now almost purple.

She suddenly thought about Clemard. This was his afternoon off. What was he doing? Was he making love with his wife? Amena . . . no . . . Amatalima—something like that. A woman four years his senior, who had had a child by another man before she married Clemard. Leslie had learned this only yesterday and it had pleasantly surprised her. She wondered, not for the first time, what he really thought of her. He was intrigued, that much she could tell.

She had been trying to pry a dinner invitation out of him, her treat, to meet his family. But Clemard had politely refused each time. Pride. He didn't want her to see where he lived, how he lived. It was unspoken but obvious. An unnecessary pride, she wanted to argue, knowing that it was easy for her to say that. For her, it would be a gesture of intimacy, a desire to break down rigid social barriers. Maybe before I leave, she thought, you never know.

Did they have sex in the same room where their children slept? Did they talk in bed the way Mark and she had? Those were the good years. She shook her head. For an instant, she saw Mark's pale face, his horn-rimmed glasses, his loose, gangly body, his love handles. You blew it, she said to him, feeling her old rancor. You treated me badly. I didn't deserve that. You could have talked to me. You could have told me you were having an affair. Just that. You could have said something. I deserved that much.

Clemard, his face and body, surfaced again. She couldn't help wondering if he ever thought about her sexually. If time and history were different, she thought, smiling to herself, then maybe. Maybe she would consider it. He was such an attractive man.

Of course, she could think that about a lot of people. Vincent, the custodian, wasn't a bad-looking man, truth be known. Nice legs. And a good drinking partner. He probably was the albino woman's lover. Maybe the baby was his too.

And there was Jeanne. Now there was a beautiful woman. Sexy. And smart. She and Jeanne and Gerard, they could have a three-some. She grinned at the thought, enjoying the fantasy. Gerard would probably freak out, she thought, laughing. He's really a little square. But I bet Jeanne would go for it.

It's the air, she mused, breathing it in deeply, luxuriating in it like a bath. All she wanted to do was have sex. Right here, on the terrazzo floor next to these little ants and that poor dead caterpillar. She needed an orgasm anyway, to relieve her cramps; they were killing her. She put her finger next to the caterpillar, pushed it, and sent the ants into a panic.

She wanted to smoke. The dull pain in her back made it un-comfortable to recline. She shifted the chair's position and pulled her legs up. The ants had regrouped, carting the caterpillar away in sections. She hoped no one would come along, discover her, legs splayed, gurney style.

A soft cry rose from the street. Alarmed, she struggled to get up. Below her, a roasted-peanut vendor stood under a tree at the bottom of the hotel driveway. She had spied Leslie on the balcony and held up a wooden tray. Leslie could see the brown sticky peanut clusters, but couldn't stomach them; they gave her diarrhea. She was still tempted, though, loving the taste of the greenish nuts and the oversweet caramel and the way you had to pry the candy from the paper with your teeth. The woman moved closer to the hotel steps, urged Leslie to come down and try some.

Leslie could see the woman looking around, probably watching for Vincent, who yelled at anyone coming onto the grounds. She shook her head, declining the offer. I don't feel well. She pointed at her stomach, making a face. I can't eat that. The woman only nodded; she wouldn't give up. Instead she extended the tray of candy, insistent. The entire exchange took place silently. I can't eat that. Leslie shook her head, Sorry. Finally the woman left.

Leslie looked up at the trees. Soon the bats would emerge from them. She had mistaken the fruit bats for birds, until the custodian had shown her one lying dead. It was remarkably soft and tiny, like a mouse with wings. And it stank.

She heard the dinner bell chime and went inside to get dressed. She flipped on the radio and found the Catholic radio station. Soeur Madeleine was speaking.

"Bonjour, Bonheur?" A shy voice was on the line. "Se Charles nan Jacmel. Mwen vle di bonjou a Marie Carmel nan Site Soley. Mande pou li vin Jacmel Vandredi matin tanpri." Hello, Bonheur? This is Charles from Jacmel. I'm calling to say hello to Marie Carmel in Cité Soley. Ask her to come to Jacmel on Friday morning, please.

She heard Soeur Madeleine repeating it: "Are you listening, Marie Carmel? That's Charles and he wants to meet you in Jacmel on Friday. In the morning. What time, Charles?"

"Dize . . . nan mache akote lekol Trinite." Ten o'clock, near the Trinity school.

"Ten o'clock . . . mark that down, Marie Carmel. Trinity school. Thank you, Charles. Who's next? What's this? Jacques Toussaint has lost his cousin Joshua. If anyone has seen or heard of Joshua Toussaint, call us here at 2-3-4-5-9 . . . We're here until ten o'clock tonight. If you have a message to communicate to someone, here's the number again, 2-3-4-5-9 . . ."

Leslie wrote it down. She could imagine the scene at the radio station right now. She had passed by the courtyard of the church earlier in the week and found people jamming the large outdoor staircase that led to the radio station upstairs, holding their little announcements to be read. It was too crowded for her to stay. But she had been able to say hello to the Canadian nun.

She turned up the sound, got out her notebook and a pen. There were another dozen people searching for missing relatives or people who had gone to the capital and had not yet returned to the countryside. The details were sometimes meager, sometimes heartbreakingly explicit. "Madame Patricia Lemurat, a message of love from your husband, Lionel. He's asking that you forgive him; he says he hasn't abandoned you and you should get in contact with his brother. Uh-oh, Lionel, that doesn't sound good." She heard the edge of humor and mild reproach in Soeur Madeleine's voice. She imagined Patricia Lemurat angrily shaking her head at her errant husband.

The notices went on for another few minutes, then Soeur Madeleine announced the upcoming news program. After a short hymn, she began with the international roundup. Leslie realized how starved she was for news; *The New York Times* was impossible to find outside of the hotels in Pétionville. The Royale carried only *Paris-Match* and *Jours de France*. She had learned a lot about Monaco's royal family, though, and why French secretaries preferred long pleated skirts on the job.

Soeur Madeleine delivered the news in a short, clipped tone, her Creole fluent. Later, the same news would be rebroadcast in French. "Coffee exports are climbing, sugar prices falling on the world market . . . In France, labor has gained a friend with the nomination of Frédéric Pepard, who will head the government's negotiating team in its dispute with the postal workers . . ." The rest of the world news was all too familiar: another meeting of Arab leaders in the Middle East, an airline merger in the United States, a murder trial in New York involving a teenage gang . . . The Washington news was equally uneventful. She went over to the desk and scanned the reports she had prepared to fax, listening with one ear as the program turned to national, then regional events.

". . . In Santo Domingo, the Haitian Minister of Agriculture will meet with his Dominican counterpart, Señor Juan Santiago Campeche, to seek a solution to the current conflict in the bateys on the border . . . The Dominicans are demanding that the laborers work longer hours to make up for the poor harvest—on the basis of a contract made between the Dominican government and the previous, Duvalier government of Haiti . . . Listen now to our correspondent in Santo Domingo, who is reporting that workers have begun deserting the camps following a rebellion . . ."

Leslie quickly turned the dial to see if the government-controlled station was carrying the same news. It was. She heard a similar recapping of world events and turned back to catch Soeur Madeleine say: "Still no confirmation on this report by our correspondent that a number of students have been arrested in several towns in the south. Again, anyone with information about this is asked to please call us here at 2-3-4-5-9. Here's the number again: 2-3-4-5-9. If these reports are true," Soeur Madeleine editorialized, "then we are seeing a veritable assault on Haitian youth. Regarding other cases, we repeat our demand for the government to carry out a formal investigation into the following cases of missing persons . . ."

Leslie wrote quickly, in her own version of shorthand: "Gerard Joseph, 16 years old, disappeared on June 2. His badly bruised body was found on Delmas 27 . . . Earlier this week at Delmas 45, a fresh corpse was discovered in the back of an abandoned truck. No one has come forward to claim the truck . . . Near Jean Rabel the police are protesting the kidnapping of four boys by Mercidieu Belvy, the local section chief, who is accused of a campaign of terror against residents of this region . . ."

After a recitation of twenty other names, Leslie's pen ran out of ink. Frustrated, she wrote the names down anyway, hoping to make some sense of inkless impressions later on. Cedric George was one of them.

She listened to the end of the broadcast, which was followed by the sound of bells announcing the evening Mass, which would be celebrated by Bishop Privat, whose nomination for archbishop had been formally announced. The first hymn was "Alelouya Granmet La Louvri Bra-li." Alleluia Almighty God Who Opened His Arms to Us. Leslie fished around in her suitcase under the bed and found a pack of Bic pens. Holding the paper up to the light, she made out the names and retraced the markings. There were only three names that she did not already have.

The dinner bell sounded again. Conch soup was on the menu tonight, and regardless of her sour stomach, she was not about to pass it up. She put her notebook under her mattress, smoothed her hair, and slipped on a shift and her sandals. Before turning out the light, she blew a little kiss to the now purplish chameleon. Watch my stuff, little guy.

22

"Julie?"

"Who is it?"

"It's Père Emmanuel. I'm outside the gate. Can you buzz me in? I think your dog is getting tired."

"I'm so sorry. I'm sending someone down right now."

A minute later, a young woman ran out to the gate. She yelled at the dog, slapped it with her rolled-up newspaper, then peered through the opening and smiled at the priest. It was Thérèse, the cook. Behind her, Dr. Sylvie stood at the top of the driveway, dressed in slacks and a light sweater.

"You caught me in my mountain wear," she joked, embracing him. "Even my family doesn't see me in long pants."

He admired her striped red-and-green slacks, tapered at the ankles. The doctor wore olive canvas boots, which matched her sweater. "You've been walking?" he asked her.

"I have." She nodded. "I went up toward Furcy to give some vaccinations."

"Polio?"

"And cholera," she replied.

"Cholera?" The news alarmed him. "Is there an outbreak?"

"Not yet." She calmed him. "It's just a precaution. But it's headed this way, from Peru. It could come here with the boats that dock at the Cape. Or with some of the people working in the camps near the border. We're not taking any chances. If it arrives here, it will mean a lot of deaths."

Dr. Sylvie led him inside through the lower part of the residence. Like most houses in this area, it was set deep into the mountain, with a wraparound balcony and roof patio that offered a 360-degree view of the landscape. It was a gorgeous setting. Inside, the decor was tasteful, a bit modern for Emmanuel's taste, with a mix of abstract Haitian paintings and small metal sculptures. The sofas were red. "I like the lilies." He pointed to one canvas. "Very delicate. Who's the artist?"

"I bought that in Martinique." She smiled. "Have you been there?"

"No," he admitted. "Is it like here?"

"A little greener. And much calmer, of course. Their Creole has some strange words in it too. But it's a good place to take a holiday. I can recommend a hotel if you ever go."

He thought about Gerard and Jeanne. That's where they should go.

"Their national team is not doing well this year," he told her. "They're usually pretty strong."

She chuckled. "Always thinking about soccer, aren't you?"

There was a standing wooden ashtray, a snake climbing a pole. A voudon object, he noted, the open mouth of the serpent the bowl for the ashes. "This is beautiful too," he remarked.

She nodded. "That's actually payment from one of my patients. I prefer it to money, in any case."

"A good deal," he said. "All I ever get are new robes and altar cloths for the church."

She laughed, leading him up a winding inner staircase with a carved wooden banister. "I was about to take my afternoon coffee on the patio. Will you join me? I'm waiting for a friend to dine with me, but that won't be for a little while. And she might be late."

"With pleasure," he said. He wondered who the friend was. At thirty-three, Julie had yet to marry, although not for a lack of admirers. Emmanuel had met a boyfriend once, but it was rumored later that he was bisexual. Of course, anyone who didn't marry was thought to be homosexual. How many people think that about me? he wondered. Probably a lot.

He knew the same rumor circulated about Julie, who rarely socialized. Looking at her back, her svelte figure and styled hair, her dangling earrings and manicured hands, he found no clues. Nor was it the kind of thing he felt comfortable asking about. But he was curious. "This way," Julie indicated. She pushed open a door. The patio was broad and pleasant, with a large Cinzano umbrella, deck chairs, and a table.

If she is a lesbian, it would explain why she chooses to live up here, rather than downtown, he thought. It's so private up here. That nurse at the hospital she's always with—what's her name again? Nicole . . . Nicole Deroncourt, that's right. She's that way. I wonder if there's anything between them. I should ask her about it. But she might be offended. Maybe if I tell her what people think about me—that might break the ice.

They settled into the round-backed chairs. Thérèse arrived with a tray bearing a blue enamel coffeepot, small demitasse cups, a can of evaporated milk, and dark, lumpy sugar in a stainless-steel bowl. "I take it black," Dr. Sylvie said. "How about you?"

"With a touch of milk," he said. "No sugar."

Dr. Sylvie smiled, putting two scoops of sugar into her own cup as Thérèse poured. "Thérèse has a meat pie that's fresh. Will you have some?"

"Are you having some?"

"Naturally." She laughed.

"A small slice, then. Just a finger. I ate at one o'clock."

Emmanuel noticed that Thérèse's arm bore a large burn mark by the elbow. She grinned at him and used both hands to carefully pour a large dot of evaporated milk into his coffee. The milk made him think of Jeanne, who had been at the student vigil, along with Edith and Victor, when he had gone the previous evening. A dozen policemen had been there too, but they made no move to arrest anyone. He had delivered the outdoor evening sermon without incident.

They settled back to enjoy the view. "To what do I owe this visit?" Dr. Sylvie asked. She drank her coffee delicately, with a little finger extended.

Would a lesbian do that? Emmanuel wondered, then caught himself. I do that. He smiled inwardly. I must be a lesbian.

The sky was big and gray, still damp from the afternoon rain.

"I had a visitor," he began, then changed his mind. "That is to say, I had a conversation with someone. Since you work at the hospital, I thought you might be able to answer a question."

"You know I'm ignorant about most of what goes on there, but certainly."

"I heard—it's nothing certain, just a rumor—that there was a body brought in from Fontamara. Last week sometime. It was in a state of severe decomposition. Do you know anything about it?"

"Nothing," she replied immediately. "But I doubt it came to us, unless it came in after I left. It's funny you ask, because I just checked the morgue for a friend of Gerard's—an American woman."

"Leslie Doyle?"

"You know her?"

"We've spoken," Emmanuel said. "But we haven't met in person yet. Actually, I told her and Gerard about a case—a young woman from Fontamara—she's been arrested."

"Is there a connection?" Dr. Sylvie spooned more sugar before helping herself to another demitasse of espresso.

"Not that we know of, although they're both from Fontamara. But we don't know why she's been arrested—the authorities won't even confirm that. Gerard went to the prison himself. And I spoke to the police in Fontamara. They say they don't know anything about either case."

"Who's your source regarding the body?" the doctor asked. "Another prisoner?"

"No—a military source," he said. "Actually a fellow who works in traffic. That's confidential. But he doesn't know much. He told me about both things, but he couldn't tell me anything else. I called the military hospital and spoke to someone I know there. He's honest enough. They didn't know anything about a corpse from Fontamara."

"I'm sure I would have heard about it if it came to us," Dr. Sylvie said. "Of course, that kind of thing happens. But I'll ask around. There's a little guy who watches the cars for us in the parking lot. If they came into the hospital from the back, he would have seen it."

"Thank you, Julie," he said, accepting more coffee. "Changing the subject, what did Leslie Doyle want?"

"She had a whole list of names of people who are missing. Including Cedric George. I don't know him. Do you?"

"We discussed it. Victor and Edith had two young men from Cedric's group visit them. They've come here to hide. But up to now, Cedric hasn't contacted anyone from their group. Or anyone else, for that matter," he added. "It's very troubling."

"I called the other hospitals after talking to Leslie." Dr. Sylvie drained her cup. "But I didn't find anything. We had only one unclassified case; I showed her the autopsy report. I have the copy with me. If you want to see it, I'll go and get it. It's for Gerard."

"I'm going to see him this evening. I'll be happy to give it to him. By the way," he added, "have you been following the case of the students?"

"I know about the arrests this weekend," she said. "Are there more?"

"No, no," he replied. "But we haven't confirmed their condition. Only one young man was released, and he says some of them—the leaders—have been beaten."

"I was going to call the prison to schedule a visit because Leslie had asked me to," Dr. Sylvie interrupted. "I'll just insist that we have to go in now. That way I can find out."

"Fantastic." He smiled. "I knew I could count on you."

"They might not let me in. You remember last time."

"You'll get in," he said confidently. "But I'll be surprised if they let an outsider like Leslie enter."

Thérèse arrived with a meat pie filled with pimientos, served cold. Dr. Sylvie got up to get the report. A few minutes later, she handed Emmanuel a copy, barely legible. He took out his glasses to read it, then turned it over.

"The fingerprints are smudged," she noted. "They're quite useless—I told Leslie that." She took her seat. "I think she was surprised when I told her we don't use fingerprints in cases here as evidence. I only had mine taken when I started working at the hospital. What about you?"

"I don't think I ever have," he said. "No, I haven't."

He silently read the report, concentrating: Male. Twenty-seven to thirty-five years old. Probable cause of death: brain hemorrhage. Estimated time of death: August 26 or 27 . . . That was two days after the attack on the Konbit office. Height: 160 centimeters. That was roughly Cedric's height.

"Wouldn't they have mentioned if his nose was broken?" he asked Dr. Sylvie.

"That depends on how many other autopsies they had to do that day." She glanced at the report, doubtful. "The intern who did this is usually very thorough. I take it Cedric George had a broken nose."

"Twice," he said. "He was tortured in the prison in Hinche. In 1983, I think." He shook his head. "It doesn't tell you much, does it?" He folded the piece of paper and put it away. "Which police division is in charge of a case like this?"

"If it's political and there's a suspicion of homicide, it goes to the intelligence police. Otherwise, it goes into a big pile and I don't think anyone looks at it again."

He made a face, knowing she was probably right.

"I'll ask about this." She indicated the report. "If it's the intelligence bureau, it won't do any good. They never tell us anything."

Dr. Sylvie watched him eat. "Anyway," she said a short while later, "as I was saying to Leslie, if you want to know how someone died, you can usually find out through an autopsy. But if you want to know how they lived, that's something else entirely. Then it's not enough to have the actual fingerprints or to know the size and weight of the organs. Then you have to look somewhere else— under the bone."

"Under the bone?" He looked at her quizzically. "What do you mean?"

"To get a true measure of the person—to really understand their life. I don't understand why these people only care about the death. I mean, I know it's the kind of work they're doing—the human rights work—but how someone lived is more important than how they died, don't you think? That's my opinion."

"And that's also why you're a doctor," he teased her. "That's your job—keeping people alive."

"I'm biased, you mean? Well, maybe. But seriously. Why do these people from the outside only care what's happening to us after someone dies or is murdered? That's the only thing that counts to them. But it doesn't count if people are hungry. You see what I mean?"

"Absolutely," he agreed. "But I do think the people doing human rights work share your opinion. I really do."

"Maybe," she said doubtfully. "But then why can't we get money from those same organizations to buy medicine or food? The only things that interest them are our reports. That's what they like—statistics. That's how they think about us—we're statistics."

Before he could reply, they heard a car honking. "That must be my friend," Dr. Sylvie said. Emmanuel stood up too. "I have to be going now anyway," he said. "I want to stop by Gerard's before it's too late. I'll give him this. And thank you for taking the time to see me. I know it's your day off."

"Mais non," she reassured him. "I'd never see you otherwise." She escorted him downstairs. "I'll call as soon as I know something."

On the way out, Emmanuel encountered Nicole Deroncourt. Aha, he said to himself as he embraced her. "Bonsoir, Nicole. The doctor is upstairs waiting for you. On the patio. I hope I haven't delayed your dinner."

"I'm the one who's late, Père." She embraced him. "The road was jammed coming up here."

Outside, he wiped away the lipstick marks she had left on his cheeks. Julie and Nicole, he mused. Interesting.

It is not only that I fear death; I cannot imagine my own absence. The idea of never again seeing those I love makes me sad. Sad is not even the right word. It hurts me, tears at my soul to know I will not have another life. I am thirty-four years old and have seen too little of the world to die now. There are too many things I must do and experience, places I have never seen except in pictures. My life cannot be in vain. I will not let my son believe the lies they say about his father. They say I am a terrorist, a coward. They say I plot against our people. I cannot let anyone believe those lies. They lie about us like they lie about anyone who seeks his freedom. They lied about Boukman, called him a traitor. We are not traitors. But they will have to catch me to kill me, I will never let them throw me back into their jail. That would be my death.

I would like to meet Fidel Castro. And Haile Selassie—he was a great leader. The Cuban people triumphed where we have failed. Their revolution is real. The only ones who say Castro is bad are the ones trying to make money for themselves; no one else says anything bad about him. I think Castro is like Dessalines—a strong man with a bad temper. Because everyone wants to kill him all the time—the Americans—so he has to protect himself. He's become hard with his enemies. The Cubans had the rich too, and the blans, but they never had the Tontons Macoutes.

Fidel Castro and Jimmy Carter. I liked Jimmy Carter. He wanted to help us. For a white man, a blan, he was honest; up to now, the only good American President. Even our good men become too hard, but it is not true they all become bad. Dessalines, Charlemagne Peralte, Toussaint, Christophe, Boyer, Pétion, Boukman, especially Boukman. He understood La Vogue; he understood how five men could be harnessed together to do something besides pull the white man's boat. But they kill all our good people. It's the same thing with Castro even though we aren't Communists. And it takes time to organize a revolution when you are too hungry to walk or think. That's why so few of us fight for a real revolution.

In Cuba they were not as hungry or poor; Castro and his men had a little money, they had education. Castro came from a good family. Look at Che Guevara. He tried to fight with a poor army and they murdered him.

Cousin brings me the news that the Dominicans have helped Luckner Zéphyr, that Tonton Macoute, given him a big house in Santo Domingo and a job. The Dominicans need a real revolution too, they suffer from the same disease we do. We all come from one land and the same bad seeds were sown here and there. The bad seeds of the French and the Spanish, all of them are bastards, their fathers were criminals chased from the prisons of Europe. Now all they know is how to exploit. They teach us their history in our schools, they forget La Vogue. They want to say Rwa Kristof was great but he lost, he was defeated. We know it was different. We say you belong to the biggest band of criminals. It doesn't matter how much of our good black blood you mix up with yours, you can't overcome your history. That is what you see in a man like Luckner Zéphyr, a black man who thinks like a blan, who has been poisoned to hate other black men. A bad white black man. And the same with those Dominican generals who give Luckner Zéphyr a big house and let him marry one of their daughters. Wait till they learn that Luckner Zéphyr is already married to his gun, Kares Tifi. Wait till they see how he treats women, without taking his boots off and holding Kares Tifi in one hand. Maybe that woman will refuse to be beaten and turn that gun on him.

That's what I tell the others. Our whole island needs a real revolution. These elections are not the answer. Look at what has happened since they said yes to the election. Not one of our candidates has received any money, any help. It is just the big men again. And none of those big men understand how we live, they don't want to. They live the way they do because we suffer. And even when they are not the richest, they forget their roots. That's why I ask, What is it we want? An election where none of our people can write their names on the ballot? A politician who stays in a big house in Port-au-Prince? No, no, that is not a solution. Bilten se papye, bayonet se fe. The ballot is paper, the bayonet is steel. Dessalines was right. The only thing to do is what we did under Papa Doc, organize in our little groups. The konbit is revolution and the konbit is La Vogue; it is just, and no man, no woman, no child is more important than another.

They think I am some uneducated peasant. The big men laugh at me, but I know I am right. It is they who have lost their courage to think as I do. When you survive like I have, you see revolution is the only real chance. That's why we must strike and refuse to work. That is the only power the big men understand. We don't have money, we don't have anything. They have taken everything away except our labor. That is why we have to demand education before the election, and an election for education. Am I witnessing a revolution? How can it be, then, that I have to run and hide, that my feet are caked with blood, that my house has been burned down a second time?

Did we really get rid of Duvalier? You want to pretend, everybody wants to pretend. But it was not only us. The Americans, they put Duvalier in the palace, they gave him the money to kill all our best people, and they let Jean-Claude steal the national treasure, and then, just like that, they put him on a jet. A criminal who deserves to have his head cut off. Koupe tet, boule kay. The Americans and the French, we know who put Toussaint in that French prison and let him starve to death. The same French. We have to think about La Vogue when we think of our enemies. We have to make the Haitian remember he is not like the American or the French or the Dominican who gives the criminal a hiding place and a big house and lets him spend stolen money.

Koupe tet, boule kay. Cut off the head, burn down the house. We have to listen to Dessalines. Look how they cut off Boukman's head. We have to bleed the bad blood from our veins. Wherever there is bad blood, blan, milat, neg. Pe Jules and Pe Thomas, they are good blans, they understand how we live. They are trying to help us. They think I should go to an embassy and seek protection. They think the Canadians will be more willing to help me than the Americans and the French. Because the Canadians suffered from the French like we do, even if they are blans too.

The Haitian blans. They say we are like animals because we burn the Tontons Macoutes. But they don't understand how they have *forced us to live. They are the ones who forget about justice. Even if the Tonton Macoute seems like the worst black white man, he is still part of La Vogue, and the blan always has the biggest whip. I agree with Edouard about that. Why is the Tonton Macoute so bad? Because he knows how the whip feels and he is afraid of it. In his being he remembers. But the blan always had the bigger gun and the blan is not afraid to use it either. The Tonton Macoute may appear more dangerous, more desperate, may kill more easily for less money, even for no money at all, only the little bit of power or pleasure it gives him, but he is still nothing compared to a blan.*

The American blans. They are the ones who had the power to get rid of Duvalier. But Duvalier was their choice, even when he turned his machete on us. They had the power because they have the money and they can buy the weapons. But they never suffered the whip. And the Haitian blans know their big houses and money protect them from the whip. And until we have a real revolution, that is true. Their logic is sound. They can use the poor black man to kill his brother and they can look down from their rich houses and say, You are acting like dogs. And what happens when we burn down even a single house of one rich blan? Then they become dogs too. Look how they buy all the attack dogs in America and bring them here to protect their property. Animals recognize one another, don't they?

I wonder what it must feel like to have a white skin, to be a blan. Like having a passport, I think. So when the revolution comes, the blan can get on the jet and the French or Americans or Dominicans will see his white skin and say, Here we will let you buy a house, we will never ask, Where does all your money come from in such a poor country?

Even if I die, if they manage to catch me and kill me, it doesn't matter. My son will avenge me, and if it is not my son, then Edouard's son, or the sons of all the others. In ten or fifty years someone will take a torch to Luckner Zéphyr's house or find some other measure of justice for what we have suffered. And then it will be a real revolution. Then I will rest in my grave.

For now all I can see with this election is the fever it causes in our people. Small dogs fighting over the smallest bone without enough meat on it, but they smell the blood inside the bone and it makes them crazy. And their noses are so close to the ground they forget to look up and see who has taken all the meat for himself. They are developing the mentality of the Macoutes, the same mentality that bites without thinking because it has been whipped too many times, only a crazy animal is left. A fever to make the little dogs crazy, to make us attack one another, that is what I am witnessing. Not a revolution.

23

"Are you sure this is where he said we should be waiting?"

Clemard's brow beaded with sweat. "It's here," he answered Leslie. But his tone was uncertain, even less certain than the day they had gone to the paupers' graves at Titanyen. And that day he had been wrong, Leslie remembered, her anger rising. It was 2:50; their meeting had been scheduled for 2:30. There was still no sign of the man. Had he already been here and left?

Was this even the place? It seemed unlikely to her. Maybe he had been unable to come, maybe there had been a problem. The thought worried her. Everything seemed to worry her now. The man had told Père Emmanuel 2:30, sharp, at the fork in the road. Where was he? Hadn't she felt on waking up that something was going to go wrong? Call it instinct, paranoia; something was off. She was tempted to say as much to Clemard, but she held her tongue. You're scaring yourself now, she told herself. Nothing's going to happen. Calm down.

She watched Clemard get out and clean the windshield for the second time in an hour.

They were perched in the S-curve of an uphill dirt road which had been hand-carved out of the mountain, or so it looked. Clemard had parked the jeep as close to the mountainside as possible; he could barely get in and out his door. Not that there was much space for Leslie either, only about two feet. Just ahead of them was the fork in the road, though it looked like nothing more than a donkey path to Leslie. It was just about where it should be on the map the priest had drawn for them.

Driving inland, they had been forced to stop a half dozen times to remove rocks, tree limbs, and plain garbage from the road. On both sides, the vertical drop of the mountain was so steep that Leslie stopped looking over the side. Instead, she helped Clemard find flat, solid stretches in the road. The exercise in concentration had left her nauseated. Luckily, they had been warned that the drive would be difficult, and Leslie had brought her Pepto-Bismol tablets.

She took two more now, and offered the cellophane packet to Clemard. He declined it with a shake of his head, his eyes avoiding hers.

Was he angry? she wondered. It was his fault for being a lousy driver. He shouldn't have pretended that he knew how to handle a four-wheel-drive jeep if he didn't, she thought unreasonably. My cousin taught me. What kind of line was that? Come on, Clemard. She tried to catch his eye. How could he be angry at her? She was the one who was angry at him. There had been moments when the trip was so bad she was convinced the jeep was going to plunge right over the side of the mountain. Several times, she thought, feeling her irritation grow.

"Are you sure you don't want any?" She offered the tablets again.

He shook his head, a tight, grim expression on his face. "No pills," he said. "I don't like pills." He wiped the windshield hard with a rag, then stood back from the jeep. He lit a cigarette, but did not offer her one. She had told him she was cutting down. Still, it irked her now that he hadn't offered. You're being a jerk, she thought, watching him smoke, it's that damn pride. Well, your pride almost got us killed, mister. What have you got to say to that? Clemard shook his head slightly, continued to ignore her. She sighed and sat back. Damn it! Where was that man? Another ten minutes went by.

Make peace, Leslie told herself after a while, looking over at Clemard. The man simply overestimated his skills. Besides, you can't be mad at him for lying. You lie all the time. Little lies, an inner voice rose to her defense, white lies. Nothing important. This was important. We almost died. Almost, she pursed her lips. But not quite.

She got out clumsily, climbing onto the hood of the jeep. Clemard had positioned himself nearby, atop a high, jutting rock. Leslie's light denim pants were covered with dust. She brushed them off. "I'm sorry we . . ." she began. "Well, I'm glad we're here." She realized how ridiculous she sounded. Clemard's face was expressionless; he lit another cigarette. The uncomfortable distance remained.

"You know, Clemard," she said, half seriously. "A little while ago I was planning my funeral. I said to myself back there, This is it, Leslie. And you know what I thought?"

He did not respond.

"I thought"—she smiled—"No, no we can't crash now, we can't die. Do you know why?"

He looked over, remotely curious.

"Because Bertrand would be right. You remember what he said? And I thought that would be terrible."

An eyebrow, a flicker of interest.

Leslie continued: "Blan Bertrand would be right," she said sarcastically, pushing herself off the hood, "and we would be dead. A terrible combination, I think."

She walked over to him and asked for the last drag of his cigarette.

"You mean you took a jeep and not my beautiful Diahatsu?" She mimed Bertrand's self-righteous tone. "Not my wonderful Japanese machine that never stalls and never slips and has such great radio reception?"

He chewed his inner lip, somewhat amused.

"Madanm Leslie—" he began.

"Leslie," she corrected him automatically. She took the cigarette from him, inhaled deeply.

"I, you know, I never drove a jeep like this one before. It's the truth."

She flicked the butt into the road. "Yes, Clemard, now I know that." She gave a short laugh. "But I must say, you learned very quickly. It's all right," she said. "It doesn't matter."

"It didn't look that hard"—he squinted—"but it's . . . it's not clear."

"No," she agreed. "It's not clear." She wanted another cigarette. "Especially," she added, "when you're climbing at an angle of forty-five degrees."

"Sixty degrees," he corrected her, breaking out into a grin. "Woy! My heart was beating!" He tapped his chest.

"Your heart was beating!" she countered. "But my heart stopped. I was terrified."

He shook his head, looking over at the jeep.

"Yah." He clicked his tongue. "Blan Bertrand—he loves to be

right." He looked at her appraisingly. "You don't like Met Bertrand. I can see that."

She nodded, admitting it. "And I don't think he likes me either."

Clemard snorted. "He said to me, Madanm Leslie is not like her father."

"You should be happy about that." She smiled, adding, "Actually, Bertrand has changed, I think. He's gotten cynical. Or maybe I just didn't notice it before—I was a lot younger."

Clemard suddenly hunched over, staring and pointing, his expression concentrated. Leslie realized that he was mimicking her, the way she had acted in the jeep, scouting for him, pointing at the rocks they were about to hit.

"If I hadn't done that we would have gone right over." She laughed defensively.

"You were panicking." Clemard nodded as he walked, hunched over like an old man, to the edge of the road, then teetered on his tiptoes, still pointing.

"Clemard! Don't! Be careful!"

He spun around; his eyes lit up. For the first time, she saw a hint of the comedian within, the class clown.

"You should be an actor," she told him when he came back, then added quickly: "Not that there are a lot of jobs for actors in Haiti. But I mean, you have talent, I can see it. That was a good imitation of me."

"I was being serious." He brought his face up to hers, alarmingly close for a second. "Because you are so serious." Here he frowned, and again she recognized herself.

"I'm not that bad. Am I?"

He cocked his head, then nodded again. "Yes—very serious. Work, work, work." He pretended to be her, scribbling at her pad.

"Méchant," she threw out. Meanie.

He scribbled more furiously. "Always working," he said. "Night and day. No sleep, no dancing, just work."

He wasn't being mean, he was flirting with her. She realized it as she looked up, caught his eyes watching her. They held the expression he had had the night of the cocktail party, when there was something he had wanted to say, and she had not known what, but somewhere she had had a sense of it. Her chest tightened.

Don't say anything, an inner voice warned. Don't start anything. He's married. He's half your age. She could feel his eyes on her.

She looked away, smiling, trying to act casual. He's beautiful, but he's married, Leslie repeated. Remember? You don't sleep with people who are involved.

She declined to meet his eyes, focused instead on the ground, on a line of banana trees. In the La Saline market, they had used the wide banana leaves as plates. She felt her face was burning.

Clemard was still studying her, a half-smile on his lips. She could feel the question hanging in the air between them. He wanted her, that's what she could feel right now, this man eleven years her junior, whose emotions were difficult for her to read, harder to judge. There was no mistaking it now, though. He wanted to kiss her. Her lips felt chapped and suddenly vulnerable; she wanted to cover her mouth. Because no one was around and no one would see them and no one would ever have to know. Tempting. She smiled to herself, still looking the other way.

"Let's stay a little longer," she finally said, avoiding the issue. "Another ten minutes," she added. "Is that okay?"

He looked at her steadily, a look that saw and understood. The woman was afraid. He nodded again. "Okay," he said.

Mr. Cool, she thought, as they waited. Mr. Cool. She already regretted that they would not sleep together, that the question had even been aired.

"Okay," he repeated, shrugging.

Okay, she said to herself, but not okay. I wish I could. Because you're beautiful.

September 3

We the undersigned, Gesner Frances, doctor of medicine, Sylvio Toussaint, doctor of medicine, and Roger Paul, doctor of medicine, certify having performed on September 3 an autopsy of the following cadaver whose identity remains unknown and whose corpse was exhumed upon orders of the Haitian government. We have observed the following findings:

At the opening of the cadaver, we find a thoracic cage divided into two segments, superior and inferior, with severe fractures of the sternum and ribs (⅓ at least). The lung cavities are filled with liquid blood (2.5 liters). The right lung weighs 325 grams, the left lung 300 grams. The heart shows a rupture in the anterior of the ventricle and in the right auricle and weighs 250 grams. The peritoneal cavity contains over a liter of liquid blood. The abdominal organs are in the proper cavities. We note a rupture of the stomach and the liver, which weighs 1,200 grams. The spleen weighs 100 grams, the kidneys 130 grams. The other organs show nothing unusual in their appearance.

The opening of the cranium reveals a severe fracture of the frontal bone and the occipital bone. The brain weighs 1,400 grams, and we note a hematoma in the left hemisphere (left parietotemporal region).

We note several wounds on the left arm and wrist, including multiple fractures; two wounds on the upper part of the right arm; a wound and cutaneous burning of the skin on the right shoulder near the clavicle.

ANATOMIC DIAGNOSIS

1. Fractures of sternum and ribs (⅓ at least)
2. Multiple bullet wounds to the thorax and superior limbs
3. Bilateral hemothorax
4. Rupture of the heart (ventricle and right auricle)
5. Rupture of the stomach and liver
6. Severe fracture of frontal bone and occipital bone of skull
7. Hematoma in left hemisphere of brain

8. Two wounds of 2 cm in diameter on top third of left arm with multiple fractures of bones and wrist
9. Two large wounds of 5 cm on upper right arm near clavicle
10. A wound of 2 cm by 2 cm on right shoulder

Signed [and stamped with the seal of the Haitian state]:

Dr. Gesner Frances   Dr. Sylvio Toussaint   Dr. Roger Paul
Military Hospital   University Hospital   University Hospital
Haiti   Haiti   Haiti

24

Gerard pulled his car up behind a wooden cart in the spot where the judge's car was usually parked. The judge had promised him a meeting. It was just after noon. Most of the offices were closed. He asked a man sitting on the steps that led down from the corner of the building, "Is anyone in there?"

The man shook his head. "They locked this door. But there's someone inside. Go around and knock."

Gerard saw a receptionist sitting behind a desk, reading a comic book. A wooden banister prevented visitors from going into the adjoining courtyard, where the judge's quarters were located.

"I'm here to see the judge," he said, shaking hands with the man. "I'm Gerard Metellus, a lawyer. We had an appointment."

The man nodded, but his expression remained nonplussed. Gerard watched as he slowly opened a drawer, rummaged around, removed a pen, then a faded blue cloth ledger. *Visiteurs*, it was labeled on the front. The man turned the book over for Gerard to sign.

"Is he here?" Gerard asked the man. "I don't see his car."

"He's out. But he'll be back." The man went over to another, bigger desk. He flipped open an appointment ledger. "I don't see your name," he told Gerard.

"We spoke over the phone. It's an important matter," Gerard added, somewhat unnecessarily. He could already tell the man had no idea where the judge had gone. "Did he say when he was coming back?"

"No." There was a knock on the door. "Who is it?" The receptionist had locked it behind Gerard with a huge iron hook. "Who's there?"

Gerard could not understand the answer. The receptionist got up and unhooked the door. A stout uniformed man stepped inside. He looked at Gerard, then at the receptionist. Gerard could tell from the bars on his uniform that he was a lieutenant colonel. A small name tag said "Dauphin."

"Is the magistrate here?" the soldier asked with impatience. "I have a message to give him."

"He's out." The receptionist thumbed at Gerard. "This man's waiting for him too."

The lieutenant colonel nodded to Gerard, but did not introduce himself. He motioned to the receptionist to come outside. The man hesitated, then followed. Not quite out of earshot of Gerard, the officer spoke: "The commander sent me. He wants the magistrate to come by headquarters—Quartier Général—at six. Don't forget, six o'clock." The receptionist came back inside. Gerard watched the uniformed man cross the street and get into a black jeep with fat tires. A woman was in the passenger seat, two children in the back. A family outing, he guessed.

The receptionist did not offer him a chair. Instead, he suggested, "Why don't you wait in the courtroom. That way you can see him if he arrives. I'm not supposed to let anyone in here during the lunch hour." Gerard doubted this; the man probably just wanted to read his comic book. But he agreed, reluctantly.

The courtroom adjoining the reception area was empty. It opened out onto the street, allowing natural light to flood an otherwise dark room. Like many of the city's buildings, it dated from the early colonial days. The furniture was sparse, even for a courtroom: a dozen long wooden benches, a small jury box, a witness chair. The judge's desk was broad, long, and unadorned. The benches looked like church pews, rough-hewn wood softened by generations of hands that had gripped them anxiously, waiting for a verdict.

Gerard surveyed the room from the archway entrance. It was completely familiar to him, down to the initials children had scratched into the backs of the benches. He walked over to the wall where the portraits of past judges—all male and hung up high to thwart thieves—looked solemnly down from a point close to the ceiling. Why would anyone want to steal any of them anyway? he wondered. They lent the courtroom a faint air of decorum, as if presiding over the stark space and the mahogany benches. He stood before each portrait, playing the game he had played so often, trying to imagine each subject's life and identity, his vices and pleasures, the kinds of cases he might have tried.

The courtroom had once been a coffee warehouse. Sometimes, in the course of a trial, Gerard imagined the men loading back-breaking bags of coffee off wooden carts, like the one outside, onto the huge scales that had hung from the beam along the warehouse ceiling, imagined wild arguments over the shape and smell and weight of coffee, the currency of the day.

He moved over to a bulletin board near another corner of the room. The typed notices posted there were old. He didn't recognize any of the cases. After reading them, he took a seat on one of the benches and sighed, feeling tired. The whole episode at the prison earlier that morning had exhausted him. The officer on duty had been needlessly dismissive, declaring that the warden was off the prison grounds. Gerard hadn't believed him. The man had also denied having any record of a detainee named Elyse Voltaire. Departing, Gerard had glimpsed several youths on their knees, their hands on their heads, in the inner corridor of the prison. Two of them he had recognized as students from St. George's College.

Gerard had dozed off when he heard the sound of a motor and recognized the judge's car. The man sitting on the corner steps hurriedly pulled his cart out of the way to let the judge move his car into the space. Gerard watched the judge give the man a gourde.

"Hello, your honor," he greeted the older man. The judge used his steel-tipped cane to climb up the stairs. They shook hands.

"Metellus . . . I forgot . . . Sorry about that . . . I had to go out . . . Follow me . . . follow me." The judge urged him into the reception area, where the surly receptionist he had already met stood up at attention. The man nodded unhappily at Gerard, as if he half expected the lawyer to be gone by now.

"Wait here a moment," the judge told Gerard. He went over to confer with the dour man.

"Let's go into my office." The judge waved Gerard over. "You can bring us some coffee," he said somewhat curtly to his aide.

Gerard watched as the portly judge settled in behind his desk. The only objects on it were a telephone, a paper blotter, a tray of onionskin, carbon paper, and an ink pad.

"So tell me, Metellus, how is your dear mother? It's been a long time since I've spoken to her. Is she well?"

"Very well, your honor." Gerard tried to remember if Judge Daniel had ever addressed him by his first name. Not that he could recall, despite the fact that their families were distantly related.

"She was a beautiful woman in her youth." The judge untied his shoes as he spoke. Gerard watched him partly ease his feet out of the shoes. A pungent smell like Camembert rose from the floor. "Always a lovely woman. She must still look pretty good." He smiled at Gerard.

"With this heat," the judge continued, moving around in his chair, "my feet swell." He rolled down his knee-high silk socks; his ankles were hairless and surprisingly delicate, given his owlish figure. The judge shifted in his seat until he was comfortable, removed a handkerchief to wipe his upper lip, then found his reading glasses, but did not put them on. He unbuttoned the top button of his shirt, and throughout a series of other adjustments, remained smiling. He looked at Gerard. "Now, what is it I can do for you, Metellus?"

"Well, your honor," Gerard began, hesitating. "It's about a client of mine."

The judge nodded, toying with his glasses.

"Her family contacted me through a mutual friend. Apparently she was picked up by some soldiers. They're convinced she's being held at the prison, but I went there and the officer on duty denied the arrest and refused to let me talk to the warden. I thought you might be able to assist me."

Gerard couldn't gauge the judge's response. He was somewhat more moderate than the other judges, but still a government lackey, and the prison fell under his jurisdiction.

Gerard noticed that, although his nails were bitten to the quick, Judge Daniel had a bad habit of picking at things. He now scraped at something stuck to his desk, the remains of food, it appeared. His fingertips were nicotine-stained.

"You're implying it's an illegal arrest?" The judge's voice remained neutral, but Gerard saw a glint of intelligence behind the benign, somewhat comic façade.

"An eyewitness saw her getting into a jeep with two soldiers." He was repeating what Emmanuel had told him, although the police at Fontamara had denied this. "She's from above Fontamara, your honor, a peasant woman. She wasn't involved in any political activities. There's no reason for anyone to arrest her." Gerard's tone was assured.

"I see." The judge sat back in his chair. His own voice, which had been neutral, now carried something else in it. Gerard felt himself being sized up.

"The warden denies her arrest, your honor. Maybe he isn't aware of it." That was impossible and they both knew it, but Gerard persisted. "I thought you could help me find that out, at least. If they're detaining her and they haven't charged her, they should release her. At least let us know the charges. It's been over twenty-four hours, your honor."

The judge kept his eyes on Gerard, then leaned forward and lifted up the receiver of a heavy black telephone, dialing once.

"Get me the warden's office," he told the person at the other end. Gerard assumed it was the receptionist. The judge put the phone down. A few seconds later, it rang.

"Hello? I'd like to speak to the officer on duty. That's right. This is the officer on duty? Who is this, Frantz? Frantz, this is Judge Daniel. Frantz, listen to me. Do you have a woman in there . . . Wait a minute." He looked up at Gerard. "What's her name?"

"Elyse Voltaire—from above Fontamara."

"Voltaire—that's right. Elyse is the first name. In five minutes. You'll call me back? We'll wait. Good."

The judge hung up. He was smiling again. "They'll call," he told Gerard.

The receptionist stepped in with a tray bearing a small silver pot, two cups, and a newspaper. The man avoided Gerard's eyes and settled the tray carefully on the judge's desk. There were two sugar cubes wrapped in paper. He left them alone.

"Do you take sugar?" Judge Daniel asked politely.

"Thank you, your honor." Gerard watched as the judge carefully unwrapped the cubes, which contained three small squares of sugar each, and dropped them into the cups before pouring the coffee. There were no spoons. The judge stirred his coffee with a fingertip, the same one that had obviously rolled many cigarettes and had just successfully pried off a lunch crumb from the desk. Gerard winced internally.

"I see another client of yours has been busy." The judge turned over the newspaper. Gerard saw Edith's picture displayed next to a story about the strike rally. He looked at the newspaper with curiosity, as if he had not already read it or known his own name was mentioned on the pages inside.

A minute later, the phone rang. "The prison? Good, good, put Vilvert on." The judge nodded, listening. His expression was concentrated. From time to time, his eyes flickered over to his coffee cup on the desk, which he fingered with a free hand. "I see, I see, of course, yes, I see, very well. Goodbye."

A short silence followed. Gerard knew something had been said. The judge spread his palms out on the desk, rubbed his round face. "It does seem there is someone being detained by that name," he said at last.

Gerard felt a slight flush of victory. "What are the charges?"

The judge smiled again. His head was slightly cocked. "Your client, from what the warden told me, was arrested for assaulting a military officer."

"Do they have evidence of that?" Gerard asked, his tone aggressive.

"I don't know if she's *officially* been charged, Metellus," the judge continued. "But it seems there is an eyewitness, as well as the officers involved."

"Your honor, if my client is being accused, she's entitled to counsel. I need to go in there and speak to her."

The judge had put on his glasses. "I know the law, Metellus," he said, allowing a trace of sarcasm in his voice. "But allow me to give you a little bit of advice regarding this matter. Be patient, Metellus. It won't help to get excited."

"Pardon me, your honor." Gerard adopted a more solicitous tone. "But my client has been illegally detained. If I understand correctly, they have not charged her. With all due respect, I am well within my rights as counsel in seeking permission to see her."

The judge gave him a cool, appraising look. Was Gerard threatening him? For a moment, the green-gray eyes seemed hard. The judge leaned back in his chair, pensive. Gerard wondered what the warden had really said to him. He knew that he was putting the judge in a somewhat difficult position. If he refused to help, Gerard could inform the press about the case. The warden would then blame the judge. Ultimately the judge was responsible for the fate of detainees, since he had legal authority over the prison. That made him more vulnerable than the warden. That, and the fact that he had been promoted to his new post only two months earlier. As far as Gerard knew, Judge Daniel had yet to challenge the army and thus his position was weak. Furthermore, he was aware that Gerard knew it.

The judge's smile was intact, betraying nothing. His mustard-tipped fingers tapped the table, debating. Suddenly he reached into a drawer, took out a slip of paper and a carbon from the tray. Gerard watched his fingers move. The judge's handwriting was flowery and elegant. He signed the authorization form, and then handed it to the lawyer.

"Thank you, your honor." Gerard put the letter in his pocket. "Thank you very much."

"Be prudent, Metellus," the judge added, his expression meaningful. "This could be a delicate affair—for both of us."

They stood up. "Your honor." Gerard shook the judge's hands and thanked him again.

Halfway across the courtyard, he heard the judge's voice and turned around. Judge Daniel stood in the doorway, socks rolled down, shoes still untied, holding his eyeglasses in one hand. With the other he massaged his big stomach. "Don't forget to say hello to your mother for me." The judge scratched his head with his eyeglasses. "Tell her I'm waiting for her visit."

"I'll tell her."

"Another thing, Metellus." The judge smiled again. "Your client—that woman? Well, I wouldn't worry too much about her. The warden gave me his personal assurances."

Gerard considered this. The last time the warden had given his personal assurances about a detainee had been the day before his client had been found outside the prison, a bullet in his back. Officially, the guards had shot him escaping. That case and the

details of the warden's "personal assurances" had been widely discussed in the newspapers. Was Judge Daniel giving him a warning?
The judge's smile was smooth. "I'll remember that," Gerard said
amicably. "Good day, your honor."

Back at the reception area, the aide looked up as Gerard entered.
The comic book was gone, replaced by a sheet of greasy bakery
paper and a half-eaten sandwich. On impulse, Gerard offered the
aide his outstretched hand, leaving a puzzled man in his wake.

25

"Why do you bring the international to see us? We have enough trouble as it is. Everyone who comes from the city brings us trouble. Do we need more trouble? I'm asking you, man, do I look like I need more trouble? You can tell that international waiting outside to go back where she came from."

The man sneered, looking around at the others. Then he glanced back at Clemard, who remained silent. The group of men and women who had just entered the small chapel looked at him expectantly. So did Wilmer, the man who had finally arrived, two hours late, to escort Clemard and Leslie to this village.

"She isn't trouble," Clemard argued back. "Madanm is here with me. Your man came to see Pe Emmanuel, to ask for help. That's why we came here. Pe Emmanuel knows Madanm. She's a blan, but she's all right."

"Who are you?" The man in the soiled yellow shirt stood up, pointing at Clemard. "Do I know your face? Who is your mother? Who is your family?"

"I told you." Clemard looked around the room, trying to reassure them. "My name is Rameau, Clemard Rameau. I'm from the city, the capital, but my family is from Jacmel. I am helping Madanm. She works for justice, for the human rights. We want to know what happened here."

"Jacmel," the bony man said sarcastically, challenging the others to support him. "I was in Jacmel once. I met a man with a face like yours. But he's dead now." At this he laughed. Two other men smiled, but did not say anything.

"I'm telling you," the angry man warned them, "talk to the international and you'll bring us trouble." He looked back at Clemard. "I don't forget a face," he said, bringing his own closer. "I'll remember yours if I need to. Don't think I won't." He gave a final glare around the room and declared, "I'm leaving. This is a bad idea." The two men who had smiled looked at each other, then quietly followed him out.

Clemard watched the man walk away. He could see Madanm Leslie leaning against a tree to the left of where the men passed, eyeing her suspiciously. She was smoking, her head turned away from him. Her bag with the equipment was by her feet.

"The army comes every afternoon," a voice interrupted his thoughts. "Did Wilmer tell you that?"

The speaker was a middle-aged woman with a pink dress held together with a safety pin at the top. She gestured toward Wilmer, a stocky man with an anxious expression. He held his machete in his left hand, tapping its flat side against his leg.

"I told him," Wilmer inserted quickly, "all about our troubles." He addressed the rest of the group. "I know Pe Emmanuel. We all know him. He sent these people to us. We can trust them. If they were bad, the army would be here already to arrest us." Wilmer turned back to Clemard. "Madanm can come in here. You don't have to be afraid of those other men. They don't know what they're talking about."

The man in the doorway waved to Leslie with his machete. She nodded, dropping her cigarette and grinding it out. The three men who had looked at her with hostility had disappeared. Were they Macoutes? she wondered. Her earlier paranoia had returned. She picked up her bag and walked over. "Don't use the camera," the man in the doorway whispered. "Wait."

"This is Madanm Leslie," Clemard introduced her. "She works for an organization in the United States. Washington," he added, pronouncing it with double s's and m's—Wassymtom.

"Jez Bous," one man confirmed, George Bush. The others laughed. There was a strong current of tension in the room.

Leslie looked around. The chapel was a low structure with a small nave and seven rough benches for pews. There was a small wooden table in the front that served as an altar. The only light came from two open doorways on either side. The chapel had been built on the only flat stretch of land; all around it were the terraced fields. Above them, but hidden behind a line of trees, were village houses.

Leslie glanced at her watch. It was almost five-thirty. She decided not to waste any more time. "I'm glad we could come here to see you," she began. "We—I—work in the area of human rights. I'm interested in knowing what's been happening around here, concerning elections and the strike . . ." She let her sentence dangle, then added: "This is not for the newspapers. It's not for the government. Se dwa moun."

Human rights. At this the group relaxed somewhat. Two of the women sat down on the floor near her. Leslie put her bag on a bench and perched next to it. She didn't remove her notebook or equipment. She could tell they felt cautious and wondered what Clemard had told them. He glanced at her and smiled: Go on.

"This man, Wilmer"—she indicated the broad-shouldered man—"he's told us a little about your troubles—your troubles with the soldiers," she emphasized, pausing to gauge their response. They were listening closely. The duo near her smiled their encouragement.

"I was told you know about what's happened in Papaye," Leslie said. "That some of you were there. Is that true?"

The group eyed one another. Finally, one of them, a man, answered. "We weren't there. But we know. We heard."

"Did you hear about a man named Cedric George?" Leslie asked. "Ti Cedric?"

Several of them nodded.

Leslie established eye contact with those who had nodded. "I'd like to interview those of you who may be able to help us. Like I said before, this is not for the newspapers, or the radio, or the authorities. This is for dwa moun—for the human rights groups. I work with them. If you give me your names, that will help, because we need to establish the source of our information. But that will be kept confidential—I won't give anyone your names. What matters is the information. First we want to find Cedric George—Ti Cedric," she corrected. "But we are also concerned about your situation here. I'll need to use this machine." She partially lifted her tape recorder out of the bag. "Because we can't just give them a piece of paper. If we only give them the paper, they say we are making it up. Do you understand? All right?" she repeated, taking out the machine. "Ça va?"

"Pa sa." Wilmer pointed to the camera as she momentarily set it on the bench. Not that.

"Wi," she reassured him, I know. She put the camera back in the bag and took out her notebook instead. She shivered involuntarily; it was cool in the room. Then she checked the tape player: "Test . . . test . . . youn, de, twa . . ." One, two, three . . . The group watched her. Leslie adjusted the volume. The women sitting on the floor nudged one another, whispering.

Leslie smiled at them. She was still worried about the men who had left, hoped they wouldn't try to steal the jeep. The hand brake was pulled up tight, but they could always slash the tires. Wouldn't we be sitting pretty? she thought.

"Bon," she said. "Nou met komanse." We can start. "Why don't we begin with you." She turned to the woman standing closest to her, extending the lavalier microphone for her to hold. "Konsa." Like that. "Kenbe la." Hold it right there. Leslie pulled the microphone away from the woman's mouth. "Bien."

She watched the needle on the recorder jump into the red from the black as the woman tentatively said, "Mwen komanse kounyeya?" I start now?

"Can you tell me what your name is and how old you are?" Leslie asked. "Then what you know about Cedric George. Or who told you what."

"The man who told me was a man I met in the—"

"Rete." Leslie stopped her, realizing she had overloaded the woman with questions. "Your name—first your name."

"Gina."

"Gina. Gina what?"

"Gina Vicaine."

"Your age?"

"Thirty-six."

"You said a man told you about Ti Cedric? When? And who was he?" Leslie checked the tape. It was rolling.

"About four days ago. He's from Hinche. But he goes to Papaye."

Leslie wrote the information down as the others watched. The woman had stopped talking.

"What did he tell you?" Leslie urged. "Anything?"

"That the army paid a bunch of men to do that thing. They're the ones who attacked the office of Konbit Papay and burned it. I know one of those men. They're the same ones who were with Zéphyr."

Leslie looked at Wilmer. Zéphyr?

"Luckner Zéphyr, the old section chief," he explained. "But he left. He's gone now."

"But his men are still here," Gina said. "They caused destruction in other places too. They're the ones who stole our pigs."

"When was that?" Leslie asked.

"Don't listen to her." Another man jumped in. "Gina, that was a long time ago," he said. "This lady wants to talk about Ti Cedric."

"I'm talking about him." Gina stood up, flushed. "It's my turn," she said to the others, holding her ground. "I'm telling you Zéphyr is the one who is still paying those men to do that. That's what I was told."

"I understand," Leslie said. "You were told that this man—the old section chief—he ordered the men to burn down the offices in Papaye. And they were paid by him. Even though he's gone away."

"Zéphyr's son is still here," Gina explained. "He has a house in Hinche. That's who gives them the money. Because Zéphyr wants to come back. Some people say he's back, but I don't think it's true, we would have seen him. But he still controls those men."

"But you don't know about Cedric George himself—where he might have gone? What's happened to him?"

Gina hesitated. "I don't know," she said, then quickly added: "but they wanted to kill him—everybody knows that."

Everybody knows that. Leslie underlined it, looking at Clemard, who had moved over to the doorway to smoke. He had heard that. He smiled at her.

"What about you?" Leslie asked the man who had interrupted Gina. "What's your name?"

He needed no prompting. "I'm Thomas. I'm twenty-nine. I live in that other village—over there." He gestured behind him, in the direction of the altar.

"Where's that?"

He named a village, St. something. Leslie would have to listen to the tape to get the spelling right. She let him go on.

"Four of them were arrested," Thomas said with certainty. "They were in Hinche, at the prison. Now they're out, but they're hiding."

"The newspaper said the army arrested Cedric's sister, a woman named Violette," Leslie interjected. "What about her?"

"She was in there, but not long."

"She left," another voice interrupted. It belonged to an older man with a grizzled face and small, penetrating eyes. He had been silent up to now. "She left," he added. "She's gone to another part of the country—far from here."

Leslie turned back to Thomas, wanting first to finish his narrative. "What else?" she said. "What else do you know?"

He nodded, stuttering as he answered, his hands animated. "I know. I—I know . . . Those men, Zéphyr's men, they're bad. They're—they're the ones who tried to chase us off our land. I don't know if he is p-paying them, but they were paid one hundred gourdes to do this."

"To set fire to the Konbit Papay office?"

"That's right. One hundred or two—two hundred."

Leslie caught the discrepancy. "Which?"

"Two hundred," he answered, his tone absolute, but, she could tell, uncertain. That meant it was rumor, third- or fourth-hand information. Leslie heard him out anyway.

"The others—the ones who were in Hinche—they were in our village, just for one night, but they were going to St.-Marc. I think that's where they've gone. You can find them there," he said with finality.

She checked her watch. This was going to take a while, she sensed.

"You"—she indicated the older man, who had gone back to being quiet. "What else can you tell me?"

He shrugged. The others were watching him, interested.

"Tell her, gran moun—old man—tell her what you know." Wilmer encouraged the older man, moved near him.

The man looked at Leslie, then at Clemard, who had flicked his cigarette outside and now joined them.

"You are a friend of the priest?" the man asked Clemard.

"Wi."

"I can trust you?"

"Wi," he answered. Then, pointing to Leslie: "And you can trust Madanm too."

The man appeared to ignore Clemard's remark. "We'll talk over here." He indicated the far corner of the room. "In private." He led Clemard by the arm.

"What are you going to tell them, gran moun?" a woman standing beside Gina complained hotly. "Why can't we listen?"

He shut her up with a frown. "I want to talk to these people. Leave us alone." He waited until the group reluctantly moved to where Clemard had been smoking, a spot too far away for them to hear what the older man was now whispering. Leslie sensed it was something about her, but she couldn't tell what. Instinctively, she felt the man didn't like her. She hesitated, then picked up the tape recorder and joined them.

"Pa sa," the man told her as she approached. Not that.

"I won't turn it on," she said quickly. "It's off, see? The light's off here."

He looked back at Clemard. "I'll talk to you. But if they find out, I could be killed." He took the cigarette Clemard offered him. Leslie immediately regretted having forgotten to offer the others cigarettes as well. She got out her notebook.

The older man suddenly grabbed her wrist. "No paper," he said. "I don't want any paper."

"I'm only going to write it down," she protested, "so I won't forget it. I don't have a good memory."

"No paper," he insisted. "Just listen."

She looked at Clemard, who shrugged. The man was adamant. She put the tape recorder and notebook on the floor, annoyed.

The older man shielded his mouth with a gnarled hand as he spoke. Leslie wondered if Clemard had already asked him his name, and presumed he had. She leaned forward to better understand him, he whispered so softly. "Ti Cedric has a cousin," he told them. "I know the cousin. He's the one who told me what happened. Ti Cedric escaped. He hid in the ravine and they went after him."

"Cedric escaped?" Clemard said just as softly. "Are you sure?"

"He escaped," the man said firmly. "He sent a message to his cousin, the person who talked to me. They killed one man but it wasn't Ti Cedric. It was someone else."

"Where is he now? Do you know?" Leslie asked excitedly, struggling to keep her voice low. The others watched them intently, straining to overhear their conversation. Leslie smiled at Gina.

"He's not here, not anymore," the man said. He held up his hand to warn the others to remain where they were. Turning to Clemard, he added, "They were planning to kill him. They had dogs."

"Who?" Leslie interrupted, whispering. "Zéphyr's men?"

No, he shook his head, licking his lips for an instant.

"The army?" she persisted.

"The soldiers," he replied. "Not the Macoutes."

"Why do that?" Leslie asked. "Because of the elections?" She wanted to write this down.

"Maybe," the man said. He seemed to be looking beyond the group in the doorway, out at something. Leslie followed his gaze, but saw nothing. The sun was getting lower, though. They would have to leave as soon as this was over.

"Did Ti Cedric come up here? Was he organizing around here?" Clemard had asked the questions.

"No, not up here." The older man sniffed, picking his nose discreetly. "He was in another place—in the mountains."

"So you met him there?" Leslie jumped in. "You saw him? When was this? Recently?" She felt slightly lost in the conversation, momentarily distracted by the lateness of the day. She remembered her earlier, unanswered question. "Do you know where he is?"

"He escaped." The man put his hand on Clemard's chest. "He went into hiding. But he couldn't stay where he was. That's what his cousin told me." He tapped Clemard's chest hard. "He's a young man, but older than you. And strong. That's why they're going to kill him."

He seemed so certain, Leslie noted. Clemard looked at her, waiting for guidance.

"Who else might know about his status?" she asked the man. "Can you take us to anyone else? Or give us some names? What about the cousin? Does he live around here?" She was breaking her own rules, plying him with questions.

"Nobody else knows anything." He indicated the group assembled nearby. "They heard it all from me."

"This cousin, what's his name?" Leslie asked.

"Delaroch."

With an *e*? she wondered, like de la roche, of a rock? Rock, she repeated to herself, trying to create a visual memory cue. "Delaroche," she told Clemard. "You'll remember it?"

"Paul," the older man volunteered, "Paul Jules Delaroch."

"Is he in Papaye?" Leslie pressed.

"No." The older man scratched his weathered face. "You won't find him. He's hiding too."

"Are you sure about this—absolutely sure?" Leslie grilled him.

He gave her a measured look. "I'm sure, madanm," he said, his tone dry.

She now realized that he was probably the village elder, which was why the others deferred to him as they did. She felt caught off guard.

He addressed Clemard, openly avoiding Leslie. "I am the one who told Wilmer," he said to Clemard. "I know Pe Emmanuel. I met him when he came to visit us this summer. He came with Ti Cedric. I heard that Pe Emmanuel was asking about Ti Cedric. That's why I sent Wilmer to tell him that Ti Cedric escaped the attack, but since then, we haven't heard anything more. And in the past week, the army has been asking about him too, sending their spies to find out if anyone knows where he is hiding. So I don't think they've caught him yet. That's all we have to tell you."

"Why make us come out here for nothing?" Clemard was suddenly direct.

"I thought Ti Cedric might come here. His cousin told him to come and see me. But he didn't."

The older man finished his cigarette. He had said everything, even if Leslie had more questions. "What's your name?" she asked him, not caring if Clemard had already asked.

"Pe Emmanuel knows my name," he told her, his tone still cool.

"Ask him. He'll tell you my real name"—he gave her a cold smile—"and my nom de guerre."

Leslie looked at Clemard, uncertain. What's he talking about?

"You fought Duvalier," Clemard said matter-of-factly, "didn't you?"

"That's right."

"Were you in prison?" Clemard added.

A small smile played on the older man's lips. He grunted, then took Clemard's hand into his own. "Feel," he ordered. "There."

"What is it?" Leslie demanded. "Clemard?"

A warm callused hand grasped her wrist; the older man pulled her arm up under his shirt, where Clemard's hand had just been. His fingers guided hers over the rough patch, the scar tissue that rose like a long bump. She felt two deep indentations, which made her flinch. Had he been knifed or tortured? She couldn't tell. He pressed her fingers, somewhat harshly, into the two spots, pushed them too hard, an ugly expression on his face.

"Ça va," she said, pulling her hand away. "I feel it. I understand," she added.

"You understand." The older man shook his head, his voice full of challenge again. "You think you understand. But what are you going to do? What are you going to do for us now that you understand? Because we understand too; we understand everything." He pointed to the room at large, shrugging. "The blan understands."

Clemard brushed her hand. Come on—he motioned with his head—it's time to go.

Leslie gathered up her equipment and bag. "Mesi," she said to the older man, who had accepted Clemard's half pack of cigarettes. Thank you. She extended her hand; he gave her a limp one in return. "Bonswa, madanm," he said formally.

She walked ahead, leaving Clemard to conclude his conversation with the older man. Maybe he would be able to get more out of him alone than with her there. Leslie was frustrated, and tired. Why had he been so hostile to her? Gina and the rest of the group accompanied her back to the tree where she had waited earlier. Clemard emerged shortly afterward with Wilmer. They said goodbye to the group as Wilmer took the lead, cutting small branches in their path with his machete. Gina trailed alongside, with Clemard in tow. The jeep was where they had left it, tires and chassis intact. There was no sign of the three men, or any soldiers.

Gina tapped on Leslie's shoulder. "Will you give me a ride?"

"Back to the capital?"

"I'll get out on the road," Gina replied, already helping Clemard remove the big rocks from behind the tires. "I have to visit someone."

Leslie crawled in, with Gina behind her. She was mentally replaying their conversation with the older man, upset at his response. Clemard was having difficulty turning the jeep around. "Clemard —wait," she said suddenly.

He looked up.

She climbed out. "Clemard, I'm driving now," she said firmly. "Please—you'll have to change places with me."

He climbed out, too surprised to protest. Wilmer, watching from the fork, waved.

Leslie adjusted the shoulder strap and the front seat for her long legs. It had been a while since she'd driven a four-wheel-drive. "Hold on tight," she warned them, releasing the clutch and the hand brake simultaneously. "This is not going to be pretty."

If the men had noms de guerre, she thought, then the women probably had them too. Did Marie-Thérèse Dubossy have a nom de guerre? What about Ti Cedric? That man had seemed so sure he would be killed. The first one who seemed so absolutely sure.

September 5
Petition for Asylum
To the ambassadors of Canada, the United States, and France:

1. My name is Cedric Milfort George. I was born January 22, 1953, in Côtes-de-Fer in the area of Bainet in southern Haiti. It has a population of 42,535 inhabitants. I have one child, who is seven, but my wife and I no longer live under the same roof. I decided to request temporary political asylum because of persecution I suffer at the hands of the Haitian army and the Tontons Macoutes, who threatened to kill me on many occasions and recently arrived at my village with guns and bayonets to murder me and my colleagues.

2. I moved to Papaye with my parents, who are elderly and unable to work. I am their only surviving child. My two older brothers both died in the prisons of the Duvaliers. I have one sister, who is married. When I was a boy, my parents sent me to live with another family and I received my primary school certification and then my secondary schooling. That is how I came to work as a teacher for the people of my village, although I also do work as a mason and carpenter.

3. In 1982 I was arrested by the Tontons Macoutes along with thirty-five other men from our area. All of us were illegally accused in the death of a land baron named Joseph Carena, who was found dead one day. We were taken to the prison of Papaye for twenty-seven months beginning March 8, 1982. During that period, I suffered ill treatment of the most cruel kind, including many blows to my hands and head because they knew I used my hands to work. I was also tortured with the djak and can no longer hear properly in my left ear.

4. When I was released from prison in 1984, I returned to my village in Papaye. I found that in my absence the army had destroyed all of the houses in our area and stolen the tools of our work collective, Konbit Papay. Along with others, we presented our complaint

to the local magistrate because many people had witnessed the section chief personally giving the orders to loot and destroy our houses. His name is Luckner Zéphyr. He had a gun nicknamed Kares Tifi— Little Girl's Caress. This man was very powerful in the region. He was the only cock that crowed. He appointed himself judge and executioner; if he decided someone was guilty, he killed the person with his gun, but he always offered to say a prayer for them. That's the kind of criminal he was. Luckner Zéphyr promised to punish me for saying over the radio that he destroyed all our houses. But the judge told him not to touch me, because the army did not want any more killings.

5. I found out from an informant who killed the baron Joseph Carena. It was the section chief, who took the land for himself. This land belonged to the people of our village before Jean-Claude Duvalier gave it to the baron Joseph as a present. The government of Jean-Claude Duvalier did the same thing in many areas, allowing the Tontons Macoutes and the rich barons who live in the cities to get their hands on the land of the poor people. Luckner Zéphyr took all control in his hands. Even though the hungry people are the ones who pick the mangoes off the trees on their own land, he now makes them pay a gourde for the fruit.

6. When I lived in Papaye I was forced to take many precautions to avoid persecution by Luckner Zéphyr and his men. They threatened me constantly. Then, in July 1984, Jean-Claude Duvalier announced a referendum to see if, Yes or No, the people would have him continue as President for Life. He did this to say to the world, and especially to the United States, that he respected democracy and human rights. But the referendum was fraudulent. The night before the vote, Zéphyr and his men came to our village and told the people that they had to vote for Duvalier. The next night, the Macoutes knocked on the door of everyone who had dared to deposit a No ballot into the box according to their convictions. And they arrested many people. Luckily, I was warned and I went into hiding for three months and four days.

7. After that my life was never secure in Papaye. I decided to work with the people in my village, to teach them how to organize against the barons, to get a better price in the market. That was the idea behind Konbit Papay.

We had groups for the youths and we taught them about their basic rights as Haitians and about democracy. That is how I came to be arrested in December 1985 and taken again to the prison. I was accused of organizing a youth demonstration against the government of Jean-Claude Duvalier. This time they used every torture they had. I was even forced to drink my own urine to remain alive. There was often no water. They beat me a hundred times and put me in solitary confinement in an underground hole. When they released me during the political amnesty I weighed 110 pounds instead of my usual 175. In my cell alone, six men died in one month from the tortures and starvation; their bodies were buried out in the fields.

8. Despite all of these terrible incidents, I was not discouraged, because I had managed to survive. I was hopeful when Duvalier was overthrown on February 7, 1986, and they promised us an election. I was also hopeful because Luckner Zéphyr and some of his men were forced to flee to Santo Domingo. Right away I started working with my colleagues in Papaye to organize for the elections, to teach our people how to think democratically.

9. Now I have been forced into hiding again. In the past three months, Konbit Papay has received many death threats. We were greatly harassed by Major Enid Fleuris, who is the subdistrict commander in charge in Papaye. He personally warned me not to participate in organizing the national labor strike to protest the poor conditions of our workers. He told me I had been identified as a subversive. Despite the statements made by the interim government to support an election, the army is not acting to protect those of us who are trying to fulfill the mandate of democracy; instead they are attacking us. They attacked us during a Konbit Papay meeting, forcing us to flee. They arrested fifteen of our group. They burned our office and stole our tools.

10. I make this declaration from a place of hiding. My friends informed me that the army accuses us of storing bombs—that is a complete lie. If they catch me, I'm sure, they will execute me. I have no choice but to seek temporary protection in an embassy. This army will not let me leave the country alive, nor do I wish to leave. But I am not safe in the streets or my home. I need refuge.

11. I testify that everything I have said is true. I also repeat that I do not wish to leave Haiti. If there was security for me and my family, my

only wish would be to live in peace in Papaye. I am a democrat and a patriot. But if I do not receive security in an embassy I am certain I will soon die.

Signed,
Cedric Milfort George
President, Konbit Papay
Haiti

Transcribed by hand by Paul Jules Delaroch, September 5, 1986. To be hand-delivered to the embassies of Canada, the United States, and France.

26

The rain beat against Gerard's office window, spilling in under the sill. He got up and shut it tighter, glancing out onto the street for a moment. There was no one in sight. In the distance heat lightning flashed over the mountains. The rain spattered off the rounded white stones that had been set into the street at the turn of the century.

He had gone back to the prison again after seeing Judge Daniel. The officer on duty had looked at his letter and handed it back to him. "You can't come in," he had told Gerard. "You'll have to come back when the warden is here."

"But the judge gave me permission. Look—it says it right here. The judge has the authority to give me permission. The Ministry of Justice is in charge of this prison and he represents the Ministry of Justice. It's the law. Besides, I know the warden is here. Just let me meet with him and show him this letter." Gerard had argued for what seemed like a half hour before giving up.

He hadn't been able to do anything for the students either, except to alert the international organizations and the press. Jeanne was meeting with the parents, acting as Gerard's courier. And no one had heard from Ti Cedric. The only positive news was the autopsy report Dr. Sylvie had passed on to him; the victim was definitely not Cedric George, although who he was remained unknown.

Where was Ti Cedric? Gerard wondered if he was even alive. It had been over three weeks. There was no sign of him. After talking to Leslie upon her return from Papaye, he had double-checked with the authorities in Hinche and Artibonite, as well as local groups and contacts he had there. No one had seen or heard from Ti Cedric, and by now, everyone agreed, he ought to have contacted someone. Unless the authorities were lying and had captured him and were holding him somewhere else, at some new detention center. The only other possibility was that they had killed him. Because he wouldn't let them worry like this. It wouldn't be like Ti Cedric.

Gerard turned to the unfinished play on his desk. He read the beginning slowly, let the judge's face be replaced by the image of a fat oily blackbird with a blue undersheen and a red cape, his yellow beak permanently stained with the dye used by repeat voters in the rigged elections, stained like the nicotine fingertips of Judge Daniel, whose feet swelled in the heat and smelled like overripe cheese.

SCENE II

(The government prosecutor ambles over stage right. His feathers are coated with grease and his eyes are bright, dilated circles of red. His beak and claws are stained orange-red from betel juice. Everyone in the country knows the prosecutor is addicted to betel seed, which he chews without stopping. Betel acts like an amphetamine on crows, making the prosecutor's movements jerky. His speech is slurred.)

PROSECUTOR

Your honor, as the legal representative for the glorious Government of Haiti, I have already presented over seventy witnesses who testified that on the day of July 12, 1966, a certain L'Espérance Fini, a Haitian national of uncertain means and moral character . . .

LAWYER *(standing)*

I object, your honor!

JUDGE

Objection overruled. Continue, Prosecutor. Give us the facts.

PROSECUTOR *(panting and out of breath)*

. . . as well as dubious lineage owing to a lack of documentation as to her father's identity and the common belief that she was the product of an illicit form of concubinage. Your honor, on this day the accused was selling food she had prepared at a stand outside the Ministry of Recreation. Due to the great heat of that day and a power blackout, the Minister of Recreation had dismissed his regular cook for the afternoon. Finding himself still hungry, he sent one of his aides to search for food. The aide brought Madame L'Espérance Fini—the accused—and her food back with him to the Ministry. It was at that point that the Minister took pity on the accused and offered her a job cooking cakes for him.

JUDGE

What kind of cakes were they again, Prosecutor?

PROSECUTOR

At first they were sweet pies of all kinds. But gradually, your honor, the cook began making rum cakes, which were a favorite of the Minister's.

JUDGE

I love rum cake myself. Soothes the stomach and the mind. Just the thing to eat during a game of canasta.

JURORS *(among themselves)*

Uhmm, rum cake!

Just the thing I like before bed!

I love to pick the raisins out!

Me, I like it with nuts and anise, and flambé!

(The jurors compare recipes for rum cake as the prosecutor continues his opening statement.)

PROSECUTOR

On the afternoon of August 11, after consuming half a rum cake, the Minister of Recreation felt particularly tired. We now know that he must have been drunk due to an unusually high degree of alcohol placed in the cake by the new cook, L'Espérance Fini. But he did not know. He retired and, according to several witnesses, did not reemerge for twenty-four hours. During that time, the Ministry was robbed of its china. There is more than compelling evidence that the break-in was timed to take place while the Minister was in a nearly drugged state. With all due respect, your honor, the Minister was in an alcoholic stupor due to Madame Fini's toxic recipe.

(To the judge's annoyance, several of the jurors appear to have fallen asleep. He can see their claws have been dipped in dye, indicating that they have received their bribes for appearing today. The next time, the judge

thinks, he will instruct the clerk to wait until the hearings are over before
paying off the jurors. That will keep them awake! He ruffles his feathers in
displeasure. The jurors who are awake smile at the judge. Perhaps this case
will prove interesting after all, they whisper among themselves, a good way
to pass the otherwise empty mornings until the ritual game of canasta,
where the crème de la crème flock each week. Only two jurors complain.
One of them, a mildly anorexic female crow, sniffs.)

My feathers are sagging in this humidity. I don't know how long I can
stand it!

(Her companion, a young male playboy of sorts, agrees.)

They didn't pay us enough. Besides, no one can see me in such bad
light. I should be flying around town right now!

JUDGE

Quiet in the courtroom! Go on, Prosecutor.

PROSECUTOR

Your honor, the accused denied the crime and claimed she had gone
home to care for her family. But a number of witnesses have already
testified that L'Espérance Fini hated the Minister and considered his great
generosity in employing her a hardship she suffered in no uncertain terms.
I repeat—in no uncertain terms. If I may quote from the witnesses we
heard in the past, your honor, for the sake of the new jurors, one witness
said, "She despised the Minister. She even told the other cook that the
Minister had a fat body like a cow's with tits."

JURORS *(waking and nudging one another)*

Did you hear that? It's a scandal!
A scandal! Oh! How delicious!
What was that? I want to hear more!

JUDGE

Prosecutor, we'll have to keep in mind there are ladies present. I understand your professional need to present the facts, but let us try not to
offend the ladies. Go on, please.

PROSECUTOR *(spreading his shiny wings broadly*
as he dips into a bow for the female jurors)
I offer my sincere apologies to the ladies, your honor.
(The lawyer clicks his teeth in disgust as the prosecutor offers a fatuous
grin to the gallery and continues.)

PROSECUTOR *(beaming now)*
Like a cow with tits, ladies and gentlemen! Is this the language an
employee uses with respect to an employer to whom she is indebted for
having removed her from the filth of the streets, for having elevated her
to a respectable level in society, to have accorded her his ultimate trust,
the trust of his stomach, his body, to her? Your honor, this case is simple
but the defense is right that it should not be closed. It remains open and
as important to the Government of Haiti as it was sixty years ago. The
honor and reputation of a government minister is at stake here, your honor,
not only the property of the State.

JUDGE
Well stated, Prosecutor.
(Several of the female jurors extend their claws for the prosecuting attorney
to peck as he makes his way to the judge's desk to deposit the witnesses'
statements.)

PROSECUTOR
Your honor, these documents were entered into the public record as
evidence during the second hearing of this case forty years ago. I present
them again today.

JUDGE
Thank you, Prosecutor. Do you have any other witnesses?

PROSECUTOR
I do, your honor. The prosecution wishes to call forward Monsieur
Jesuis Imparfait to the witness stand.
(There is a creaking sound, and the door to the witness room opens, stage
right. A slight, bald man wearing a polka-dotted green shirt and a red hat
takes a hesitant step forward. He carries a roll of paper under his arm and

a small portable desk. He takes his place in the witness chair next to Judge
Arsenic. There is something about him that looks familiar to the lawyer,
but he cannot place it. The clerk lifts the witness's left hand. His index
finger is stained pink, his middle finger turquoise, his little finger yellow.

A fat female crow in the jury box, Madame Telenovela, whispers
excitedly.)

Look! His third finger is turquoise. That means he was here in 1986—
I heard it from very good sources that turquoise dye was used by the court
then. And before that it was yellow—yes, I'm certain of it. Monsieur
Imparfait must be our historic witness. He must be a rich man by now.
When the court recesses, I'm going to ask him to be my partner in canasta.
His memory must be superb!

(By now, the lawyer is convinced he has seen this man before, but he
cannot recall the incident. He removes his spectacles to study Imparfait.)

CLERK
State your name and date and place of birth for the court, if you will.

WITNESS (in Creole)
Jeswit Impafe, Potoprens, Ayiti.

JUDGE
In French, please, Monsieur Imparfait! According to the laws of the
State, Decree Number 484 of the Official Language Act, Creole is no
longer an acceptable language for trade or law, except in the marketplace.
Though this courtroom seems to have served as such for the counselor, it
is the official embodiment of the principles of the glorious monarch who
presides above us. I refer to none other than the Chief of Chiefs, a small
man but a great man, our symbolic father and fraternal brother, Napoleon
Bonaparte!

(All eyes are upon Napoleon, whose riding breeches in the portrait are
sullied, but whose tricolored hat is held aloft in the air.)

WITNESS (in French)
Jesuis Imparfait, a scribe, your honor. I had been working as a scribe
at the time I met that woman, L'Espérance Fini.

CLERK

Do you swear to tell the truth and nothing but the truth to this court upon pain of immediate execution if you say things later found to be unfavorable to the truth of fact as His Excellency, the great Justice Arsenic, interprets this to be?

WITNESS (*confused*)

No próblem, your honor.

(*The lawyer has raised his hand. He now recognizes the witness, Jeswit Impafe/Jesuis Imparfait, as none other than J'Étais Plus-que-Parfait, a witness subpoened by the prosecution during a previous hearing of this case.*)

LAWYER (*protesting*)

Your honor? Your honor, I believe the court is being deceived!

JUDGE (*glaring*)

Deceit, Counselor! That appears to be the sole province of the poor unfortunate whose honor you so vainly seek to uphold. First you accuse the court, now you accuse the Government's primary witness. I warned you before—I'll have no interruptions! As it is, we may have to delay our game of canasta—and the President will not be happy!

(*puffing up his chest, pontificating*)

In any case, Counselor, deceit, like truth, is a matter of interpretation. Since I am the only one who can establish the facts, I am the only one who can judge deceit. Do I make myself clear? Hasn't Monsieur Imparfait sworn to be truthful upon pain of execution?

LAWYER (*raising his eyes heavenward*)

Yes, your honor. But I am convinced that this man appeared before Judge Barbancourt during the second hearing of this case. He said his name was J'Étais Plus-que-Parfait. I have court documents to prove it is true . . . if you'll just give me a minute to find them . . .

(*The lawyer riffles through his briefcase full of yellowed documents. He pulls one out, but it crumbles in his fingers.*)

(*The judge leans forward to study Jesuis Imparfait, who smiles sweetly*) and waves his colorful fingers at Madame Telenovela, sitting in the front row of the jury box. She removes a handkerchief from her purse to wipe her eyes, which are brimming with tears. She blows Imparfait a tragic kiss, already acting the part of a devoted wife moved by false accusations against her maligned husband.)

JUDGE (casting an approving glance at the rapport developing
between the socially prominent Madame Telenovela
and the Government's star witness, Imparfait)
You are Monsieur Imparfait, aren't you?

WITNESS
Yes, your honor. I was Imparfait when I woke up this morning.

JUDGE
You were Imparfait this morning. Very well. But this man is convinced you were Plus-que-Parfait. Can you explain this difference to the court?
(The lawyer is furiously looking through his briefcase. A pile of yellow crumbs pours out as he overturns the briefcase, frustrated)

WITNESS
I am Imparfait; I was Plus-que-Parfait. I am no longer the man I was, your honor. I legally changed my name. I had been working as a scribe forty years ago, when I was still a young man. Later I changed my name to Imparfait.

JUDGE (leaning back, pleased)
By all means, continue, Monsieur Imparfait.

WITNESS
As Plus-que-Parfait, I had been working as a letter writer for the citizens of this fair city, but I could see that I had to change—to modernize. The population of Port-au-Prince—especially the young people—had been complaining about my style. They had been taking their business else-where. But even by then I had felt a need to change. My grandfather, Passé Historique, was a firm believer in this philosophy: "One cannot stay living in the past without advancing in the present." That had always been

his motto; it became mine the day I changed my identity. I became Imparfait and I never regretted the change. I tell young people, many of whom are brokenhearted, "Love lives in the memory of the past, but you must live for today."

(There is spontaneous clapping. The blind clerk is forced to escort Madame Telenovela out of the courtroom, she is so moved by her future husband's passionate regard for life.)

JUDGE *(smiling)*

A wise man you are, or, I should say, you are being.

PROSECUTOR *(handing the judge a letter)*

Let it be entered as evidence, this document testifying that the man before you today is not the man he was in the past. Judge, Jesuis Imparfait has explained it to you in his own words. He is a changed man. And according to the laws of our glorious State, his testimony must be heard today, as he is the only living witness to the events of this case.

(The prosecutor flies over to the painted cart and grabs the scroll with his claws, then flies over Judge Arsenic and drops it on the table.)

JUDGE *(smiling broadly)*

Thank you, Prosecutor. The court accepts this evidence that Monsieur Plus-que-Parfait is a member of the distant past and that Monsieur Imparfait is a modern man. What happens in the present is necessarily related to the past, but to brood upon actions as they occurred relative to past actions . . . Well, I can understand your decision to change your name, Monsieur Imparfait. A modern man must keep pace with the times. If there is any doubt about your statement, I will consider it my prerogative to confer with Judge Barbancourt, who presided over this court during the second hearing of this case in . . . Clerk, what was the date?

CLERK

I wasn't born yet, your honor.

JUDGE *(ignoring him)*

Never mind. What Monsieur Imparfait has said reminds us that truth is like love: over time, what is false will be forgotten; what is true will remain clear in our memory. Objection overruled, Counselor. Prosecutor, you may proceed with your questions.

PROSECUTOR

Monsieur Imparfait, you say you knew the accused, L'Espérance Fini. Can you recall for this jury, which is not familiar with your prior testimony, the events which caused you to come into contact with her?

WITNESS

Yes, sir. It was in August of 1966, if I remember correctly. I worked as a scribe, as I told you earlier. I sat at my desk on the corner of the Rue Mauve attending to my customers.

PROSECUTOR *(interrupting)*

The Rue Mauve, your honor, no longer exists. It was located at the intersection of the Rue Rouge and the Rue Bleu. I submit as evidence Exhibit Two, this letter, from L'Espérance Fini to her mother, Madame Toujours Pas Fini, as it was written by the hand of Monsieur Imperfait.

PROSECUTOR *(handing the letter to the witness)*

Will you read this letter for the court, please, Monsieur Imparfait? What did the accused say to her mother on the date of August 10, on the eve of the attack on the residence of the Minister of Recreation?

(The lawyer has finally located the ancient document entered into the court dockets on February 7, 1986. It is written in the pluperfect form and signed: Jete Pliskepafe.)

WITNESS *(reading loudly, in the imperfect tense)*

"Dear Mother, I waited to hear from you for more than a month before I decided to send this letter. I hoped for some news from you that I might return home. You asked me about the job? I wanted to say then how terrible this Minister of Recreation was. He acted like an evil man in his actions toward me, his cook! Why did he act this way? He forced me to stay after dark to cook his rum cakes; that was the excuse. The Minister of Recreation wanted me to ignore my husband and my children to come to the kitchen to cook for him late at night.

"Do you understand, Mother? He asked me to do things—evil things

—but I refused. I said to him, 'I will cook your rum cakes but you must leave me alone in this kitchen.' I had no more patience for him. So he was looking for an excuse to beat me—I'm certain of it. I took the key to escape the Minister of Recreation, who was in the habit of locking the Ministry with me inside baking his rum cakes. So I gave the key to my friend to come and rescue me if the Minister of Recreation asked me once again to come to him. By then I decided to leave the job, and planned to leave. But before that, I wanted to explain to you about my unhappiness with the Minister of Recreation, who is a liar and a bad man. Your daughter, L'Espérance Fini."

PROSECUTOR (*nodding gravely*)

Thank you, Monsieur Imparfait. Your honor, Counselor, distinguished jurors . . . Can there be any doubt from this letter written in Monsieur Imparfait's own hand that L'Espérance Fini detested the Minister of Recreation? No, there cannot be. Here we have evidence that she stole Government property—the key to the kitchen door of the Ministry of Recreation—and gave it to a friend. A friend of the accused, perhaps, your honor, but a thief. Your honor, I present Exhibits One and Three, the letter and the key to the kitchen door.

(*The blind clerk, moving forward, accepts the evidence, which is then shown to the jury for their perusal. Madame Telenovela has returned and is cooing at Monsieur Imparfait like a pigeon. Meanwhile, the lawyer is trying to attract the judge's attention. He waves a tattered document in his hand. But the judge is distracted, having spied a pornographic magazine featuring topless Taiwanese trapeze artists in the cart bearing the constitutions.*)

LAWYER (*rising*)

Excuse me, your honor—your excellency . . .

(*Several of the male jurors fly over to the cart as well. They whistle and shriek; Madame Telenovela is impressed to see that Jesuis Imparfait keeps his eyes ahead of him.*)

LAWYER (*waving*)

Justice Arsenic—your honor? If the court will permit, I must challenge this testimony! There are certain discrepancies in the letter Monsieur

Imparfait has read. By changing the action under discussion from the far past to the recent past, we can see even more clearly that L'Espérance Fini was actually threatened by the Minister of Recreation, not merely afraid of being threatened as her testimony in the pluperfect tense suggests.

In the original letter, for example, she says about the Minister of Recreation (reading aloud): "Why HAD he BEEN ACTING this way? He HAD BEEN FORCING me to stay after dark to cook his rum cakes; that HAD BEEN the excuse." But today Monsieur Imparfait's statements indicate that the Minister of Recreation FORCED my client to stay after hours—that WAS the excuse. I believe such discrepancies speak directly to the issue of intent, of cause and effect, and of premeditation—important issues that affect the facts of this case. Your honor, are you listening?

(The clerk feels his way along the banister and accepts the worn document from the lawyer. Then he approaches the judge, bumping into the female jurors, who pinch his feathers with their beaks. They feel piqued by the attention being given to the topless Taiwanese trapeze artists. Only Madame Telenovela refrains from pecking the clerk; she slyly extends a painted claw forward for Jesuis Imparfait to admire.)

JUDGE *(looking up)*
What was that, Counselor? What's that you have? Another letter? Well, Counselor, one letter from that poor unfortunate client of yours is enough to convince this court that she suffered from that great common social malady—female hysteria. Her delusion that the Minister could harbor anything aside from the most honorable intentions, well, I do not have to say it, Counselor, but I will: that is outrageous. Your client has provided us with a grotesque display of chicanery. Clerk! Burn the letters at once!

(The clerk, standing stage left by a column with a candle in its holder, nods. Before the lawyer can act, the clerk has ignited the letter. As if on cue, the orchestra in the kitchen strikes the notes to "La Marseillaise" and the jurors begin to sing along. Madame Telenovela makes her move. Landing on Jesuis Imparfait's head, she begins to whisper sweet nothings in his ear and offers to preen him.)

JUDGE *(impressed and envious)*
Plus-que-Parfait . . . now Imparfait. Perhaps with this dear lady's encouragement it will now be Monsieur and Madame . . . Future Condi-

tionelle? What do you think, ladies and gentlemen of the jury? Is it time for canasta? . . . So be it! The court is adjourned for today and indefinitely!

JURORS *(clapping and dancing)*

Hurrah!

Chic alors!

(One of the jurors, the playboy, does a series of double and triple somersaults in the air, flying at breakneck speed around the room. He leads the other jurors out of the courtroom. All of them except for Madame Telenovela have forgotten about the case of L'Espérance Fini. Madame Telenovela, whispering seductively to Jesuis Imparfait, asks, "Darling, about the Minister of Recreation. What was it that he did to her that was so evil? You were so coy not to tell us, I mean, the details of it. Was she pretty?"

(The lawyer finishes putting his papers into his briefcase. He walks over to the pile of ashes that once proved the innocence of his client, L'Espérance Fini. He will give them to her family. It is not much to offer, the smallest token of justice. He brushes the ashes into his brown paper bag. The clerk moves around the jury box, sweeping into a pile orange peels the jurors have dropped. The market vendors have woken and are preparing to depart. A light rain falls as the lawyer exits the main door.)

BLACKOUT

END OF ACT ONE

Gerard pulled the page out of the typewriter and set it on top of the others on the table. He looked at the last paragraph for a long time. Inside, something began to break up, the dull ache he had been feeling for days. Tears welled, of relief and sadness. He closed his eyes. Before him flashed a succession of faces: Madame Paule; Jeanne; Oncle Louis leaning on a walking stick outside the house at Kenscoff; his mother in bed, her shortwave radio in hand; then himself, at age ten, a choirboy, singing; and Ti Cedric, arguing at a meeting; Leslie, her hair graying at the roots; old R. V. Singh, clapping his hands together and laughing; Bishop Privat, accepting the nomination with General Lucerne by his side; then Father . . . his own father.

A face looked at him, a white-haired man in a dark suit with heavy black glasses, shirt sleeves rolled up, a bottle and a glass beside him. He was cutting limes with a hunting knife. Gerard, he said, Don't ever let me down, son. Everything I've sacrificed, I've done it for you. Be a good son, don't stay away too long. Come back to us, son. And, son, don't ever disrespect your mother, do you hear me? Do you see this belt I'm wearing? I won't be afraid to use it on you. Now go on, leave me. I have work to do.

Gerard fingered the pages of the play. You were a bastard, old man, he said to the face still before him. I wanted to tell you that the night you were dying. But I was still too good a son, wasn't I? So listen to me now. You beat my mother. I saw the marks on her face. And you had four mistresses, you weren't content with one or even two. I saw it all. Every time you came back late at night. I watched you take off your shoes outside. I knew everything about you. May you rot in hell, Father, for what you did to her. Do you hear me? For what you did to all of us. You and your kind. Do you hear me, Madame Paule? My father was a Macoute. That's right. But you probably knew that, didn't you? All of you probably knew it. A Macoute who beat his wife and children. And yet you still trusted his son. You still trusted me, didn't you?

⤳ 27 ⤳

Riding in taxis in Haiti made Leslie feel her own discomfort, her own boundaries, as if a layer of protection was being chipped away. She enjoyed the hot breath of the child held in its mother's arms next to her. He smelled soft and sweet as only an infant can. She rubbed his foot and he smiled. His mother didn't seem to notice.

Leslie had turned down Clemard's offer to drive her up to Pétionville; it made no sense for him to drive down from Bertrand's to pick her up, only to have to drive down again later and then come back up to drop Bertrand's car off before going home to wherever it was he lived. He had yet to offer her an invitation to his house. Leslie was still determined to pry one out of him.

The drive up took much longer than it had the night of the American Club reception. The taxi made frequent stops to pick up and drop off passengers. The mother and child got out; a teenage boy carrying three eggs in a handkerchief got in. The car was so low to the ground that they could feel every bump. They passed the nearly completed Hôtel des Artistes, then Kentucky Fried Chicken and the office building of one of the presidential candidates.

The plaza next to the restaurant was just ahead. She tapped the driver on the shoulder to get out, handing him blue two-gourde notes so worn the numerals were almost illegible, the paper soiled with the greasy residue of thousands of fingers. Imprinted at the top was *Banque de la République d'Haïti*, one of the banks through which Duvalier had funneled millions, transferring state funds into secret Swiss accounts and dubious investment projects. Gerard had shown her some of the bank documents this week, photocopies of checks written out to dozens of Duvalier family members and acolytes. What had impressed her were the almost monthly six- and seven-figure checks written out simply to "Cash" that the First Couple had blithely withdrawn from the government's accounts and deposited directly into their personal accounts. They had clearly seen no need to hide their activities, a point Gerard had underscored by telling her, "Duvalier considered the state's money to be his; he made no distinction at all. That's why he continues to argue that he didn't steal it. He was using his own money, in his opinion."

The bottom of the gourde read: *This bill conforms to the Constitution of the Republic of Haiti and is payable to the bearer in legal tender of the United States of America at a rate of five gourdes to the dollar.* Could there be a better summary of a postcolonial relationship? Leslie wondered. The driver extended a coin with a worn-off face; she told him to keep it. Up ahead, a half dozen white jeeps with blue *Organization Internationale* license plates were parked in front of a terraced building. The taxi driver honked and waved, passing her.

The restaurant was noisy and full of white people. An early Elton John–Bernie Taupin song blared from a Technics compact-disk player. The machine was mounted on the wall above the bar. A jagged red neon line dipped and peaked on the electronic panel. Everyone was drinking; it was like happy hour in the States, an oversized television set broadcasting, via satellite, a U.S. baseball game. Leslie heard English all around her. The foreign aid set, she thought wryly. Groups of animated young people talked loudly at the bar. Several wore CARE T-shirts; another the jacket of an organization she did not recognize. My peers, she mused with detachment.

"Ms. Doyle?"

Leslie turned.

"I was sitting over there." Peter Samuels pointed. "I got here early." They shook hands. "I'm sorry we didn't get a chance to talk at that reception," he said. The embassy officer motioned for her to follow him toward the back of the room. "I've been terribly busy this week. This is the only free time I've had. You didn't have any problem finding it, did you?"

"No, no problem. I took a group taxi."

The bar had seemed familiar to her upon entering; now she knew why. She had been here before, with Father, but it had been a nightclub then. She had been shy of her eighteenth birthday; she remembered that too, because she could drink in Haiti and not at home and she had liked that. Her braces hadn't been removed yet, and she had that terrible acne then. Smiling at the memory, she looked around for other recognizable objects. That was the time we went to the Citadel with Bertrand, she thought. She recalled the harrowing small plane ride they had made to the Cape.

"What would you like?" Samuels asked, waving the waiter over. He was drinking a beer. "They've got great frozen drinks. Planter's punch, piña colada—that kind of thing."

"I'll take a piña colada." She gave him a friendly smile.

On the phone she had had a mental image of a dark-haired heavyset man, due to Samuels's deep, measured voice. But he looked like a high school jock turned businessman: chino pants, a green Lacoste shirt buttoned to the top, and brown loafers.

The Special Assistant to the Under Secretary for Political Affairs was also younger than she had expected. He was a medium-sized man with a trim, athletic build and somewhat handsome features, around forty-five, she guessed. His fair skin was sunburned, his pale blue eyes almost the same color as Mark's. That's one strike against you, she thought. Plain wire-rimmed glasses gave him a faintly academic air.

"Here are the handouts we give to the media." His tone was businesslike as he offered her an oversized envelope. "I hope they're helpful. Whatever's not in there, just let me know. We don't tend to issue stuff that often these days."

She glanced at the contents, which included several press releases on the political situation, the elections, and, she noted with satisfaction, a report by USAID on rural self-help projects. That would save her some legwork.

"You might want to talk to our development officer too," he suggested. "She's in Washington for the week, but she'll be back next Monday. She's got a good feel for these kinds of things."

"What's this?" She pulled out a Xerox. *Travel Advisory: Dos and Don'ts*, it read.

"Oh, that's our little tourist guide." Samuels chuckled congenially. "You know, the best restaurants, where you can find a toilet in the local village—all the good stuff."

She smiled again, appreciating his sense of humor. The embassy brochure sternly warned U.S. residents to avoid political demonstrations and traveling after dark. She turned to the section marked *Water*.

"They don't mention Culligan," she told him.

"What's that?" He leaned forward.

"Oh, just a rumor I heard. That people fill empty Culligan bottles with tap water and sell them in the markets."

"Didn't hear about that one yet." He signaled the waiter. "But it doesn't surprise me. They're clever that way. This place is the greatest recycling center in the world. Have you ever seen what they can do with a tin can? It's amazing. Same as in Africa—toys, tools, lampshades, you name it."

She watched him out of the corner of her eye. Samuels was definitely less of a stuffed shirt than the Haiti desk officers back in Washington. She could feel herself loosening up a little; she had been nervous about this meeting all day.

He pointed to a huge barrel by the bar. "Should we have some peanuts? They're the best thing about this place." His smile seemed genuine.

"Sure." She settled back into a deep, cushioned seat while he got up to fetch some peanuts.

From here she had a view of the roadside market, which was winding down for the day. Groups of women stood with baskets or burlap bags on their heads, waiting for the tap-taps that would take them to the suburbs. Madanmsaras, Leslie thought, wondering if Elyse Voltaire was one.

When Samuels returned, he dropped a handful of peanuts on the table. Leslie hoped she wouldn't regret eating them.

"This place used to be a nightclub," she told him. "I came here a long time ago, when I was seventeen. It's completely changed."

"Oh, really? I've been told people don't go out the way they used to. Must've been more fun back then."

He had thin lips, not very sensuous, and small, evenly spaced teeth. She counted a dozen gray hairs on his head.

Together they looked over at the outdoor dancing area behind the bar, which was decorated with hanging Japanese paper lanterns. "Pretty, isn't it?" Samuels remarked, waving to an acquaintance, who returned the greeting.

"Very nice." She wondered if he was CIA or not. The embassy political officers usually were; Gerard had thought it likely.

Her drink was as strong as the one the bartender had made at the

Royale. She looked at Samuels's hands, his fingers square and blunt. A pragmatist, she thought. His forefinger was unusually long, the sign of a leader but not a Napoleon. More of a follower, a company man. He wasn't wearing a wedding band, which surprised her; she thought marriage was a prerequisite for foreign service officers.

"You said you're from Washington?" His tone was still amiable. "Whereabouts exactly?"

"Adams Morgan—the hippie section," she added, joking. "Actually it's really a yuppie area now; the hippies can't afford it."

He smiled. "Any relation to Paul Doyle?"

"Uh-huh." She sipped the drink, then cleared her throat. "He was my father. But he passed away—of a heart attack."

"I'm sorry to hear that," he said. "I took a postgraduate economics course at the American University, so I'm familiar with his work. He was a smart guy."

Samuels absently separated the peanuts into three little piles. Had he brought up the subject of her father to let her know he had checked up on her? "He was a good man," Leslie replied. "He loved the Caribbean."

"Is that how you got interested in Haiti?" He cracked the shells in his teeth, then picked the nuts out of them.

"We used to spend the summers wherever he was teaching. Then about ten years ago I started working with migrant workers; a lot of them come from here. I was teaching ESL—you know, English as a Second Language? That's when I learned Creole. I started doing development work after that and now my interests have sort of merged."

She had already told him in their phone conversation that she was here to investigate self-help projects on behalf of the Funding Coalition. Of course, if he was CIA, he would already know that. Samuels had an all-around nice guy demeanor, Leslie thought, bland but intense. He reminded her of a nurse shark: his hands never stopped moving either.

To her left, the CARE group broke into raucous laughter; one of the young men had dropped an ice cube down a female colleague's shirt. Another woman, who had identified herself to the room at large as Sherrie, was holding forth on the difficulties of delivering vaccines to rural villages: "So the jeep broke down and there we were, totally stuck, the mud is six inches deep. We end up having to buy all these Cokes in this village so we can put the vaccines in the cooler. I mean, it was just too much. You should have seen these guys carrying buckets of ice with the vaccines on their heads. I mean, we're talking pri-mi-ti-vo!" Sherrie had a braying laugh; it filled the room. Leslie looked at the group, caught Samuels's eyes, and smiled.

"Peace Corps." He thumbed in the group's direction. "A good bunch of kids. But after spending six weeks out in the field, they come in here ready to tie one on." He spoke of them with almost paternal affection. "The only perks we get here are weekenders to Miami," he added. "But at least the cable reception is good." He looked over at the television. "Except when it's hurricane season. Ever been here then?"

"Once. I think I slept through it, though."

He laughed. "Gives you a new appreciation of Mother Nature. You wouldn't want to get stuck at sea in one of those."

Was he making a reference to the boat people?

"There was a little storm when I flew in," Leslie said. "It gave me a few final thoughts."

He chuckled.

"So," he said after a long pause, "you said on the phone you had a couple of questions?" A businesslike tone was back in his voice. "Shoot."

They had established the ground rules for a conversation earlier. It would be off the record, only for background, unless stated otherwise. Samuels carelessly brushed the peanut shells onto the floor; one fell by Leslie's foot and she pressed down on it until it snapped.

She had prepared a series of written questions, but she decided not to use them. She knew what she wanted to find out, though she was still unsure how much she should reveal about her own motives. If he was CIA, she worried that any information she gave him could fall into the wrong hands. Samuels was cracking open the peanuts with a thumb and finger, separating the seed from the shell in a single deft movement.

"Maybe you could tell me how you—how the embassy sees the

situation. What our position is, that sort of thing. I mean, beyond what's in here." She gestured to the information packet he had given her.

"Which situation?" he asked. "Are we talking generally?"

"Generally," she replied. "Just your overview."

Samuels laced his fingers around his glass and pursed his birdlike lips. "Well, that's easy enough. You can put this on the record. The United States government supports the efforts of the Haitian government to bring about democratic change, and the Haitians have promised to hold free and open elections. We will assist them in pursuing that goal. How's that?"

"Sounds very official." She smiled. He was treating her like a novice.

"Well, that's our position. That's what Uncle Sam thinks." The note of congeniality was still in his voice, but it was serious. He's going to make me work, Leslie thought.

"How about off the record?" she asked. "Don't you have a personal opinion?"

"Sure, but they don't pay me for that." He answered matter-of-factly, rolling a peanut through his fingers like a magician trying a card trick.

"Off the record," she persisted. "No quotes. I mean, they must pay you for *that*."

It was a little jab, but he smiled appreciatively, quickly popping another peanut in his mouth.

"Generally, things are pretty smooth," he replied. "You read the papers. The political parties are starting to get organized. From our perspective, the government is cooperating with the organization of the elections. Of course, the economy is still pretty shaky, but you can see it picking up here and there. I mean, you have to have a perspective. Things have been chaotic here for a long time. So we don't expect change overnight."

"There's still a lot of theft and corruption," Leslie said, framing her queries as statements. "The day before yesterday I spoke to a representative of the World Bank. He told me it's a serious problem." She deliberately tried to make herself sound naive.

"It's definitely a problem, but we're talking about a country that's run on patronage. That's certainly not going to go away tomorrow. And the authorities are aware that it's a problem. I don't see the issue as being a problem of corruption; it's a need for some infra- structure. Once you've got that, you'll be able to cut down on the black market and all the scams. Without government control, it's anybody's game."

She pressed on. "As I mentioned earlier on the phone, the reason I'm interested is that our donors hear the same reports and they're naturally concerned. Not only about the sale of foreign donations on the black market but also about the military seizing the deliveries after they're in the warehouses. I'm trying to get a clearer picture of what's really going on."

He shrugged. "Well, I'm certain if you looked hard enough you could probably find some isolated case where a soldier—maybe even a group of soldiers—has taken charge of a shipment. It happens. But I think that's the exception. Things have improved. Talk to these folks in here." He gestured to the Peace Corps group. "They'll tell you we're getting good cooperation at all levels of government, including the army and the police and the customs officials. So we're happy. We've definitely seen progress. I mean, you're always going to have people trying to take advantage of chaos, but there's no large-scale theft, nothing like you're suggesting."

"Interesting," she replied, unconvinced. "I've gotten exactly the opposite story from other people. For example, the human rights groups say the army is using an anti-drug campaign as a pretense to go after people who support the elections. I'm sure you've heard that." She hoped the change of subjects sounded natural, casual.

He made a face, dismissing her suggestion. "Teledjol—you know that expression?—the rumor mill? Well, it's on overdrive in this country. If you want to talk about elections, let's do that. The first thing you'll find is that a lot of these groups, especially radical leftist groups, don't want an election. They may say they want one, and theoretically they do, but not now. Because now is too soon. They know they wouldn't stand a chance if an election was held today —they don't have the support. So you've got quite a number of people who are willing to say a lot of things in order to derail a process they publicly support. You've got to look beyond the rumors and see what people's motives are. From our perspective, we're satisfied that things are moving along in the right direction. We're seeing evidence of it every day. We are one hundred percent behind the goal of elections. Hell, it's our goal."

She didn't believe it. Or him. It was a complete party line. She tried another tack.

"What about all the arrests I've been reading about? Can you tell me anything about that?"

"Nothing you don't know. Like I said, we read the same papers. There are incidents in which they've picked some people up—God knows, it's like the Wild West out here—but they've released them after questioning."

"I just read the new Amnesty International report," she said, choosing her words carefully. "They have a long list of people they claim are being detained as political prisoners."

Samuels smiled. "Don't get me started about those folks," he warned. "Their August bulletin—is that what you're talking about? Because, trust me, there isn't a lot of meat to it. That particular report was way off the mark."

She was surprised by his reaction. His tone remained calm, but she had clearly struck a nerve.

"What do you mean?" she asked.

"I mean, quite simply, they don't distinguish fact from rumor. You read that report, you'd think the whole country was one big prison. You'd think Baby Doc was still running the show." He shrugged.

"But they are arresting people," she cut in. "Right? I mean, that's been on the radio and in the newspapers. It's not just Amnesty International saying it."

"No one is saying incidents never happen. But Amnesty International and groups like that tend to exaggerate things. They hear someone's been picked up for stealing and suddenly it's a case of torture and the whole family's been kidnapped. But the funny thing is, every time we ask Amnesty to provide the evidence, the hard, concrete evidence, they don't have it. They do have a lot of people willing to make statements and accusations, but that's all. And, trust me, you can get anyone in this country to say just about anything, especially if it's against Uncle Sam. You've heard about the American Plan, haven't you? Well, that's us: we're the enemy. But go to those villages, talk to those people, and you'll find out the truth. It isn't close to what Amnesty International says.

"The thing is," he continued, "Amnesty is like all these human rights groups. They're not-for-profit, but they still have to do something to justify those grants. They've got to generate their reports, whether or not they're true. That's the thing that bothers me so much. Because groups like that end up undermining their own credibility. And I think it's because they're really not that interested in figuring out the truth. They've got a political agenda; it just happens to be called human rights. But what it ultimately comes down to is bashing us, as in the U.S.—Uncle Sam—no matter what's really going on. It's got very little to do with the truth."

Samuels took a long sip of his beer, finished his glass, and picked up where he had left off. "No one"—he signaled the waiter—"is going to deny that abuses occur. That would be foolish. This is Haiti, after all, and Haiti is a violent place with a lot of problems and a lot of poverty. But we denounce the serious abuses wherever they happen. Let me level with you." He leaned forward conspiratorially. "The truth—if we're talking about it with a capital T— is that there's a total breakdown of law and order in Haiti. That's really the bottom line. Most of these guys in the army can't even spell their own names. So yes, you absolutely have a discipline problem. But you also have a lot of ordinary crime taking place, a lot of daytime theft where the soldiers are called in to help. And it becomes awfully easy to blur the two, which is what the human rights groups like to do. The way I see it, it's a deliberate blurring. But it hardly adds up to what they call a campaign of abuses or whatever—"

"Terror?"

"Terror," he acknowledged, his tone sarcastic. "It's easy to throw the word around, but it's a lot of malarkey. You have to be very organized to carry out a campaign of terror. This army and what exists of this government are not organized. What you're witnessing is a lack of good policing. But it's not overtly political; it's civil in nature. There's an important difference."

Malarkey. She was stuck on the word. It was so quaint. She had heard everything he had said and was weighing his logic. Though she disagreed with him, Samuels was not stupid.

The waiter returned, and Samuels ordered another beer for himself. She had not finished her drink and declined another.

"Even if Amnesty is exaggerating"—she took up her theme—"which for argument's sake I'll say is possible—since they rely on local groups to inform them and, as you mentioned, it's hard to get concrete proof—people are still disappearing. Something's happening. I hear their relatives on the radio. Frankly, I believe them. They're completely convincing. Everybody can't be making it up."

His reply was calm, still matter-of-fact. "Everybody . . . who? There's a lot of chaos," he repeated. "People, as you say, move around. The point is that the Haitians—including the folks in the military—are trying to move forward. And they're doing it against huge odds. So yes, you can find people in the army who are opposed to the election, just like you can find them in all the different sectors, but you've also got some professionals. Take General Lucerne, he's a professional. He's trying to get the army in shape—and out of the political stuff. He's more or less supportive of these elections. I wouldn't say the same about all the others, because they're more rigid. They'll accept some reforms, but they're frightened by too much change. So your strategy is to find the professionals and support them. That's our position," he emphasized. "That's what we're focusing on, and that's really the important stuff. Without guys like Lucerne, you won't have an election."

Lucerne. The one who had humiliated Marie-Thérèse Dubossy, ordered her to strip. Samuels was avoiding a real answer, putting forth soft rhetoric.

"I'm not disagreeing," she said. "But what about all these missing people? They're not just on the move."

He sat back and shook his head wearily. "You've got people going over the border every day. It's like a fishnet, big holes in border control. You've got boats leaving all the time, they don't want to tell anybody where they're headed. It all boils down to infrastructure. That's what we're trying to support. You deal with that and everything else falls into place. Until then, you'll see all kinds of abuses.

But it's not systematic. And it's not a campaign of terror. There are no secret prisons. Anyone who says differently is sadly misinformed."

They were clearly deadlocked. Leslie smiled. For now, she wanted Samuels to think she was, if naive, a well-intentioned outsider. She backed down a bit.

"I understand what you're saying. And I appreciate your being so frank."

"Hey"—he shrugged—"we do our best." He asked a moment later, "Anything else?"

"What about a guy named Cedric George?—they call him Ti Cedric."

"Sure—the guy from Papaye. What about him?"

"He's been reported missing. You know about that?"

"We've gotten a report, yes. But we don't know anything about it."

"But the military has denied having him, right?"

"That's my understanding." Samuels suddenly shifted in his seat, then expertly cracked his neck. "Excuse me." He smiled. "I get a stiff neck sitting for too long. I sat in meetings all morning." He sighed and asked more directly, "Why are you interested? Is he a friend of yours?"

"No, but a friend of a friend," she said. "They're very worried."

"These political guys are pretty good at keeping a low profile when they want to." Samuels sniffed, tweaking his nostrils. "I'd wait a bit and see if he doesn't turn up. From what I understand, this guy's survived some rough stuff in his time."

"My friend," Leslie broached the subject carefully, sipping her cocktail, "wondered if Ti Cedric might have contacted the embassy to try to get protection. Any chance you know about that?"

"Even if I did, you know I couldn't tell you." Samuels sat back. "But, in fact, I don't know about anything like that. Makes my life easier, though." He was joking, she saw.

How could she know if he was telling the truth? Samuels's expression was benign; he seemed to be fairly relaxed.

"I mentioned to you in my letter that I'm trying to get inside the prisons," Leslie said after a long pause. "I don't know if it's the kind of thing you could help me with. But I'd like to see for myself what the conditions are like."

"Which prison?" Samuels asked. "Here in Port-au-Prince?"

"Well, I'd love to go inside Fort Dimanche"—she smiled—"but I don't think they'd let me in."

"It's closed."

"Some people claim it's still being used."

He didn't comment.

"I've petitioned the warden at the penitentiary here. But I haven't gotten a response yet. It's been two weeks. Do you have any access?"

"Not really," he said. "That's domestic stuff. We don't get involved in that. You'll have to deal directly with the government on that one. But hey, why not ask Amnesty? They're the ones who know how to do it. They had a group in there not long ago."

"I tried them. They don't have a mission planned right now."

"Well, I'm sorry, but there's nothing we can do, Ms. Doyle. That's just out of our domain."

"I understand. I just thought I'd ask."

"Why not ask your lawyer friend?" Samuels suggested. "He ought to be able to help you."

Leslie was taken off guard. So he knew who Gerard was. And that they were friends. That meant he also knew more about Leslie than he had been letting on. She felt exposed.

"I'll ask him," she replied lightly, masking her surprise. "I just thought I'd ask you first."

Samuels's expression remained enigmatic. Could he tell when she was lying?

"Madanm?" The waiter swung by offering another round. Her glass was not quite empty, but she let him take it away. "Good thing we're talking business," she joked. But Samuels didn't laugh; he was studying his drink. Leslie fingered a new bracelet she had bought that afternoon. What was he thinking?

The waiter set down a fresh drink. She took a few sips, toying with a maraschino cherry. "What do you think will happen with the elections?" she asked after a few sips. "Everybody seems to think they'll be violent."

"Everybody?" He arched his brow. "You keep using that word.

Are we talking now about people who don't want an election?" The slight edge of challenge was back in his tone.

Leslie suddenly wanted to tell him that he had a bad haircut, that he would look better with different glasses and a different style. She felt her own hostility building up, and moved to keep it in check, smoothing the tablecloth to brush aside the peanut shells.

He cocked his head, as if trying to decide something about her. Then he smiled. "Since we're on background, and since you asked and you seem like a reasonable lady, I don't have any problem telling you." He inched his chair farther forward. "You really want to know what's going on? Right?"

"I do," she said, thinking, It's about time.

He wiped his mouth, then took a long swallow of beer. "Well, you won't find anybody at Amnesty saying this," he began. "Hell, for that matter, you won't even find many people in Washington willing to go on record. But the fact of the matter is that Haiti is a total and complete mess. That's right," he repeated slowly, "a-total-and-complete-major-mess."

She folded her paper napkin into triangles, listening.

"How can anyone seriously talk about elections in this place?" he asked quietly. "I mean, honestly. A democracy? In a country where maybe eighty-five percent of the people can't read? You understand what I'm saying?"

"I think so," she ventured. "I mean, I'm not sure I agree with you. People can vote even if they can't read."

"Let me explain." He pursed his lips. "Based on my experience—and I've been here four years—Haitians wouldn't be able to recognize a free election if it knocked on their doors and introduced itself." She saw that he was perfectly serious. I wish I had my tape recorder, she thought. I want this.

"Haiti is a joke, except nobody's laughing, because it's really not that funny, unless you have a sick sense of humor, which a lot of people seem to have, at least around here." Samuels looked around the room, then back at her.

Leslie lowered her eyes. She decided Peter Samuels was a singularly unattractive man.

"We talk about democracy," he stressed, "with a big D—Democracy in Haiti, right? But what are we talking about? Anyone who really thinks there can be democracy in Haiti is either hopelessly naive or too stupid to be taken seriously; you can take your pick. I've met a lot of people lately—journalists in particular—who qualify as both. But really, the biggest joke is on us, because we end up throwing our money at countries like Haiti without ever getting results. It's like pissing in the wind, if you'll pardon the expression. And we've been doing it here for an awfully long time."

Leslie drank her drink slowly.

"No one is even pretending we can solve Haiti's problems anymore," Samuels added. "Hell, the situation is too far gone for that. But the problem is, we can't get out—we're stuck. And it's the folks like Amnesty International who denounce our policies who would be the first to scream if we stopped supporting this process."

Under it all, he's just like Bertrand, Leslie thought. Just a shark—all nerves, no heart. Just another Ivy League racist. She felt disappointed.

"You know why?" he asked suddenly.

"Why what?" She had missed the question, preoccupied by her train of thought.

"Because they don't want to live in a democracy. That's the irony. Because democracy is hard work. You know, it's a lot easier to let the army run things and complain."

She had heard it before.

"I'll give you an example," he said. "There's this fellow who works in our embassy cafeteria; a little fellow, nice guy." Samuels sniffed again, wiping his nose on his napkin. "We have a coffee machine there. You know the kind—you plug it in and put in the filter." He mimed filling a coffee filter and slipping it into the machine.

Leslie took another swallow of her piña colada. I might as well get tight, she thought.

"That way we can have hot coffee in the morning. No big deal, right? So what does Mr. Efficiency do? He forgets to plug in the machine—every time. Or he says he forgets." Samuels shook his head. "So if I want a cup, I have to wait, and by then it's actually faster just to boil water for a single cup and use Nescafé than it is to make the whole pot. Now, I go through this routine about once a week with this guy. And the man is not dumb. He knows exactly how the machine works. So what? He still forgets? He's lazy? When all he has to do is turn it on? Because look, the guy the night before has left it clean and ready to be used again, you see. I mean, it just blows my mind—it's ridiculous." Samuels bit a peanut in half, not bothering to remove the shell.

"He just refuses to do it." Samuels's tone had grown bitter. "And that's how they all are. What I'm saying is, show them a way to improve something and they'll act like you're asking them to commit a crime. You'll hear every last one of these fellows talk about democracy, but they have no notion about it—none at all. They don't have any desire to work with one another. They would rather fight. It's easier, that's really what it comes down to. It's beyond laziness. I don't know, it's kind of pathological."

Pathological, oh yes. Leslie swallowed. I should have seen this one coming. The Haitian pathology. But she couldn't let this one slide. She had to say something. What?

Before she could formulate a response, Samuels added: "I'm a realist, Ms. Doyle. I see this every day. I lived in Africa for ten years; I saw it there too."

Yeah, she was tempted to fire back, and it's called racism. She suddenly felt defeated, wanted to be back in her hotel, drinking with the custodian instead. Pathological, she repeated to herself. She couldn't believe he had actually used the word. Didn't he know it was politically out of fashion? Clearly, he'd been away for too long.

"That doesn't mean Haitians aren't sweet and generous and have a lot of other wonderful qualities, because they do," Samuels continued. He seemed oblivious to her reaction. "I mean, their songs and their artwork, they're really fantastic. But that's not reality—that's imagination. And what I'm talking about is a refusal to deal with reality."

"Don't," she said finally, keeping her voice even, "don't you think that what you're talking about is a question of education? Or culture? Or an issue of survival? Maybe the guy in the cafeteria thinks the coffee machine will take away his job. I mean, I don't really know what you're trying to say. If there are any conclusions to be drawn about this man and the coffee machine, it's that something is being imposed on him that doesn't make any sense to his life; it's his form of resistance."

"Resistance? No way." Samuels rejected the idea flat out. "Now you're giving me the liberals' line. I'm talking hard facts. That man is not going to lose his job. First of all, he's got one of the only secure jobs in this damn country." He made no attempt to restrain his sarcasm. "That's the thing too. People don't want to face facts. All these journalists who come down here with their armchair statistics. They've already made up their minds before they get here. They're no different from Amnesty International. As far as they're concerned, the United States is just Big Brother and the Haitians are innocent victims. Well, to me that's a pretty myopic view—it's tunnel vision. And it's not helping the Haitians either."

Another Darwinian, she thought, survival of the fittest. The conversation was tiring her.

"I'm a realist," Samuels repeated, "and our kind is not too popular these days. But hey, another six months and I'll probably be out of here."

This was good news. "Where are you going?" Leslie asked, vaguely curious.

"Don't know." He patted back his hair. "If I'm lucky, France. Or Italy. Somewhere where the water's clean."

It was a joke, but she was not amused. Their conversation had hit a wall. Samuels was simply an asshole.

"If you go to France, you can say hello to Baby Doc," she remarked dryly.

"There you go," he agreed. A minute later, after signaling for the waiter to bring the check, he added: "That's another little fact people have got wrong."

"What?" she asked, confused. "Are you going to tell me Duvalier's not in France?"

"No, he's in France. But they complained about the guy until they finally got rid of him. And who are they going to put in his place? Every last one of these guys is a little dictator. You should see how they run their campaigns."

Well, we're not very democratic ourselves, are we? she thought. But she held her tongue. What was the use?

Samuels handed the waiter a credit card before Leslie could offer to pay. "Don't worry about it," he said. "Them's your tax dollars at work." He smiled, a little crooked grin.

"Thanks," she replied. She wanted to wipe it off his face.

Samuels stood up to take his leave. "If there's anything else I can help you with, Ms. Doyle, just give me a call." She rose to shake his hand. "And don't worry," he added, "most of the people in Washington agree with you. But I'll guarantee it, spend a couple of years here and you'll see it my way."

Don't count on it, she thought, adding a bit coolly: "Thank you for your time."

She followed him out with her eyes, watching as he got into a white jeep and drove away. Then she lit a cigarette and mentally replayed their conversation.

Pathological, she thought, smoking and exhaling slowly. What a wretched man!

FUNDING COALITION
1816 H Street NW (Suite 5M)
Washington, D.C. 20433
Phone: 202-477-2230
Fax: 202-477-2247

September 11
Mr. Victor Corelli
Assistant Secretary-General
Executive Office of the Secretary-General
Room S-3802-D
United Nations Plaza
New York, N.Y. 10017

Dear Assistant Secretary-General Corelli:

I am the project coordinator for the Funding Coalition, a nonprofit organization based in Washington, D.C. My current mission is to assess the political climate in Haiti with regard to funding for grass-roots and development projects and with regard to the status of foreign donations to Haitian groups. To that end, I have undertaken an investigation of the general human rights situation in Haiti and the electoral climate. As reported by Amnesty International and local human rights groups, the situation has deteriorated in recent weeks, and political violence has reached new levels in several areas of the countryside.

Please find enclosed a summary report of recent human rights violations that have occurred in Haiti, primarily in the northwest. As you will note, the disappearance of regional activists who are organizing for the elections is particularly alarming. Local human rights groups have identified several members of the Haitian armed forces in connection with these disappearances or with attacks on clergy, peasant groups, and, in recent weeks, student groups.

In view of the Secretary-General's mandate to help oversee democratic elections in Haiti, I hope you will share my findings with him and others in your office. I understand that several groups, including Amnesty International, have requested that you send a delegate or fact-finding mission to Haiti to investigate the current situation. I would like to urge you to consider this step. I have spoken to local Haitian human rights groups over the past week, and there is no doubt that paramilitary forces, acting in concert with soldiers, are actively opposing the organization of the electoral campaign through assassination, kidnapping, and illegal detentions, as well as torture.

I am sending copies of my report and this request to the following agencies: UN Director-General for Development and International Economic Cooperation; UN Office for Special Political Affairs; UN Centre for Human Rights (NY/Geneva); State Department Haiti Task Force; Inter-American Commission on Human Rights; Amnesty International; Americas Watch; Lawyers Committee for Human Rights; National Coalition for Haitian Refugees; International Legal Commission on Human Rights.

For more details regarding the individual cases mentioned in my report, I respectfully suggest that you contact the Haitian human rights organization Dwa Moun (Port-au-Prince, phone: 34954; fax: 34989) or Gerard Metellus (Port-au-Prince, office phone: 20064; fax: 22473), the attorney who is helping Dwa Moun and other groups to determine the status of Haitians who are reported missing or dead in the capital as well as the countryside.

Thank you for your attention to this letter. If you have any questions regarding the content of my report, or other matters, please contact me in Haiti c/o the Hôtel Royale, phone: 24133. I can also receive faxes via Mr. Metellus's office. Again, I urge you to share these findings with the Secretary-General and delegate a human rights mission to Haiti in the coming weeks.

Sincerely,

Leslie Doyle

Project Coordinator

28

Dr. Sylvie stood at the entrance to the hospital, a medical bag in her hand. "Nervous?" she asked Leslie, who nodded through the car window. In the front seat, Clemard reached behind to unlock the back door. The doctor got in.

Dr. Sylvie had gotten dressed up for the visit. She wore gold earrings in addition to her pearls. Leslie had deliberately dressed down, not wanting to attract any more attention than she usually did as a blan. She had chosen a slightly drab denim skirt, a short-sleeved flowered blouse, and slip-on leather shoes with flat heels—in case they suddenly had to run. She knew it was unlikely they would encounter any trouble at the prison—a sudden shooting or prison riot—but the flat shoes reassured her. Dr. Sylvie, by contrast, wore her usual high-heeled pumps.

"We got lucky—if you can call it that," Dr. Sylvie said. "I suppose it's due to all the publicity in the press about the students. By letting us in, the authorities can show they're not hiding anything. Of course, we don't know what they'll let us see. Did you bring some kind of identification?" she asked Leslie.

"I have a letter from my organization," Leslie replied.

"We'll try not to use it," said the doctor. "Let me do the talking."

Dr. Sylvie quickly caught them up on new developments. Just yesterday, she had spoken to a young intern who had been at the hospital when an army vehicle arrived to deliver an unidentified body to the morgue. "They apparently decided not to bring it in," she explained. "The intern said it was quite decomposed. He was told they eventually took it over to the military hospital. But Père Emmanuel has a good source there and they denied receiving it. Nor did any of the private funeral parlors take in a cadaver in that kind of physical state."

"So you think they just got rid of it?" Leslie wrote down this information in a new pocket-sized notepad she had bought expressly for the prison visit. Dr. Sylvie had already warned her it was unlikely they would be able to interview the prisoners in any detail, but she had stuffed the pad into her deep skirt pocket anyway. There had been no question of bringing in a tape recorder.

"I would assume so." Dr. Sylvie shrugged. "What's odd is that they came to our hospital in the first place; usually they go right to the military hospital. It's as if the soldiers weren't sure of their orders. At least that's what the intern concluded. So something's definitely off there."

"Did you tell Gerard?"

"I talked to him last night. Which reminds me, he wants us to call after our visit."

"What about Père Emmanuel?"

"Gerard was going to get in touch with him. Unfortunately, he's in the provinces today. He won't be back until this evening."

Clemard stopped the car a short distance from the mustard-colored prison entrance. They could see a guard standing in the gateway.

"I'll wait here for you," he told them. "Kenbe fem." He had not wanted to accompany them. It seemed too risky, he had told Leslie. His family didn't want him to go inside. What if he was detained in there for no reason?

The guard at the entrance did not move aside, but instructed another soldier to find out if the visitors could enter. After a few moments, a higher-ranking mulatto officer wearing a khaki uniform came out of the building. "Come in," he said politely.

Inside the reception area, he instructed them to take a seat and wait. He knocked on a door to someone's office, then sat down behind his desk. Leslie thought he must be the garde du jour—the day officer. She wondered if he was the man whom Gerard had met when he went to see the judge.

The door opened and a very dark mulatto with a receding hairline stepped out. His starched tan uniform was unbuttoned at the top button. It was General Lucerne. But what was he doing here? They had expected to see the warden.

"Doctor," the general greeted them, extending his hand to Dr. Sylvie, then Leslie.

"This is Madame Leslie Doyle, General Lucerne." Dr. Sylvie introduced her in a solicitous tone. "She's the one I mentioned who would be accompanying me. I wrote that in my letter to the warden."

"Henri Lucerne." He nodded, his hand unusually soft and damp. A sensualist, Leslie thought automatically, releasing it quickly. She remembered Samuels's comments about Lucerne. A career officer. A moderate professional.

The general had brown eyes ringed with pale blue. He was a handsome man, very self-assured. He wore four gold rings, a gold watch, a gold identity bracelet. A small gold religious medallion peeped out from his shirt. His striking eyes searched Leslie briefly. She wondered if she should present her letter from the foundation. Before she could decide, the general ushered them into the warden's office.

A moment later, the officer on duty in the other room knocked and entered. He took Dr. Sylvie's medical bag and looked through it. Dr. Sylvie smiled. "It's just my equipment," she said. General Lucerne's eyes moved from the doctor to Leslie, then to the papers on the desk. Leslie recognized Dr. Sylvie's handwriting: it was their request to visit the prison.

"The warden is out today," the general said. "I'll be accompanying you. If you're ready, we'll begin." Dr. Sylvie looked at Leslie quickly, then nodded.

"Allons-y," she said. Let's go.

They walked out of the reception area into a narrow corridor. The ancient facility was made of concrete and limestone. Armed guards were stationed at various points along the inner corridors, their Uzis held at attention.

They were escorted by two prison guards in blue uniforms. One had an enormous belly and thick muttonchop sideburns. Rudolphe, Leslie read on his name tag. She couldn't tell what rank he or anyone else had; the bars and stars meant nothing to her. Back at the reception area, she had read a notice on the wall delineating the hierarchy of the military and the symbols accompanying each position. There were so many. She had never been able to remember if a lieutenant had a higher rank than a captain anyway, only that a private was the lowest, which appeared to be true here too.

All of the guards were armed; the general was an exception. He walked ahead of them, listening as one of his men whispered something which made him laugh. Leslie wanted to know where they were going.

"This is the women's section," General Lucerne said, indicating a closed metal door they had just reached. "We can come here after we've seen the other prisoners."

Leslie decided to speak up. "Are these all common prisoners, General?"

"Yes, madame." He turned to her, his manner formal and somewhat gallant. He had a superb physique for a man his age. He walked with authority and had a slight spring in his step. He added, for her benefit: "There are no political prisoners in Haiti anymore."

They walked past another metal door, which was also locked. The prison was laid out like a maze, with rectilinear inner courtyards surrounded by interconnecting corridors. A blue-uniformed guard stood before a high metal gate and saluted crisply.

The fat aide, Rudolphe, opened the gate and pushed it forward. The other uniformed guards passed before them, hands on their holstered pistols. General Lucerne was next, followed by Dr. Sylvie. Leslie slipped in last. The door closed behind her. She heard it being locked by someone on the other side.

A hundred pairs of eyes stared at them. The men were standing together inside the small courtyard. They immediately started shouting questions: "General, may I ask you something?" "Gade, madanm—psst." The uniformed guards glared at them; one raised his weapon. The men fell silent, but followed Leslie's group. The general directed them toward the small concrete building, which Leslie guessed was the clinic. She had not known they would be visiting the male prisoners; whether Dr. Sylvie was surprised or not was impossible to gauge. The Haitian woman merely kept a brisk pace with General Lucerne, saying nothing.

Leslie had also expected cells, or barred rooms, some signs of detention rather than this large, open-air cement courtyard. It was obvious from clothing left scattered in corners that some of the inmates slept out of doors, without cover. The cement floor had great cracks in it; a gutter full of leaves and slime ran along the side of one wall. Their toilet.

Attached to the concrete building was a kind of dormitory with two dozen bunk beds, most of them without mattresses or bedding. Leslie felt eyes tracking every movement she made, every gesture. Some of the prisoners discreetly acknowledged her; others still mouthed "Madanm." Their eyes expressed fear as well as hope; at least there were witnesses to their plight.

They entered the clinic, Leslie trailing behind Dr. Sylvie and the general. A wooden examining table and an old-fashioned dentist's chair were the only objects in the small, dilapidated front room. Leslie felt a tug on her arm. Dr. Sylvie pulled her through an open doorway into a larger room. A standing screen was placed at the far end. General Lucerne stayed behind, advising the prisoners outside to disperse. Behind the screen lay two men, one in a bed, the other on the floor. Dr. Sylvie crouched beside them.

The man in the bed had been severely beaten. His eyes were bloodshot and swollen almost shut, his cheeks puffy. He had sores on his lips as well as his forehead. Dr. Sylvie tried opening one eyelid, then another. She gently took his blood pressure and temperature. Other prisoners looked in to see what was happening. Several tried to catch Leslie's attention. "Blan!" they mouthed. "Blan!"

"Is he drinking?" Dr. Sylvie asked. No one answered her. She called the big man over. "He refuses to drink," Captain Rudolphe told her. The patient moved his hands over his crotch. Dr. Sylvie hesitated, then carefully unbuttoned his fly. Leslie swallowed dryly. In place of the sex organ was a mass of grayness and blood, unrecognizable by its bloated shape. Dr. Sylvie looked at the captain, his gut bulging over his thick belt, then back at General Lucerne, who was out of earshot. She did not say anything. Leslie could feel her own heart beating.

"He got into a fight," a voice said behind them. It was one of the younger uniformed guards. Leslie caught his eye and the man looked down.

"These men need immediate medical attention, Captain," Dr. Sylvie told him. "You can see they are in critical condition. They need to be transferred to the hospital. I can't do anything for them here.

"Won't you help me, Leslie?" Dr. Sylvie asked quietly, not waiting for his response. She crouched beside a young man who lay in a pool of urine on the floor between two beds. Dr. Sylvie's face was grim. The youth was scarcely a teenager. He was frail, and his mouth and tongue were coated with a thin white film. He wore only a dirty pair of underpants.

Distressed, Leslie helped the doctor grab the youth from behind. She felt the sharp boniness of his ribs, while Dr. Sylvie quickly slipped her arms under his legs. The youth had no energy; he was dead weight. With difficulty, they managed to lift him back up to the bed. The uniformed guards, who now kept their distance, did not move.

"I suppose this one doesn't drink either," Dr. Sylvie said sarcastically to the captain. He looked uncomfortably at her, then at the general for guidance.

"General Lucerne," the doctor called out. "You have to transfer these men to the hospital right away. They are very sick. They both need transfusions."

The general, Leslie saw, had only pretended to be uninterested. "Are you taking note of that?" he asked Captain Rudolphe, who nodded. "The captain here will make sure your recommendations are followed," he told the doctor.

Dr. Sylvie fished two small jars used for taking urine samples from her bag. "Could you bring these men some water, please?" she asked the captain. "Here." She handed the nearest guard the jars. "Use these." The guard hesitated, then went off.

As they waited for him to return, Dr. Sylvie wrote down instructions for each of the two men. "These patients are completely dehydrated," she informed the room at large. "If they don't get liquids, they will die." She handed the prescriptions to Captain Rudolphe.

The guard returned shortly with two jars of cloudy water. He handed them to Dr. Sylvie, then resumed his post at a distance. His expression was closed; he refused to look at Leslie. Shame on you, Leslie was saying to the guards with her eyes, This is inhumane.

The man with the festering genitals was unable to drink; the water spilled onto his cheeks and chin. Dr. Sylvie held his hand for a few minutes, then said something that Leslie could not hear. The man was crying. She turned to look at Captain Rudolphe, whose expression was indifferent.

Leslie wondered if the man had been beaten before or after he fell ill. She held his head and back upright while Dr. Sylvie lifted the cup up to his lips. It was painful to watch him try to drink. His entire body shook from the effort. She wondered how he had survived even this long. Leslie tried to avoid staring at his gangrenous sex organ, which had oozed pus and blood. To urinate would be torture; it was unimaginable. She finally looked away, her hands clammy with sweat.

She stayed with the man a few more minutes while Dr. Sylvie gave the other youth some water and questioned him, whispering and writing things down. She was prodding under his arms; the boy was grimacing. Leslie could see the doctor's fingers moving over the skin, feeling tenderly, examining a lesion on his leg. She wondered if the boy had AIDS; his appearance was similar to that of the young woman they had met lying on the gurney in the hospital corridor. The prisoners in the courtyard turned to watch them file out. Leslie gave them encouraging smiles, but she felt devastated. Ahead of them, the general was telling Dr. Sylvie that the two sick men had been seen the week before by a military doctor, who had assured him of their condition. Hearing that, Leslie felt like rushing the general, shaking him, gagging the lie. She wanted Peter Samuels to be here, to see the bedsores on the beaten man's hips, his swollen hands and feet, his missing teeth. A professional, she heard Samuels's description of Lucerne again, a political moderate. She privately gritted her teeth, then exhaled heavily. You're an evil man, her eyes bore into his back. What's going on here is evil. Evil and inhumane.

She took another deep breath before entering the women's section, worried now about what she might encounter. This courtyard was much smaller than the courtyard of the men's section. Several women stood on the far side, in the open doorways of small rooms that appeared to be their sleeping quarters. General Lucerne, followed by Captain Rudolphe, led Dr. Sylvie and Leslie into a small building, a chapel of sorts. There were several old-fashioned manual sewing machines inside, the kind you advanced with your hand,

and a few wooden benches. On one wall was a faded print of St. Paul, and on another, facing the sewing machines, a crucifix made of woven palm leaves. The room seemed to serve an all-purpose function. Next to it was a tiny concrete room in poor condition, the walls pockmarked, the paint peeling. It held a wooden cot and a cabinet. This was the women's clinic.

Leslie looked around for a metal pipe protruding from the ceiling—that's how Marie-Thérèse Dubossy had described the shower in the infirmary in her testimony. But there was no pipe, only an empty Mylanta bottle on its side on the shelf.

Outside, the guards were assembling the women; they heard several names being called out. Leslie wanted to go back out to the courtyard to see if Elyse Voltaire might be among them.

"I'll leave you now," General Lucerne said, as the first woman was ushered in. He watched as Dr. Sylvie once again removed the contents of her medical bag. "If you require anything, the good captain will relay it to me," he added, exiting.

The huge man stood right next to Leslie, who was forced into a corner; the clinic was too narrow. His gun was out of its holster; he held it casually, loosely. Outside, Leslie knew, the other guards stood with their weapons drawn as well. The atmosphere here and in the courtyard felt tense. Leslie could feel the big man's presence like a weight.

"They can answer yes or no," he told them, referring to the women. "Those are my instructions."

Dr. Sylvie listened to the first woman's heartbeat, then placed her stethoscope on her stomach and lower torso. "Do you feel well?" she asked the woman, who was slight yet wiry, her hair twisted into a dozen nappy points. The woman looked inquiringly at the big guard. Can I answer?

Dr. Sylvie encouraged her. "Wi ou non?" Yes or no?

"Wi."

She opened her mouth to let Dr. Sylvie flash a slim light down her throat. The doctor put her thermometer under the woman's armpit and left it there. She tested her reflexes, then took her blood pressure. Throughout this, Leslie smiled at the woman, who identified herself as Lilliane, before the guard cut her off. "No talking, just yes or no," he barked. Five minutes later it was over; there could be no vaginal examination under these circumstances. "You're all right," Dr. Sylvie told her. "But remember to drink a lot of water."

Leslie smiled at the woman as she exited. She felt frustrated, wanted to talk to them. Beside her Captain Rudolphe stood stonily, his uniform shirt coming out of his pants in the back. Dr. Sylvie read Leslie's mind. Not now, she said with her eyes, maybe later.

Another woman was led in, then another and another. After a half hour, four women had been examined, each claiming to be well. The Haitian doctor worked swiftly and assuredly but always gently, Leslie noted, admiring Dr. Sylvie's sangfroid. Under Rudolphe's intent gaze, a woman around twenty, quite pregnant, lay down on the cot. Dr. Sylvie ignored the big man, slapped a manicured hand under the woman's dress, felt her stomach, her womb.

"Are you more than thirty weeks?" she asked.

A nod. "Wi."

Dr. Sylvie wrote something in her pad. "I'm going to send some vitamins for you," she told her, looking up to Captain Rudolphe as she did. He looked away. "We'll try to get you transferred to a hospital to have your baby. All right?"

The woman was not reassured. She slipped off the cot; the guard led her away.

There were rings of sweat under Dr. Sylvie's armpits. Leslie herself felt thirsty and tenser than ever. The captain stared at her with a languid, intimidating expression. She tried to appear insouciant. In the meantime, her eyes continued to roam, mentally capturing every detail of the experience, the graffiti on the wall in several places, the names of women. She decided to move closer to the doorway, despite the guard blocking it. On the outside, women who remained to be examined sat on the cement floor of the courtyard, next to a hand-drawn well. Leslie tried to make out what they felt, their expressions were so flat.

A minute later they heard shouting. One of the guards whispered something to Rudolphe, who said aloud, "Non!"

"What is it?" Dr. Sylvie interrupted, stepping past the smaller guard and pushing her way out into the courtyard. Leslie followed her. Over Dr. Sylvie's shoulder she saw a half dozen women—girls—standing close together beyond the well. Their heads had been shaved; they looked like vulnerable children. All wore identical blue dresses. Leslie recognized a school uniform. These had to be the arrested students. Dr. Sylvie walked toward them, ignoring Captain Rudolphe's warning: "No, Doctor! No, madame! You can't talk to them! It's not permitted! Madame!"

She turned on her heel and faced him. "These girls are from the lycée, aren't they?" The expressions of the girls confirmed this. Leslie held her breath, wondering what Dr. Sylvie was going to do. Then the moment passed.

The doctor came back toward Leslie and the big guard. She was smiling at him. "Captain, why not allow me to examine these girls? That way I can make sure I've done my job." Behind her, the girls waited, expectant. Leslie counted six of them; they looked odd, with their shaved heads and long dresses and hard shoes. She smiled discreetly. They stared back at her, not daring to do the same.

"I have my instructions," Captain Rudolphe replied. He ordered the girls back into one of the rooms where they were being held. Huddling and holding hands, they went back inside, glancing all the while at Leslie and Dr. Sylvie. Do something, their expressions implored.

"Are we almost finished yet?" the huge man asked, angered. Leslie could see he was worried now, maybe that he would be blamed for the incident.

"There's one more," another aide informed him. "But she doesn't want to come out."

"I know who she is," the big captain spat. "Get her out here." The guard yelled something into one of the rooms. "Voltaire! Vini-m pale-o!" Voltaire! Come here!

.

A big-boned young woman wearing a gray dress stepped out. She eyed the group warily, then looked down, her fingers interlaced before her. Leslie recognized her immediately, her insides tightening. Elyse Voltaire looked older and stronger in the flesh than in the Xerox of her school picture. She walked uncertainly toward them, covertly glancing at the other women, then at Leslie and Dr. Sylvie.

Captain Rudolphe wore an odd expression, close to a sneer. Leslie sensed there was some kind of relationship between him and Elyse Voltaire. He led her into the clinic ahead of them, but not before Leslie said softly, "Elyse?"

Elyse Voltaire spun on her heel, her eyes round. "Blan?" She searched Leslie's face, not recognizing it.

Captain Rudolphe, who had observed the exchange, inserted quickly: "No discussions—just the examination." He eyed Elyse Voltaire menacingly. "Hurry up," he commanded. "I know there is nothing wrong with you."

The young woman's skin was hot; her breath sickly. Despite her large, bony frame, there was a roundness to her hip area. "Are you pregnant?" Dr. Sylvie whispered, adding aloud: "Ou ka di wi ou non." You can say yes or no. Captain Rudolphe was talking to another guard, distracted for a moment. The medical exam began. Leslie watched, desperately wanting to tell the woman, We know all about you. We've been in contact with your relatives. We're trying to get you out.

"Go get the chief," Captain Rudolphe said abruptly to an aide a few minutes later. To Dr. Sylvie he explained, "I'm sorry, madame. We'll have to end the visit now." He gave Elyse Voltaire another dark look. Leslie caught it, but did not understand what was being communicated.

"I've just started, Captain," Dr. Sylvie protested firmly. "We'll only be a few more minutes. This young woman isn't well. She has a fever." The doctor slipped the thermometer under Elyse Voltaire's armpit. Dr. Sylvie felt her glands, examined her eyes, throat, and ears. "Have you had a cold?" she asked.

Wi, Elyse Voltaire nodded.

"A hundred and one—a little temperature." Dr. Sylvie showed her. "That's not too bad. Sit up now and breathe deeply. I want to check your lungs." Leslie watched as Dr. Sylvie moved the metal disk around Elyse Voltaire's chest and back, feeling a strong sense of déjà vu. This was her dream, some part of the daydream she had

had about Marie-Thérèse Dubossy. Dr. Sylvie suddenly whispered something to Elyse Voltaire, who nodded.

Lie back, the doctor had instructed. She slipped the stethoscope under Elyse Voltaire's dress, her brow furrowed in concentration. What is it? Leslie wanted to know. She kept empathetically smiling at Elyse Voltaire, trying to communicate telepathically: We know who you are. We've been trying to get you out of here. Your family knows you're in here. They've been worried about you. But they're safe. Don't worry. Captain Rudolphe edged closer to check on what was happening. Leslie saw Elyse Voltaire avert her face to avoid his eyes. Had he beaten her? she wondered. There was definitely a personal relationship here.

What was Dr. Sylvie feeling? The doctor was still bent over the woman's belly. "Draw up your knees for me, will you? Captain, can we please have some more space." He shrugged, moving back a little.

Dr. Sylvie was feeling and prodding, still moving her stethoscope around.

"Everything okay?" Leslie ventured. Dr. Sylvie merely nodded.

"Turn onto your side," she told Elyse Voltaire, who complied. "Now the other side," the doctor said, helping her roll over. "Okay, on your back again. All right. That's good. You can sit up."

What had she observed? Dr. Sylvie pulled a sheaf of papers from her bag, separated one from the pack. "I'm going to ask them to take you to the hospital for an X ray," she told Elyse Voltaire. To the captain, she added: "She has to sign this form. Without it, they won't authorize the procedure."

He looked at the form suspiciously, then relented. "Sign here." Dr. Sylvie handed Elyse Voltaire a pen. Leslie saw that her handwriting matched the signature that had been on the back of the school picture. She still felt pressure to somehow communicate with the woman. In a few minutes, the opportunity would be lost. Dr. Sylvie had warned her about that possibility, but Leslie refused to accept it. There has to be some way, she thought.

"Are you ready?" The captain suddenly touched Leslie on the arm; she jerked away instinctively, stung by the contact. He added: "The visit is finished, mesdames. It's time to go." He jerked his thumb at Elyse Voltaire. "You—go back to the others. Now!"

Leslie opened her mouth to protest, but Dr. Sylvie stopped her. "We're going, Captain. No need to get excited." She whispered, "I'm sorry, Leslie."

A smaller guard let them out; the steel door to the courtyard fell shut with a loud clang. Another guard came to lock it with a chain and padlock. As he fumbled with it, reopening the door for an instant, Leslie glimpsed Elyse Voltaire standing against the nearby wall, watching what was happening. Their eyes met again. Leslie gave a little discreet wave. We won't forget you, she promised, regretting that she had failed to say something; don't be afraid. She saw Elyse Voltaire's hand move slightly by her side; she was waving back.

"Mesdames." General Lucerne met them midway in the corridor, his displeasure evident. "I'm afraid the visit will have to be cut short." He offered no further explanation. Leslie assumed he had been informed about the incident with the students and their recognition of Elyse Voltaire. "The captain will escort you out," he said, stepping aside to let the bigger man take the lead. "As you can see, madame," he said to Leslie, a smile briefly reasserting itself on his face, "we lack the proper materials and resources to care for extreme cases. That's why we appreciate the assistance of private citizens like Dr. Sylvie and yourself. But we are making improvements. We have nothing to hide, as you can see for yourself."

Leslie looked down at her feet, amazed at his gall. "Will those men be transferred to the hospital?" she asked him bluntly.

"I've already seen to it, madame. We didn't realize the gravity of their condition."

The general extended his damp, warm hand. "Good day, mesdames." They passed ahead of him to depart.

They were forced to wait a moment for the guard with the key to catch up to them; he had stayed behind to talk to the general. In that instant, Leslie saw an old woman, stooped and gray-haired, emerging from a doorway across the way. She held a silver bucket and a broom whose end was dirty and dripping wet. Her eyes were milky, one pupil turned inward. "No, I can't wait—I can't see!"

Marie-Thérèse Dubossy's voice rang in Leslie's head. "My eyes are hurting—my eyes burn!" The woman turned the corner and was gone. The guard had pushed open the gate; Leslie saw blue sky. She followed Dr. Sylvie out. The whole visit had taken just over an hour and a half.

Outside, nothing had changed, though Leslie felt it should have. The street was bustling, tap-taps pushed up close to one another; pedestrians ran after them, clambering into the back. Dr. Sylvie walked ahead of her on the sidewalk toward the car, talking about the serious condition of the two men in the clinic. There was only a slim chance they could save the first one; the penis was septic. The younger boy was close to dying of AIDS. "I was wondering why Lucerne was there and not the warden," Dr. Sylvie said grimly. "The warden obviously didn't want those men dying in his care. General Lucerne has more authority to authorize a transfer; otherwise it could take several days. This way they'll die in the hospital." She added: "They used us." She bit her lip, sighing: "It's like a game to them, really. But when someone's life is at risk, you're forced to play along even though you know they're manipulating you."

Clemard drove up, waving. Leslie looked over at the prison, the high mustard-colored wall. Elyse Voltaire was inside there, on the other side of a half foot of concrete, but it was another reality, another world entirely. It was hard to believe she had just been in there.

"Did you hear what I said?" Dr. Sylvie was looking at her. "Leslie?"

"What?" She had not heard.

"Elyse Voltaire? Now that we have her signature, we have the evidence we need that they're holding her. Gerard will be happy. It should help to get her out."

Of course! Leslie felt foolish, she had been so overwhelmed by the experience she had forgotten all about that goal. "I wondered why you asked her to sign that form, and not the others," she said, impressed. "Do you think it will really make a difference?"

"I hope so—we can only try," Dr. Sylvie replied. "But with what we saw today, Lucerne will definitely be on the defensive now. He's going to have a lot of explaining to do. I predict they'll let those students out by tonight—you'll see. Because they know I'll call the press as soon as I get home." She had a little triumphant smile. "The fat captain knew I was up to something, didn't he? But what could he say? His vanity is our victory. He didn't know the hospital rules and he was too proud to admit it." She laughed harshly. "It's always their downfall."

Clemard had opened the car doors for them. "We saw Elyse Voltaire, Clemard," Leslie told him as soon as she got in. Dr. Sylvie climbed in the back. "And some of the students—the girls. They shaved their heads. I'll tell you all about it."

Clemard smiled, happy to see they had been successful. They quickly took off for Gerard's office.

"Do you know something?" Dr. Sylvie remarked a minute later. "It was quite unusual." Without waiting for Leslie to answer, she said, "You saw that she's pregnant?—Elyse Voltaire. I assume over three months, but I didn't want to say anything in front of the guards. They're rougher on the women if they know they are pregnant. She's not showing much. Anyway, there were physical signs, of course, though not many. But it was strange, I couldn't detect a heartbeat. Usually at that point you can hear it. It was very odd. Enfin"—she shrugged and tapped Clemard's shoulder—"nou fin we tou, hein?" We've seen it all, right? She turned to Leslie. "By the way, did you notice the dates written on the wall, near the names? Some of them are over fifty years old. I never noticed them before. There's a little bit of history for you. You should include that in your project."

"I will." Leslie smiled back at her, her thoughts turning to Marie-Thérèse Dubossy. She looked back at the prison. In her mind's eye the old woman with the cloudy eyes stood at the end of the corridor, holding the dripping mop, then disappeared. Another world—Leslie faced forward again—another reality.

From St.-Raphaël to St.-Michel-de-l'Atalaye, from Camatche to Ennery to Petite-Rivière-des-Bayonnais. Over to Souvenance, to snatch the star off the temple peristyle, wear it over my heart. Across a plain of candelabra, cactus grabbing my pants, all the way to Gonaïves, town of misery, of fatras, human garbage, 500,000 living on a palm of sand, that is all the bay has left them. A curve of sand to dig their hands into, to cup the water to drink, to plant the stick in, to build the house, to build the life. I could stay there for weeks, fish for eels at night. Then the day would come and the big wave would wash over me and the sea would pull me under the houses. Would that be freedom? Pull me into the current all the way to Ile de la Tortue. I think about who has died there. What for? Or I could go north to Coridon instead, find myself a hiding place in the old Sedren copper mine, a thousand hiding places in the Montagnes de Terre.

Look at this map. There is no piece of land that would not welcome my tired feet, give me a corner of rock to make a pillow for my aching head. Bombardopolis, where I have a cousin. Môle-St.-Nicolas, where Christopher Columbus, that bastard, first set his dirty foot. Now the Americans want to build a base there. Well, let them, let them. It's not a holy place, not anymore. Jean-Rabel . . . there the blood of my brothers is still watering the fields. How many massacred, how many? And Cabaret? How many there? More than I can count. I would stumble across their faces if I tried. Port-de-Paix, what kind of peace has it known? None, none that I can remember.

I could go west, to Anse-à-Chouchou, or Bas Limbé, but the worst Macoutes are hiding there too, the most cowardly. Or pretend I was a beggar and take my place in line at the foot of the Citadel, selling limes for the tourists to rub on their faces as refreshment. Slip myself into a cannon, sleep for years in the rusty inside of Henri Christophe's cannon until this bad period passes. Or find his hidden body and suck up the silver bullet he used to kill himself

—another coward—and use it on them when the time comes. Or steal an ass, disguise myself as a woman, ride sidesaddle like some madanmsara to the little market near Pignon. But what good would it do me, what good?

Thomasique, Thomonde, Mirebalais, there are many good places for me to rest. Saut-d'Eau, holy place. Slide my legs and feet covered with these sores into the waterfall, heal them to walk another hundred nights without sleep or thought. I could avoid Poste-Rouge then, avoid Thomazeau, avoid the places the enemy is waiting for me. Go the long way around, through Croix-des-Bouquets, where the guards are always drunk, going off with women at night instead of keeping their watch.

That is one way. Or break into the empty house of some bourgeois bastard in Pétionville. Hah! My strategy has its merits. And if the dog-soul Americans won't open their doors to me I'll knock on the French and impress them with my pretty words. Or the bastard Canadians—tell them I've never seen the snow.

Life, life, I'm on the run now. I've put my hand up to the four corners of this land. Everywhere I stop I can feel the big wind but no bonanj, no guardian angel to comfort me, no spirit to show me which road is safe. North, south, east, west. I'm like a franginen, a true African, don't you see me sniffing at the roots of every veritab, every tree of knowledge, tell me which way to go? So I can forget the false promise of the white man and his government. Rasin ginen. African roots. Franginen with veritab roots. Then I could skip across the mountains from Kenscoff to Jacmel, find a warm place to sleep on the beach at Raymond-les-Bains, go searching for some treasure left behind by Bolívar and his army, some weapon they forgot, not knowing I would need it now.

Amnwe, now I can hear the dogs. Sen Jak, can't you hear the dogs? Se chyen ki la. The dogs are there. They disturb my sleep, I do not dream. They smell my fear. Every time I sniff a tree, they come to mark it too. Anmwe, I say. Sen Jak pa la. Se chyen ki la.

29

The ball rose in a high arc, forcing two heads to rise above the pack. Emmanuel opened his mouth, anticipating the collision. "Aye!" he said sympathetically as the two players crashed, then fell to the ground. He watched carefully as the old referee rushed forward, singling out the taller player. A fight was breaking out on the field.

The other player in the striped jersey, Maimonides, was a youth Emmanuel knew well. He was arguing with the referee, showing him how the ball had flown upward, how his opponent had jumped on his back to try to butt the ball. Emmanuel cheered out loud as the referee relented: the ball was returned to the Haitian team. They were ahead, 3–2. This was the closest and most exciting game in the series. Emmanuel looked over at Joseph, the elderly caretaker. Joseph had tipped his chair back and was smoking his pipe contentedly. Emmanuel winked at him. "Ou we sa?" he asked. Did you see that?

Joseph shrugged. He did not understand soccer well enough to bet on it; he was a numbers man. In the morning, he would wager a small amount on the national lottery, and often bet in the neighborhood domino games. He had won a small black-and-white television and promptly donated it to the parish. That way Emmanuel could watch the news and Joseph could get the lottery results right away.

The reception was best in the courtyard. Every night for the past week, he and Emmanuel had set up the television on the courtyard wall after the Confession period was over. Last night, several parishioners had stayed after Confession to watch. This evening, Emmanuel had had a surprise visit from Didier, his colleague from Labadie, and Père Lantz, who had ostensibly come into the capital for the archbishop's inauguration later in the week. Emmanuel was glad to learn Didier's hearing loss might not be permanent, but the news about Père Sansaricq was upsetting. After a psychological evaluation, he had been recalled by his superiors.

Didier had other bad news. They had received new threats against holding election meetings at the parish; the latest one had come Sunday, a threat to burn down the church. Père Lantz had also received warnings. Didier had written a letter to be sent to the Papal Nuncio, which Emmanuel had signed. Emmanuel had also convinced them of the necessity to make a statement of some kind during the inauguration ceremony, when the international press would be in attendance. The two priests felt a boycott of the event could jeopardize their positions, and they already felt too vulnerable. They favored a group statement instead and had agreed to draft one to show Emmanuel.

Joseph suddenly clapped. Emmanuel looked at the repeating image on the screen. The older man got up to adjust the reception, moving the wire coat hanger he had attached to the antenna. The players were blurred, and now zigzagging. "To the left, Joseph, more, no, less, there, that's good." Inside, the telephone rang. It was probably Emmanuel's mother; she usually called about this time. He had forgotten to call her earlier. On the screen, Maimonides had just scored a goal; no, he had missed. The telephone kept ringing, then finally stopped.

Emmanuel got up during the commercial. The wooden box with the telephone in it was locked. He found the little key hanging on a peg by the door. His mother's number rang and rang, but no one answered. She must have unplugged it and gone to sleep. He glanced at his watch. It was after her bedtime. He remembered Victor's party, which would be starting about now. Maybe he would swing by after the game was over.

"Pe?" It was Joseph yelling. Father?

"What is it, Joseph?"

"Someone's asking for you. Out there. Look."

"Who's there?" Emmanuel asked. He could see a hand waving over the top of the high courtyard wall. "Who's there?"

There was no answer. Joseph looked at the priest. He gestured toward his rifle. No, Emmanuel shook his head.

"Whoever you are, come around the side," he said loudly. "The front door is locked." They saw the hand waving again.

"I'll go," he told Joseph. "Don't worry. Stay here and tell me what happens in the game."

He passed through the empty chapel, around the hall to the side room where they kept extra chairs. He unlocked the door and pushed it open. A squat, bowlegged man with a barrel chest was standing there, dressed in the blue uniform and cap of a traffic policeman. He was nervous and uncertain, pulling on a few wisps of his graying beard.

"I didn't mean to scare you," he said. "I was knocking out there for ten minutes, but nobody answered. I heard the television and went around out back."

Emmanuel smiled. He recognized the rich, nasal accent from Les Cayes. "Jean-Marc Benjamin?" he asked. "I recognize your voice. Come in."

"I called you on the phone too, but nobody picked up." The policeman stepped inside hesitantly, removing his cap.

"I thought it was my mother calling," Emmanuel said. "We're watching the football match."

"I was listening to it on the radio in my truck," Jean-Marc said. "Is it still three to one?"

"The other team just scored a goal. It's three to two." They stood inside the doorway. "You didn't come for Confession, did you? Because that ended an hour ago."

"No—it's something else." The policeman turned around to look outside. "Can we talk somewhere privately?"

"Certainly." Emmanuel smiled. "We'll go to my office. Follow me." He closed the door behind the policeman and bolted the lock, then led him along the dim hallway, noting as he turned around that Jean-Marc Benjamin walked with a slight limp. The policeman gave him a brief, nervous smile.

There was only one chair in the office. "I left the other chair in the courtyard," Emmanuel apologized. "I can go get it."

"No, Pe, it doesn't matter." Jean-Marc dismissed the idea. "I can't stay anyway."

Emmanuel sat down and eyed his visitor with curiosity. He was slightly different than he had envisioned, neither tall nor thin. The policeman looked disheveled; his blue shirt hung out and the bottom of his pants and his shoes were spattered with mud.

"What's on your mind?" the priest asked, searching for his glasses.

"They just let that woman out," Jean-Marc said hastily. "Just a little while ago. I thought you would want to know."

"Which woman?" Emmanuel asked sharply. "Elyse Voltaire? That woman?"

"And some students," the policeman added, shifting his weight and looking out the window at the courtyard. From here, the glow of the television was visible. "I don't know who they were, but they had on school uniforms. I think they're the ones the radio was talking about."

Emmanuel nodded. He took out a piece of paper and wrote this down.

"Tell me exactly what you saw," the priest said. "Which officers were present?"

"I was inside, talking to my friend. He works there on the night shift. He does the job I told you about—the job I used to do. They took them out while I was there. My friend told me who she was."

"How did he identify her?"

"He said he knew her. I didn't ask."

"And the students, did he know who they were too?"

"He doesn't know how many are in there. These were just the girls. But they have boys in there too."

"How many?"

Jean-Marc made a face, uncertain. "I only saw a few, maybe four or five. It happened quickly," he added. "I don't know if they let more out earlier or after. It wasn't prudent to stay there."

"I understand." Emmanuel was mentally composing a message for Joseph to take to a neighbor down the road who had a walkie-talkie. They would have to monitor the police traffic to find out if others had been released.

"Tell me about their condition. Were they badly mistreated? Any signs of torture?"

"I don't know, Pe, it was too dark to see. I just saw them for a second as they were coming out. But there were soldiers there. Like I told you, I couldn't stay there. My friend told me to leave. But Captain Rudolphe was there and he's General Lucerne's man."

"What do you mean, 'his man'?"

"His man," Jean-Marc stressed. "He works directly for the gen-

eral. He protects him. Everybody knows Rudolphe. Gwo Toro—
that's what we call him—a big bull. He's the one who's in charge
of torturing the political prisoners."

"What about the woman, Elyse Voltaire? What did you see?"

"They let her out with another woman. But my friend didn't
know who the other woman was."

"What else? Anything?"

Jean-Marc grimaced. "It's a bad thing, Pe—they shaved them."
He looked down, then added: "Not Voltaire, though, and not the
other woman. They weren't shaved. Just the students."

The news depressed Emmanuel. "I'll have to inform the families
of the students right away," he told the policeman. "In case they've
been left to make their way home alone. Do you know if they were
being taken somewhere?"

"I don't know." He then added, wanting to be more helpful: "But
I'm sure General Lucerne gave the orders to release them. That's
why Captain Rudolphe was there. He executes all of the general's
orders."

"I'm going to give the caretaker a message." Emmanuel stood.
"And I have a telephone call to make. Wait for me a moment, will
you? I'll be right back."

Emmanuel closed the door behind him. The policeman leaned
against the desk. There were purple flowers in a vase on the windowsill and, folded over a hanger on the back of the door, a long
red sash with the letters INRI inscribed in gold. A Bible lay on the
desk, and another book. He didn't turn it over to see what it was.
Instead he felt inside his shirt, against his back, where he put the
envelope he had taken out of the file drawer when his friend had
gone to the bathroom. No one would think to look in the drawer
till morning; there was no way they would suspect him. Jean-Marc
exhaled, still anxious about having taken it.

"I'm back," Emmanuel said a few minutes later, entering with
the chair he had brought in from the courtyard. The game was even
again, 3–3. He had given Joseph the message to take to his neighbor
after the game was over. And he had tried calling Gerard and Victor,
but neither had been home. They were at the party. "Sit down."
He gestured to the policeman. "Rest a minute."

Emmanuel sat down in his own chair and quickly wrote out a press release, making a carbon copy for the television station as well. Although it was too late to broadcast tonight, he would leave the note with the night watchman at the radio station to give to Soeur Madeleine, who was in charge of the 6 a.m. newscast. Emmanuel included all of the details the policeman had mentioned, attributing them to a source inside the prison, but he did not name Jean-Marc or General Lucerne and his aide, Captain Rudolphe.

Jean-Marc watched him, saying nothing. "Pe?" he interrupted finally. "Can I show you something?"

Emmanuel looked up immediately. "What's that?" Without taking his eyes off Jean-Marc, he signed the press release and folded it.

"I—I brought you . . . this." Jean-Marc struggled to remove the envelope, ended up pulling out his shirt in back to do so. "Here."

Emmanuel took it, eyeing the manila envelope carefully. "What's this?" he asked, weighing it in his hand. He could feel little, hard objects inside. When the policeman did not respond, he turned the envelope over. Sunday's date was written on the back.

"I thought you might be able to do something with it," Jean-Marc said quietly, rubbing his chin. "But I'm not the one who gave it to you, okay?"

"Who is?"

"Nobody," the policeman said. "Anyway, not me."

Emmanuel looked at him thoughtfully as he opened the envelope and slipped his hand inside.

A watch. A ring. He pulled them out. The ring was gold and was imprinted with an emblem. There was also a black leather wallet, shiny and worn, stuffed with papers. That was all. Emmanuel put the objects on the desk between them. "Someone's personal effects, I assume," he said. "Am I right?"

The policeman confirmed this, but remained silent.

"Have you looked in here?" The priest indicated the wallet. When there was no answer, he repeated, "Did you?"

"I looked," Jean-Marc muttered. "That's why I thought I should bring it to you." His expression was guilty; he looked down at his shoes.

Emmanuel removed the cards, one by one. Serge Moïse, from Bossou. He knew the area, it was near La Chapelle in the Artibonite. Levelt and Léopold St.-Germain, brothers from Les Cayes. Denis Ferila, a member of the Coopérative Jeunesses des Cayes. Emmanuel felt his heart quicken. Cedric Milfort George. Sex: M, 34 ans. Résidence: Grande Rue, Papaye. Date de naissance: 8-10-52. Nationalité: Haïtien. He turned the driver's license over to read the back, then flipped it over again. Cedric's face was grainy, his chin and neck underexposed. Merde alors! Emmanuel swore to himself. Shit!

Jean-Marc chanced a look at the priest, who had closed his eyes. "I didn't know anything about it, Pe," he started. "I'm sorry. I would have told you if I knew anything . . ."

Emmanuel raised a hand to stop him, needing a moment of silence. Chastened, Jean-Marc watched him get up, cards in hand, to look out the window. The priest wore a tight expression, his head shaking slightly.

After a while, he turned around. "I knew this man," he said, holding up the driver's license. "He was a very fine young man, very brave. Ordinary, like us, from the countryside, but also exceptional, because he never lost his courage. When someone is tortured like he was they rarely know how to laugh. But Ti Cedric loved to laugh, do you know that? He loved to tell jokes. And yet he was a serious organizer. He never stopped organizing." Emmanuel paused, then addressed Jean-Marc: "Are we sure he's been killed? Don't they take the personal effects of the prisoners when they arrest them?"

"None of these people are in the prison. I checked. There's a book where they write down that kind of thing."

"The personal effects, you mean?"

"When they arrest someone, they are supposed to write it down in the book. Those names weren't in the book. I checked myself, when my friend wasn't looking, because I wanted to be sure. That's when I got the idea to bring the envelope to you."

"So we have to assume they were probably killed. Would you know if they went to Titanyen? Could you find that out?"

"I already checked that too, Pe. The truck went out as usual on

Wednesday and Friday and took the dead from the morgue and hospitals to Titanyen. But there weren't any bodies on Sunday, which is the date written on the envelope. So they didn't take the truck we usually used. But it could have been another group."

Emmanuel sat down heavily, taking all this in. He spread the identity cards out on the desk. "What about the corpse from Fontamara—the one you first told me about? Could it have been one of these people?"

"I really don't know, Pe," Jean-Marc said honestly. "I told you, I don't know anything else. This is everything I know. But I can ask my friend tomorrow—he might know more."

Emmanuel studied the policeman. My somnambulist, he thought wryly, the man with the honeyed voice. "What made you come and tell me?" he asked him. "Couldn't you sleep?"

Jean-Marc shrugged, slightly embarrassed. "I—I didn't plan it. Really," he said. "I wasn't even thinking about doing something like that. I could get fired for taking it. But when my friend showed me the envelope . . . I don't know. I recognized his name"—the policeman pointed to Cedric George's identity card—"and I was curious. When my friend went out to go to the bathroom, I took the envelope back out of the drawer. I don't even know why—I just did it. And then I checked and didn't see their names in the book and, I don't know . . ." He added: "I thought about our conversation, you know, and that maybe you would know what to do with them. Anyway, I can't put them back now. It's too late."

The policeman paused and eyed the priest slyly. "I think it was fate, Pe. Don't you? It was more than luck."

"What do you mean?" Emmanuel rubbed his forehead, exhausted. He was thinking about what he was going to tell the families. That the personal effects of their loved ones had been reported, that their loved ones were presumed murdered, but that no one knew where their bodies might be recovered, there was no concrete evidence, nor had the guilty party been identified. He knew the families were going to want to recover the bodies and properly bury them, to assure the spirit's passage into the next world. Until then, they would not rest, would cling with a stubborn faith to the belief that their loved one might still be alive. How many times had he witnessed this? Too many.

"More than luck," the policeman repeated softly, interrupting Emmanuel's train of thought. "I was thinking about what to do—about my problems. And you were looking for that woman. It's more than luck that I ran into my friend—I rarely see him. Like it was my destiny."

"I see." Emmanuel smiled ruefully. "Destiny—but not God?"

"A little of both maybe. Pe," he said a moment later.

"What?"

"It's the general who's doing those things."

"What things?"

"The attacks. Against the people organizing the strike. That's what my friend heard. General Lucerne has been put in charge. He sends his men to find young people and pays them to be spies and make trouble. They're San Manman."

San Manman. Bon-a-rien. Vakabons. Those without mothers. Good-for-nothings. Vagabonds. A death squad made up of youths heartless enough to shoot their own parents if the order was given. Ruthless thugs, many of them street orphans loyal only to the men with the guns and the money. Under Papa Doc, youths had been recruited into a vanguard teen militia tacitly under his control. Now the San Manman were warring death squads willing to take on the army. They respected no one and killed everyone.

"Can you get me any names?" Emmanuel asked him. "Find out what military units are involved, what other officers."

"I'm sure Captain Rudolphe is part of it. Anyway, I'll find out. But I have to be careful. They'd kill me—bang! No hesitation." He gave a short, rough laugh. "I should go now, Pe. It's late."

Emmanuel stood up. Through the window, a sliver of moon had emerged between the clouds. The courtyard was lit by the dim glow of the television. The game was ending. Ti Cedric's face appeared before him, his eyes and mouth laughing. The image changed. Ti Cedric stood on a platform at an outdoor meeting wearing a straw hat with Konbit Papay painted on it, shouting, urging his comrades to join the national peasant movement.

Another fallen one, Emmanuel thought, looking up at the crucifix on the wall. Do you hear me, Lord? Among the best. And the bravest.

Jean-Marc had turned over the book on the desk. The *Confessions* of St. Augustine. Emmanuel watched him flip the pages. The Confessions of the man from Les Cayes, he mused, turning his gaze to the identity cards loosely piled together on the desk. "Levelt and Léopold St.-Germain—they're from Les Cayes—did you know them?" he asked.

"No."

Emmanuel walked over to the desk and picked up the pile of cards, put them back in the wallet. "Jean-Marc, I'm going to ask you another favor. A big favor. You can say no, but I hope you won't."

The policeman waited expectantly.

"I want to know what happened to them—all of them." He tapped the wallet on the desk. "I need your help. I'm going to ask you to do that for me, to go back to the prison, to look around, to find out if another truck might have gone to Titanyen recently, or some other place. I know we probably won't be able to find out, but you never know, and I want to really try. Would you do that for me?"

The policeman sucked on his teeth, deliberating. "I won't tell my wife," he finally answered. "I'll send her to Les Cayes to stay with my family, in case something happens to me. You never know. But I'll do it. I'll even go back to Titanyen, if you want. But not tomorrow, because they would suspect me. I'll have to judge the right moment. And, Pe," he added, "I wanted to thank you—for what you said to me about my troubles. I've been thinking about it a lot. I think maybe now, maybe if I do this thing for you too, that I'll sleep better."

Emmanuel considered the policeman. "I'm glad to hear that, Jean-Marc. You know"—he fingered the watch and ring on the table—"you didn't have to bring me these. From a poor man," he added, "it was an act of charity."

"Even if I took them?" the policeman asked.

"What do you think?"

Jean-Marc debated the question. "If the army or the Macoutes killed those people, then that's wrong. And they've kept their things. That's also wrong. But I took the envelope to give it to you and you can give it to their families. That's a good thing, I think. Isn't that what God would think?"

"Why don't you ask Him yourself," Emmanuel suggested as he moved to open the office door. "Let me know what He says."

They shook hands. "Thank you, Jean-Marc," Emmanuel said. "I'll be waiting to hear from you. Call here or just stop by. If I'm not here, Joseph will know where to find me. Day or night, it doesn't matter. I don't sleep that well either," he added with a smile, escorting him out.

After the policeman left, Emmanuel went back into his office, turned off the light, and knelt before the small crucifix. He prayed for the brothers, Levelt and Léopold St.-Germain—had they shared their last moments together? Then for Edouane Albert, electrician, and Serge Moïse, from the Artibonite, where Emmanuel's grandmother lived. Denis Ferila, a young soul, and Letoit Jean-Baptiste. Emmanuel stretched his hands upward and then bowed his head until it touched the ground. Ti Cedric, my brother, my friend, wherever you are, whatever has happened to you, may God keep you, may the Lord take you into His bosom and protect you on earth or in heaven. Amen.

Emmanuel prayed for the soul of the mysterious corpse from Fontamara and thanked God for the release of Elyse Voltaire and the students. He asked God to speak to Jean-Marc Benjamin, who had entered into a holy dialogue and was seeking His forgiveness. He asked God to help Père Sansaricq, whose spirit was destroyed, and Didier, who might never hear properly. Give us Your blessing, Father, we who await and worship You, today and for the rest of our eternal lives. Amen.

The football match had ended. The national anthem was playing; that meant their team had won. Emmanuel could hear Joseph singing along in his low, slow voice. "I am feeling weak tonight, Saviour," he whispered, rising at last. "I am tired. I no longer know which way to go. Talk to me, tell me what to say to them. I don't know what to tell them anymore. I don't know what they should do. I need Your wisdom, Your divine grace. Please, Lord, hear my prayer. Have mercy on us. In the name of the Father, the Son, and the Holy Spirit. Amen."

30

"Why do you suppose they did it?" Victor asked Leslie.

"Did what?"

They sat in Victor's backyard. Inside, Gerard was talking on the phone. Since Père Emmanuel had come to tell them the news, the party had ended, but the stream of people coming and going only swelled.

"Shaved their heads," Victor said. "Do they do that in American prisons? It's like the Nazis." He shook his head, disgusted. "These people have lost their humanity." He puffed up his cheeks and loudly expelled his breath. The labor leader's wiry arms were covered with thick hairs; he tugged at them, pensive. "They're going to have to pay," he added, more to himself than to her. "It's not going to be the way it was before."

Leslie glanced at Edith, who was wearing a bright green shirt-and-pants combination. Victor's wife had taken off her shoes and was sitting huddled in a corner beside José. They were conversing in low tones, the photographer unloading his camera. He had returned from the Dominican camps only this morning, full of stories of abuses. Another group entered the house and several unfamiliar faces peered back at them through the kitchen window. Bonjour, they waved, then disappeared indoors.

"They're all with us." Edith called over to Leslie. "The chauffeurs' syndicate."

Victor was talking to them about Ti Cedric. Leslie took out her notepad. Clemard had gone to buy some Sekola soda.

"I didn't know him well, but I know he liked to play."

"To play?" she asked. "What? Sports?"

"No." Victor smiled. "Theater—acting. He organized that for the children. He loved children. He only had one child, you know. After the torture, he couldn't have more. But if he could, he would have had twenty. He couldn't live with the mother. Her family was against him. He was too political. They always blamed him because the first time they came to arrest Ti Cedric, he wasn't there, so they beat her instead."

A trio of young men wandered into the backyard through the back gate. Victor followed them with his eyes. "Ti Cedric was always being watched, just like we are," he continued. "Over there it never stopped. Right after Duvalier fell, the next day and the one after it, they were the worst. Because the little Macoutes were terrified in the countryside. They knew that the people were going to come after them, and burn them, which happened. So before the people could do anything, the Macoutes arrested people like Ti Cedric and beat them badly. That's the way they think over there. Here, we have always been more protected. But over there, if you're an activist, you have to be so careful. You have to watch your back all the time, and you don't have as many people to help you in an emergency. I bet if Ti Cedric had been living in Port-au-Prince, we could have protected him. We had people who lived like him hiding for years under Duvalier. Even now, I know a dozen people who don't sleep in their homes at night. And this is a so-called period of liberalization."

"Victor, isn't there any chance that he escaped?" she asked. "I mean, I know that's not likely, given the circumstances, but it seems that some of the people here tonight feel he could have gotten away, or that he's taken refuge in an embassy."

Victor shrugged, his expression doubtful. "He's been gone over three weeks, right? They went after him with dogs—that much we know. He was headed for Bois-Rouge; he never went there. Maybe he knew they were waiting for him at Thomonde, that's possible. He escaped without taking anything with him. So, yes, they could have found his identity card when they raided his house, before they burned it. I agree with that. But if the man went across the border, why wouldn't he have contacted us by now? That's where it doesn't make sense." He sniffed, accepting a cigarette from Leslie, who lighted one of her own. "In my bones, Leslie, I don't have confidence. I feel they got him. Who knows," he added, grimacing, "maybe they've made him into a zombie, like Narcisse. You've heard of our famous zombie, haven't you?"

She hadn't. "How long was Narcisse missing?"

"Narcisse? I think about thirty years. They buried him, and then one day he walks into his village. Can you imagine? They had him working the fields as a slave. They do that with poison; it saps the person's will. As if you were in a coma."

"Have you ever met someone in that state?"

"A zombie? No." He dismissed the notion. "But they brought in the experts from all over the world to examine Narcisse. I have a book about his case, if you want to read it."

"I'd be interested," Leslie replied. "And anything else you have that I might like. I haven't read that much Haitian literature."

Victor suddenly touched her on the leg, raising his lecture finger. "It's important not to fantasize," he cautioned. "It's important not to fool ourselves. Ti Cedric is probably dead—that's the most logical explanation. Even if all these other stories exist. You understand? Our problem is that we don't like our reality. We prefer thinking something else. And a lot of outsiders are the same way. But the reality still exists. And we can't escape it." He sighed. "We just have to change it, somehow."

There were plastic cups left on the ledge of the wall where guests had been drinking earlier. One of the newcomers gathered them and filled one with a large dose of rum. He had just heard the news about the students and shook his head darkly. "We have to crush them," he said angrily to Victor. "Macoutes," he muttered, pouring the rum sloppily. He was drunk, and bound to get drunker.

Leslie heard her name being called. Through the sliding glass door she saw Gerard talking on the telephone. I'll be ready in a minute, he gestured to her.

"So you're going to go to see the woman tomorrow—Elyse Voltaire?" Victor asked, changing the subject. "Gerard told me." Before she could answer, he put his finger in the air to silence her. There was something out in the streets. Leslie strained her ears, listening for whatever it might be. A dog barked, but there were no gunshots. It's nothing, Victor concluded.

"We're going to go up to her village tomorrow," Leslie answered. "But I don't know if she'll be there. When I went with Clemard last week, it was deserted. I wanted to go up tonight, but Gerard thinks it's too difficult." She looked at Victor. "What do you think?"

"I always follow Gerard's advice," he said, helping himself to some rum directly from the bottle. "The road's difficult. It makes sense to wait until morning."

She studied Victor, trying to imagine what his prison experiences had been like. "You were in prison under Duvalier," she said to him softly. "Have you ever written about it?"

No, he dismissed the idea. "I got lucky," he said matter-of-factly. "They only beat me, but not badly enough, because I survived, right? One of the officers knew my family, so they spared me." He turned to her. "That's how our prison system works. You either know someone or you die. But even if you survive, you've seen so much you feel you want to die. That's how I felt afterward."

He paused, lifting his finger again. This time it was real. A single shot, followed by another. "It's coming from the market," Victor said. "I'm sure of it."

He turned back to Leslie. "You've been talking to my wife about the women. Well, the women suffered in ways people can't imagine. But the children too; they threw the children in with the parents. You didn't see any children when you went in the other day, did you? But we have children who were born in the prisons, and quite a few died in them too. There's another history we don't like to talk about." He cocked his head, still listening to the night. Then he yawned. "Gerard tells us you're thinking of staying longer. You'll need some time to do a project like that—it's ambitious." He smiled. "You'll just have to move here."

"I wish it was that easy. Unfortunately, I have a lot of commitments and my little girl's just started school. I don't know how it would be for her if I brought her here. And I don't think her father would agree. We have joint custody," she added.

"A difficult situation," Victor commented. "But at least you had the courage to divorce. Here, people stay together because the family wants it. And then everyone is miserable."

Gerard stepped out to the backyard. He was tired and needed a shave. It was past three in the morning; he had been on the telephone for two hours, talking to reporters, informing parents, trying to confirm the information Père Emmanuel had brought them. Until a half hour ago, they had not been able to reach Papaye or Les

Cayes to inform the relatives of those whose names had been on the cards.

"It seems that all but two of the girls were let out," Gerard said. "We'll go in the morning and try to get them." He sat down awkwardly next to Leslie. "I'm exhausted," he said. "I need seventy-two hours of sleep."

"And the boys—were they mistreated?" Victor asked.

Gerard nodded and took a swig from the rum bottle Victor passed him. "They made them kneel with rocks in their hands. All day." Gerard wiped his mouth, then took another swallow. "They shaved some of them, like the girls. Dr. Sylvie is going to examine the whole group tomorrow. After that we'll organize a press conference with the parents."

"Did you tell the press about Ti Cedric and the others?" Leslie cut in.

"No—only about the students." Gerard was sweating; his stringy hair clung to his forehead. "I want to contact all the families first." He took a puff on Victor's cigarette. "I'll call from the office later; the line might be working by then. Anyway, a few hours isn't going to make much difference in this case."

"What do you think, Gerard?" Victor asked. "Edith and I were talking about Peter Samuels earlier. Do you think the Americans know what General Lucerne is up to?"

"Now there's a good question," Gerard said, blowing the smoke into a ring. He handed Leslie the bottle. "But I don't know the answer." He stroked her knee affectionately. "Que penses tu?" What do you think?

"They would have to, wouldn't they? If their intelligence is any good. What about you, Victor?" She took a short sip before passing the bottle back to him. The rum stung where she had bitten her tongue. She checked her watch. Clemard was taking a long time. Would he have given up and gone home without telling her?

"It's like everything else," Victor said. "We're always asking, 'What's the position of the United States in our affairs?' And we'll keep asking the question because it's not clear. I gather you got the impression from Monsieur Samuels that the Americans favor the elections, that it's not just a façade. So why give their support to

Lucerne—unless it's to keep an eye on him. Or to control him. Or—and we have no choice but to think this—because they agree with him. He's their man; he's doing their dirty work."

"You know who Peter Samuels resembles?" she said to Victor. "Not physically, but in his opinions? Bertrand. He has the same kind of paternalistic attitude, except someone like Samuels hides it better. Bertrand's is classic postcolonialism."

"Parfait," Victor agreed. "Hey, Gerard." He set the bottle aside. "Here's news. Edith is thinking of running for the Senate. As an independent candidate. Just to bother Bertrand. What do you think?"

"Ti Malis," Gerard said aloud. "La Sénatrice. It rhymes. It could be a good slogan." Edith looked over, amused. "The only problem is that she'd probably win," he added. "And then she'd be really unhappy."

They laughed, but there was sadness behind their laughter. Gerard leaned his head against Leslie's shoulder. She ruffled his hair. Victor narrowed his eyes, gazed at the bottle. "C'est pas juste," he said. "It's not fair. Not now. Not after all Ti Cedric suffered."

Gerard nodded slowly, his head still resting against Leslie. She put her arm around him, feeling there was little to add.

"Emmanuel is saying a Mass for them next Sunday," Gerard informed them. "Maybe we'll have gotten some other news by then. But I doubt it," he added, more for his own benefit than theirs. He looked heavily at Victor. "How many is it now?"

"Forty-two," Victor said. "I was counting earlier."

For Leslie's sake, Gerard explained: "We keep track, Victor and I, Edith too. Between us, that's the number of friends or colleagues that we've never seen again. We know for sure the majority were murdered, but the others . . ." He spread his hands apart in the air. "Disappeared. From one day to the next."

José was packing his camera bag. The photographer got up to leave. "I want to have these developed by tomorrow morning," he told them. "For the press conference." He tapped his camera bag. "Leslie, I have more pictures that I never printed. You can come and look at them at my studio."

"Thank you, I'll do that," she said, rising to embrace him. "I'm staying a few more days anyway, so I have some time. I'll be at the hotel until Wednesday, then I'm hoping to go to the Cape."

Gerard got up to walk José out. While he was away, Victor said to Leslie, "It took me a while to distinguish the gunshots. I measure it like the thunder after lightning," he explained, counting slowly. "One, two, three . . . You can usually tell from the delay what kind of weapons are being used."

"Thanks for the tip," she said, thinking, I can probably use that in Washington too.

"You started to tell me earlier," Victor said. They heard Gerard talking on the telephone inside the house. "Your ex-husband opposes your plan to live here?"

"It's not that," she replied. "I mean, it definitely depends on Marisa, because I don't want to take her out of school where she just started. But children can adjust, and I'm sure I can work something out with Mark—that's my ex-husband—if I insist. Unfortunately I don't have the money for the project yet. I've only gotten funding for this initial phase of research. I have to go back and apply for grants and they can take a long time. So it would be a year before I'm really prepared to move here. Even that would be fast."

"My wife is waiting for me," Gerard said, sitting back down. "Jeanne was beginning to get anxious. Do you still hear the gunshots?" he asked Victor.

"They've stopped," he confirmed. "For now. I'd suggest going the long way around. That way you'll stay clear of it."

Edith came over to sit on her husband's lap. "What are we doing?" she asked Victor.

"I'm trying to get drunk," he replied matter-of-factly, kissing her on the shoulder. "Want to join me?"

Edith held his head back to study him, pursing her lips. Leslie watched them exchange a serious look. "Give me some rum, Gerard?" she asked, pointing to the bottle. "And a cup," she said, pointing her chin. Leslie leaned over and got a cup for her. Gerard poured. "To Ti Cedric," Edith said simply, looking at Victor. She took a large sip, then sniffed and cleared her head.

"To Ti Cedric—our compatriot," Victor echoed, doing the same.

There was a long period of silence after the toast. They finished the bottle and started another. Leslie looked around at the group. Edith's toenails, she noted, were badly chipped. The Haitian woman had a habit of nervously twisting her hair at the nape. Leslie tried to imagine her addressing a huge crowd while soldiers trained their submachine guns on her. People in America have no idea how these people live, she thought to herself. This is not their image of Haiti at all. She looked at Gerard, his angular face grave but flushed. He was picking at a chip in the terrace parquet, absorbed in thought. Edith caught her eye. For a long second, they looked at each other; the Haitian woman extended her hand to Leslie, who took it, squeezed it, then dropped it, self-conscious.

"Do you know any of the students who were released?" she asked Edith. "I assume they're the same girls we saw when we went in. But Dr. Sylvie told me she thinks they were keeping some other students in a part of the prison we didn't go to."

"I know two of the girls," Edith said. "We're going to go with Dr. Sylvie to see them tomorrow. If you want, you can come with us." Victor massaged his wife's shoulders. "That feels good," she murmured, leaning into him. "Does your husband do that to you?" she asked Leslie.

"She's not married, chérie," Victor said quickly.

"Not anymore," Leslie clarified.

"Ah." Edith nodded, sensing a faux pas. "You're a free woman," she added lightly.

There was only a momentarily uncomfortable pause. Victor broke it: "Leslie's going up with Gerard to try to find Elyse Voltaire tomorrow. So she can't come with us. But I thought we could all meet around four at our house and schedule the press conference for six o'clock. That way the television will have to carry it live and won't be able to edit it."

"Smart man." Edith patted him on the hand. "That's fine with me."

José's jeep pulled out of the driveway below with a screech. He honked.

"Did you see his pictures of our rally?" Edith asked Leslie. "It's a shame you were away in Papaye on that day. You could have met some of the women I told you about who are organizing in the garment factories. Maybe we can arrange for you to meet with them before you go. I heard you saying you're thinking of staying longer?"

"Hopefully another week, if I can get the flight," Leslie replied, accepting a fresh cigarette from Victor. "Share this with me?" she asked Edith, who agreed. "Gerard told me the rally almost turned violent. Weren't you frightened?"

"Not at the time," Edith said, turning her neck under Victor's fingers. "I get so involved when I'm speaking I forget about everything else. If I stop I'll lose my concentration. But afterward"—she shook her hands dramatically and laughed—"woy!"

Leslie took a deep drag, then handed the cigarette to Edith. The Haitian activist smoked elegantly, drawing the smoke in with a long pull and exhaling to one side. Something in her manner reminded Leslie of Greta Garbo.

"I don't think they were planning to shoot," Edith continued. "They just wanted to intimidate us. Plus, there were too many foreign journalists. Those people are our best protection."

"Monsieur Samuels was there," Victor put in.

"He was the one with the binoculars, chéri?" Edith asked, turning her head to see Victor nod. "I figured he was with the American embassy, because the police left their group alone." She shrugged, handing back the cigarette to Leslie.

The breeze had picked up. Leslie looked at the palms blowing above the backyard wall. A rooster began to crow, its inner clock premature. The night was still clear; they could see several constellations. Leslie spotted Venus and what looked like the Little Dipper. Edith yawned and got up. "I need to sleep, darlings," she told them. "Victor, are you ready?"

"Will we see you around four?" Victor asked Leslie and Gerard. "At our house?"

"We'll be there," Gerard said. "I'm sure Jeanne will come along too."

"Ciao." Edith leaned down to embrace him, then Leslie. Victor hung behind her, then did the same. They went off arm in arm.

Leslie felt envious. Such a dynamic couple. She looked over at Gerard. They were the only ones left in the backyard.

"You know, I don't know what happened to Clemard," she said. "He went off about an hour ago."

"Pardon, Leslie." Gerard tapped his head, apologetic. "I completely forgot to tell you. He called and I told him I could drive you back. So he's gone home. I trust that's all right."

"That's fine," she said. "I was just worried."

"He called a half hour ago. I don't know why I didn't remember. I got five phone calls, one after another."

"It doesn't matter," she reassured him. "It's fine. It's probably better for him. We had a long day together. I went out to Léogane, to see that development project."

"Right—you told me you were planning to go. So how is it over there?"

"Well . . . honestly? It's very hard to judge. I saw what they're producing. A lot of baskets and handicrafts, some ironwork. It seems fine. But the real issue is how to sell and make a profit. They supposedly have an agreement worked out with an organization in Denmark, which will pay for the shipping and take care of distribution in Europe, but one of the people there told me things were very slow."

"They're one of the groups asking for your support?" Gerard helped himself to another half glass of rum.

"One of twelve," she said. "I've only managed to visit four so far. Obviously, I won't be able to visit all of them."

"I can always check things out for you," he offered.

"Thanks, Gerard," she said. "But I think you've got enough on your hands right now. Speaking of which," she said, "do you know who Père Emmanuel's source is?"

"I have my suspicions." He smiled enigmatically. "But no, I don't know for sure. Emmanuel is very secretive, even for a priest. He was like that when we were boys. He used to make us mad because we knew he had secrets and he would never tell us. But everybody told him everything. He just inspires people to trust him. But, you know, it doesn't matter, because he always finds some way to help us. The others try to hide behind their Christian vows, but not Emmanuel. Every time, he is there, pushing them and pushing us to take a position, to go further. And yet he manages to preserve his own position. He won't be compromised. That's very unusual here in Haiti."

"It's unusual anywhere," she stated. "But you do that too. You don't compromise."

"Me?" he scoffed. "I constantly compromise. I just try to hide it, that's all." He saw she didn't buy it. "You don't believe me? Ask Jeanne. She'll tell you."

She tapped him lightly on the chin. "I don't believe you."

Gerard had parked his car down a dark, empty street, illuminated only by a distant streetlamp. They rolled down the windows partway to listen for the gunshots and drove in silence. Occasionally a dog barked as they passed houses in the night. At the first major intersection, Gerard leaned forward and opened the glove compartment. He pulled out a folder. "This is for you," he said. "But it's my only copy, so don't lose it."

She edged out the contents. "A play?" she asked curiously. She read aloud: "*Afternoons at the Palace*, a play by Hervé Paule. Gerard, is this yours? It is, isn't it? When did you write it? You didn't tell me you were writing a play. Gerard, this is wonderful," she exclaimed, thumbing the pages. "I can't wait to read it!" She looked at him, shaking her head. "Talk about keeping secrets. I'm so surprised."

He looked pleased. "Don't get too excited. It's just the first act. I'm not sure what's going to be next. But you can tell me what you think, and be honest—I can take it."

"Honestly, I'm impressed." She pecked him on the cheek. "Congratulations. I know I'm jealous," she added. "A play! That's so ambitious!"

He grinned.

"Did Edith tell you?" Leslie asked as she put the folder away in her bag. "She's talked to two women. One was a prisoner here, the other one had a mother in jail in Jérémie. I'm going to take their testimonies before I go."

"You're going to do a lot of things before you go," he teased her. "Are you sleeping?"

She laughed. "You know, Gerard, I feel like I've been here much longer than three weeks. So much happens every day. No wonder people here age so quickly."

"Are you telling me I'm old now?"

"I wish I had known it was your birthday," she said sincerely. "I would have brought you a birthday present. Anyway, I hope I look as good as you do in ten years. Look at what happens to me in this heat. My hair is a disaster."

Wrong, his look said. "You look better than ever, Leslie. I don't care what that foolish ex-husband of yours told you. He *was* a fool, you know."

"You're nice to me, Gerard." She smiled. "But my hair is a mess." She wanted to change the subject.

The street narrowed, making it hard to see the potholes. Leslie recognized it as the long one that led to the side entrance of the Royale.

"Gerard," she said after they had squeezed past two parked cars, "if Elyse isn't there, what should we do? Do we know where Pierre is? The cousin whom Père Emmanuel spoke to?"

"We can swing by the parish before going," Gerard suggested. "He actually mentioned that they might not be in the village. I think they were going to take the grandmother somewhere."

"Grann? Is that her name?"

"We tend to call anyone who's elderly Grann. Like 'gran moun,' it just means 'old one.' Emmanuel didn't give me another name for her."

"I have to talk to her—to Elyse," Leslie said with sudden passion. "You can't believe how frustrating it was not to be able to say anything when I was right next to her."

"I do know," he said. "I have to deal with that every time I try to talk to a client. They put us in a little room with the guard right there and expect the client is going to talk freely. It's absurd."

"I wonder if she'll know who that woman is."

"Who's that?"

"The woman I mentioned to you that we saw as we were going out. She looked blind. I keep thinking about what a coincidence it was. That tape you gave me, with Marie-Thérèse Dubossy's testimony, and seeing this woman with those eyes. I keep fantasizing that it's somehow her." Hearing herself, she thought about Victor's earlier remark. "I'm sure it's not her," she added quickly, "but it's still kind of remarkable."

Almost all of the lights were off at the Royale. "Here you are, Madanm Leslie," Gerard said, imitating Clemard. He had told her that Clemard had a little crush on her—had she noticed? Leslie had strenuously denied it. She got out and pounded on the locked gate. Then Gerard got out. They sat on the hood of the car to wait. "It's so late," Leslie said, looking over at the wall around the hotel to see if she could spy any lizards. "I'll never be able to get up in four hours."

They heard sounds. Someone was awake.

"This city is so different at night," Leslie said. "It's a completely different place. I can see why people get scared. It's so quiet."

He looked affectionately at her. Without a word, as if the night had been building up to it, they embraced, hugging each other tightly, rocking. Gerard stroked her long hair.

"It's been a long night," he said. "Are you okay?"

"Uh-huh." She smiled. "I'm fine. A little overwhelmed, that's all. This is a lot for me to absorb." She squeezed him tighter. "I wanted to tell you. I really like Jeanne—a lot. I'm glad we've finally met. I was a little worried, to be honest; I didn't really know what to expect." She hesitated. "Did you tell her anything? About us, I mean. I mean . . . you know what I mean . . ." She let the question dangle.

His fingers were soft on the back of her neck. "I told her that you were a fantastic woman. That probably made her jealous. But Jeanne is very secure. She knows I'm devoted to her." He added, more seriously, "I told her we were good friends—we are good friends, aren't we?"

"Thank you for inviting me to come, Gerard," Leslie said earnestly. "I needed the push. I think I was afraid."

"Understandably," he said. "But not so afraid that you didn't come, which is the essential thing."

"What about you?" She disengaged herself from him. "How are you feeling? You looked so sad earlier."

He shrugged. "I don't think I even know the answer," he said honestly. "It's very hard. This news about Ti Cedric, it's—what is it like? Like something that makes me feel quite helpless, frankly. I don't know what else I can do besides what I'm doing and I just want it to stop. And I know others feel the same way. But it won't, not for a long time, I think. I look at Victor and Edith—they get so angry. That's how I should feel. Edith—she's furious; that's what makes her so powerful. But I don't feel that, I never felt that. I usually just feel bad, very bad. Bad for everyone. For Ti Cedric, for his family, for his son. I even feel badly for myself. This is what we have to live through but nobody should have to. It's not that I even have hope, like Emmanuel and Victor have hope. I don't have that vision that we are going to succeed, not even that. But I lived through Duvalier, and that, I suppose, is a miracle in itself." He stretched, adding: "Nou la. You know the expression. We're here. Right? We're here and we're waiting. For that one day when it will all be over. That's all we can do—that's all any of us can do. And one day it will be over, although I don't expect it to be in my lifetime."

They saw a light bobbing its way through the darkened hotel. It was Vincent.

"I talked to Ti Cedric's sister, Violette, a little while ago," Gerard told her, "but not the rest of the family. She was expecting something like this, I think. She's going to come here in a few days. I'm going to pursue a formal investigation and we need her help to do it." He pushed himself off the hood and looked down under the chassis of the car, then got up. "Will you be able to stay for the Mass?"

"I'll find out tomorrow if I can postpone my flight. I don't see that the weekend will make any difference. As long as I show up for work on Monday morning."

"Met!" Vincent, the custodian, shouted, recognizing Gerard. "Mwen vini." I'm coming. He held a large ring of keys and was shirtless.

"Good thing we're not being chased by anyone," Gerard mused. "It looks like he's been sleeping."

"Or drinking," Leslie whispered.

He gallantly helped her off the hood.

Vincent opened the gate; Leslie slipped in. "I'll see you in a few hours," Gerard said. "I'll bring my thermos of coffee. I think we'll both need it."

Together Leslie and Vincent watched the car slip away. The custodian kept his flashlight trained on the driveway.

"Alors, Vincent," Leslie teased him. "Were you dreaming?" He grinned, and led her into the hotel.

"*One day* . . ." Gerard's words stayed in her mind as she climbed the staircase. She went out to the terrace to see if she could spot his car, but he was gone. The mountains were mere shadows and the air was humid; it was going to rain again. She searched the sky for signs of the bats, then turned in. One day . . . She yawned, lifting the mosquito netting and slipping in fully dressed. One day in court for every night like this. That should be part of their new constitution.

31

They walked without stopping or talking. Their muscles hurt; Elyse had a cramp in her side. Her calves were stiff. The clouds were moving quickly; it was going to storm. She looked over at Luz, whose expression was worried.

"Tengo hambre," the Dominican woman said. I'm hungry. Elyse nodded, quickening her step. They saw headlights in the road and hid, crouching behind a bush. The car did not stop; the headlights missed them. Luz crossed herself, holding on to Elyse for support. The market was ahead of them. There would be people sleeping under the closed stalls. Elyse wanted to avoid being seen, to avoid anybody who might report to the police two women hurrying away in the darkness.

"This way." She pulled on Luz's arm. "Let's go into the ravine."

The bushes were wet, branches struck their faces. Ahead of Elyse, Luz tripped, then slid, grabbing on to a thorny vine for balance. "¡Ay!" she cried out. Elyse hushed her, maneuvering between indistinguishable gray shapes. The garbage from the market was dumped here, old cans, decaying fruit. Her foot sank ankle-deep into soft mud; she swore. Just above, they could see the darkened stalls. There were no signs of human activity.

Farther on, several small goats were grazing. Elyse and Luz moved quietly past them; the goats scampered away. They came upon a stretch of mud houses, also devoid of signs of life. It had taken them five minutes to go around the perimeter of the market, but the way was clear.

"¡Jesús!"

She turned around. Luz had twisted her ankle; she cursed under her breath.

"N'ale." Elyse pulled on her arm. Come on. "Pa ka rete." We can't stop here.

They both heard the shot at the same time. Luz looked fearfully at Elyse. "Dios mío," she muttered, rubbing her sore ankle.

"N'ale!" Elyse whispered more vehemently. A small whimper

escaped Luz, but she followed Elyse's command. "Nou met ale nan simitye," Elyse told her. We'll go in the cemetery. They made their way toward it, and slipped into a side entrance.

There were people sleeping inside the large crypts; Elyse knew they should stay away from that part of the cemetery. She took hold of Luz's hand and they climbed on top of a crypt, grasping for balance the metal wreaths that decorated the tombs. The crypts were so close together that they didn't have to set foot on the ground. Elyse watched for rats anyway; there were so many here. They proceeded at an angle, and Elyse guessed that they would be able to exit at a point beyond the intersection where a policeman was usually posted, even at night. Another gunshot sounded, farther away. They froze, and then continued. The police would never think to come in here.

Luz suddenly grabbed her shoulder. "No puedo," she implored. I can't. Reluctantly, Elyse agreed, and they rested, taking refuge behind a vault decorated with white tiles. Luz was hunched over, staring at her reflection. Elyse moved closer to her, held the Dominican's face in her hand and examined a large, puffy bruise on her left cheek. The older woman pulled back her lip to show Elyse where a tooth had been knocked out and where her tongue was bloody. "Aquí." She gestured. Here. They hit me here, and here. Elyse shook her head in sympathy. "Pa fe rien," she comforted her. It doesn't matter. "Nou libere." We're free.

There had been no time to plan. The big man had come for Elyse and the other girls and had ordered them to follow him. At the entrance, she had found Luz, her dress torn, her hair wild around her face. Something had happened to Luz, something bad. Get out of here, the guard had ordered. To Elyse he had said, Keep your mouth shut next time. Remember, we know where to find you.

They had not known what to do, where to go in the middle of the night, whether to stay with the schoolgirls or go by themselves. They stood at a distance from the prison, unsure, frightened, wondering what to do, when the first shot rang out. The girls ran without looking back; Elyse and Luz had gone in the opposite direction, toward Fontamara.

"Vin avek mwen," Elyse urged Luz anew. Come with me. We can find your family tomorrow, your children. It's safer if we stay together. Come on. Luz rearranged her hair and wiped her bloodshot eyes. She sniffed back little tears. "Vin," Elyse repeated gently, tugging on her shoulder.

They kept close to the inner wall of the cemetery, arriving at a dead end in the far corner. The wall was high. Elyse climbed first, Luz pushing from below. Then Luz tried, with Elyse pulling. The Dominican was heavy and her ankle ached. Finally, she scaled the wall. There was no one in the street and they ran across it. A dog had heard them and started barking. Luz froze. "Pa rete!" Elyse pushed her. Don't stop!

They kept away from the streetlight at the end of the block and moved behind a tree when a car suddenly appeared from a side road. It's not the police, Elyse reassured Luz, don't worry. They waited until the car was out of sight, then headed for the bay. There were stores along the road here, all of them shuttered. They slipped past the Baptist mission and the small bank, then a grocery store. To the left a little road led to the water.

A few sailboats had been pulled up onto the shore. Elyse thought about her dream, looked for rounded black rocks, but there were none. This was still the bay; the water was flat and brackish. A cow was tethered to a tree in a field to their left, asleep standing up. Elyse thought about milk, about pulling on the cow's teats, about her baby. The baby had to grow now. Because the baby was sleeping, she could feel that. She knew it was still waiting. Up ahead was the road home. They paused to listen for more gunshots, but heard nothing, only the wind, picking up force.

They walked another half hour. Luz had to rest. They drank water from a small stream that crossed the road. The water was full of grit. The cramp in Elyse's side was so sharp that she had to knead it as she walked. She recognized a borlette lottery stall ahead, locked up. She tried the latch, but it would not give. Huge red dice were painted on the side of the stall. My dream, Elyse thought, pointing them out to Luz, who nodded without comprehending. Luz spotted several mangoes that had fallen near the stall; they hungrily shared one. It was overripe and wormy, but it was food.

A tap-tap approached. Elyse flagged it down. There was a passenger in the front seat next to the driver. "Pa gen kob," she said to them as the vehicle stopped. We don't have money. "Lapolis vin lage nou." The police just released us. "Nou pa kriminel." We're not criminals. "We li!" Look! She thrust Luz in front of her, showed them the bruise, explained how they had been illegally arrested and released now in the middle of the night, to make their way home on foot. Would they accept the mangoes as payment? Please. They only had a short distance to go. Please. Elyse pointed to Luz's foot. My friend twisted her ankle. She can't walk well. Help us out.

The driver looked at the passenger, an old man, who shrugged. "Monte." He thumbed toward the back of the tap-tap. Get in.

A woman with a huge burlap bag sat in back. They took a seat across from her. The woman had overheard the conversation. She stared at Luz, curious, then shook her head, understanding. Elyse smiled at her. Luz leaned her frame against Elyse and probed her bruised body, trying to gauge the extent of her injuries. Here—she took Elyse's hand to feel her rib—and here. "Nou libere," Elyse whispered to her. We're free. Luz nodded.

Elyse rubbed her face, which was dirty. She massaged away her cramp. Mwen la, Grann. She spoke to her grandmother. I'm coming. A few more minutes and they would be there.

The tap-tap dropped them off beyond the police station. "Bon chans," the driver said, accepting the mangoes. Good luck. The other passengers looked ahead, not meeting their eyes. "Mesi." Elyse grasped the driver's arm. "Mesi anpil." Thanks a lot.

The waterfall was to their right. "Tann mwen," she told Luz. Wait here. But the other woman did not want to be alone, even for a moment. Luz followed her into the thick bush, around a mapou tree. Elyse paused to trail her finger around its trunk, to feel the ancient wax that had dripped from candles onto its branches. It was a petwa tree, holy. They were nearing the stream. Elyse took a deep breath. She remembered the moment so clearly, the corpse shining in the moonlight, the little black cloud of dragonflies buzzing above it, and the smell. "La." She pointed out the spot to Luz. There. It was over there.

She moved a few steps closer and saw the tree. The one where she had left the medallion hanging for Sen Kristof to find. Sen Kristof, who had carried the infant Jesus over the water, who was Rwa Agwe, who had sent his queen, Metres Agwe, to help her. She needed protection now. Where was it? She felt around the tree, the branches, farther up the trunk until her hand grasped a chain, then the medallion, exactly where she had left it. "We li!" she cried triumphantly. Look at it! She showed it to Luz, then slipped it over her head. This was his protection, she said in her mind to Grann. Now it's my protection. He left it for me.

The village couldn't be seen through the foliage, it was too dark. Elyse waited until the moon emerged from behind a cloud, then spotted the opening to the path up to Grann's house. She climbed instinctively, helping Luz, who grunted behind her. It's up there. She pointed ahead for Luz. We're almost there. There was a heavy smell of smoke in the air. Perhaps they had had a feast. Elyse let Luz's hand go to scramble up the last part, pulling on a frail branch to step up into the clearing. Then she froze.

"Manman!" She rushed forward toward the charred embers of what had been Grann's house. "Woy!" she screamed, putting her hands over her ears. "Woy! Woy! Woy!" She pushed on the black-ened stump of the center pole, kicked at the embers, then ran toward the next blackened circle. They had burned down the entire village . . . Pierre's house . . . Hyppolite's . . .

"¡Chica!" Luz ran up behind her. "¡Chica!" Luz grabbed her, tried to pull her away from the embers. "Makout!" Elyse cried out. "Kriminels!"

"Vámonos," Luz implored her, frightened. Let's go. Let's get out of here. She tried to drag Elyse away, but Elyse was stronger. Her knees sank into the ashes, which were cold and wet. She held up the charred end of what looked like a chair leg, crying. Luz looked around behind her, worried. "Chica," she repeated, "vámonos." She put her arms around Elyse.

"Grann," Elyse muttered, "kote Grann?" Where's Grann? "E Pierre—kote li?" And Pierre—where is he? "Kote tout moun?" Where is everybody?

Gone, Luz gestured, escaped. They're not here. Come on. She slowly led Elyse away, patting her on the back, murmuring unintelligibly in Spanish. "Grann," Elyse asked her again, "kote granme mwen?" Where's my grandmother? At the edge of the clearing, she turned back, looking at the ashen debris one last time.

Grann had escaped. Pierre had taken her away. Ignatius might be with them. She had seen them escaping in her dream. She had to find them now, to join them. Metres Agwe, she prayed. Sen Kristof. Pa bliye mwen. Don't forget me.

In my dream, she thought to herself as Luz led her down toward the waterfall and the road, in my dream I remember there was smoke. I thought it was the fever, the fever that killed my mother. But now I understand. Metres Agwe was trying to show me. Now I have to find them. She looked over at Luz. You have to help me. I have to find Ignatius. I have to tell him, to warn him not to come back here. If he didn't come already and leave with the others. We'll find your family, then you can take me to the border. You know where those camps are. Take me there, will you? Maybe we'll find a boat. Because look what they did to you. They won't leave you alone either. We can't stay here anymore.

We'll help each other, she said to Luz. I'll help you. That's the only way. That's what you told me, remember? We'll go back and find your children and then we'll find Ignatius and Grann. I have to find Grann. I can't stay here alone. And I have protection now, that dead man's protection. Metres Agwe, she gave me a dream. She won't let me down. She'll help us find them.

It began to drizzle. Elyse wiped the ashes of Grann's house from her arms and legs. The hem of her dress was filthy. "No importa," Luz said. It doesn't matter. "Mira la mía." Look at mine. You don't have to clean it now. But Elyse did; she had to. Even after she waded into the cold stream and wiped the dress hard between her fingers, she could still smell the fire in it, just as she could still smell the sulfur in the water, the smell that had been inside her all these weeks. The smell of the dead man.

Down below, near the beach, they sought cover from the storm. Lightning forked over the distant horizon; thunder echoed across the water. The wind scattered branches, whipped their dresses around them. They were quickly soaked and huddled together until it subsided, until the night paled into a gray dawn.

Farther along the shore, a fisherman was repairing his nets. He took the dead fish they had gathered from the tidal wash and added them to his catch. There was dry wood under his beached boat, he told them. They could make a fire and warm up. He offered them some fruit and listened as Elyse told him what had happened to her. She described her dream in detail, from the Carnival procession to the streets flooded with red rain, to the babies floating on rafts out to sea, then held out the medallion for him to examine.

They sat with their backs against his boat and breathed deeply. Elyse slowly unbraided her hair and looked out at the sea, which turned muddy near the shore. The storm had tossed a fine layer of glistening black stones onto the beach. In my dream, she told the fisherman, these stones turned into eyes. They watched me escape.

Epilogue

Who is it that pushes my hand along this page in the dark? Is it the great wind, la mort, or the warmer current, life, which never forgets the oars, La Vogue, which dipped into its waters? The soil and the sea, salt and blood and bone of human suffering.

My child will walk the earth in my bones, and if not my child, then sister, lover, friend. The bone is stronger than the lash. What destroys the flesh cannot grasp what lies inside the heart. Who pushes my hand along the page? Whose blood inside my bones? Boukman? Or the French who cut off his head and displayed it for all to see?

Bad blood and La Vogue push my sad bones across this page. God have mercy on my soul. I who have never felt whip or gun. I who forget to kiss the soil, lick the ground, taste the salted seasons. I who am left here as witness, passive eye in the center of a terrible storm. I ask you, Who moves my hand along the page?

They disturb my sleep. A generation that cannot be washed away by the great storm, the one that steals the next dawn. Whenever I lie in silence and dream. Wherever my spirit slips out to wander, buffeted by history and memory. I hear their voices riding on the wind. Nou la. Nou la. Nou la.

J3/4 ¢